ROCK REDEMPTION

NALINI SINGH

NEW YORK TIMES BESTSELLING AUTHOR

eISBN: 978-1-942356-32-5
ISBN: 978-1-942356-35-6

Cover image by: Jenn LeBlanc/Illustrated Romance
Cover design by: Croco Designs
Book design by: Maureen Cutajar/www.gopublished.com

ROCK REDEMPTION

BROKEN

KIT SMILED WHEN THE elevator doors opened as soon as she pressed the button. Stepping in with a thudding heart, she fought the urge to flat out grin. She was going to see Noah again! She hadn't made the concert despite her best efforts, but she knew he wouldn't mind. Noah had been her biggest supporter during her struggle to move from daytime-soap actress to the big screen.

Now she'd won a part in *Last Flight*, a movie based on a heartrending book set in the war-torn Congo. It had such a small budget that the wardrobe department was made up of clothes the actors and crew had brought in, but she could already tell the movie was going to be a stunning emotional journey. Though the *Last Flight* team hadn't been able to get permission to shoot at the location itself, they'd all soon be departing for another part of Africa that would stand in for the Congo in the location shots.

That trip would swallow up the majority of the budget.

Before that, the filmmakers were trying to shoot as many of the interior scenes as possible in as short a time as possible. The schedule was grueling, but Kit was in it for the long haul.

Not only did she love the script, this movie might finally earn her the title of serious actress. For a woman who'd spent her entire career fighting not to be dismissed as a rich girl dabbling in the art, that meant everything.

After cleaning off the on-set makeup she'd worn today to affect a gaunt, ill look, she'd put on her moisturizer, then added just a touch of mascara and a light lip gloss. Noah had seen her without her "face" on many times, and he liked her just fine. With him, she could be herself, no shield of glamour required.

In return, rock star Noah St. John was just Noah with her, that smile he saved for her lighting up the dark gray of his eyes as he teased her by calling her Katie. It was a little crooked, his private smile, and more than a bit wicked. Gorgeous already, that smile made him irresistible. And it was for her, just for her.

She hugged that knowledge to her heart.

The elevator doors opened on the VIP floor.

She wouldn't have been able to get up here without a special key card, but Noah had cleared her with the hotel staff as he always did. The man at the desk tonight had been very discreet, slipping her the card and the number of Noah's room in an envelope. Kit knew she and Noah would be found out one day soon—someone would sell a story to the press or just trust the wrong person with the information. But for now, the two of them could be private, could learn one another without the glare of intrusion that was the eye of the paparazzi lens.

It helped that she didn't have much of a profile. Noah's was in the stratosphere, of course, but he was also known to like women, so even if the paps scented the news, they likely wouldn't rush to hunt down the story. She was just another woman in a long line to be linked to Noah.

Kit's stomach dipped, smile fading as she walked down the corridor.

She'd known the members of Schoolboy Choir since the first week the band—young and broke and in stubborn pursuit of their dream—arrived in Los Angeles. She'd been waitressing at the time, determined to support herself and to break into the business on her own. Her folks had thought she was taking independence too far, but it had been important to Kit that she not ride on their coattails. She'd even taken the stage name of Devigny rather than using the well-known and distinctive Ordaz-Castille moniker.

Noah, Fox, Abe, and David had come into the diner late one night while she was the only one on duty. At first she'd been wary. fresh off a construction job, they'd been dirty and dusty and frankly rough-looking. But then she'd realized the four were composing a song together, one of them drumming his fingertips on top of the table while another one sang softly, with interruptions from the others about cadence and rhythm.

Smiling as she realized they were just like her, striving to make it, she'd told the group they didn't have to be quiet since it was only the five of them in the diner. They'd grinned and asked her to be their audience, and she'd found herself listening to what would eventually become the group's second number one single.

Fox, Abe, and David she'd gotten along with from the start.

Not Noah.

Everything was too intense between her and Noah, too bright and sharp and demanding. She might've given in to the raw heat that shimmered in the air whenever they were close to one another except that Noah changed women like other men changed T-shirts. In for a night, gone the next.

Five months ago, things had... changed. Kit and Noah had become friends, and though they'd never so much as kissed, their relationship was the most intimate one she'd ever had. Her heart ached with missing him when they were apart. He knew her dreams and she was starting to glimpse his, and they were slowly, beautifully, making their way from friendship to love.

Maybe tonight they would finally share their first kiss.

Her blood pounded at the memory of how close they'd come last time. She'd been able to count each one of his eyelashes, feel his breath against her skin, see the staccato beat of the pulse in his neck. A single inch and their lips would've touched.

She might explode when that happened, she was so ready.

Taking a deep breath as she reached his door, she didn't knock. He'd told her to just walk in; the last time she'd knocked, he'd still been in the shower, cleaning up after the show, and she'd ended up going in on her own anyway. Kit felt her silly, goofy smile break through her self-control as she tapped the key card on the doorknob to open it.

When the door stayed locked, she looked down.

"Idiot," she muttered, realizing she had to insert the card at this hotel. "You'd think you were fifteen and about to meet your crush alone for the first time."

Except that was exactly how she felt. Happy and excited and bubbling with love. Never had she felt this way about a man. She could see the promise of forever in Noah's eyes, and it captured her heart, her soul, held it prisoner.

Chest tight with the emotions inside her, she pushed the door open. Music filtered out, low and lazy. Her smile grew deeper. There was always music around Noah. Even when he was reading a book, he'd told her he had music on in the background.

"It's like another heartbeat," he'd said to her once. "I miss it when it's not there, even though I might not consciously notice it when it's present."

That made so much sense to her, gave her another insight into his mind.

About to call out his name as she stepped into the living area of the suite, something made her stop, dread coalescing into a dark and viscous intruder in her gut. The lights were on, the music was on, and she could see the remnants of a room service tray, so Noah was around, but...

That was when she saw what her subconscious had already noted and processed.

A high-heeled shoe lay on the carpet by the room service tray. The shoe glittered under the lights, sparkly gold with a four-inch stiletto heel.

At that instant, it felt as if that heel were embedded in Kit's chest, the pain of it burning and burning. She knew she should turn around and leave, but she couldn't. She had to know, had to be sure. Noah meant too much for her to make a mistake or to have doubts.

Heart squeezing and lungs barely drawing in enough air to keep her from passing out, she made herself walk across the floor to the open bedroom door. And as she walked, she saw the other shoe by that door, along with a knot of black cotton that was a T-shirt flung off without care to where it landed.

Fingers curling into a fist, she brought it to her mouth, trying to plug the agony that was churning inside her, keep it from erupting into a scream that would never end.

Then her eyes landed on the glittery pile of sequined fabric that might have been a dress, and the agony twisted.

Keeping her gorge down only because she refused to crumple, not here, not where he could see her, she took the final step to the door.

Her heart just… broke.

Noah was on the bed, beautiful as always, his golden-blond hair falling over his forehead and his back muscles bunched beneath his tattoos as he braced himself on his arms above a woman whose face Kit couldn't see but whose breasts sat large and high on her chest.

The sheet hid Noah's lower body, but there was no mistaking what he was doing, his hips moving in a distinctive, unmistakable motion. He was beautiful even in that, a part of her noted, like music given physical form.

The thought made her want to laugh, and she knew she was a second away from hysteria.

Noah looked up at that instant, his eyes meeting hers across the room, and everything in her froze, went numb, the shards of her splintered heart stabbing her from the inside out.

CHAPTER 1

KIT GROANED AT THE sound of her phone. Reaching out blindly toward the nightstand, she hurled mental curses upon herself for forgetting to turn it off so she could catch some uninterrupted sleep before her four-a.m. makeup call.

It'd be fun and great for her career, her agent had said when recommending Kit take the superhero flick. Coming off two serious and emotionally wrenching projects, Kit had taken Harper's advice and jumped on board the high-budget, high-octane venture. Unfortunately, Harper had forgotten to mention the four hours it would take to put her into the head-to-toe makeup required for the role. Daily.

"What?" she snarled into the phone without checking to see who it was.

"Hey, Katie."

Every cell in her body snapped wide awake. Lifting her eyelids, she just stared at the ceiling through gritty eyes. Her heart thumped, her throat moving convulsively as she swallowed. She hated that he could still do this to her, *hated it*, but her visceral response to Noah wasn't something she could stop. She knew because she'd tried for the past two years and three months.

"Noah," she said flatly. "Do you know what time it is?"

"Two fifteen," he answered.

Kit should've hung up. God, he'd *hurt* her. So much. But there was something in his voice that had her sitting up. "Are you drunk?" One thing she knew about Noah: no matter his bad-boy rep, he was *never* wasted. He might give a good indication of it, but look closely and those dark gray eyes were always sober.

"Probably." A silence, followed by, "I just wanted to hear your voice. Sorry for waking you."

"Wait," she said when he would've hung up. "Where are you?"

"Some dive." He took a deep breath, released it in a harsh exhale. "I'm sorry for being an asshole. I wanted to tell you that. I don't want to go without saying that."

"Noah," she said, a horrible feeling in her stomach. "Where exactly are you?"

"The Blue Flamingo Inn off Hollywood Boulevard. Far, far, *far* off." He laughed, and it held no humor. "It has a neon sign of a blue—surprise!—flamingo that's flashing right through my window. Looks like someone stole the curtains."

Having already grabbed her laptop, which she'd left beside the bed after answering some e-mails before sleep claimed her, she found the Blue Flamingo Inn. But Noah was already gone, having said, "I love your voice, Kit," in an oddly raw tone before hanging up.

He didn't pick up when she called back.

"Damn it! Damn it!" She shoved aside the blanket under which she'd been buried, having turned the AC to ice-cold as she usually did at night. Shivering, she tugged on a pair of jeans and an old sweatshirt over the panties and tank top in which she'd gone to sleep.

Pulling her black hair into a rough ponytail to keep it out of her eyes, she ran through the house, phone in one pocket, credit card and driver's license in the other. In the kitchen, she grabbed her keys off the counter and shoved her feet into the tennis shoes by the door that led to the garage.

She was in her car and on the way to the motel three minutes after Noah had hung up, mouth dry and an ugliness in her gut. "Please be okay, please be okay, please be okay," she kept saying, the mantra doing nothing to calm her down, but at least it kept her mind focused.

She wanted to call Molly and Fox, or the others in the band, but no one was currently in the city. Schoolboy Choir had completed the final show in the band's hugely successful tour just over two weeks earlier. Day after that, they'd all gone their separate ways to recharge and regroup.

"Much as I love these guys," David had said with a grin that reached the dark gold of his eyes, "I've been looking at their ugly mugs daily for months. We need to go blow off some steam separately before we start snarling at each other."

At the time, Kit had nodded in understanding, having had that same experience while working on location for long periods. Tonight, however, she wished the others were all here, not scattered across the country, because something was very wrong with Noah.

"Noah doesn't do drugs," she told herself as she drove as fast as she dared, not wanting to risk getting pulled over and further delayed. "He isn't the kind to—" She couldn't say it, couldn't even think of Noah ending his life. "*No*," she said firmly, her hands white-knuckled on the steering wheel. "Noah isn't like that."

He might be a bastard, but he'd never hurt his friends and family by committing suicide. His sister was only twenty-one, and Noah adored her. If nothing else, his need to protect Emily from their overbearing parents should keep him from doing anything stupid... anything irreversible.

Her phone began to beep. Reaching out, she pressed the button to activate the Bluetooth speaker and microphone. "I'm fine," she said to her security service.

"Casey's in the car behind you."

Kit's eyes flicked to the lights in her rearview mirror, un-surprised the bodyguard had caught up to her even though she'd taken off like a bat out of hell. She'd hired Casey and Butch and their team because they were damn good, but to-night she needed to be alone; whatever happened, Noah would shut down if a stranger walked in beside her.

"Tell Casey to go to this location and wait." She read off an address about five minutes from the Blue Flamingo. "I'll call him if I need him."

"Don't turn off the GPS tracker on your car. That's not the best part of town."

"I know. I won't." Kit wanted privacy for this, but she wasn't stupid, not with a stalker who'd been frighteningly per-sistent in his efforts to get to her. "But make sure Casey doesn't follow me, Butch. I need privacy for this, and if you breach that, even to protect me, I can't trust you anymore."

"Any hint of trouble and you hit the panic button," Butch ordered. "Understood?"

"Understood." Kit was officially their boss, but the two men had become friends to her, they'd been watching over her for so long. Icy and dangerous as they were in public, they treated her like a younger sister in private. It was part of the reason she liked the two ex-Marines so much. The men who worked under them were younger but just as dedicated and professional.

Ending the call, she followed her GPS's prompts as to the shortest route to the motel. Butch's call had kept her mind busy for a couple of minutes, but now the fear came rushing back. Using the Bluetooth system, she called Noah again.

No response.

Should she alert the paramedics or the cops? What if she was wrong? What if Noah was just passed out, drunk? It would end up all over the media. Noah would never forgive her.

That risk Kit would've taken, but the idea of exposing Noah to strangers while he was vulnerable... No, she couldn't do that. "You'd better not have done anything stupid, Noah."

Trying not to panic, she drove past run-down businesses and anemic palm trees, the street corners host to small groups of working girls and boys, their pimps hovering in the background. Noah wasn't just off Hollywood Boulevard—he'd managed to find a hidden pit of darkness in amongst the sleek and shine. It was a damn good thing her car didn't draw attention.

She'd jumped into the trusty brown sedan that was the first car she'd ever bought on her own. It was old enough and dusty enough—she'd been meaning to take it to the carwash—that she was probably being visually tagged as another middle-aged husband searching for a cheap thrill.

A possible customer for the pros, but not worth carjacking.

Thanking the car that had gotten her to more casting calls than she could count, she ignored the sideshow and carried on.

The Blue Flamingo Inn appeared out the darkness in a screaming blue blaze. Turning into the lot, she found that the neon sign was the brightest lighting in the place.

A bulb flickered on an upstairs landing of the U-shaped building, and there was a yellow-tinged bulb inside what looked like the manager's office, but that was it. The entire place was dark and grimy and a great location to get mugged—except the thieves had probably given up on this place, it was so sad and dilapidated. Parking the car in the nearest spot, she went to get out and realized she had no idea of Noah's room.

Remembering what he'd said about the flamingo flashing through his uncurtained windows, she looked around and zeroed in on three upstairs rooms from where the sign had to be brightly visible. She'd try those three first before waking up the manager and blowing Noah's cover.

Grabbing the pepper spray she kept in the cup holder, she got out after making sure there was no one else around and locked her car. Then she ran quickly to the stairs that led up to those three rooms. All three were dark, but two of them had some limp-looking curtains. Cupping her hands over the sides of her eyes as she pressed her face to the window of the third, she felt her breath leave her in a painful rush.

Noah sat on the edge of the bed, bare-chested and with his eyes on his hands. His shoulders were slumped, but he was very much alive.

Pulling away from the window, she bent over, braced her hands on her knees, and tried to breathe. The air hurt going in, coming out. At least two minutes later, she gripped the skinny metal railing, pulled herself up and, breath still a little ragged, went to knock. Then something made her try the door. It turned easily in her hand.

"Wrong room," Noah said without looking up. "Unless you're looking for a quick fuck. Then I can oblige you."

It was a kick to the gut. As was the sight of the condom wrappers on the floor and that of the obviously used bed. She almost stepped back, almost left. He'd never know, never realize how desperately worried she'd been tonight... and then her eyes fell on the nightstand and the syringe that lay on it.

Ice formed in her gut again.

Striding across the carpet, she picked it up. "What the hell is this, Noah?"

"Kit?" He looked up, his pupils hugely dilated. "I can smell you. You always smell so good." Reaching out, he touched her thigh. "I guess I must be really drunk if I'm imagining you here." With that, he grabbed the bottle she hadn't seen at his feet and took a swig.

Holding the syringe with one hand, Kit pulled away the bottle with the other and slammed it on the nightstand. "What," she said again, gripping his jaw to force him to meet her gaze, "*is* this?"

An unconcerned shrug. "Something to make me high as a kite according to the dealer."

"Jesus, Noah, you don't even know what it is and you were going to shoot up with it?"

"Couldn't do it," he said on a harsh laugh. "Kept hearing your voice in my head telling me you have no fucking respect for people who fucking space out on drugs. And now I'm hallucinating you." He swiped out at the bottle, missed when she grabbed it first. "Gimme back my whiskey, Hallucination Kit."

"I'll give you your whiskey." Taking the bottle, she went into the tiny bathroom and poured the liquid into the cracked and stained sink.

Noah got up and followed her. His face fell. "Don't do that, Hallucination Kit. Now what will we drink?"

Ignoring him, she finished with the bottle and depressed the plunger of the syringe while holding it over the sink. Once it was empty, she put it on the narrow back ledge of the sink so the maid would see it straightaway. Hopefully the cleaning staff had a process for disposing of needles. "Where's the vial?" she asked Noah after dumping the bottle in the garbage.

Noah just looked at her, his jaw bristly and dark. It had always fascinated her that he could be so blond and yet have such dark stubble, eyebrows, and eyelashes. She'd always had to fight the temptation to bite at his jaw, taste him. Today, however, all she wanted to do was hit him. "Where. Is. The. Vial?" she repeated deliberately. "Noah!"

When he still didn't answer, she pushed past him, his muscled chest warm under her touch, and began to open the drawers in the nightstand. They proved empty, and there was no other furniture in the room aside from the bed. Going to her knees, she looked under the bed, caught the glint of glass. The vial had rolled underneath, likely after Noah knocked it off the nightstand.

It was empty and unlabeled.

Throwing it in the trash in the bathroom, conscious of Noah watching her with an intensity that felt like a touch, she began to search the bed for his T-shirt, careful to touch things only with the tips of her fingers. She couldn't think about the

14

fact that he'd been fucking some other woman in this bed not long ago or she'd throw up.

"You want to fuck, Hallucination Kit?"

She'd jerked up her head, intending to flay him for the question, when he said, "I don't want to. Not with you."

And the bastard kept kicking her, kept hurting her. "I wouldn't sleep with you if you were the last man on the planet." Having found the tee, she threw it at him. "Put that on."

He did so, oddly compliant.

"Noah," she said, worried again. "Did you take anything else? Pills?"

"No, because Kit hates drug addicts. I drank. And then I ran out of booze so I went and bought some more and drank again."

Since she could smell the booze, she had to believe him on that point. "When was the last time you ate something?"

Another shrug.

Kit could've left then, but she couldn't abandon him here. Regardless of how much he'd hurt her, he'd once been her friend. Her *best* friend. "Come on, let's go get a burger." When he didn't move, she held out a hand despite how deeply she wanted to maintain distance between them for her own sake. "I'm hungry."

His eyes went to her hand and he moved at last, coming over to close one big hand around her own. His fingertips were callused from playing the guitar, his skin tougher than her own, his temperature hotter. The contact was a shock to her system, anger and pain and hurt entwined.

Swallowing it all down, she tugged him out of the room and to the car. "I'll go pay the manager," she said once she'd unlocked the car.

Noah laughed as if she'd told a crazy joke. "I might be drunk and hallucinating, but I know this place is prepay."

Right, of course it was. "Then get in."

The smell of alcohol and of Noah filled the car as she drove them out of the seedy area. "What are you doing back in LA? I thought you were in Hawaii?" Fox had mentioned that fact in passing when she'd had dinner with the lead singer and Molly the night before the couple left for their road trip down the Pacific Coast Highway.

No answer from Noah.

When she glanced over at the passenger seat, it was to find that he'd either fallen asleep or passed out, his head leaning against the window. Stopping at the lights, she reached out to check his pulse to make sure it was a natural sleep. He mumbled something at the touch of her fingertips, his pulse strong.

Relieved, she alerted Casey she was on her way back, then drove straight home. Once there and parked inside the garage, she went around to open Noah's door and was faced with the prospect of either leaving him in the car or trying to haul him inside.

"Noah," she said, forcing herself to grab one of his muscled shoulders and shake. "Wake up if you want to sleep in a bed."

"Not your bed," he mumbled.

Kit tried not to let his words draw blood. "Yeah, you've made that clear. Now get up."

Eyes opening, though his lashes were heavy, he stumbled out and wrapped one arm around her shoulders. "Hi, Katie." He nuzzled at her hair. "I missed you."

Tears so close to the surface that they were about half a minute away at most, she managed to bully, push, and lead him to one of the spare bedrooms—where he flopped facedown on the bed and went immediately back to sleep. Realizing he was wearing his boots as well as his belt with its heavy silver buckle, along with old black jeans, she thought she should do something to make him more comfortable, but she'd hit her limit.

She paused only long enough to put a blanket over him because she knew how much he hated her liking for cold temperatures at night. Leaving the guest bedroom, she went into her own, stripped off, stepped into the attached shower, and cried until she had no more tears in her.

Her chest hurt by the end, her throat was raw, her nose stuffy. But she was an actress, knew all the tricks. Grabbing a cold pack from the fridge, she lay down on the bed with it over her eyes. She still had forty-five minutes before she had to leave for the studio. Plenty of time for her to become Kathleen Devigny again, sophisticated, talented, and far too intelligent to have her heart broken a second time by a rock star who had never loved her like she'd loved him.

CHAPTER 2

NOAH WOKE TO THE sound of a drumbeat loud enough to reverberate through his bones. "Cut it out, David," he muttered, wondering why Schoolboy Choir's drummer was practicing inside his skull.

When the drumming continued unabated, he opened his eyes a slit and saw white sheets with tiny blue flowers. There were even green leaves around the flowers. He ran his fingers over the sheet, felt the texture, focused on the flowers and leaves again. This wasn't home. And he never stayed overnight with anyone.

Eyes flicking fully open even as another part of his brain identified the scent in the air—evocative and fresh and painfully familiar—he sat up. Too fast. His head swam.

He groaned and, holding his head in his hands, closed his eyes for another minute until things settled down. Then he glanced around the room.

The walls were a warm cream, the bedside tables honey-colored wood, a stained glass Tiffany lamp on one side; the colors from the lamp were reflected in the abstract painting on the wall in front of him. On his right side was a large window that looked out onto what appeared to be a private green haven. He could see the pebbled pathway, knew that if he walked down that path, he'd find himself in a painstakingly maintained Japanese garden.

Inside was a pond bordered by large stones covered in a fine, velvety moss. A small wooden seat was positioned beside a miniature maple tree, right at the perfect spot to look into the calm of the pond as a cherry blossom tree cast its shadow on the water.

Go right and he'd eventually reach the end of the garden outside the kitchen. There was a picnic table in that spot, along with two benches, under the spreading branches of a leafy green tree. Go left and, after several minutes, he'd find himself at a moss-covered wall—because this place *was* a haven, secret and contained.

Noah knew every corner of it... or he had. Kit had probably changed everything by now. She was always out there. She had a service that maintained the lawn out front and made sure the wooded area on her property was free of any damaged or dangerous trees, but the garden was hers.

"It gives me peace," she'd told him once, her eyes shining and open. "I walk out there, put my hands in the earth, and the stress of the day just falls away."

Shoving off the blanket tangled around his legs, Noah got out of bed. He was still wearing his boots, and it felt like his belt buckle had embedded itself in his gut. It made him laugh even as he winced, and the laugh had his head pounding like it had a live jackhammer buried in it.

"Shit." Having collapsed back on the bed, he forced himself to get up, winced again. He smelled like a fucking distillery.

"Christ." Stumbling into the bathroom, he threw some water on his face, then used one of Kit's fluffy white towels to dry off. Not only did he smell like he'd bathed in whiskey, he looked like he'd been on a three-day bender. "Impressive, Noah." He'd achieved that result in a single night. And Kit had seen him like this. Great. Just fucking great.

Leaving the bathroom, he walked out of the bedroom. "Kit?" he called out, gritting his teeth as his head pounded in time with his heartbeat.

All he heard was silence. The door to her bedroom—just down from his—was open. Looking in carefully, he saw her bed neatly made and piled with a ridiculous number of pillows. He'd once asked her what the point was when she only needed one for her head and she'd rolled her eyes. "Only a man would ask that question."

He fucking missed her voice, her smile, *her*. That's why he'd called her. It was coming back to him, flashes of what he'd done. He knew it would all eventually appear. That was his special curse: he could drink himself to oblivion, something he usually only ever did while alone inside his house, but he remembered *everything*. Sometimes it took a day before it all came back, but it always did.

He was already getting grainy, blurry images of Kit picking up a hypodermic, shock and horror on her face.

Fuck, fuck, fuck.

Walking into her sunny kitchen, he saw no sign of her. What he did see was a note propped up next to a large bottle of aspirin. He ignored the pills and picked up the note.

You're probably still over the limit to drive, and in case you're idiotic enough to think you're not, I'm taking all the keys. Call my car service when you get up and they'll take you home. I'm at the studio.

At the bottom was the phone number for the car company. He flipped it over in the hope she'd written something else, but that was all. A stabbing in his heart, he crushed the paper in his hand. He had to get the fuck out since it was clear Kit didn't want him here. Not that he could blame her.

Having shoved the piece of paper in his pocket because he was pathetic and wanted something of hers, even if it was only a terse note, he thrust a hand through his hair and winced again at the smell of alcohol. He couldn't go anywhere like this unless he wanted to attract attention, and that was the last thing he needed today.

Back when he and Kit had been friends, he'd left a few things in the closet in the spare bedroom. Wondering if there was a chance she hadn't thrown it all out, he went back to the room and opened the closet.

It was empty.

There went that idea, he thought, about to close the closet door when he noticed a box up on the shelf. Pulling it down, he found his stuff. It had been thrown in there in a mess, but he had everything he needed.

A long, hot shower made him feel a little more human. Afterward, he chucked his dirty clothes into the large garbage can beside Kit's garage—thanks to her stalker, she paid a company to come in and personally pick up and dispose of her garbage, so no one would be digging through it and discovering his clothes. He *did not* want to remember the night he'd almost done the one thing he'd sworn never to do, no matter how bad the hell inside his head.

Returning to the house, he began to pull on his boots over bare feet.

He couldn't call Kit's car service without linking his name to hers. Everyone knew Kit was friendly with the band, but if he was picked up alone from her house, even at three in the afternoon—*Jesus, he'd been out of it*—it would fuel all kinds of rumors. The only reason they'd escaped that during their friendship was because he'd been very careful not to put her in the line of fire.

He could call the service the band used when they wanted to party and didn't want to drive, but the driver they usually used was out with a broken leg and Noah didn't know the new guy well enough to trust he'd keep his mouth shut. He'd walk out except that no one walked in neighborhoods like this—he'd probably get picked up by private security before he got a hundred feet.

He knew Kit's own security guys were professionals who never blabbed about clients; he'd ask one to run him up the road, then grab a cab once he was far enough away that his name wouldn't be connected to Kit's. She deserved that much at least from him. No way was he messing up her life with a tabloid feeding frenzy.

He was on his way out to see if he could touch base with one of the security team when Kit's home phone rang. He half smiled at the stodgy male voice that came on asking the caller to leave a message. The recording had come with the machine, and Kit used it so random callers wouldn't realize whose house they'd reached. He had his hand on the front doorknob when Kit's voice filled the air.

"Noah, are you awake? Are you alive?"

Gut tight and breath shallow at the sign that maybe she hadn't totally written him off, he grabbed the handset. "Yeah, awake and alive and about to bounce from your place."

A pause before she said, "What's wrong with your phone?"

He took it out of his pocket. "Dead battery."

"So..."

"I'm good." He shoved a hand through his hair. "I fucked up, Kit. I'm sorry. I shouldn't have called you."

"Yeah? So you should've just sat in that fleapit and shot poison into your body?" Anger vibrated in her every word. "Damn, I have to go. We need to talk. *Don't leave.*"

The dial tone sounded in his ear before he could reply. Putting the handset on the cradle, he sat down on a nearby sofa and pulled off his boots. It wasn't even a decision that he'd stay. This was the first time Kit had talked properly to him since the night he'd willfully destroyed the best thing in his life.

Self-disgust built in him, but he was used to that. It had lived in him most of his life. He'd done what he had to protect Kit, but he'd hurt her, and that made him a bastard. If she wanted to take a few shots at him, he'd stand there and let her pummel him bloody. It'd be worth it if she'd just talk to him again.

KIT WALKED INTO HER house at seven that night to the smell of something delicious. Even dog tired as she was, it made her mouth water. A hot, prepared meal sounded like her idea of heaven right then. She'd been planning to eat one of the refrigerated meals she bought by the dozen.

It wasn't that she was a terrible cook—okay, yes, she was a terrible cook, but she enjoyed trying. Except with such an intense filming schedule, she had zero time. She was either at the studio or sleeping. Thank God she only had two more days to go.

And all of that, she thought as she detoured to her room to drop off her purse and kick off her flats, was just an attempt to distract herself from the fact that Noah was in her house. She could smell him in the air, and this time, there was no alcohol. Just Noah.

Warm and intrinsically male.

Fisting her hands, she made herself remember what he'd done, remember the sight of his body moving sinuously on another woman's. It twisted up her gut, but the sick feeling was coupled with an anger that had been growing and growing and *growing*. Tonight it drove her out of the bedroom and to the kitchen, where Noah was stirring something on the stove.

He looked up with a wary smile, his jaw still shadowed but his hair clean and his T-shirt white, his jeans a faded blue. She knew those clothes, had been telling herself to throw them out since the hotel-room ugliness. Pathetic as it was, in the month after it happened, she'd hurt so much with missing him that she'd even put on his T-shirt once.

"Hey," he said. "It's not gourmet anything, but I found a pasta sauce mix in your pantry and some spaghetti."

"Why?" she asked, the question too violent to be kept inside any longer. "Why did you do it, Noah?"

His expression grew dark. Switching off the stove, he gripped the edge of the counter. "Because that's what I do, Kit," he said, his voice gritty. "I fuck women. As many as I can."

She flinched but didn't back down. "Don't you do that," she said across the distance between them. "Don't you give me some pat, Noah St. John-is-a-bad-boy answer. Did what we

had together mean nothing to you?" They hadn't slept together, hadn't even kissed, but the thing growing between
them, it had been rare, precious. And he'd shit all over it.

"It meant everything," Noah snapped back, his eyes blazing
at her with an intensity the world never saw. "But I'm never
going to be that guy, Kit. The one who makes you happy."

"I *was* happy. So were you." She hadn't imagined his
crooked, sexy, private smile or the welcome in his eyes. She
hadn't imagined the hours they'd spent talking. She hadn't
imagined the music he played for her or the way he called her
Katie just to rile her up.

"I wanted you as my friend!" Noah's eyes glittered, strands
of golden-blond hair falling across his forehead. "I didn't—
don't—want to sleep with you!"

The blow landed again, just as hard as it had when he'd
said it at the motel. No, harder, because he was sober now.
Feeling brittle and bruised, she gave him a tight smile.
"You've made that crystal clear."

Noah's head fell forward, shoulders slumping. "Shit. That
didn't come out right."

"Don't worry, Noah, I get it. You're just not that into me,"
she said, mocking herself.

Noah's laugh was broken. "Kit, I—" He shook his head. "It
doesn't matter."

"Say it." She needed this dream to die a final death.

His head jerked up, dark gray eyes brilliant with fury and
with a need so vicious it rocked her. "Why can't you just be
my friend?" he asked, his arms rigid he was holding on so
hard to the counter. "I fuck everything female that moves. I
don't want that with you."

The bruise was so painful by now that it pulsed... but for the first time since he'd told her he didn't want to sleep with her, she actually *heard* him. Maybe because she hurt so much she was numb, her mind oddly clear as a result. As his words echoed in her skull, she thought of all those hours when they'd watched old movies together, or sat in a hotel room running lines, or the day they'd gone to a go-cart track after disguising themselves so they wouldn't be recognized.

They'd raced like maniacs, then eaten burgers that fell apart they were so huge, and Noah had laughed. No sophistication, no edge, pure happiness. He'd grinned the same way the day she'd gotten the part that had launched her career into the big time. Noah was the first one she'd told, his arms like steel around her as he lifted her off her feet and swung her around.

"I knew you'd do it!" he'd said, his confidence in her a buoyant force that had made her believe she could conquer every hurdle.

He'd been her friend, the best friend she'd ever had. He was the reason she'd tried out for the part in *Last Flight* in the first place. He'd told her not to call herself "just a soap actress," had driven her to the casting call himself, had *held her hand* until she'd walked inside; he'd been waiting when she came out—exhilarated, nervous, and relieved that she'd made it through without embarrassing herself.

Noah's smile had held open pride.

I fuck everything female that moves. I don't want that with you.

The words flayed her, destroyed her, but there was also something in them that cut through the hurt and made her pause. Noah never spent any non-sex time with the women he slept with—not one ever saw him twice. He didn't cook for them, didn't drive them to auditions, certainly didn't pull out his guitar and ask their opinion on a new piece. The *only* woman with whom Kit had known him to do all those things was... her.

Kit didn't know what that meant, didn't even know if she could handle being Noah's friend while he added notch after notch to his belt, but she knew she couldn't shove him out into the cold. The memory of the fear she'd felt on the drive to that motel burned like acid on her bones. No matter what Noah had done, how much he'd hurt her, she couldn't imagine a world where he didn't exist.

She'd keep an eye on him at least until the rest of the band returned to LA.

After that... Kit had no answers. All she knew was that Noah was bad for her... and that part of her would always miss him.

CHAPTER 3

NOAH SAT ACROSS FROM Kit at the little picnic table she did still have at one end of her garden. It was illuminated by beautiful paper lanterns that bathed everything in a soft light that probably flattered most people. It only hid the purity of Kit's beauty, the mobile curve of her lips, the sparkle in her eye.

Neither was in evidence tonight, he knew that, but he liked to imagine them, liked to imagine her smiling at him as if she couldn't wait to tell him about her day and to ask about his.

And her laughter when he pointed out something ridiculous; he'd never heard better music. What he wouldn't do to hear her laugh again.

Yeah, you'll do anything except stop being an asshole.

He didn't know what they were doing here tonight. He didn't know if Kit had understood what he'd said to her. He adored her, and because he did, he would *never* touch her. The instant he did, he'd ruin her, ruin everything. He didn't want their relationship tainted by sex—if they even had any kind of a relationship.

Most probably she was just making sure he didn't end up in another dive about to shoot up. Kit had always had a soft heart, and Noah was bastard enough that he was going to take advantage of that to have her in his life, even if only for a day or two.

"It's not too bad, right?" he said, having inhaled his own serving of spaghetti. "Probably not in your diet though." Kit loved food, loved trying new dishes, but she had to maintain a strict dietary regime to stay in shape for her newest role.

Noah knew that because he followed every tidbit about her in the media.

"Body paint and Lycra hide zero sins," she'd said with a grin in a recent television interview. "I'm eating a burger with all the fixings and having two bowls of ice cream the day we finish filming. Oh, and I'm ordering a full-fat creamy latte every morning for a week!"

Noah had downloaded the clip of her laughing onto his phone, watched it so many times that he'd lost count. Eyes dancing in self-deprecating humor, she'd been the Kit who meant everything to him, the one who'd once dropped ice cubes down his back after he refused to stop calling her Katie.

Tonight she shrugged. "It's only two more days till we wrap. A little spaghetti won't kill me." Finishing off the last bite of her small portion, the rest of her plate having been filled with salad, she drank from the glass of chilled water into which she'd squeezed some fresh lemon juice. "And it was delicious, way better than anything I can cook."

"In that case, I admit I ate the fish salad thing you had in your fridge."

Kit's lips didn't curve at his confession. "I'm seriously jonesing for a burger. With extra pickle and jalapeño relish and a big pile of french fries."

His memory of her interview collided with the reality of their conversation, of the fact he was here with her and she was talking to him like he was a friend. Hope flickered, bright and anxious as a puppy. "That food truck you like?"

A small nod as she reached for a slice of the orange he'd peeled and cut up for dessert. He knew all about Kit's sweet tooth, had learned during their friendship that the fruit would give her a sugar hit while not compromising her film diet. During the course of *Last Flight*, she'd had to become a gaunt shadow of herself; he'd hated seeing her that way, but Kit's body was part of her art, an instrument she used as necessary.

About to offer to take her out to the food truck soon as the movie wrapped, he took in her face as she rubbed absently at her forehead and frowned at the purplish bruises under the gorgeous amber of her eyes. "You need to get to sleep," he said, realizing she must've only had four or five hours last night what with having to come rescue his useless ass.

"Not with spaghetti sitting in my stomach." She reached for another piece of fruit, the deep golden bronze of her skin shadowed by the delicate leaves of the tree that rustled above the picnic table. "I'll stay up for another hour, have a bath, wash off the stress of the day."

"You've already showered." He'd caught her damp hair when she came in.

"Best way to get rid of the last of the body makeup. Not as relaxing as a bath." She stood. "Stay the night."

He looked up, held her gaze. "I won't go there again." He'd hit rock bottom last night, but he still hadn't used that hypodermic. "You don't have to watch over me." Even he wasn't enough of a bastard to keep her on the hook worrying about him.

Kit wrapped her arms around herself. "What would you do if you found me drunk and alone with a needle full of poison? Would you trust me when I said I was fine?" She didn't wait for an answer. "Stay the night, drive home tomorrow. I'll sleep better if you stay."

The last words were so quiet he barely heard them, but they shredded him. He wouldn't have left now if his life depended on it.

Watching Kit walk away after picking up the plates, he wanted to say something, anything, to make her stay. But Fox and David were the ones who had the words. Noah wrote songs sometimes, but words didn't come as easily to him as the music, and he didn't have his guitar tonight.

Getting up, he decided to go for a walk. Kit's home had extensive grounds, not because she was particularly acquisitive, but because it had been the most secure property on the market when her stalker kicked into high gear. The fucking creep had broken into her previous home and ejaculated on her bed, then left her an "I love you" card and flowers.

She'd thrown out the bed the instant the cops were done processing the scene, but the incident had haunted her, making it impossible for her to remain in her cozy and inexpensive-to-rent town house. Add in the rising media pressure—photographers had started camping out on her damn doorstep and trying to peer through her windows—and it had made sense for her to get a place with enough land that her home was isolated in the center, far from the prying lenses of both paparazzi cameras and that of the stalker.

The cops, studio security, her friends, everyone was taking the threat dead seriously, but the fucker was still out there.

31

According to news Fox had passed on to Noah, the disturbed man had shipped Kit a box containing a wedding gown and a ring two months ago—so they could "renew their vows." It had been followed a week later by a letter naming her a "slut" and a "whore" because she'd been snapped while out to dinner with one of her costars.

Noah wanted to get his hands around the coward's neck, wring it until the pathetic man could no longer terrorize Kit. The only good news was that Kit's security measures seemed to be working. She'd had no unpleasant surprises in her new home.

He'd been walking for about ten minutes when he saw movement in the shadows in front of him. "Butch," he said, recognizing one of Kit's bodyguards.

The broad-shouldered and heavily muscled man, his dark blond hair worn in a military crew cut, was dressed in black cargo pants and a black T-shirt rather than the suit he wore when out and about with Kit.

"Hey, Noah." He held out a hand and they shook.

"Any problems?"

Butch rubbed his jaw rather than responding to Noah's question.

"I know you don't talk about your clients' business," Noah said, appreciating that about the man. "But you know I care about Kit."

"Yeah, I know. All you guys do." Falling into step beside Noah, he said, "I'm glad you're staying with her, to be honest. I've had a bad feeling lately—I think the nutjob's back, and he's watching her. I brought in two extra men to cover her and the house around the clock, but then she took off last night. I can't protect her if she won't let me."

Noah wanted to kick himself for having put Kit at risk. "Won't happen again." He made a vow then and there not to get falling-down drunk ever again. It was a vow he'd broken before, but then it had only been about him—now it was about Kit. And Kit was everything. "Any physical signs of the stalker?"

"No. But I know he's out there. Years of instinct, man."

"I believe you." It was Noah who'd recommended Butch and his team for this job, though Kit didn't know that. Fox had passed on the information without mentioning where the rec came from. "You have my number, right?"

"Yeah."

"Call me if you don't want Kit to be alone." He'd come, even if he had to bed down in the garage.

"Will do," Butch promised. "If she fires me for talking to you, you owe me a job."

Noah slapped him on the shoulder. "How about a starlet who's currently falling out of limos and into cocaine?"

The burly ex-Marine snorted. "Hell no. Not after Kit."

Noah understood that. Kit was extraordinary. She'd come through the ranks to the bright glare of fame without losing sight of what was important: at the top stood her friends and family. For them, she'd do anything.

As a struggling actress when she'd been cast in the soap for what was originally meant to be a bit part, she'd barely had two extra cents to rub together. Nevertheless, she'd opened her tiny apartment to the junior makeup artist on the show when the other woman was evicted after falling behind on her own rent.

Becca and Kit were close friends to this day.

Kit had helped so many people in similar ways. Her nature was all the more extraordinary given how she'd grown up—as the only daughter of a supermodel and a tennis ace. He had no idea how she'd turned out so normal. He just knew she had.

Far more normal than Noah.

KIT HAD EXPECTED TO spend the night tossing and turning, but she slept more soundly than she had since the day the stalker broke into her previous home. It didn't take a genius to figure out the reason why. Apparently she could hire the best security in the world, but all she needed to feel safe was to have Noah in the house.

Annoyed with herself, she got out of bed in the dark and stumbled to the bathroom to have a quick shower to wake up. That done, she dressed and grabbed her purse. When she stepped out of the bedroom, she was startled to see a light in the kitchen. Her heart thudded until she saw Noah's half-naked body moving about in there.

"What are you doing up?" Nobody should be up at this hour; if the studio wasn't paying her, she certainly wouldn't be.

"I know you don't like to eat this early," he said with that old crooked smile, "but I made up one of those healthy sea-weed things you like and put it in this." He held out a travel mug, drawing her eyes to his chest. The ink there was relatively simple—the biggest work was on his back. "So you can drink while they're slathering you in makeup."

"You didn't have to do that," she said, feeling awkward and not at her best. She couldn't deal with a bare-chested Noah

34

this early in the morning. Especially when he was all mussed up and yawning and lazy-looking. It made her want to walk into his arms and snuggle against him while he rubbed his bristly jaw against her hair.

Grabbing the drink, she headed to the garage entrance instead—to find he'd opened it for her.

He leaned against the entrance as she got into the black sports car she'd bought before the stalker forced her to pour all her money into this property and hiring security. She put the drink in the cup holder and pushed the garage-door opener.

"Still not a morning person, I see."

"Shut up," she muttered. "It's not morning. It's the middle of the night." With that, she closed her door and backed out of the garage. The last thing she saw as she left was Noah standing in the doorway haloed in light, and she thought about how wonderful it would be to wake up to him every morning.

"Enough, Kit." Slamming her hand on the steering wheel, she focused on the road, conscious of Casey behind her. When she had to stop at a red light, she sipped from the drink Noah had made her, all the while asking herself why she didn't just run the light. It wasn't as if anyone else was on the road.

The answer, of course, was that she was too much of a goody-two shoes. Kit didn't need a shrink to tell her that she'd overcompensated for her crazy upbringing. When your parents partied till five in the morning every weeknight, you either joined them, or you put on noise-canceling headphones and locked your bedroom door so drunk party guests looking for the bathroom wouldn't wake you.

Kit had chosen the second option.

Pulling into the studio lot, she picked up the travel mug and made her way to Makeup. Casey fell in with her, but neither one of them spoke, the bodyguard concerned with keeping an eye out for threats. Nothing had happened on the studio lot as yet, but no one was taking any chances.

"Only one more torturous morning wake-up to go!" she said to Becca when she entered the brightly lit glare of the Makeup trailer. "Only two more days of being an avocado-green superhero!"

Her currently pink-haired friend held up a pot of body paint, her nails black with tiny pink hearts. "Aw, shucks, and I thought you liked being slathered in this goo." Becca fluttered her eyelashes, her mascara dark against the cream of her skin. "Green is such a flattering shade on your skin, and those tiny horns. Oh, baby."

As Kit laughed and went to change into the high-cut Lycra leotard that provided a base for her transformation, she tried not to think about the fact that the house would be empty when she got home.

CHAPTER 4

NOAH TOOK KIT'S OLD sedan, leaving soon after she did. It didn't take him long to drive from Kit's Pacific Palisades home to his place overlooking Venice Beach. Fox and David had places out in the Palisades too, but Noah liked the vibrant energy of Venice, and he didn't mind driving over when they decided to jam at Fox's place—as they'd been doing more and more since the lead singer hooked up with Molly. Fox's girl had a way of making everyone feel welcome.

His place was exactly as he'd left it, including the mess in the bedroom. He'd thrown things at the walls, punched a hole in one, torn off the blinds, and generally had one hell of a pity party. No more, he thought, *no more*. He'd put Kit's life at risk with his actions, and that wasn't going to happen again. Not even if he had to stay awake for the rest of his fucking life to escape the nightmares.

Flicking on every light in the place, he began to clean up. First he picked up everything he could, then he tried to see if he could fix the blinds. It took a while and two of the slats were cracked, but the blinds opened and closed. Not that it mattered. He'd taken Fox's advice and had the builders put in reflective glass for the windows. No fucking pap was going to be sneaking photos of him with a long lens.

He didn't care what they did while he was out in public, but this was *his* space.

Heading into the kitchen afterward, he got himself a glass of orange juice and sat at the counter, the sunshine hitting his back. It poured in through the doors he'd slid open, the pool sparkling under the dawn sunlight. He had trees and other greenery around the pool to cut down the heat, spent a lot of time out there working on his music.

He thought Kit would like his pool, but he didn't know because he'd never brought her to his house. They'd always ended up at her place; he'd crashed in her guest bedroom any number of times. He'd just never been able to take the next step, invite her here even as part of a group, and that just showed how fucked-up he was.

He probably had no chance in hell of ever winning back her trust.

His phone rang even as the bleak thought passed through his head. He glanced at the caller ID, ready to ignore it. But it was one of the few people he could stand to speak to today. "Hey, Foxie," he said, ribbing the lead singer with the hated moniker so often used by groupies. "Where are you?"

"Molly and I got back last night," Fox said. "Want to come over for breakfast? I've been working on something, could do with your input."

"On my way." He wasn't in any shape to be alone, and the drive would help clear his head, especially if he got on the Pacific Coast Highway, had the salt air and crashing blue of the ocean on one side as he drove.

Leaving Kit's car in the garage, he got into the gleaming black of his fully restored 1967 Mustang convertible and headed out. Since the roads were no longer clear, he popped in a demo CD a hopeful group of musicians had sent the band through the mail. Might as well use the travel time for good. He, Fox, Abe, and David didn't advertise it, but Schoolboy Choir had a policy of not simply blowing off the hopeful and the desperate. They divided up any demos that came in and reported back to the others.

Most of the stuff was, unfortunately, enthusiastic but uninspired. This one, however, had potential. Schoolboy Choir had been moving slowly into backing some up-and-coming talent, and he decided the four of them might have to listen to more from this band. The next demo made him wince and pull it out after a minute, and so it went.

Good or bad, the music was better than the madness in his skull.

Pulling into Fox's drive after using the remote gate opener Fox had given him, he roared up to park in Fox's garage, which his bandmate had left open. He slipped the Mustang behind the hot red Lamborghini Aventador the lead singer and his fiancée had taken on their road trip. Given its gleaming state, Noah had a feeling Fox had spent the morning cleaning and polishing his pride and joy.

The man had millions, but he trusted no one else to care for the Aventador.

The sheer normality of that had Noah grinning as he got out and walked through the open front door. "Hey, you two decent?"

"Damn it, Noah, your timing sucks!" Fox called out.

"Don't listen to him, Noah," countered a laughing female voice with a naturally warm timbre that reflected Molly's personality. "He just ignored me for an hour while he fussed over Red."

Noah walked upstairs and into the open-plan kitchen/living area to find Fox squeezing Molly from behind while she laughed, her brown eyes lit from within.

"Red, huh?" He took a seat at the counter, the couple on the other side. "I always knew your love for that car was unnatural."

"Molly's the one who named her," Fox pointed out, pressing a kiss to Molly's neck before releasing her and reaching out to bump his fist against Noah's. "She and Red have a close personal relationship."

"It's true." Molly moved around the kitchen as she grabbed the ingredients for what looked like blueberry pancakes, her pretty yellow-and-white sundress skimming her curves. "She's a gorgeous beast, and it was incredible exploring the PCH in her."

When she returned to the counter to place some eggs on it, he saw that her skin carried a faint hint of sunburn. Unlike Kit's naturally bronzed complexion, Molly's hated the sun. "You forgot your hat," he said, thinking of his meal with Kit, of how her skin had glowed in the soft light from the paper lanterns.

"No, she didn't," Fox growled, dark green eyes focused on the woman he loved so much he'd had her name and claim to him tattooed across his heart. "She just kept whipping it off to sunbathe."

"Worth it." Molly's expression was unrepentant as she blew Fox a kiss before returning to her breakfast preparations.

"We're going all out today," she told Noah after using a hair tie she'd had around her wrist to pull back her silky tumble of black hair. "Fox and I stopped off at an all-night grocery store on our way home."

"Blueberry pancakes." The lead singer put a fresh mug under the spout of the coffee machine Noah still hadn't figured out. "With fucking bacon." He hauled Molly in for a kiss, his free hand sliding down to rest possessively on her hip. "Damn, but I love you."

A little breathless, Molly scrunched up her nose. "Be still my heart."

Fox's grin exposed the lean dimple in his left cheek. Whatever he murmured to Molly had her blushing and standing on tiptoe to press a sweet kiss to that dimple.

Noah thought of the small, stark-faced boy he'd met the first day of boarding school, so alone and determined not to cry. He could see no trace of that grieving child in the strong, happy man in front of him, a man who was a brother to him in everything but blood. There were relatives, and then there was *family*. Fox was family.

Noah would celebrate Fox's joy, would never let his friend know how much it hurt him to see Fox have the one thing that was forever out of Noah's reach. At least one of them had made it. "Get a room," he ordered. "*After* you feed me."

Laughing, Molly pushed Fox away. "Go sit with Noah. This breakfast is on me." A glance at Noah. "He's earned it—he stopped at every single antique shop along the way."

"You have *no* idea how many there are." Coming around with two steaming mugs of coffee, the lead singer passed one to Noah, then grabbed a stool beside him at the counter.

"And I swear the staff and customers have their own secret language. They say things like *provenance* and *patina* and *upcycle* like they're words actual people use."

Grinning as Molly stuck out her tongue at Fox, Noah said, "So when are you two doing the wedding deal?"

"We were thinking six to eight weeks." Molly mixed up the pancake batter with quick, competent hands. "I want to do it at home, so we don't have to worry about finding a venue, and everything else we can organize on short notice."

"What about the dress?" Noah asked. "Isn't that like a big deal?"

"What the fuck do you know about wedding dresses?" Fox scowled. "You have a secret addiction to reality TV I don't know about?"

"Yeah, I'm all 'say yes to the dress already, lady.'"

Molly snorted with laughter at Noah's deadpan response.

"My cousin got married last year," he said after taking a sip of his coffee. "You know, Keira."

"Crazy Keira?"

"Yeah, she lived up to her name. Serious bridezilla, and apparently she was psycho about the dress. Emily told me Keira threw a full-on tantrum in the bridal salon because the pearls on her dress were a size too small or something." His smart, sweet, funny sister had considered recording the incident for Noah but had been scared off by the wrath of the bridezilla.

Fox looked at Molly, his expression softening in a way it only ever did when he looked at the woman he adored. "You planning to go nuts on me, baby?"

"Maybe a little." Molly winked. "But not about the dress. Once Charlie arrives from New Zealand, she and Thea and I are doing a girls' trip to that vintage wedding-dress shop I saw."

Charlie, Noah remembered, was Molly's best friend, Charlotte. As for Thea, she wasn't only the band's publicist, but Molly's sister through their shared father, a hypocrite of a man who'd died while Molly was a teen. In Thea's case, the paternal relationship had been merely biological—she considered her stepdad to be her true father.

"I'm going to ask Kit too if she's not on location," Molly added.

"We all still heading to Bali for David and Thea's wedding?" Noah asked as the simple sound of Kit's name made his entire body ache with a need that wasn't ever going to go away.

"Yes!" Molly beamed. "It'll take longer to put together though—her parents and David's parents both want a big ceremony." She flicked on the cooktop. "Food coming up pronto."

IT WAS OVER AN hour and a half later, after a breakfast from the heavens, that Noah and Fox walked out to take seats around the metal table beside the infinity pool. Molly was inside, on the phone with Charlotte; her laughter occasionally drifted outside.

"You're a lucky man," Noah said to Fox, his hands hanging between his knees as he leaned forward with his forearms braced on his thighs, staring out over the clear blue waters of the pool to Santa Monica Bay in the distance.

"I know." Fox strummed the acoustic guitar he'd picked up on their way outside. "What do you think of this?"

Noah listened, made a suggestion, the music easing the scars on his soul as it always did. Didn't matter what kind. As long as it was music. Listening to Fox's strumming, he watched the sunshine glitter on the water and tried to let his mind drift, go empty.

It proved impossible.

He kept seeing snapshots of the past twenty-four... no, it was closer to twenty-nine, thirty hours: Kit's scared face as she asked him what was in the syringe, waking up on soft white sheets with tiny blue flowers, watching Kit drive off with a scowl on her face.

"You going to tell me what happened?" Fox said about ten minutes later. "And don't bullshit me, Noah. I've known you too long."

The fact was Fox knew more about Noah's demons than anyone else in the world. They'd been assigned as roommates at boarding school, both only seven years old at the time. Fox had heard him scream at night, had found him huddled, shivering in the corner, more than once, a stolen kitchen knife in hand.

Fox hadn't told on him then, and in all these years, he'd never once betrayed Noah's secret. Not even to Molly. Noah had worried about that when the two first became serious, but Fox had been blunt: *It's not mine to tell, and Molly understands that—just like I understand there are things she can't tell me about Charlie.*

Certain in his trust in Fox, Noah said, "I hit rock bottom." He had to admit it, had to get the pathetic, dangerous nature of his actions burned into his brain cells. "Ended up in a no-tell motel with a fifty-dollar hooker and a vial full of poison to

ROCK REDEMPTION

pump into my veins. I thought it would make the noise in my head go quiet."

Fox stopped strumming the guitar. "Fuck." His voice was like gravel, his hand fisted on the polished wood of the guitar. "Why didn't you call me?"

"I called Kit."

A long silence. "And?"

"And she came, saw me at my worst again." He gave a harsh laugh. "I'm such a prince I dragged her out of her house at half-past-who-the-fuck-knows o'clock in the morning."

Starting the music again, Fox didn't speak for another five minutes. "I know you don't want to hear this, but I'm going to say it anyway—you need to talk to someone. It's getting worse, not better."

Noah clenched his jaw, his teeth grinding against one another. "I can't talk about it. Not to a stranger." He had enough trouble talking about it to Fox, and they never actually talked about what lay at the root of all his problems. He'd told Fox when he'd been a child, alone and scared, but that boy was long gone. "Fuck man, I don't even want to think about it."

"But you are thinking about it. Every night," Fox pointed out. "If you're serious about Kit—"

"No." Noah sliced out a hand. "No, Fox. I want her in my life, but I won't pull her into the hellhole that's my messed up head. She doesn't need to know." He held his friend's eyes. "She *never* needs to know." He couldn't bear it.

"You know I won't say a word." The other man thrust a hand through the dark brown of his hair. "But it's eating you up from the inside. You sleep even less now than you did when you were a kid, and you're drinking so much it's worse than with Abe."

Noah couldn't dispute either charge. He might not have ended up in a near-coma like Abe, but it wasn't for lack of trying. "I poured all the liquor at my place down the drain." He'd done it in the middle of fixing the blinds.

"You know it's not that easy."

"Then I'll do it hard." Because no way was he ever checking into rehab or any other place where they could fuck with his head.

"Damn, you're a stubborn asshole." Fox passed him the guitar. "Play something while I get us more coffee."

Losing himself in the music, Noah stayed at Fox and Molly's until almost five in the afternoon. At which point he got in his car and drove not to his own home but to the studio lot where he knew Kit was filming the superhero flick. Thanks to Noah's own contacts, he had no problem getting past security or finding his way to a park outside the right sound stage.

He waited for an hour by her car before he saw her walk out with Casey. Kit sometimes rode with the slender black bodyguard and driver, but she generally preferred to live her life as normally as possible. And in a stalker-free world, Kit wasn't the kind of woman to have guards and chauffeurs.

She froze for a second when she saw him.

Shaking off her surprise as Casey nodded to him and peeled off to get into his own car, she walked over, her glorious hair damp and plaited into a loose braid. "What're you doing here?" No expression on her face.

It wasn't Kit standing in front of him, he realized, but cool, sophisticated Kathleen Devigny.

His gut clenched. "I was hoping I could take you out to dinner to say thanks."

Opening the car door, she dumped in her purse. "I'm exhausted. I need to get to bed."

Gripping the top of her door as she got into the driver's seat, he drew in the fresh scent of her. "Tomorrow?"

"Wrap party's right after we shoot the final scene. Will probably go late."

Noah knew he shouldn't keep pushing when she was giving him a large, flashing "go away" signal, but he couldn't make himself leave. "What about the day after?" he said. "We'll go someplace where you don't have to think about green superheroes or four-a.m. makeup calls."

"No, Noah."

When she pulled at her door, he released his grip on it, well aware he'd already pushed far beyond the point where he should've stopped. He couldn't blame her for her response; he was a bad bet even as a friend. He'd only stuck with Fox, David, and Abe this long because the three were as stubborn as he was... and in different ways, they needed him as much as he needed them. Kit didn't need him, and so he didn't know what to offer her to make her come back into his life.

CHAPTER 5

KIT MANAGED TO MAKE it home and inside the garage before she gave in to the sobs that had been building inside her since the moment she'd walked out of the studio and seen Noah waiting for her. It had been like one of her stupid daydreams come to life—daydreams he'd stomped to death under his boot.

Crying so hard that it hurt, she clung to the steering wheel and told herself to stop. But she couldn't. All she could think about was that night, the night when Noah had hurt her more than anyone ever had before.

Kit had learned not to believe in people a long time ago, courtesy of her parents. It wasn't that Parker and Adreina Ordaz-Castille were bad people; they loved Kit, but they weren't exactly reliable or steady. When Kit was a child, her father would play with her for hours sometimes, promise to take her to get ice cream the next day, only to cancel because a friend asked him to go sailing.

Some months she'd be lucky to see him at all around his business and social engagements. Other months he'd focus all his attention on her, charm her into believing his promises…

only to disappear back into his busy life just when she'd hopefully invited him to a school play or some other small thing that meant a lot to her.

It had been either feast or famine.

As for her mom, Adreina would take Kit shopping, spoil her, but though she'd promised Kit some mother-daughter time, she'd invite along her girlfriends. Kit had craved alone time with her vivacious and always-in-demand mom. Just an hour when she didn't have to vie against adults for Adreina's attention, when they could talk about little-girl things.

But if Adreina wasn't with friends, she was at Parker's side as they enjoyed their active social life together. Midway through her eighth year on the planet, Kit suddenly realized she hadn't actually seen either parent for a month. Late nights meant they were asleep when she got ready for school, at business meetings or modeling shoots when she came home after school, and from there, they'd been going straight to dinners and parties.

Kit's nannies had been nice, but they changed so often she knew not to get attached—Adreina always fired them when she decided to be a stay-at-home mom, which happened about four times a year and usually lasted all of three weeks.

By the time of Kit's ninth birthday, it had become easier not to expect anything emotionally from either Parker or Adreina—that way she was never disappointed. Instead, any time her mom or dad kept a promise or remembered something important to Kit, it had been a nice surprise that gave her pleasure.

She'd never again been as terribly hurt by their benign neglect.

And somewhere along the way, she'd started applying her rule about not expecting anything from people to everyone she met. It had stood her in good stead in show business. Then she'd become friends with Fox, Noah, Abe, and David. The four men had kept their word when they'd said they'd do something—whether it was meeting her for lunch or dropping by to move her stuff from her tiny first apartment to the town house.

After her life exploded following *Last Flight's* success, the guys had been there to help her through it, far more used to A-list fame than Kit was. When she'd needed dates for awards shows or other red carpet events, Abe, Fox, or David would always make time to go with her, aware that she was nervous and needed to be with someone she trusted.

Even before, when she'd been on *Primrose Avenue*, the soap that had paid her rent for years, one of the three men had stepped in whenever she needed a plus one. But Noah... Noah hadn't ever been her date, not even before what he'd done during the filming of *Last Flight*.

They'd always had too much chemistry for her to be comfortable with him the way she was with the other guys. Until one day he'd heard her talking to Abe about a book she'd recently read and called her up that night to tell her he'd just finished it himself. They'd spoken for an hour, and by the time she hung up, the chemistry had started to change into something deeper, more dangerous.

It had continued to change, call by call. Eventually they'd moved from books to movies, and he'd come over to her place to watch old black-and-white films full of glamour and wit. They'd played chess in the garden, and he'd even helped her plant the leafy tree that shaded the picnic table. When the band went on tour, she'd started to fly in for visits, somehow always ending up in Noah's room.

Where they'd done nothing sexual, nothing physically intimate. But they'd been intimate nonetheless. In those hotel rooms, they'd spoken to each other about far more than movies or books or chess. She'd told him about her parents, about how she'd spent every childhood birthday she could remember with a different nanny, and of her dreams of breaking into movies.

Noah, in turn, had told her that his parents had shipped him off to boarding school when he got to be a handful.

Apparently I was too much stress. They much preferred not having to see my face every day.

At the time, she'd thought that moment a crucial one in their relationship. Kit had never felt as close to a man as she had to Noah—she'd trusted him, relied on him, to the point that she'd ignored her own instincts about his insatiable sexual appetite. Until that horrible night. It had felt like being backhanded across the face.

That hadn't even been the most awful thing.

When Noah's eyes had met hers, she'd seen the truth— he'd done it on purpose, orchestrated things so she'd find him fucking another woman. He'd clearly realized what she felt for him, and he'd wanted to make certain she didn't start to think he felt the same. Humiliating and hurting her had obviously been easier than just telling her to her face.

Her eyes swollen and her throat raw, Kit pressed her head to the steering wheel as the tears finally faded. She felt worn out, beaten. As an intelligent woman, she knew the best thing to do would be to cut Noah out of her life. Only she wasn't about to give up the other guys and Molly and Thea just to avoid him.

And the worst, the absolute *worst* thing was that a part of her still wanted to see him, still missed him.

She got out of the car, then trudged her way to the house and to the fridge to get some water. The instant she opened the door, she remembered Noah doing the same yesterday, and that made her mind ricochet to the motel and to the syringe full of God-only-knew-what that Noah had considered pumping into his veins.

Her hand slid off the fridge, the door shutting on its own as she pressed the cold bottle of water to her forehead. It throbbed, both from her tears and from the memory of the breath-stealing fear that had gripped her that night. Regardless of how much she might want to forget Noah, to shove him out of her life, she had to accept that she'd be a wreck if she lost him so completely.

"So what are you going to do, Kit?" she asked herself.

There was no magical answer.

AN HOUR LATER, SHE was lying in bed staring up at the ceiling when she realized her mind was going around in circles like a hamster on a wheel. Grabbing the phone, she called Molly. The other woman and Kit hadn't gotten off to the best start—and the fault, Kit knew, had been hers. She was protective of the guys and untrusting of anyone she didn't know. But Molly was a rare creature in Hollywood: a warm, loving human being who was fiercely loyal to her man and to her friends.

She'd quietly become a deeply trusted friend of Kit's, someone without an agenda and honest to the bone. Becca was wonderful too, but the makeup artist was so much on Kit's side that her advice was often one-sided. She was the kind of friend who'd cheerfully help Kit bury a body.

Molly, in contrast, never sugarcoated her answers, conscious Kit needed a sounding board who saw her flaws as well as her good points. She'd help bury that body too, but not until she'd grilled Kit on the facts and made her own decision as to the merits of the hypothetical murder. And, critically, she was friends with Noah as well, knew he was far more than just a promiscuous rock star.

"Hi, Molly," she said when the other woman answered. "Did I wake you?"

A laugh. "It's only eight thirty, Kit."

"Right." Kit groaned. "This filming schedule has reset my entire body clock. I'll be fast asleep in another few minutes."

"I can't wait to see the movie." Molly's smile was in her voice. "Charlie's a huge fan of the series, and she got me hooked when we were in high school."

Kit hadn't yet met Molly's best friend, but she had a feeling she'd like the other woman. "Want to come to the premiere as my date?"

"Are you *serious*?" Molly uttered a wordless sound of excitement on the heels of her question.

"Absolutely." A smile tugged at Kit's lips, the other woman's joy was so infectious. "I was going to go on my own, but it'd be fun to have the company."

"I'd love to!"

They talked about the future premiere for a while longer

before Molly said, "What's the matter?" Her voice was gentle, caring. "You don't sound like yourself."

Kit had called Molly for a reason, but she still had to fight to speak; it all just hurt too much. Like a cold, icy weight sitting on her chest, crushing and crushing. "It's about Noah," she said, having already trusted the other woman with the ugly truth of what Noah had done.

The only other people who knew were Becca and Fox. Seeing Kit nearly every day thanks to their shooting schedule, Becca had picked up on Kit's giddy happiness then on her devastation, and connected the dots.

As for Fox, he'd bumped into her in the corridor after she ran out of Noah's hotel room, had held her safe while she sobbed, her heart in pieces. He'd kept her secret too, never let on anything to David and Abe, though the other two band members had to have guessed something was going on with her and Noah.

Now, Kit didn't betray the fact Noah had ended up stone drunk in a dive on the wrong side of town, saying only that he'd come back into her life. "I don't know what to do, Molly." The confession emerged in a rasped whisper. "I know he's not good for me, but"—she curled her fingers into her palm, admitted the truth—"I still miss him. Like a part of me was torn out and there's this hole there."

"Do you want to try again with him?"

Kit was shaking her head before Molly finished asking the question. "I'll never trust him again." How could she ever forget that horrible scene he'd set up for her, ever forgive him for humiliating her with such cruelty?

"I can understand that," Molly replied. "What you said,

about having a part of you ripped out—perhaps you need to find a way to allow that wound to heal."

"By accepting Noah in my life?"

"I'm not going to tell you to do that, Kit, not after the way he hurt you. I will ask a question though—if he disappeared from your life forever, would you be happy?"

Kit thought of her panic the night Noah had called her, the cold terror that had gripped her throat and squeezed. "No." Her breath hurt. "What am I going to do, Molly?"

KIT GOT THROUGH THE next day by focusing on work with grim-minded determination; she even managed to laugh at the wrap party.

"This is relief laughter," she said to Cody, one of her costars. "No one needs to wear that much makeup." Her hair was still heavily damp from showering the cosmetics off. "You have no idea how tough it is to wash off full-body avocado-green goo."

The chiseled-jawed actor pressed a kiss to her cheek, his teeth gleaming Hollywood-white against the ebony of his skin. "You were a babe, even in green."

"Still not dating you."

"Why not?"

"You're gay. I don't want to be your beard."

Cody wrapped an arm around her shoulders. "You sure?" His dark brown eyes turned soulful. "I'd be the best boyfriend you ever had. No pressuring you for sex, willing to share chores and happy to go shopping."

Kit snorted. "You hate shopping and you have a gazillion maids." Hugging him around the waist, she leaned into his muscled warmth. "And sex would be nice." Too bad her body wanted a man who'd made it clear multiple times that he didn't want to "fuck" her.

"If you insist." Cody sighed. "I'll pop a pill, get it up."

"You're a riot." Leaving him with a mock punch to the rock-hard abs that decorated the bedrooms of teenage girls across the country—regardless of the fact that he was, in fact, openly gay—she went to talk to Becca.

It was an hour later that she slipped out. Cody left with her and Casey, eager to head home to his steady boyfriend. That didn't stop the incorrigible flirt from teasing Casey—who was about as straight as they came. Fighting not to laugh as Casey gave Cody the cool Marine stare that said he was not amused, she wasn't ready for Cody's sudden swearing.

"Damn it to hell! Some asshole's slashed my tires!"

Ice trickled down Kit's spine. "I'm so sorry, Cody. It might've been my stalker." The disturbed man had never before struck inside the studio lot, but…

"Nah, I don't think so, babe," Cody said, hunkering down to look at the tires. "Everyone knows I play for the home team, so no reason for your stalker dude to get his panties in a jealous knot. Probably just some fuckwit getting his rocks off."

"I agree with Cody," Casey said, a frown in his eyes as he took in the damage. "Your stalker believes you two are married, and Cody's no threat to that." He squeezed the other man's shoulder. "I can organize a tow for you."

"Thanks, man." Cody rubbed his face. "I'm gonna call my sweetheart for a ride." He leaned into Kit's tight hug. "Aw, don't look so pissed, Kit. It's only tires—gotta remember that and not let this gutless weenie ruin our night."

"Gutless weenie?" she said on a surprised laugh.

"Yep. No guts and a tiny dick."

Kit and Casey stayed with her fellow actor until his boyfriend arrived. As the two men were happy to wait together for the tow truck, Kit and Casey got into their respective cars to head out of the lot. Kit hadn't touched a drop of alcohol at the party. She needed her head on straight tonight.

Taking a deep breath, she turned in the direction of Noah's home.

She was halfway there when it struck her: she'd never actually been to Noah's house. Back when they'd been close, it hadn't been a big deal. Noah had said he liked the feel of her place, first at the town house, then at her current home. It had made her happy at the time, but now...

Her fingers gripped the steering wheel so tight that her bones pushed up white against her skin. "No way am I inviting myself to his house if he doesn't want me there." And since this was one conversation she didn't want to have in public, she turned the car around. Behind her, Casey was probably wondering if she was lost.

Sending Noah a message at a red light, she didn't check for a response until she was home.

On my way. –Noah

He always did that, always signed his messages. As if she might forget who he was, despite the fact he'd been one of her most frequent contacts at one time. When she'd ribbed him about it, he'd shrugged and given her that crooked smile she could never resist.

Not back then.

Heart aching at the sweet poignancy of the memory, she

put her keys and phone on the kitchen counter, then hunted in her freezer until she found a couple of gourmet pizzas. Even she couldn't mess up pizza. She turned the oven dial to the correct temperature and, while waiting for it to heat up, went into the bedroom to change into black yoga pants and a fitted dark blue T-shirt.

Hair mostly dry at this point, she combed it into a loose ponytail, her eyes on the mirror and on a face the tabloids had called "fugly" when Kit had been at the awkward adolescent stage. As in, how could two people as genetically blessed as Parker and Adreina Ordaz-Castille sire such a fugly child?

Those same tabloids now called Kit "a mix between Grace Kelly and Sophia Loren." She snorted. Yeah, no matter how much smoke the media blew up her ass, she wasn't about to get a big head. Neither was she about to forget that Noah would rather sleep with random groupies than with her.

A jagged breath.

Heading back into the kitchen, she slid the pizzas into the oven and began to make a green salad. She went to grab a bottle of wine halfway through, froze. No, she wouldn't give Noah alcohol. Not until she knew if the other night had been a one-off or if he had a drinking problem.

She decided to make iced tea instead, heavy on the honey. Noah had a liking for the stuff, though she didn't know where he'd picked up the taste.

The kitchen was redolent with the smell of bubbling cheese when Butch called to say Noah was heading up to the house.

It was time.

CHAPTER 6

THROAT DRY, KIT WAITED for Noah to knock before she padded to the front door. Pride wouldn't allow her to stand there waiting for him. Never again would she wait for Noah St. John.

The impact of him hit her all over again the instant she opened the door. He was wearing another pair of faded blue jeans and his favorite scuffed boots with the metal rivets, but his short-sleeved shirt was crisp black with a black-and-red design on one side. His hair was damp, his jaw freshly shaven. She knew if she leaned in close, he'd smell of the sea breeze of his aftershave and of the raw masculine heat that was Noah.

Hand tightening on the door, she stepped back and called on all her theatrical training to sound normal, unruffled. "Come in. I made pizza."

"I picked up dessert."

It was only then that she realized he was holding an insulated bag from her favorite ice cream place.

"Peanut butter fudge." That heartbreaking smile, the song lyrics tattooed on the inside of his right wrist catching her eye as he lifted the bag. "No more superhero body paint, right?"

Kit's calm facade nearly cracked. Noah had talked her into dessert more times than she could count during their earlier… whatever it had been. "Thanks."

Taking the bag, she carried it into the kitchen and put the tub of ice cream in the freezer. She was putting the insulated bag on one side of the counter and trying not to be hyper-conscious of Noah's presence when the oven timer went off.

Grabbing at the distraction, she put on oven mitts and pulled out the two pizzas.

"Planning to indulge?" Noah asked, his gray eyes solemn though his lips smiled.

"I know you inhale pizza." She'd wonder where it went except that she knew he ran for miles at night, long after the rest of the world was asleep. It was a truth she'd discovered when he'd crashed in her guest bedroom once. She'd woken and gone to the kitchen to grab a glass of water, caught him coming back in, damp with sweat and breathless.

He'd shrugged and grinned that off too, saying he ran after midnight because of the peace and privacy afforded by the darkness. She'd accepted the explanation, but like so much about Noah, it didn't make sense in hindsight. Except for one notorious incident where he'd lost his temper with a frankly aggravating photographer, he didn't seem to care about the paparazzi or the public snapping photos of him.

"This looks like seriously fancy pizza," he said now, picking up a piece that dripped with cheese.

"Careful. It's hot."

He bit in anyway, groaned in pleasure, the strong column of his throat moving as he swallowed.

Kit's breath caught. Stifling the visceral response, she jerked away her gaze and passed him a plate before getting one for herself. She grabbed a slice, some salad, and took a seat at the table.

"Is that iced tea?" Having taken the opposite seat, Noah got up and brought over the pitcher she'd forgotten on the counter, its sides frosty with condensation.

"Thanks," she said when he poured her a glass.

They sat, ate. In silence.

It was excruciating. Awkward beyond bearing.

"I miss you."

Throat choking up at the roughly uttered words, Kit poked a fork at her salad.

"Kit." Noah reached across with a careful hand, closing it over her own. "I'm sorry." It came out gritty. "I fucked up. Bad."

A punch of anger had her snapping up her head. "You did it on purpose."

"Yeah, I did."

His admission brutalized her all over again, but he held on when she would've pulled away her hand. "I didn't know how else to show you how bad of a bet I was," he said, curling his fingers into her palm.

"So you had me walk in on you with another woman?" Kit demanded, ripping away her hand because he had no damn right to touch her; he'd thrown away that right. "You didn't have enough respect for me as a friend to just *tell* me you weren't interested?"

"I'M MESSED UP," NOAH said flatly. "Seriously messed up." It was all he could say; he couldn't tell her the why of it, couldn't bear for her to know.

"That's not an excuse." Her eyes, those passionate amber eyes, blazed at him. "We're all a little messed up."

"Not a little." Getting up, he strode to the other end of the kitchen and back. "Not even a lot. I'm messed up on a level nothing will ever fix." He'd accepted that a long time ago. "I'll never be someone who deserves you... but I need you." It was so fucking hard to say that, to admit vulnerability and lay himself open to her rejection.

Kit was the only woman who could make him bleed, make him beg. "Be my friend, Kit. Please."

Kit's eyes shimmered. Ducking her head, she pressed her face into her hands, her fingers trembling.

Noah hated himself for what he'd done to her, hated that he hadn't just let her go, but he *couldn't*. Going to her, he hunkered down beside her chair and gripped the back of it so he wouldn't give in to the urge to touch her again without her permission. "I'm sorry." The words were inadequate, but they were all he had. "I'm so sorry, Kit."

Seeing her like this, Noah wanted to punch himself, kick himself. If anyone else had hurt Kit this way, it was exactly what Noah would've done. "I don't expect you to forgive me, but please don't shut me out." His blood roared in his ears, his face flushing burning hot then going ice-cold when she didn't raise her head. "I can't breathe knowing you hate me."

Kit looked at him at last, her face ravaged by tears. Then she was in his arms, that stunning tear-wet face buried against his neck. He held her as she cried, and he called himself a selfish bastard, and it was true, but one other thing was also true: "Day or night, rain or shine, I'll be there for you," he whispered against her ear, his hand cupping the back of her head, and his arms around her.

His hand was the one that trembled this time. "Just be my friend." Laugh again with him, remind him that life wasn't only nightmares and pain, make him feel as if he could be a better man if he tried hard enough. "Don't give up on me. Please don't."

"I want a promise," she said after too long, her tears having soaked the shoulder of his shirt.

Wary, he looked at her as she sat back up, her eyes puffy and her cheeks shining with the remnants of her tears. There were some promises he simply couldn't make, some promises he was too broken to keep.

Taking a shuddering breath, she said, "Promise me that you'll never again even *think* of doing what you almost did in that motel room." A harsh demand. "You promise me, Noah, because I can't go through that again."

"I promise," he said without hesitation. "Never again."

Kit grabbed one of the pretty napkins she'd put on the table and wiped her face before dropping her hand to her thigh, her fingers clenched around the napkin.

He waited, his pulse a huge, loud thing that drowned out his breathing.

"Okay," she said, so softly it was less than a whisper. "We'll be friends."

KIT DIDN'T KNOW WHAT she was doing agreeing to be Noah's friend, didn't even know if they could salvage that relationship from the wreckage. But ten minutes later, as she watched him pull the ice cream from the freezer, she couldn't deny the need inside her.

As she'd confessed to Molly, she'd missed him too. So much.

She wished she didn't, would do everything in her power to bury that need going forward. It wasn't the right way to enter into a friendship, but it was the only way she might survive it. "One scoop for me," she said, when he began to dish out the dessert.

"You sure?" A sinful, tempting smile. "You love this stuff."

Butterflies in her stomach, an acute pain in her heart. "I'll get sick if I start eating too much rich food at once—and I already had pizza."

"Right, I never thought about that." Putting a couple more scoops in his bowl, he placed both bowls on the table before returning the tub to the freezer.

The light caught on the gold of his hair, the strands silky and bright and just long enough to slide forward until he shoved them back with a thrust of his hand. She'd always loved Noah's hair, always wanted to touch it. Taking a quiet breath that hurt going in, she forced herself to look away.

Noah wasn't for her, would never be for her.

"So," he said, sliding into his chair, "are you excited about your full-fat latte tomorrow morning?"

She'd made that laughing comment in an interview. It messed her up to know he'd watched it, remembered. "I decided to save the lattes for next week, when my stomach's had time to recover from the movie diet." It was all but impossible to sound natural when her emotions were a black turbulence inside her.

"You know who to call if you want company." Noah's voice was easy, but the renewed awkwardness between them was a living, breathing entity.

Kit didn't know what to say, so she just ate a spoonful of ice cream to cover her nonresponse. "What are you and the rest of the guys planning to do now the tour's over?"

"Work on a new album. We've got some material and ideas already, but it's time to sit down, start putting the pieces together." He shrugged. "Fact is, we could put out an album next week if we wanted to, but it wouldn't be *us*."

Kit understood what he meant. Schoolboy Choir was so successful not because they released album after album, but because the albums they did put out were stellar. "That song," she said. "About the sparrow. Will it be on this album?" Noah had sung it to her when they'd been friends but had said it wasn't ready for recording.

"No. It's not exactly Schoolboy Choir material."

"What are you talking about? It's amazing." A harsh, beautiful ballad of such heartbreaking vulnerability that it had made her cry.

Noah just shrugged.

Before, she would've pushed, but she didn't have that right anymore. Couldn't have it for her own emotional health. "Well," she said, "if you don't release it, record it for me. I'd love to hear it again."

"You'll just have to put up with me." A devastating smile. "I'll sing it to you anytime you want."

There was a time when Noah's offer would've made her go all melty inside. Now it just hurt.

"Sorry," she said with another forced smile. "I think I'm

beginning to fade. Had an early start." It wasn't a total lie; she'd been at the studio at four a.m. as usual, but she wouldn't be going to sleep so soon after eating.

Which, she belatedly realized, Noah knew after her comment the night he'd made her spaghetti. Instead of calling her on it, however, he got up. "I'll help you clean up."

"Don't worry about it." A yawn cracked her mouth. "Drat, sorry again."

This time, his smile reached his eyes. "You really are beat." Leaving the dishes, he walked to the front door, her by his side. "Do you think you'll be up early again tomorrow?"

She made a face. "Three twenty on the dot, I'm guessing." It would take at least a week to break out of that rhythm.

"Want to come do something with me?" Shoving his hands into the back pockets of his jeans, he wouldn't quite meet her eyes. "Since we'll both be awake at that hour."

Kit frowned. "What would we do in the middle of the night?" It wasn't until the words were out that she realized how suggestive they sounded.

Thankfully, Noah didn't seem to notice. Rubbing the back of his neck, he said, "I was thinking I'd pick you up at four thirty, and it'd be just before six and getting light by the time we got there."

Kit wasn't certain she was reading him right—Noah was never hesitant or nervous... but he was sure giving that impression right now. "Where?"

Shoving both hands back into his pockets, he finally met her gaze, a slight flush on his cheekbones that floored her, smashing right through her defenses. Noah never blushed. It was simply not in the Noah St. John repertoire. Except he was rocking on his heels and that color hadn't receded.

He was impossibly gorgeous.

"To go for a flight."

Kit felt like a parrot, but all she could say was, "A flight?"

"Yeah, I, um, got my pilot's license, bought a small two-seater plane."

Her mouth fell open. "Since when have you been taking flying lessons? Do the guys know?" No one had ever mentioned it.

"A while." He ran a hand through his hair, gave her that lopsided grin, only this time it held a piercing edge of vulnerability.

At that instant, he looked younger than she'd ever seen him.

"You're the only one who knows. I didn't want to say anything until I actually did it," he added. "Had the license, I mean."

Wonderfully astonished and fighting the urge to kiss him, he was so beautiful right then—so *her* Noah—Kit just stood there.

His smile began to fade at the edges, daylight swallowed by night. "You don't have to. I just thought—"

"Yes," she interrupted. "Yes, I'd like to." She couldn't kick the gift of trust back in his face... and she'd promised to be his friend.

As she'd already admitted, no matter how much he'd hurt her, her heart would break forever if Noah was no longer in the world. That didn't mean she was going to fall back into the trap of loving him. It was time she said good-bye to a dream that had held her hostage even when she'd believed herself free: beautiful, gifted, broken Noah St. John was simply never going to love Kathleen "Kit" Devigny.

Sliding to the floor with her back to the door after Noah left, Kit stared at the hands that always wanted to touch Noah when he was near and shook her head. Her tears were silent this time, the hot droplets erasing the last traces of the dream.

CHAPTER 7

NOAH MANAGED TO SLEEP that night, thanks to a trick he'd discovered on the Internet. He'd put in a search term in desperation one night and hit on a video of rain falling in someone's backyard, and before he knew it, he was asleep in his chair. He'd woken five hours later with a stiff neck and the video still playing in a loop.

He'd immediately bought the download.

The rain sounds didn't work every time or even mostly, but they did that night. Thank God. He'd never have risked taking Kit up otherwise. He had an excellent reaction time, but fatigue could dull even the best instincts.

Awake in plenty of time, he showered and shaved, then pulled on his favorite old jeans and a dark gray T-shirt, wondering what Kit would think of his little Cessna. White with blue markings, it was parked in a hangar beside a small private airfield. As far as the sixty-something owners of the airfield and hangar were concerned, Noah was simply another weekend warrior who worked in the city and came to play with his toy in his off time.

He'd deliberately chosen a place that was out of the way,

but he'd lucked out with the owners being uninterested in any music but country. Blissful anonymity was the result.

He grabbed his wallet and the keys he needed to access the hangar and plane, then got into the black SUV he kept beside his Mustang—no sense screwing up his anonymity by driving a distinctive car. This early, traffic was light enough that he'd make it to Kit's with time to spare.

His heart beat a little too fast, his fingers tapping on the steering wheel.

When he glimpsed the lights of an all-night grocery store up ahead, he made a snap decision and swung into the parking lot. He grabbed a cart and got a few things for brunch as well as the one snack Kit could never resist. He wanted this to be a good day for her; to do that, he couldn't allow himself to imagine it wouldn't work, that he'd lost her forever the night he'd done the unforgiveable.

"Wow." The pimply-faced teenage cashier's mouth fell open. "Are you really you?"

Noah didn't perform for the fame, but he also didn't disdain his fans. They were the reason he could be free to live the music inside him; without that music, he'd be dead or huddled in some damn psychiatric ward. "Depends who you think I am."

The teenager gulped. "I recognize that voice and that tattoo on your wrist." Hand trembling, he put down the drink he'd been about to scan. "Wow. C-can I…" He just held up his phone in a wordless question.

"Sure." Taking the phone since he was taller, Noah snapped a photo of himself with his arm around the kid's shoulders, the teenager giving two thumbs-up and grinning so hard his face was about to crack.

The photo-taking attracted the attention of the night manager and the only other clerk on duty. By the time Noah finally left, traffic had thickened as early commuters tried to beat the chaos of LA traffic, but it was still manageable and he arrived right on time.

Kit came out of the house as he stepped out of the car. Dressed in jeans that hugged her legs, flats, and a kind of floaty tunic top in white with three-quarter-length sleeves, her hair in a ponytail, she looked fresh and pretty and like his Kit. Not Kathleen Devigny, Oscar-nominated actress on the way to superstardom. Just Kit.

"I wasn't sure what to bring," she said. "I have my phone and some money. Anything else?"

"No, we're good." He didn't fight the happiness that was sunshine in his blood; Kit alone could make him feel that way, as if he was an ordinary man out with a woman he adored.

"Let me set the alarm. I've already alerted security we're heading out." A glance over her shoulder. "I told them not to follow today."

Noah braced his arm against the top of the SUV, shaken by her trust. "I'll park the SUV in the hangar so no one can get to it while we're in the air." Up there, she'd be safe in his hands.

Five minutes later, she was snug in the SUV.

After grabbing coffee from a drive-through, they drove in silence for over twenty minutes. It wasn't as awkward as dinner had been, but neither was it as comfortable as they'd once been together. Noah had destroyed that. He'd done it deliberately with his eyes wide open. He'd hurt the one person he never wanted to hurt... and he knew without a doubt that it was the best thing he could've ever done for Kit.

No matter what happened from now on, she'd never forget or forgive the cruelty of his actions. It would keep her at a safe distance, where he couldn't hurt her in far more vicious and irrevocable ways. Where he couldn't stain her with his ugliness.

His hand tightened on the steering wheel. "Do you like the superhero movie?" he asked, needing to hear her voice, to have that much of her at least. "I mean, I know the green gunk and early starts got old, but do you have a good feeling about the final product?"

She shifted in her seat, the movement sending her scent his way, the freshness of soap and water licked with a faint trace of her perfume. It was subtle and elegant but with a hint of the earth, exactly like Kit.

"It's good fun, has amazing stunts, and the plot makes sense, wonder of wonders," she said after a thoughtful pause. "There was even some actual emotional acting required." Her tone was a little too nonchalant.

"The script was phenomenal, wasn't it?"

"Yep." She laughed at being caught out. "Great cast too. Even if Cody did keep hitting on me."

"Maybe you should hit back, make him uncomfortable."

"Hah, nothing makes Cody uncomfortable." Sounding more at ease, more like herself, she told him about the stunts she'd done herself. "The best was sliding off a motorcycle. Worth all the time it took me to learn it."

"Jesus, Kit." His fingers squeezed the steering wheel. "That's dangerous."

"That's why it's called a stunt. I ended up with a scraped elbow but no other bruises."

Fighting his instinctive protective response, he said, "I'll be first in line to see the movie."

She didn't ask him to go with her. No surprise. Kit never asked him to accompany her to an event. He understood why: at first, there'd been too much chemistry between them, the sparks hot enough to burn. Then... then it had become too important.

Noah would give anything to stand next to her while she shone bright, but he didn't trust himself to be able to keep his emotions hidden when she glowed in front of him. He was fucking proud of her, and he wanted to tell the whole world. Especially the assholes who turned up their noses and belittled her accomplishments by insinuating that her parents had bankrolled her.

He'd seen her work double shifts at the diner, watched her schlep to audition after audition and come back disappointed but determined to try again. Not once had she fallen back on the Ordaz-Castille name—and since she'd made no attempt to court publicity during her teens, no one had recognized her. She'd simply been another young, hopeful actress.

Kit had earned her place in the limelight, and she'd done it on her own terms.

"Did you like New Zealand?" she said before the lengthening silence became painful, full of all the words they couldn't say to one another. "I never asked."

Because she'd refused to talk to him then. "Lots of water and sunshine, and the South Island's crazy beautiful. Me and Abe, we took off for a week to one of the national parks, did white-water rafting, bungee jumped, even walked on a glacier."

"It sounds incredible." She sighed. "I've always wanted to go down there, never had the chance."

It was on the tip of his tongue to say he'd go with her, that they could hike through the sprawling parks full of snow-capped mountains and pristine rivers, camp under skies so clear you could nearly touch the Milky Way at night. No photographers, no stalkers, nothing but a wild beauty that would suit Kit's grounded nature.

He bit back the offer just in time; she'd agreed to come with him today, but he was under no illusion that their new relationship was anything other than brittle. "You'd love it," he said through the renewed tension in his gut. "If you can swim it, climb it, ride it, jump off it, or hike it, New Zealand's got things covered."

Kit had so many questions about the small country that the rest of the drive passed by without further silences. The sky was beginning to lighten in the east when he punched in the code to open the gates to the isolated, no-frills airfield and drove through to the hangar.

"Here she is," he said once they were inside and by the plane. He patted the side of the Cessna, his nerves in a knot.

It mattered what Kit thought. Always had. Always would.

"She's not what I expected." Kit ran her hand along the buffed-clean paintwork. "I mean that in a good way." A smile. "I expected a new, glossy plane, but she's got age, character."

Noah took a breath. "Yeah, she's got a few miles on her." Her imperfections were part of why he'd fallen in love with the machine. "I like to think she's seen the world and now she's showing it to me."

74

KIT FELT HER HEART hitch at the evocative beauty of his words. It was at times like these that it was so difficult to keep her distance from Noah, fleeting moments when he showed her a piece of himself. A real piece, part of the heart he kept hidden so deep that most people never knew it existed. To the rest of the world, he was simply a bad-boy rocker, the most scandalous member of Schoolboy Choir, the one who provided the best photo ops and led the most hard rock lifestyle.

Abe's former drug use had been tabloid fodder, of course—the paparazzi had hounded him when he was discharged from the hospital after his overdose, but Noah's liaisons with endless women made for much prettier pictures, especially when he was snapped with a leggy model, actress, or other woman famous in her own right. If he'd kept a little black book, it would've been overflowing with A-list names, but Kit knew Noah didn't keep any records—a man only did that when he wanted to see a woman again.

"Ready to go up?" he asked, the light in his eyes almost boyish. "Wait, hold on a sec. I bought some stuff for brunch."

As he went to the car to grab the bags, she found herself hesitating. It was early now. If he planned on having brunch with her, that meant they'd be together for hours. She wasn't sure she could handle that, but the light in his eyes, she hadn't *ever* seen that. Not even their first time around.

She was such a sucker. She had to say no, had to back off before she placed herself in harm's way again.

"Done." He put the grocery bags in the plane, turned. "We can catch the sunrise if we take off now."

Kit inhaled, held the breath before releasing it in a slow exhale. "Noah, I'm—"

Smile fading, he met her gaze, the dark gray of his eyes empty of that bright, unexpected light. However, instead of offering to take her back to the city, he braced a palm against the plane and said, "I'm not giving you up, Kit." His jaw was granite. "You're too important to me."

Not important enough.

She barely bit back the angry words. They'd been through that, and if she kept dwelling on it, it would only make her bitter and broken, and poison whatever relationship remained between them. "What are we doing, Noah?" she said quietly. "You know this won't work." They'd never been meant to be just friends: they could be either passionate lovers or sworn enemies.

There was no middle ground.

"It can work," Noah said, as if he could *will* a simple, uncomplicated friendship into being. "But only if you give it a shot." He stepped closer, close enough that she could feel the heat of his body. "Don't throw in the towel on me, on us." A pause that held like a dewdrop on a spider web, caught between sparkle and shatter. "I need you."

Her chest ached.

She apparently still had a mile-wide weak spot when it came to Noah exposing his need. He showed it so rarely, asked for something even less. And she *had* promised to be his friend. She owed it to who they'd once been to give the attempt this one chance at least. "Let's go watch the sunrise."

That sunrise was spectacular, coming over the San Gabriel Mountains and bathing the world in a deep gold kissed with pink, but it didn't hold her attention, not with Noah beside her. He was competent and efficient at the controls, a haunting lightness to him.

"You really love this," she said, her voice soft with realization.

"Up here, it doesn't matter who you are, what your sins." His gorgeous voice poured into her ears through the headphones, made her stomach flutter, her thighs clench. "It's total freedom. No expectations. No judgments. Just endless sky."

Kit had never understood why Noah was so deeply unhappy. On paper, his life seemed picture-perfect. Born to a wealthy couple, his father a powerhouse lawyer and his mother a political lobbyist, he'd had the proverbial silver spoon in his mouth since the day he was born. He also openly adored his younger sister, Emily, had invited her along as his plus one to the music awards last year.

Even if it was about shitty parents, that was no cause for such deep anger at life.

Kit knew countless people with parents who couldn't care less. Some grew up and dealt with it, others were constantly badly behaving teenagers trying to get their parents' attention, but no one she'd ever met had been this *angry*—least of all anyone who'd found a passion in life and followed it. Her acting had been her lifeline, but while Noah lived for his music, it didn't seem to penetrate the hard shell of his anger.

"Look."

CHAPTER 8

FOLLOWING NOAH'S POINTING FINGER, she saw the tiny figure of a lone hiker waving up at them before the man continued on his journey and they flew on. Noah was right—it was stunningly peaceful and freeing up here.

"I heard about your cosmetics deal. Congratulations."

Fisting a hand against the impact of his voice so intimately close, her pulse rapid, she said, "It's not a sure thing yet. Papers still to sign."

"You know they won't back out. They'd be idiots if they did."

"I feel like such a fraud." It was the first time she'd admitted her fears aloud. "I'm no model." All of Adreina's closest friends were fellow supermodels, so Kit had grown up around inhumanly perfect people, knew without a doubt that she wasn't one of them.

"But," she added, "it's such an amazing opportunity that I couldn't turn it down. Harper says it'll grow my brand, and the money will be welcome." Kit had earned a good amount with *Last Flight,* thanks to the profit sharing deal she'd signed in lieu of payment in advance; at the time, no one had expected the movie to turn into a blockbuster, so the contract had been generous.

Unfortunately, being forced into a premature property purchase by the combined efforts of her stalker and the paparazzi had put her in a deep financial hole. She now had a monster of a mortgage; her security team didn't come cheap either. Neither did the gardening team she'd had to hire to maintain the property. The instant she let things go, rumors would start, and right now she needed to fake it until she made it.

"The cosmetics deal will get me mostly out of my mortgage hole unless something goes horribly wrong—like if I break out in a sudden case of acne."

Noah snorted. "That's what airbrushing is for."

Laughing, she shook her head. "I'm not kidding, it's in the contract."

He shot her a disbelieving look. "*Acne?*"

"Not that specifically—any facial injury or outbreak or general hideousness," Kit said, her shoulders shaking. "They can airbrush the ads, sure, but if a paparazzo gets a real-life shot of me looking unacceptably rough, there goes my value as a promotional asset."

If Kit hoped for a renewal after the initial one-year term, she had to make sure she looked good even if she was heading to the gym or popping out to grab groceries. "There's also an 'unacceptable weight gain' clause, but hey, at least my lawyer got the 'moral turpitude' one struck out."

Noah scowled. "You should've told the assholes to shove it where the sun don't shine."

"Giant mortgage, remember?" She shrugged. "It's almost like another acting gig for me, and to be honest, the cosmetics people treat me nicer than most directors."

"You're fielding movie offers left and right." Noah angled the plane east in the crystalline blue sky. "You don't have to do anything that makes you unhappy."

He was so protective of her, always had been. He'd come to her town house in the middle of the night when she'd freaked out after catching a photographer peering through the window; he'd also made the police take the stalking seriously from the very start. That protectiveness was part of the reason why his betrayal had hurt her so badly. It was as if he'd become a different person that night, a person who didn't care about her at all.

"That's just it." Chest hurting, she looked out the window. "The cosmetics deal will give me the freedom to sign more movies like *Last Flight*. Not that I didn't have fun doing the superhero movie, but my heart tends to sway toward script-driven dramas."

"YOU'RE AN AMAZING ACTRESS." Noah loved watching her on-screen. "Whatever you choose, you make it better."

"Some scripts can't be saved, Noah." An unexpected laugh.

His lungs began to work again. He'd caught Kit hesitating and choosing her words several times during the flight, and her body language... there was distance there. Distance he'd created, so he couldn't fucking cry about it now.

"Harper got this one offer for a movie about erotic insect-women who wanted to sex men to death." She was no longer staring out the window, her smile like sunshine. "I was meant to be the insect empress, and oh, I got to wear the 'diamond' string bikini."

Noah tried very hard not to imagine Kit in a string bikini; the last thing he needed was a hard-on. Kit was flat out the sexiest woman he knew. "Tell me you still have the script," he said, managing to pull off a light response.

"I might have saved it."

He smiled. "Was that the worst one?" Talking to her this way, it felt like having his Kit back again. "No wait, I want to know something else more."

"What?"

"Did Hugh make an offer yet?" he said, referring to the owner of the most well-known adult magazine in the world.

"Yep. Hundred grand."

"Pfft. Total lowball. Hold out for at least nine figures."

Open laughter. "I don't think they paid that much even for Abigail Rutledge, and she's the reigning queen of the A-list."

Noah was suddenly sorry he'd brought up the topic. The idea of random men jacking off to Kit's naked body made him want to punch out the lights of every other male in the fucking world. "Would you do it?" he forced himself to ask. "Pose nude for the right money or the right photographer?"

"Nope. And I won't do nude scenes either—it's in all my contracts. If the director wants a flash of breasts or whatever, they bring in a body double. No exceptions, and I don't care if the stance loses me roles."

Noah unclenched his jaw. "You feel strongly about it." Good. So did he.

She took a long time to reply, her face pensive when he glanced over. "I love my mom, and I think she has the right to showcase her body any way she chooses." The last words were

81

soft and fierce both. "But… when I was in junior high, boys in my grade were ogling the nude spread she did at forty-five. It was the 'Mrs. Robinson' issue, and it spread through the male population of the school like wildfire."

Noah suddenly realized he'd seen that spread; every man of a certain age probably had. He was fairly certain one of the boys in his class had tacked it up on the back of the door to the gym locker room.

Feeling a little ill, he shook his head. "Hell, Katie." The affectionate term just slipped out, but lost in her memories, Kit didn't seem to notice.

"It wasn't the first time—she'd done spreads when she was younger, but I wasn't old enough to be bothered by it then." She reached up to fix her headphones. "I wasn't ashamed of her. I think she's the most astonishingly gorgeous woman I know, and I admire her confidence." Love and pride entwined. "It was just weird and uncomfortable to know that the boy I sat next to in math class, or the boy who was my crush, would probably go home to jerk off to pictures of my *mom*."

"They use it against you?" Noah asked, furious at the thought of her being bullied.

Hugging herself, she rubbed her hands up and down her arms. "A few snotty remarks, the odd snigger, one dipwad plastering my locker with the spread, but that was it. My classmates were all from prominent entertainment or sports families, so my mom was hardly the first parent to be in the media.

"Drugs, cheating, white-collar crime, public drunkenness, you name it, one of the parents had been busted for it." She blew out a breath. "But it mattered to *me*. I want to have children, Noah, and I don't want any child of mine to ever be put in the position of knowing other kids are passing around naked photos of Mom."

"I get it," Noah said, awed by her strength. If that had been him he'd probably have spent his entire school life bloodying noses and breaking jaws. "Good thing you weren't a boy."

"I should call you a sexist pig for saying that, but in this case you're right. Can you imagine going over to a friend's house and finding nude photos of your mom pinned to the walls?"

Noah shuddered, skin crawling. "Thank God I'm never going to be a father—some of the shit I've pulled is insane." He'd been photographed in bed with three half-naked women for Christ's sake. It had been for a magazine editorial, but still. "How the hell would I ever explain any of it to a son or a daughter?"

Kit shifted in her seat to face him. "What do you mean you're never going to be a father?" A pause. "I'm sorry—that was insensitive."

"No, it's all right—it's not medical. I just know I won't make a good father, so I'm not going to saddle some poor kid with Noah St. John as a dad."

Regardless of his mood or the demons in his head, he was always very, *very* careful. The one time he'd had a scare, it hadn't been because he'd fallen down on the job but because the condom had torn. Thankfully, the groupie he'd been screwing at the time had been on the pill, so he'd dodged that bullet.

He'd put a private eye on her to make damn certain, because if he had fucked up and fathered a kid, he'd have taken responsibility—financially at least. "I'm actually thinking of getting it taken care of permanently."

"*What?*" Open shock. "Noah, you can't do that. What if you change your mind?"

"I'm not a good bet as a father, Kit. You know that." He met her dismayed gaze. "Would you want me as the father of your child?"

Her face froze. Not saying a word, she turned to stare out the window.

It felt like a punch to the solar plexus. "Exactly," he said quietly.

But Kit didn't stay silent. "You could be a great father," she said without warning. "It'd involve trying and working hard and being accountable rather than burying yourself in whatever hell it is that makes you so angry." Her words vibrated with emotion.

The bones in his jaw grinding against one another, he didn't respond.

"You have to make a choice, Noah." Harsh words. "I made a choice as a child to not let my parents' lifestyle damage me to the extent that I ended up a druggie or a self-destructive waste of space. Whatever it is that's behind your behavior, you made the opposite choice."

How could he tell her that he was *surviving*, that it was all he was capable of doing? He could've been dead a hundred times over by now. It would've been so easy to give in, to surrender to the pain, but he'd refused. "I didn't," he gritted out. "I made the choice to *live*."

He could feel Kit's eyes on him, incisive and penetrating... and he realized what he'd said, what he'd nearly betrayed. "Look down," he said, slamming the door shut on the memories that made him feel soiled and desperate and used up.

"I'm pretty sure that's a mountain lion. You can use the binoculars over on your side."

Kit didn't reach for the binoculars. "Noah," she said, her voice soft, private. "What happened?"

"Nothing original." He tried a cynical smile. "Drugs and all that—I was addicted as a teen, decided to get clean." It was a lie, but one he had to tell. It was far better that she think him weak in that respect than that she know the truth. Kit couldn't know. He'd die before allowing that to happen.

KIT KNEW NOAH WAS lying.

It was as obvious to her as a flashing neon sign. And given that he knew her low opinion of drug addicts, the fact he'd confessed to that to get her to stop asking questions made her blood run cold. She wanted to take back her earlier harsh words, wanted to start all over again. Because she was beginning to understand that whatever had scarred Noah, it had nothing to do with the usual small tragedies of life, the things she'd seen growing up.

It had been something bad enough to make a boy want to end his life.

Shaken and not knowing where to go from here, she folded her arms and stared out at the view. It was far greener than immediately around Los Angeles. "Where are we?"

"Near a private landing field I know." A short pause. "Actually, it's mine."

He'd given her so many surprises today that she took this one in her stride. "So you'd have a place to land where no one knew you?"

"Yeah." A lopsided smile. "There's nothing else around for miles."

She could see it now, a cleared strip surrounded by what looked like acres of trees. "How *much* land did you buy?"

He just laughed and took the plane down, and as her stomach dived, she allowed herself a moment of weakness and let that rough, masculine sound wrap around her.

A few minutes later, Kit stepped out of the plane and, stretching her legs, took deep drafts of the air. Grass and trees, birdsong and the gentle rustle of leaves in the wind, there was nothing of civilization within sight but the plane Noah had just landed. "Do you plan to build here?"

"I have a small cabin a little bit farther in. Other than that, I think I'll leave it." A shrug. "Don't need anything bigger." He hesitated before saying, "I was planning for us to picnic nearby, but do you want to go see the cabin?"

Kit knew she should say no, put a stop to the increasing emotional intimacy between them. But this was the first, the *only* time Noah had invited her to a place that could be thought of as his home. "Yes," she said. "I'd like to see it."

His smile, it wrecked her.

"Let me grab the food."

Taking the smaller bag since he had a picnic blanket as well, she walked toward the trees with him, spied an overgrown path. "You haven't been here for a while?"

"Not since before the tour—but the cabin should be fine. Unless the squirrels decided to stage an attack. Probably banged the door down with hammers shaped from acorns."

She couldn't not smile. "You should write children's books." The visuals he occasionally came up with were brilliant.

He erupted into gales of laughter, the warmth in his eyes contagious. "Can you imagine a parent buying a kid's book penned by Noah St. John?" Not waiting for her answer, he pointed with his chin. "There it is."

Wrenching her attention from him, she saw a log cabin beside a stream kissed by sunshine. "Noah," she breathed. "It's perfect." The clearing in which the cabin stood was all lush green grass and wildflowers, like an image from a fairy tale.

"The cabin's not very well put together," he told her. "I did it and it won't fall down on us, but it wouldn't pass any inspections." Smile fading, eyes shadowed, he looked at the small building. "I guess I just wanted a secret, private place where no one expects anything from me."

"Thank you for sharing it with me." It was hard to keep her voice steady when he'd just told her this wasn't his home.

It was a piece of his heart.

CHAPTER 9

"L ET'S SIT OUTSIDE," SHE said through the renewed ache in her chest. "It's so pretty by the stream." It would also be easier than being shut up in a cabin with a Noah who was acting more and more like the man for whom she'd fallen so hard she was still bruised from it.

Putting down the food, he snapped out the tartan-patterned blanket—dark blue with lines picked out in red and white. Pretty, and one she'd seen before. He'd pulled it from the trunk of his car one day, spread it out in her garden, and lazed in the sun while she finished weeding.

The garden hadn't been finished then. It was Noah who'd helped her hoe the beds. That day, however, he'd been a complete sloth because he hadn't slept the previous night. He'd told her it had just been a bad night, and Kit had believed him. It was only later that she'd realized Noah didn't sleep much at all.

He'd slept in her garden, however, under the shade of the cherry blossom tree that had been one of the first things she'd planted. Giving in to need, she'd watched him. His lashes had been dark against the gold of his skin, his cheekbones defined and his jawline shadowed. There was no question that Noah was incredibly good-looking, but Kit was surrounded by good-looking people on a daily basis, had been since childhood.

It was what lay beneath Noah's looks that had compelled her: the drive, the passion, the talent, and, she'd believed, the capacity to care. She hadn't been wrong about the latter. Noah *could* care, and care deeply, but—

"Kit."

Jerking, she said, "Sorry, thinking about a project I've been offered." It was the first thing that came to mind as an excuse.

Light reflected into the dark gray of Noah's eyes. "Anything exciting?"

"It's the same writing and directing team as *Last Flight*." Kit went down to the blanket and began to set out the food. Noah had bought croissants, sunflower and linseed rolls, cold cuts and little miniature spreads, as well as fruit.

Holding up an apple, she raised an eyebrow. "I'm impressed."

"You should be." He folded himself down onto the blanket and emptied the other bag. "Juice, water... and cupcakes for dessert."

Kit gasped at glimpsing the miniature vanilla cupcakes with chocolate frosting. "Noah!" She pointed a finger at him. "You know I can eat a whole package of those by myself!" Cheap and prepackaged the cupcakes might be, but she adored them a thousand times more than the expensive gourmet versions.

He moved the cupcakes under her nose. "No more painted-on superhero costume." A wicked smile. "Or I can eat them all."

Grabbing the package from him, she went to put it aside, then said to hell with it and opened it. "We need coffee."

"Give me a couple of minutes." He got up, jogged into the house, moving with a masculine grace that was addicting to watch.

Stuffing half a cupcake in her mouth, she forced her attention to the stream that sparkled under the sunshine. The water was so clear she could see the pebbles beneath, the grass around the edges lush but not too tall. Since Noah hadn't been by for a while, the grass itself had to be of a variety that stayed short.

She finished the second half of the cupcake, moaning at the taste. Putting the package aside after taking a second cupcake, she peeled off the wrapper and started to eat that one much more slowly. As she ate, she tried to think of anything but Noah. She failed.

"Coffee, as ordered."

Looking up, his denim-clad thighs threatening to highjack her attention, she accepted the mug he held out.

"Only instant." He came down to the blanket with his own mug in hand, close enough that their shoulders would brush with another inch of movement from either one of them. "It's caffeine though, right?"

"Your generator's pretty quiet." She'd heard it start up, but it hadn't been intrusive.

"I bought it online." A grin. "Had no idea how to work it— and the instructions were in Swedish."

EVEN AS KIT LAUGHED, Noah knew he remained on shaky ground. It didn't matter. Not today, not with her joy sinking into his bones. He'd shit on their friendship once, would slit his fucking wrists before he ever hurt her again—and if it took a lifetime to convince Kit, then it took a lifetime. He was in this for the long haul.

"Play that new Carina song," Kit said when he pulled out his phone to play something in the background.

He cued it up. "Don't tell Molly I have this. She changes the channel if Carina ever shows up on TV."

"Can't blame her after the way Carina flirted with Fox in that interview. But man, the woman has a voice."

"Do I get any of those cupcakes?" he asked when she reached for a third one after eating the second one with infinite care. He loved that habit of hers—she'd inhale the first one, then nibble at the rest.

"Hmm." She counted the remaining cupcakes with an ostentatious concentration that made him want to kiss her.

Fuck. He could not be having those thoughts about Kit.

"Well, since you were smart enough to get a twelve-pack," she said, her tone serious, "I suppose I can spare a couple."

Ripping off the wrapper after she handed him one, he ate the whole thing in a single bite. "Cheapest gift I ever bought." He tried to stare at the stream, but it was impossible not to look at her when her absence had been a hole inside him nothing could fill.

"So cheap yet so delish." Licking at the frosting, she picked up her coffee and took a cautious sip. "Not bad for something that's been in the cottage for so long."

"Makes you wonder what chemicals are in it, doesn't it?" He took a second cupcake. "Just like I wonder what's in these cupcakes—you know they don't expire for months, right?"

"I don't care. Not when they taste this good." Fourth cupcake finished, she rested by drinking more coffee. "So, the tour was successful?"

"Yeah, it was good." Schoolboy Choir had sold out shows across the country, added extra dates. "Glad to be home though."

Hands cupped around her coffee mug, Kit said, "You have any specific plans for the new album, or are you just going to jam and figure it out?"

"We want to stretch ourselves." It was time to go back to their roots, dig for the music that made their souls burn.

Frowning in concentration, Kit turned her body toward him. "A change in direction?"

"No, just… growing." It was the one way in which Noah *could* grow. Music had always been his freedom, perhaps because he'd found it afterward. There was no taint to it. "Did you know Fox and I started to learn music together?"

Pure delight in Kit's smile. "At boarding school?"

"Yeah. It was the one class in which we always behaved. Mr. Denison was convinced the other teachers were making up lies about us being troublemakers." He chuckled. "We send him tickets to our concerts when we pass through Houston—that's where he lives now—and damn if he doesn't always attend."

Sitting cross-legged on the picnic blanket, Kit peeled the wrapper off a cupcake and gave it to him before taking one for herself. "He must be proud of you."

"I think he is." Far prouder than either one of Noah's parents. "Last time he came backstage, he brought his wife and told her how Fox and I were the only two students he'd had who wanted to learn to read music so much that we used to haunt his office."

"You didn't meet Abe and David till later, right? When you were thirteen? I think I remember David saying something like that once."

Noah nodded. "Yep." Unlike Fox and Noah, David and Abe had families who loved them. They hadn't been shipped off and forgotten... or hidden.

In Abe's family, boarding school was a proud tradition; his folks had come to see him every visitation weekend, had taken him home each vacation.

David's folks hadn't been able to visit that often—Alicia and Vicente Rivera hadn't had the funds for it. But David had received the best care packages, full of home-baked goodies, a letter, and articles his family had clipped for him from neighborhood papers. Those care packages had grown bigger after the four of them became friends, Mrs. Rivera including enough for Noah, Abe, and Fox as well.

She'd even written them all.

If Noah'd had a choice, he'd have gone home with Abe or David come vacation time. Either one of his friends' families would've opened their doors to him and Fox. But he hadn't had a choice. Noah's father couldn't stand to look at him, but he wasn't about to be accused of neglect. So Noah had to go home.

The only thing that had made it bearable was having Fox with him—his friend would've rather gone to David's or Abe's too, but he'd always said he wanted to go home with Noah.

Noah would never forget that act of loyalty.

"Did you like boarding school?" Kit's husky voice cut through the memories.

"It was better than home." Kit knew he had a dysfunctional relationship with his mother and father. "That was how I

93

thought of it at first, but after a while, yeah, I did enjoy it. Mostly because of the friendships." Quite frankly, he wouldn't have made it the first month, much less the first year, without Fox.

His need would've made him feel unequal in the friendship, except that Fox had needed a friend just as badly for different reasons. If Noah had parents who, in public, acted as if he mattered, all the while ignoring him in private, Fox's mother had flat-out abandoned him for her shiny new family.

So they'd become one another's family, brothers not by blood but by choice.

"Your classmates must've pulled a few interesting stunts," he said, and, when Kit answered with a wry nod, he asked another question. He wanted to hear her speak, see her smile... fix what he'd deliberately broken.

IT HAD BEEN A strange, oddly wonderful, and terribly painful day. Kit didn't know quite how to process it, so she just shoved everything aside as she'd been doing since the moment Noah picked her up. Living in the moment was the only way she could deal with this.

"Thanks for the flight," she said as they headed to the car early that afternoon. "It was beautiful." No lie there, no need to watch her words.

"Anytime," Noah answered with a smile before his phone went off. "Give me a sec." His expression darkened when he saw the name on the screen, his answer a brusque "Yeah?"

Walking on to give him privacy, Kit was nonetheless aware of the curt nature of his conversation. He'd unlocked the SUV using the remote by the time she got to it, so she climbed inside and put the picnic blanket and the detritus of their meal in the back.

His jaw was set in a hard line when he got in, white lines around his mouth. "Did you want to stop anywhere on the way home?" he asked after driving out of the hangar, getting back out to lock it, then sliding into the driver's seat again.

"No." Kit knew she should keep her distance, but that wasn't who she was when it came to people she cared about—and hell, that was the wrong direction to take. She couldn't care about Noah, not that much. But she did. Despite everything, she did, and it was tearing her apart. "Bad news?"

Blowing out a breath, he turned on the music.

Kit kept her silence though frustration churned inside her. He'd always done this with certain questions. Just ignored them. Back when they'd been close, she'd excused it as him not wanting to talk about things that were too personal. Only later had she realized that she didn't really know much about Noah beyond his current life. Except for the odd comment about his troubled relationship with his parents, his entire past had been a no-go zone.

As a result, she wasn't expecting him to speak, was startled when he did.

"It was my father."

Kit took in his rigid shoulders, the hand gripping the steering wheel with bruising force. "What's happened?"

"Nothing. I've been ordered to show my face at some charity gala they're sponsoring not this Saturday but the next."

Kit frowned. "You don't do anything you don't want to do, Noah." Anyone who'd had even limited contact with him knew that.

"Yeah, well, he brought my aunt Margaret into it. Aside from Emily, she's the only person with an actual heart in my family, and she's the head of the charity."

He *had* mentioned his aunt once when Kit complimented him on a shirt he was wearing. He'd said it was from his aunt—she couldn't remember why they hadn't spoken more about it, but then Noah was very good at distracting her, intentionally or not. "So you'll go?"

His hand tightened further on the steering wheel. "Yeah. Fuck." Exhaling loudly, he seemed to consciously flex his fingers before curving them around the leather again. "I don't suppose you want to subject yourself to a couple of hours of social torture?"

Kit froze.

"Shit, sorry." Noah shoved a hand through his hair. "Forget that. No need to ruin your Saturday night too."

There it was, the out she needed. But she also saw the angry tension in his body, and she remembered the syringe and the motel room and her terror at the thought that she might lose him forever. "I'll go," she said before her mind could override her heart. "The idea of rocking a glam gown will motivate me to move during my sessions with Steve."

Kit liked to eat, but given her profession, that meant she had to stick to a strict exercise regimen—including a two-hour session booked for later today. But even though she'd been known to call her trainer Macho Steve, the Evil Personal Trainer, she generally enjoyed the workouts. "Plus my being snapped at a big event will make my publicist happy."

Noah's responding glance was unexpectedly grim. "How about if you get caught being my date? What's Thea going to say to that?"

She shrugged. "I've been photographed with the band so much no one takes any hookup rumors seriously anymore." That wasn't quite true, but her PR person could spin it that way.

Thank God Thea had decided to take Kit on as a client. Thea hadn't really had the time, not with handling Schoolboy Choir and a few legacy clients, but when she saw Kit beginning to drown under the deluge of publicity after *Last Flight*, she'd stepped in.

"You sure?" Noah returned his attention to the road, his shoulders no longer as stiff, his jawline relaxing. "It won't be fun."

Kit's heart tried to read hopeful, romantic things in Noah's response to the idea of her company. She shut it down with teeth-clenched will. "That's what friends are for."

CHAPTER 10

NOAH FELL ASLEEP AT three that morning, was awake by six. As far as nights went, it hadn't been a bad one. He'd slept deeply from start to finish. After showering and shaving, he pulled on a pair of jeans so ragged he found new tears in them daily, grabbed a mug of coffee and his guitar, and went to sit by the pool.

Though he'd meant to work on new material, he started to play the song about a sparrow caught in a net, its wings broken, who somehow found the strength to fly free. Kit saw hope in that song, saw courage. Noah didn't have the heart to tell her it was about death. Because that sparrow with his broken wings would never be able to fly. He'd fall to the earth, lie bleeding until he breathed his last breath.

The only possible freedom was the final one.

Noah sang softly as he strummed the guitar, fully conscious that this song could be seen as a suicide note. It wasn't and never would be. He might've fucked up when drunk out of his skull, but he'd never consciously chosen death. That meant little though, not if he was holing up in motel rooms and shoving poison into his veins. The choice might not be a conscious one, but it was still a choice.

Like the choice he made at eleven that night when the nightmares became too loud, the demons too vicious. It was painfully easy to find women who wanted to screw him. At least the pitiless god who'd given him this life had also given him looks that made women gravitate toward him. He picked up a starlet who had lips plumped up with filler and breasts taut with silicone, and he fucked her against the brick wall behind a club after she gave him head.

When they were done, she called him "baby" and slipped him her number. He didn't even know her name until he glanced at the little piece of paper. Waiting until she was back in the club, he scrunched up the note paper and threw it in the dumpster not far down the alley. Then he walked down the street and toward another bar bursting at the seams.

There was a line, one he could've easily circumvented, his face so well known that he didn't have to introduce himself to the bouncers. But he didn't even have to go that far. Two giggling brunettes in skintight minidresses waved at him, and when he smiled and crooked a finger, they squealed and ran over. He walked them back to his car, drove them to his place—the place to which he'd never once invited Kit.

He didn't take them into the house, however, but into the little guesthouse his architect had talked him into. There was nothing of him in the guesthouse. It might as well have been a hotel room. But it had beds. He picked one—and then he spent the next three hours fucking both brunettes.

It didn't silence the screams in his head, but for the moments that he was this base, rutting creature, he wasn't Noah any longer, and if he wasn't Noah any longer, then he didn't have to be that scared little boy either. He just became nothing. Empty.

Afterward, he slapped one of the brunettes on the butt and said, "I've called you a car."

She gave him big, hurt eyes. "You're kicking us out?"

"You knew the deal." The hurt was well-practiced. "If you wanted the white picket fence, you wouldn't have come home with me." Noah's reputation left no room for misconceptions or false hopes; he'd never made any effort to hide his activities and proclivities.

The brunette got up with a sniff while her companion leaned over and tried to kiss Noah. "No kissing," he snapped, hauling her back with a hand fisted in her hair. He didn't know why he'd made that stupid rule—it wasn't as if it changed anything, but his heart insisted on thinking that it did, that he could keep part of himself pristine.

Clean.

What a load of bullshit. And yet he still couldn't make himself kiss any woman on the mouth. He sometimes wondered what people would say if they knew Noah St. John, Bad Boy of Rock and King of the One-Night Stand, had never been kissed. "That's the car," he said to the women when there was a buzz on his phone.

Getting out of bed, he pulled on his jeans and then walked them to the door, because now that he'd managed to drain himself to numb emptiness, he wanted to sleep. He *had* to sleep. If he missed this window, he might not sleep again for days.

He hauled open the door. "Thanks for a nice time, ladies," he said, because he wasn't a total bastard. Not all the time anyway.

Pouts disappeared, replaced by sultry smiles. Placing one hand each on his chest, they leaned in as a unit. "Thanks, Noah. Anytime you want a good time, call us."

Her friend took out a phone. "Mind if I take a photo of us together?"

Noah knew that photo would end up online or in the papers. Where before he wouldn't have given a shit, now that Kit was back in his life, even if only as a friend, he found himself shaking his head. "No souvenirs." He smiled, using it like the tool it was. "Be good and I might use those numbers you left by the bed."

They giggled and waved before getting into the damn car at last.

Eyes so heavy he could barely keep them open, he nonetheless managed to get himself to the house, collapsing into bed thirty seconds after he entered the front door, his mind blanking out.

When he woke, dawn was pink on the horizon. A glance at the clock on the bedside table told him two and a half hours had passed.

A good night's sleep.

TWO DAYS AFTER THE picnic with Noah, Kit walked out of a meeting with the director and the writer of *Last Flight* with a spring in her step. Their new project—still in the planning stages—sounded remarkable, and she was more than ready to be attached on the understanding that they'd negotiate a contract once Terrence and Jade got the financing sorted.

Kit knew her agreement would assist the duo to get the

funding they needed, and she was fine with that. Without the risk the two had taken by casting her in *Last Flight*, she'd still be knocking on doors and attending open casting calls with a hundred other hopefuls. Kit wasn't about to turn her back on them, especially with a script this poignant and complex.

"Kit, hold up."

Turning, she smiled at Terrence. Tall, with shaggy black hair against olive skin and bright hazel eyes behind silver-rimmed frames, the writer was one of her favorite people in the industry. "You don't have to give me the hard sell, Terrence. I'm convinced."

"Excellent." Putting his hand on her back, he smiled down at her, his features fine-boned and his camouflage green T-shirt sitting easily on a body lean with muscle. "In which case I can put my efforts into convincing you to have dinner with me tonight."

"With Jade?"

Terrence shook his head. "Just you and me." His expression softened. "What do you think?"

"Oh." She fiddled with the bound copy of the script she held in order to give herself time to think. She'd always liked Terrence, but she'd never thought of him in a romantic way, mostly because she'd been hung up on Noah. She had to get over that. Why not with a man she respected and admired?

"Okay," she said. "But not anyplace celebrity—I'd rather we go somewhere we can actually eat and talk." As opposed to see and be seen.

"Us poor writers can't even get into those celebrity places." Terrence's smile was wry as he thrust his hands into the pockets of his buff-colored cargo pants. "The maître d's look at me like I'm some hobo who crawled in off the street." A grin that reached his eyes. "I know a nice neighborhood Italian place."

"Sounds good. Shall I meet you there?"

"I can pick you up if you don't mind."

She knew what he was asking. If he came through her gates, the paparazzi would start salivating and snapping; if not immediately, then soon enough. "That'd be lovely," she said, her breath tight in her chest. "Six thirty?"

"Yeah." Smile deep, he offered her his arm. "I'll walk you out."

"No, go back to Jade—I'm sure you two have tons to discuss. I'm heading next door to pick up Becca so we can grab a coffee together." Her friend was working on makeup designs for her next gig. "I'll see you tonight."

As she left, she was aware of her heart thundering, her blood a roar in her ears. Terrence was a nice guy—a good-looking, smart, funny guy—but he wasn't the one who'd provoked the raw emotional response. It was only Noah who got to her that deep. But Noah wasn't for her.

Moving on from him, *really* moving on, was terrifying and freeing… and heartbreaking. She'd dated since that ugly night, but part of her had held back, secretly hopeful. No more. It was time to erase that hope, walk away from it forever.

Ducking into a restroom on the way to the makeup trailer where Becca was working, Kit locked the door and tried to stifle the sobs that threatened to break out of her. Her chest hurt, her body ached, her eyes burned, and her breath had turned choppy. Two tears rolled down her face, but she managed to swallow the rest, managed to learn to breathe again after five minutes of trying.

After washing her face at the sink and patting it dry with tissues from the dispenser, she dug around in her purse for her compact and lipstick and repaired the damage. She was good at hiding it, had learned all about makeup from her mother. Adreina had taken her in hand for two weeks after she turned fifteen, given her lessons.

Kit planned to teach her own daughter too—*if* that daughter wanted it. At fifteen, Kit had still been in the fugly stage and sitting in front of a mirror with a supermodel by her side had only highlighted her flaws. Despite that, she'd loved those hours with her mom, just the two of them for once—and Adreina had never once put her down. Rather, her gorgeous, confident mother had told her to look bullies in the eye and say fuck you.

Those memories were some of the most cherished of Kit's childhood.

Checking her face afterward, she caught her own eyes in the mirror. The camera apparently loved her eyes—the critics raved about how expressive they were, how much she could communicate with just those two amber orbs.

Today her eyes revealed bruised pain and a searing sense of loss.

Becca would take one look at her and know something was wrong, regardless of the stellar job Kit had done on her face. Kit couldn't handle her friend's perceptive mind right now, so she did what she tried very hard never to do with her closest friends: she put on a mask.

Closing her eyes, she took a deep breath and thought of a bit part she'd played right when she'd started out in the industry. It had been of a "girl next door" whose only job had been to smile and flirt with the coffee guy who was the heart-throb, thus giving the heroine a reason to act jealous. It hadn't been the greatest script, but it had paid her rent that month.

It was also perfect for today. Her eyes filled with cheerful joy, her lips curved, and suddenly she wasn't Kit anymore but that happy, uncomplicated girl next door. If only the trans-formation wasn't simply skin deep.

NOAH PICKED ABE UP around seven, the two of them having decided to grab a bite together after the keyboard player got into the city. "Any preferences?"

His mahogany skin gleaming with health after his camping and hiking vacation, Abe rubbed his hand over his clean-shaven skull. It was a very conservative look for the other man; he usually rocked color, with patterns razored into his close-cut and tightly curled hair. Noah hadn't seen this look since soon after they first arrived in Los Angeles as eighteen-year-olds full of dreams.

"Remember that Italian place your bud Esteban showed us last time he was in the city?" Abe said after a second's thought.

"Yeah." Noah had enjoyed that restaurant too. It was run by a family of six who all seemed genuinely happy to be part of a family business. No hidden surliness or frustrated ambitions.

The eldest son, Luca, worked the door and took care of the guests. The father was the head chef, with the only daugh-ter in the family his apprentice. The mother was a pastry chef in charge of desserts, and the two younger sons waited tables.

One was studying management, the other human relations, both in preparation for opening a second family-run place.

Noah knew all that because Luca had sat down with him, Esteban, and the guys during their first visit. They'd ended up being the last people in the place that night, but rather than hurrying them out, the kitchen had sent out extra platters full of delicious bites, and the younger sons had kept topping up their drinks.

Needless to say, the five of them had left a gigantic tip.

"Here." He passed Abe his phone. "Give them a call while I drive. They might be full up—it was a popular place the last time we were there. Number's under Meluchi."

Abe made the call, and from what Noah heard, it appeared the person on the other end well remembered their table. "We in?" he asked Abe after the other man hung up with a laugh.

"Yeah." Abe put the phone in the cup holder. "They're setting up an extra table for us on the patio. Apparently it won't have a view, but fuck the view, I want the *food*."

Noah grinned. "Yeah." He glanced reflexively at his phone when it vibrated, but it wasn't Kit's face that filled the screen, the shot one he'd taken back before he'd destroyed them. She was laughing in that photo, her eyes crinkled at the corners and her hair coming loose from the careless bun in which she'd knotted it.

"I'll grab it." Abe picked up the phone. "David, what do you want?" he asked with the casual rudeness that was only acceptable among men who'd been friends for so long that politeness would be considered a sign of trouble. "When? Yeah, I'll tell Noah. We're going to that Italian place."

A pause.

"Fuck you, man." Abe laughed and hung up. "He's bragging about not needing to date us now he has Thea."

"If ever a man deserved to win his woman," Noah said, "it's David." The drummer had been crazy in love with the band's tough-as-nails publicist since forever. One look and boom, he'd been a goner. Noah, Abe, and Fox had all watched that love grow deeper and more indelible day by day and had winced silently when Thea appeared oblivious.

Turned out she wasn't. The way she looked at David... Noah would've never believed Molly's sister had such tenderness in her. It was obvious she thought David hung the moon. "What did he want?"

"To invite us over on Sunday afternoon for a barbeque. He and Thea are talking wedding stuff and they want to torture us." Abe folded his arms across his chest, his muscles bulging. "Me, I'm running off to Vegas if I'm ever stupid enough to walk down the aisle again."

Noah snorted. "Your mom would scalp you, and you'd whimper like a baby."

Abe was silent for a while. "Actually, I think she'd be fine with it. Sarah and I had the big wedding, and you know what my mom asked me the day of my wedding?" The keyboard player stared through the windshield. "If Sarah was a woman I'd run off with if given the chance." He shook his head. "I laughed back then, but she was serious. She wanted to know if I loved Sarah enough that I'd do that, just take off with her."

Noah didn't know how to react. Abe's marriage and divorce were treacherous waters. The divorce had led him back into the cocaine habit he'd managed to quit six months earlier, then later into alcohol. The marriage, on the other hand, had seemed happy enough. Sarah had never quite meshed with the band, but they'd all accepted her because she was Abe's.

"Would you? Have run off with her?" he finally asked, knowing he'd be no kind of friend if he didn't step through this unexpectedly open door.

Even as he asked the question, Noah knew his own answer when it came to Kit. If he'd been normal, if he hadn't been so ugly inside, he'd have sweet-talked her to Vegas in a heartbeat. He'd have lied and cheated and charmed just so she'd be his. And he'd have woken every morning feeling like the king of the fucking world.

CHAPTER 11

ABE'S OWN ANSWER TOOK a long time in coming. "I don't know," he said at last. "No secret that I wasn't in a good headspace when I married Sarah." Grief thickened his voice. "Not that it matters. She didn't exactly hang around when I wasn't the perfect rock-star trophy husband anymore."

Noah knew Abe was referring to his problems with drug addiction. "You know I have your back, man, but living with a cocaine addict can't have been easy." Abe had once punched Noah while in the fog of drugs; Noah had no idea what had gone on behind closed doors between Abe and Sarah, but he did know that she'd changed from a hopeful, somewhat shy twenty-one-year-old to a brittle, angry twenty-four-year-old by the time of their divorce.

"Yeah well, she landed on her feet." The furious undertone to Abe's voice made Noah's instincts prickle. Until right then, he hadn't believed Abe was hung up on Sarah; they'd parted in too much anger, their divorce a battleground of lawyers and bitter demands.

Sarah had asked for Abe's keyboard collection even though she didn't play. Abe, in turn, had accused her of cheating when Sarah just wasn't the cheating kind. In the end, he'd kept his keyboards and Sarah had suddenly caved and accepted a settlement after months of refusing to sign the divorce papers.

At the time, David had wondered if the two were drawing things out because they didn't actually want to be divorced. Noah had disagreed, especially since Sarah had been pregnant with another man's baby by then, but now...

"I don't know," he said. "Her fiancé's a bit of an asshole who keeps her on a short leash from what I've heard."

Abe went very, very still. "He hurting her?"

"No signs of that—all I heard is that the guy's a control freak," Noah said evenly, suddenly dead certain Abe's feelings for Sarah ran far deeper than the other man had ever admitted. Maybe his marriage had simply become collateral damage in the devastating loss that had scarred Abe the same year he married.

"He's a smug fuck too." Abe's words were dark. "You should grab that parking spot up ahead. We're not likely to get anything closer."

Noah parked, and the two of them got out to walk the rest of the way. They hadn't bothered to disguise themselves since the worst that would likely happen in this low-key neighborhood would be a teenager or two asking for an autograph. A minute later, they passed a lanky boy strumming his guitar as he sat on the stoop in front of a small, neatly kept apartment building.

The kid's double take was funny enough that Noah walked up to him and, taking the guitar, strummed a few bars. "Here's where you're faltering." He'd heard it as they walked.

"This is what you do to fix it." Putting his fingers on the strings, he showed the kid how to compensate for the fact he had a pinky that was missing its top half.

The kid's eyes locked on his fingers, deep grooves between his eyebrows. Taking the guitar from Noah when he held it out, the boy did exactly what Noah had demonstrated. The smile that bloomed on his face was worth all the shit that came with fame. "I didn't think I could do that," he said, repeating the riff before he looked up, hope incandescent in his deep brown eyes. "You think I could be like you? Go all the way to the top?"

Noah wasn't sure he should be encouraging a sweet, normal kid to join his world, but dreams were dreams. "Don't see why not." He tapped a finger against the boy's temple. "Trick is not to try to do what everyone else says you should do—you have to figure out your own unique style. That's what I did."

Flexing his left hand, he held it out so the boy could see the fine scars that spider-webbed it. "It had the hell crushed out of it when I was about your age." A car accident after he stole his father's Beemer following an argument during a rare vacation week when Fox wasn't with him. His friend had been forced to stay an extra week at school as punishment for an infraction Noah couldn't now remember.

"It's never going to be as strong as my right hand." It throbbed at night sometimes, a bone-deep ache.

"Wow." The kid touched his fingers to Noah's hand. "I never knew that."

"Most folks don't."

He and Abe spent a few more minutes with the kid, and Noah gave the teen his number before they left. It wasn't something he did often—kids tended to brag, and he had no intention of dealing with thousands of messages. But he didn't think this kid would boast. Having the number would be enough for him. And if he did ever call, it'd be because he couldn't figure something out.

Heading back down the street afterward, they made it to the restaurant right on time.

"This is bad." Abe glanced at his watch with a scowl. "We're being way too well behaved. What's next? No shenanigans on tour? No raising hell? Punctuality is a slippery slope, my friend."

Noah snorted. "Screw bad behavior. I want to eat."

"Noah, Abe." Luca Meluchi came over and shook their hands, his grip that of a man who spent his off time fixing up and flipping houses. "Like I told Abe, I squeezed in a table for you on the patio, but it's kind of stuck in a corner."

"Every seat here is the best in the house." Noah grinned. "And forget about taking our orders. Just feed us."

"Done," Luca said with a laugh, and led them out the side door and onto the patio.

Seeing the soft semi-darkness of it, the tables romantically small and lit only with candles, Noah glanced at Abe. "Don't try anything."

"You should be so lucky," the bigger man said as they were shown to their shadowy and tight corner, the table right up against the back wall of the restaurant. "You're not my type." With that, Abe grabbed the seat that put his back to the rest of the people out here, which meant Noah ended up with his to the restaurant wall, his view of the other tables uninterrupted.

It was the seat he'd have chosen given first pick—and he knew full well Abe was aware of that.

Luca came out right then with a loaded antipasto platter and they dug in.

"I swear this is the only place I actually eat eggplant," Noah said, reaching for more.

"I'm all about the olives, man. And those weird pickled pepper things."

"Those are goo—" Noah froze, his eyes on the woman who'd just stepped out onto the patio.

Never would he mistake Kit's profile for someone else's. About to raise his hand, alert her to his and Abe's presence, his brain finally caught on to the fact that she had a male hand on her lower back. That hand was attached to a man who looked vaguely familiar.

"What's so interesting?" Abe looked over his shoulder, blew out a breath. "Dude works with Kit, doesn't he? I remember him from that awards ceremony."

Noah's brain clicked. "He wrote the script for *Last Flight*—she liked working with him." All at once, he could remember every good thing Kit had said about her date. "Terrence Gates."

"Maybe they're working together again." Abe returned his attention to the platter.

"Yeah, Kit mentioned a new project," Noah said, but from the way the guy had just reached out to touch Kit's hand across the table, it was obvious this was a date. He knew he should stop looking, stop watching, but he couldn't help himself. The candlelight caressed Kit's face, made her skin glow and her eyes sparkle. Or maybe the glow was because of Gates.

They hadn't sparkled for Noah in a long time.

"Shit man, we can leave, eat somewhere else."

He jerked his attention to Abe's keen gaze. "No. If we do, we'll only draw attention to ourselves." Right now, their position made them all but invisible to Kit and her date.

Abe leaned in close, the candlelight throwing shadows on his face. "Then stop staring at her." A grim order. "I don't know what you did to mess it up with Kit, but you did. Now live with it." Pausing to take a drink of the ice-cold water one of Luca's brothers had placed on the table as they took their seats, he said, "She looks happy. You want to change that?"

Noah's hand clenched around his own glass. "No." Forcing his gaze off Kit, he tried to keep it on the food. He knew it was delicious, but he couldn't taste a bite because he was trying so hard not to look at the only woman who had ever been his friend.

LEAVING TEN MINUTES AFTER Kit and her date finally headed out, Noah and Abe didn't speak much. When he would've dropped the other man off at his place, Abe shook his head. "You know what I learned when I ended up drinking myself into the hospital?"

"I don't need secondhand therapy." Noah's hand flexed and tightened on the steering wheel.

"Yeah, well, you're going to get it. You can't be alone tonight, Noah. You're going to go do something stupid."

"I won't." He swallowed. "I promised Kit."

"There are plenty of kinds of stupid, and I bet you can find a loophole of stupidity."

Noah wanted to disagree, couldn't. "What do you want to do?"

"Go do something stupid together." Stretching out in the passenger seat, Abe grinned. "Let's go have an impromptu party at Fox and Molly's. We'll shanghai David and Thea along the way."

"You shanghai Thea. I'm not feeling that stupid."

Abe laughed and Noah felt his lips twitch. It was good to have friends who gave a shit.

And friends who laughed and joined in with their plan for a party, complete with junk food Abe and Noah had picked up along the way. Noah ended up with a guitar in his arms. He always had one nearby. This one had been in his car. Not one of his more expensive ones in case it got stolen, but a solid model. Feeling the strings thrum under his fingertips, he found a calm that was so often missing in his life.

It was Fox who'd given him music, having already had a basic command of the guitar thanks to his grandfather. He'd taught Noah the beginnings of it the week before their lessons properly started. Noah had found a sweet salvation in the strings. When he played, he could forget for a while, go to another place.

Kit had once called it a meditative space.

Noah didn't think of it like that. He thought of it as escape.

So he played for his friends and with them, and when David drew Thea into a dance, he increased the tempo and the rhythm while Fox took a pair of drumsticks David must've had on him and drummed out a beat on a side table. Abe, meanwhile, had Molly in his arms, the two of them swaying together with the ease of friends.

115

Noah had wanted to dance with Kit for so long, to feel the music through her body. He'd never permitted himself the pleasure, never allowed himself to put his hands on her. Because whatever he touched, he destroyed.

Continuing to play when Fox broke off to grab Molly's ringing phone to pass to her, he segued into a romantic little ballad that let David twirl Thea. Schoolboy Choir's usually sharply dressed publicist was barefoot and in an at-home outfit of white shorts and a cherry-pink top, the straps fine against her honey-gold skin, her black hair sleek down her back.

I could do what David did, win my girl.

It was a tiny whisper, from the boy he'd once been. Noah ignored it. If he tried to be with Kit, he'd mess her up so badly nothing would ever put her back together again. Friendship was all he could aim for, hope for.

Coming back into the room after having taken her call by the pool, Molly went back to dancing, this time with Fox. Abe relaxed in the armchair next to the one where Noah sat and, after a short pause, began to sing.

Abe didn't have Fox's ferocious vocal cords, but he had a bluesy tone to his voice that was perfect for this night, this moment. And the words he sang, they were gentle, undemanding, yet compelling all the same.

"You could go solo," Noah said when the song ended.

"So could you, dipshit."

Lips curving, Noah shook his head. "Me? I'm just a pretty face."

"And I'm just a schmuck piano player."

Fox, having caught their conversation, spun Molly to hold her from the back, his arms crossed over her waist. "And David's just the drum guy, while I can sing some. We are who we are together."

"We're better than who we are alone." David sat down, tugging Thea onto his lap, her long legs hooked over the arm of the chair as she wrapped one arm around his shoulders.

"You aren't better," Thea said with an arched eyebrow. "You're phenomenal. Split you up and you'd be good, perhaps even great, but it wouldn't be this magic."

"I'm too lazy to go solo anyway," Abe drawled. "At least this way, I get a breather during concerts when you showboats take over."

"Fuck you," Fox and Noah said in stereo while David fist-bumped Abe.

And he was okay. For tonight, for this instant in time, he was okay. As long as he didn't think about the fact that some other man was probably putting his hands on Kit right now.

CHAPTER 12

K IT CRAWLED INTO A cold bed and stared up at the ceiling. She'd had fun with Terrence, but when he'd kissed her good night, all she'd felt was a keening, horrible pain. Because it wasn't Noah, wouldn't ever be Noah.

I fuck everything female that moves. I don't want that with you.

Those words were important, she knew that, but they also hurt. So much. It would've been easy to say yes to the invitation in Terrence's eyes, to ask him in, to lose herself in his body. He was handsome and kind and her friend.

And she couldn't use him that way.

"I'm not ready," she'd admitted to him. "I… I'm getting over someone."

To his credit, he'd cupped her face with slender writer's hands that felt too smooth against her skin, kissed her on the forehead. "I was starting to get that vibe." A warm smile. "Feel free to rebound on me. Anytime you need a date or a plus one, I'm here for you."

Throat thick with emotion, she'd hugged him tight. "Thank you," she'd whispered, drawing in his scent—and that scent, it wasn't right, wasn't of the man she should've been hugging.

It was all so frustrating and stupid.

"And," Terrence had added, "I'd like to keep seeing you if you don't mind. We can go as slow as you like. I don't want to stop and try to start all over again now that we've discovered we can have a good time together, just the two of us."

Kit's heart had hurt, but she'd nodded. "Yes, I'd like that." Then she'd remembered her one prior engagement. "I promised Noah I'd go with him to a charity gala next Saturday, but we're not dating or anything."

Terrence's smile had been open, his hazel eyes clear. "I know that, Kit. Everyone knows you and the Schoolboy Choir guys are tight—if you'd intended to date one of them, you'd have done it by now." A deeper smile. "I won't throw a jealous fit if the tabloids report it as a clandestine love affair."

"Clandestine love affair?" Kit had laughed. "Careful, or people will start to think you're a writer or something." At his chuckle, she'd hugged him again. "You're a good man."

"Yes, I am." A kiss on the cheek as they drew apart. "I can also be an amazing boyfriend."

Yes, Kit thought, Terrence would be a great boyfriend. He was intelligent with a warm personality, and beautifully creative. Over dinner, they'd talked not only about the industry, but about the deep history of storytelling as well as about travel and how it changed a person. Terrence was also as passionate an advocate of Kit's talent as an actress as she was of his as a writer.

They were perfect for one another. If only she could forget Noah.

She shoved off the comforter after an hour of tossing and turning, then padded into the kitchen and made herself a cup of herbal tea. She didn't particularly like the taste, but oddly enough, it did usually put her to sleep. Not tonight.

Going out into the cool but comfortable air of the garden with the half-finished drink in her hands, she took a seat on one of the picnic-table benches and thought about how Noah's eyes had a way of becoming a silvered gray when he truly laughed. One of her favorite memories of him was from this garden: he'd been lying on his back on a blanket, all lazy and relaxed as they played Worst Rumor while she tidied up the area, tugging out a weed here, clearing up leaf detritus there.

It was a game he'd made up. They had to one-up each other with false celebrity rumors. Of course, half the time they ended up debating whether something was false or not.

Okay, I have a good one, his voice said in her head. G&V *is reporting that Bleu Flavell killed and ate his pet pig Pigiligi during a drug-fueled rampage and is now in therapy to get over the trauma.*

Lies. Kit remembered rolling her eyes at the ridiculous claim. *That pig has its own room in Bleu's house, complete with a bed and a personal groomer and chef. No way Bleu's touching a hair on its body.*

Yeah? So why hasn't Pigiligi Flavell been spotted for the past week, huh? And Bleu did have that blowout party last weekend.

Eyes burning at the memory of their ensuing hilarious attempts to uncover the truth, she stared at the spot where he'd lain. "Stop haunting me." It was a whisper.

Music sounded, soft and gentle.

She'd brought her cell phone outside with her, had been debating whether to text Molly or Becca on the off chance they'd be awake and available to talk. But the name displayed on the screen wasn't of either of her two closest women friends. It was of the man she'd come out here to forget.

She knew she should ignore the call. It would be the sensible, the healthy thing to do. But then she thought of the way he'd asked her to be his friend, of how he'd exposed his need when he never allowed anyone to see his vulnerability, and felt her resolve break. "It's two a.m.," she said into the receiver.

"I was passing by your place, figured I'd try my luck."

Noah had no cause to pass by her place. "Go home."

"I tried." A quiet pause. "Molly made me a bed at her and Fox's place. I snuck out."

He was fine, Kit thought. He wasn't drunk or in trouble. He was just… "Go home," she said again. "There's nothing for you here."

"How about my friend?" It was a rough question.

Kit pressed a hand over her heart, pushing into the ache within. "She's sitting here thinking about the shopping she has to do tomorrow for her mother's annual luncheon." Adreina organized a group mother-and-daughter luncheon for her and her friends every year, and no matter what, Kit would never hurt her by refusing to attend.

Unfortunately, it meant a new outfit head to toe. Her mother insisted. "Make an effort, Kathleen," she'd say in a throaty voice that still carried faint hints of a Venezuelan accent. "If you don't wear the latest styles, people will think your career's sliding and you're pinching pennies."

The worst thing was that she was right. With Kit's career on the rise, the media, the industry, the audience, they were all watching her like hawks. She might worry about her mortgage, but everyone else was interested only in whether she gave the impression of a financially secure A-list actress.

"That come around again already?" Noah's voice sank into her bones, into her blood, into every part of her.

She wanted to scream at him to get out, to leave her be, but he kept on haunting her, kept on becoming part of her. "Yep," she said and rose to her feet. "I better go to bed so I'll be bright and shiny for the shopping trip tomorrow."

"Good night, Kit."

"Good night, Noah." *Why can't you see me like I see you?*

KIT WAS BOTH SURPRISED and not when her phone rang at ten the next day. "Want some company for that shopping trip?" was Noah's response to her hello. "I'm about to reach the gates to your house."

Her fingers clenched into her palm. "You really want us plastered all over the tabloids?"

"Nobody believes we're a couple, not after we so totally debunked the last lot of rumors."

Those rumors had begun when a very smart reporter picked up on the edgy chemistry between Noah and the soap actress Kit had been at the time. However, when Noah made it clear he was dating everyone *but* Kit and Kit started dating a costar, the rumors had died a quick death. Their demise had been helped along by the fact she and Noah had both laughed it off, as had the other members of the band.

In one memorable quote, Noah had said, "Date Kathleen? It'd be like dating my sister."

So yes, he was probably right about the tabloids not making a big deal of it. "Since when do you like shopping?"

"I've been watching that show with the designers. I can make it work."

Her lips twitched at the well-known catchphrase. That was the thing with Noah—he could charm, but he also had a great sense of humor. Sometimes it was wicked, other times sarcastic, occasionally quiet, but the only people who ever saw it were those he trusted. That list was very short.

Stop it, Kit. Stop trying to make yourself special to him.

Only she knew she *was* special to him. He might not want her as a lover, but he valued her friendship. Maybe what she needed to do was desensitize herself to his presence, really beat it into her head that all he wanted was to be friends—if she didn't avoid him, if she repeatedly exposed herself to his indifference to her as a woman, sooner or later, her heart and her body would get with the program.

"Fine," she said on that pragmatic and painful decision. "I'll tell Butch to buzz you in."

Having been about to head out anyway, she was waiting for him when he rolled up in that black Mustang that was all grunt and swagger. "Do you know how much gas this car guzzles?" she asked when she slipped in, not waiting for him to come around to open her door. "I thought you were going to sell it?"

"Turns out I can't part with her." Turning the car around after giving the steering wheel an affectionate pat, he drove back toward the gate. "I happen to know that you buy perfume that costs as much per spritz as a tank of gasoline."

Damn it, he knew too many of her vices. "My taste in expensive perfume is all my mom's fault." Adreina had given her the specially blended perfume on her eighteenth birthday

123

with the instruction that she was now a woman and should have a signature scent.

Kit hadn't expected to like it—her mother's taste in perfume ran to the sultry and voluptuous—but Adreina had surprised her with a clean scent that carried just a touch of the earth. It fit Kit perfectly. "And anyway," she added, "I've never actually had to buy it. Mom gives me a bottle every birthday." It delighted Adreina that even after all these years, Kit preferred that perfume to all others.

"Talking about your mom, does she know you're not rolling in it after your house purchase?" Noah zipped through a yellow light that changed to red halfway through. "Since she's asking you to spend up for her luncheon."

"Neither of my parents have any idea, or they'd throw so much money at me I'd drown in it." Undependable Parker and Adreina might be, but loyal and protective they most certainly were; it was a duality Kit had accepted long ago.

Noah's glance was perceptive. "You won't tell them though, will you?"

"I won't be in such a tight spot as soon as the cosmetics deal is finalized. Another big movie or two, and I'll be home free, no pun intended."

"Would you have gone to your folks anyway?"

"You know I wouldn't." Noah came from money, as did Abe, but Kit knew the two men hadn't used any family money to build Schoolboy Choir. No, Fox, Abe, David, and Noah had done it on their own from the ground up. All four men equal and all four men proud of what they'd achieved.

Kit had always been envious of their since-childhood friendship. She'd had friends in school, of course, but no one with whom she'd bonded deeply enough that they'd stayed in touch after graduation. Not anyone's fault, just the roll of the dice. Becca was her longest-standing friend. They'd clicked at their very first meeting on the set of *Primrose Avenue*, been close ever since.

And now she had Molly too. She could already tell that friendship would last.

"Hey." Noah's voice, a curious smile. "Where did you go?"

"Just thinking about a coffee date I have with Molly." They planned to go to a little place Thea had recommended.

"Anyway," she said, "my folks both earned their wealth." Parker's parents had ensured that he had the best tennis coaches and could attend the most elite training camps, but he was the one who'd put in the court time; he was the one who'd begged off from nights out and vacations away.

Kit was pretty sure her father had never gone on a spring break blowout, gotten drunk and partied. He'd been too driven, too dedicated to his goal of achieving a Grand Slam— which he'd done not once, but twice. As for Adreina, she'd been born dirt-poor, clawed her way out through sheer grit and determination. It was partly why she lived so flamboyantly now.

"I want to stand on my own feet too," Kit said, remembering the pleasure of her first paycheck, of how good it had felt to know she'd earned it through her own hard work. "I bet you've never taken money from your mother or father either."

Noah's expression turned grim. "I have a trust fund that's been gathering interest and dust for decades. I should donate it or something, but..." He shook his head, his golden hair catching the sunlight and making him appear a young god.

"Let's not talk about my nonrelationship with my folks—I heard your dad's going to be organizing one of the big tennis tournaments, right?"

"Yes." Despite his pleasure-seeking lifestyle, her father had never lost his interest in, and passion for, the game. "Mom's really excited and already making plans for the parties she'll throw the players and their teams post-match."

Noah shot her a dark look before returning his attention to the road. "It kind of weirds me out that your parents actually still like each other. Like, for real."

Kit laughed, unsurprised. Celebrity marriages did not, as a rule, last, especially when you were talking two giant egos. "It occasionally surprises me too." Her mother could appear so shallow, her father so self-involved, but while they were flaky parents, they were devoted lovers.

"The thing is," she said to Noah, "Mom and Dad *always* back each other. They argue in private like the two passionate personalities they are, but in public, say a single bad thing about one to the other, and you're persona non grata." Kit loved that aspect of her parents' marriage.

"And though it makes me squirm to even think about it, my parents continue to find each other hot." She shuddered. "While I was still in high school, I once walked into the conservatory at our family home to find my naked mother straddling my clothed father." She scrubbed the heels of her hands over her eyes as Noah's laughter, deep and unrestrained, filled the car. "I'm pretty sure she was undoing his belt at the time."

Cheeks creased in a huge grin, Noah said, "What did they do?"

"Mom looked over and said, 'Kit, dear, not now. Your father and I are discussing something.'"

"*Discussing something?*"

Shoving at his arm when he snorted with laughter again, she giggled. "Well, I guess they might've been, but I just backed out and shut the door. Then I went and found a sock and put it on the door to warn the staff and my grandparents, who'd just arrived. It was Christmas—which might explain the red ribbon tied into a big bow below my mom's breasts." She shuddered again. "Mom was holding another ribbon. I *do not* want to imagine where that was intended to go."

"Ho, ho, ho, Merry Christmas to Parker."

She was the one who snorted this time. "Shut up."

Noah was still grinning when he pulled into a parking garage off Rodeo Drive, the open, unshadowed pleasure on his face threatening to undo all her resolve.

Careful, Kit. He's not for you.

She had to repeat that until it sank in, until she could look at Noah and not feel that hole inside her tear open all over again.

CHAPTER 13

WALKING OUT OF THE garage, they made their way to the street. A skinny, black-haired photographer with an improbable handlebar moustache popped out from seemingly nowhere seconds later and began to click away. "Come on, Kathleen! Give us a smile, love!"

Kit complied because it was the easiest way to get rid of this particular pest. "Enough, Basil," she said when he continued to back down the sidewalk, camera pointed at her and Noah. "There're only so many places that want photos of me dressed down in jeans and a white T-shirt." She was well put together, her hair brushed back in a sleek tail and her face lightly made up, heels on her feet and the T-shirt fitted, but it was hardly tabloid gold.

That was on purpose. Kit had studied actors and actresses who managed to land big deals without being constant paparazzi fodder, intended to follow their lead: be classy, be elegant, don't hang out at the celebrity hot spots, and don't wear things that shouted for photographers to take snaps.

"Why do you do this to me?" Basil put a hand on his heart, his English accent incongruously posh. "I don't suppose you

128

two will hold hands? I can sell it as a secret romance. It'll be great for both your profiles."

Noah, dressed in ripped black jeans and a black T-shirt featuring a band he loved, paired with his usual scuffed boots, gave the photographer the finger instead, careful to time it so it was between shutter clicks.

Basil swore but walked off to stalk more financially rewarding targets. Forgetting him because, in truth, Basil was one of the more reasonable paps Kit ran into on a regular basis, she nodded at an upcoming boutique. "In here."

There were four other women inside already, including a glossily put-together clerk. Every single one—from the eighty-something matriarch with a face kept youthful by an excellent surgeon, to the ten-year-old in sparkly sneakers—took a deep breath when Noah walked in behind Kit, having held the door open for her.

Kit couldn't blame them. He was impossibly beautiful, but he wasn't pretty. No, he had that hard edge that said he'd break hearts and beds too. Women gravitated toward him. Was it any wonder that he took advantage?

Hand fisting at her side, she forced herself to smile as the clerk came over.

"Ms. Devigny," the clerk said, her curly hair ruthlessly tamed into a neat knot and her body clad in a black tunic-style dress. "It's so good to see you. I have a lovely dress I think you might like."

"Thank you, Hailey." Accompanying the rail-thin part-time model to the back wall of the boutique, she examined the jewel-green sheath dress with a gorgeous design element on the right side of the lower half.

"The beading is hand-stitched," Hailey told her. "Just a touch, so it's light enough for daytime but can be dressed up for the night if you're going day to night."

"I like it," Noah said from behind her, her body prickling with a primal awareness of his masculine presence. "It's too long for you though."

He was right. The dress looked as if it would hit her at the wrong part of the calf, and it couldn't be brought up without ruining the beading. "I'll try it anyway, just in case."

When she did, she found her and Noah's doubts were justified.

"Hey, Kit," he said from outside the large changing room. "Fashion show."

Opening the door, she stepped out to twirl with a hand on her hip. "Definitely too long but I wish it wasn't."

"You make it look gorgeous," Noah said, and for a moment, as their eyes caught and held, it was too much, too painful, too beautiful.

Thankfully, Hailey hurried over right then to exclaim over the dress, though she, too, had to admit it was the wrong length. She showed Kit three other pieces, but nothing worked.

"Next stop is on the other side of those traffic lights," she said to Noah after they left the boutique.

"What's with that dress?" He was pointing toward a designer piece in red leather in the window of an exclusive salon. "It looks like a deranged serial killer took a shredder to it."

"Fashion, darling," Kit said in her best fashionista voice. "You clearly have no taste, no *je ne sais quoi*."

"Nope," said the gorgeous man who constantly wore disreputable jeans and whatever T-shirt he could find, and looked hotter than any other man on the planet. Right now he had a thick metal chain going from the front left pocket of his jeans to the back. That was dressing up for Noah.

Dropping the phony accent as her traitorous, addicted-to-Noah body threatened to focus on the way his butt looked in those jeans, she said, "The dress is a monstrosity. Want to go ask the price?"

"They let you ask the price?"

Kit shrugged, they looked at each other, then went in. Keeping a straight face at the five-figure price tag was difficult, but they managed it until they were outside and past the shop.

Barely.

"What are you wearing to the gala?" Kit asked once she'd caught her breath and they were safely across the street. "I assumed it was black tie." Thea had already lined up a couple of designers who wanted to put Kit in one of their gowns.

"Yeah, it is." A sigh. "I'll put on a fucking penguin suit because it's my aunt's deal."

"I've never seen you in a tux."

"And you probably never will again," he muttered as he pulled open the door to the boutique that was their destination.

She saw the dress at once: a dark, dark pink that was *almost* red, it was sleeveless and had a classic A-line set off with a thin black belt. The neckline was almost straight across with the barest curve while the back zipped up all the way. It had a 50s vibe to it that appealed to Kit. Paired with the discreet dia-

131

mond earrings her paternal grandparents had given her on her twenty-first birthday, it would be perfect for the luncheon.

This time she didn't come out and show Noah the dress. Because if he complimented her again while looking at her as he'd done in the other boutique, the anger and frustration and love inside her might erupt into a scream, her fists pounding at him as her fury spilled over.

Shaking, she took a deep breath and put on the mask again.

Noah was smiling when she stepped out, but it faded almost immediately and she knew he'd seen the mask. Too damn bad. "Got it," she said, and took the dress to the counter before the clerk could come over.

The two of them left the boutique in silence after she paid.

"Noah!" The call came from two excited female voices.

Figuring they were fans of the band, Kit waited a few steps away so Noah could sign autographs. Except these women didn't want autographs. The top-heavy brunette threw herself into Noah's arms. "Tuesday night was a-*mazing*!" she squealed.

Even as Kit's stomach lurched, bile burning her throat, the other brunette stroked a hand down Noah's arm. "We haven't been able to stop talking about it." Giggles as Noah extricated himself. "If you want us to come over tonight, we're *so* ready."

Noah managed to peel them off, his charming expression never changing—but Kit knew that look. It was the one he used with people he didn't particularly want to talk to, and yet he'd obviously slept with both these women. What did that make him if not a user? Of course, the women appeared to have gone to his bed with open eyes, but it just seemed wrong that he could dismiss them so easily.

Feeling sick about the whole situation, she avoided his gaze and was about to walk away on her own when she realized Basil was lurking in a doorway not far in the distance. If she did what she wanted to do, the shots would be all over the tabloids tomorrow, telling a story she didn't want anyone to know.

So instead, she maintained her bored waiting face and the next time Noah looked over, pointed at her watch. As if she was nothing more than a friend annoyed by the delay. Grinning, he took his leave of the women, who both pouted in disappointment.

He didn't say anything about the incident and neither did she. Good. Because the humiliating thing was that while Noah had been fucking not one but two women, she'd been lying alone in bed, trying to get over him.

Part of her heart finally, *finally* turned to stone.

NOAH KNEW THE MOOD was broken. For a few wonderful hours, he and Kit had managed to recapture the friendship that had made him understand joy, but it was now as out of reach as the moon, the atmosphere in the car tense enough to snap.

"Noah," Kit said into the silence. "Do you like women?"

"What kind of question is that? You know I like women."

"No, you use women. But do you actually *like* them?"

He scowled. "Sure. I like you and Thea, Molly and my sister, for starters."

"Then why do you treat your lovers that way?" Turning in her seat, she looked at him with eyes he couldn't read, the shutters down and locked. "As if they're worth nothing?"

Noah couldn't believe she wanted to talk about this. "Jesus, Kit, they weren't my lovers. They were just women I—" He cut himself off before he spoke words even he knew would make him appear an asshole. "We weren't lovers."

"Have you ever had one? A lover?"

Yeah. You. They might've never so much as kissed, but during their friendship Kit had known him better than any of the women he'd fucked ever would. He'd given her his heart in the songs he wrote that weren't the hard rock for which Schoolboy Choir was known, and she'd held that heart cupped safely in her hands.

"No," he said aloud. "Why settle for just one?" It came out a brittle question.

Kit shifted to stare out the window.

They didn't speak again until she got out of the car at her house. "Thanks for the company," she said and was gone.

ENTERING THE HOUSE, KIT went to her room and hung up the dress so it wouldn't wrinkle. Then she sat on the edge of her bed and, for the last time, faced all of her most secret dreams when it came to Noah and accepted that none of them were going to come true. The end. Run credits.

No tears this time, just a quiet and soul-deep grief.

Not only for her lost dreams, but for Noah and the terrible thing that haunted him. If he ever shared the cause of his demons with her, she'd be his friend, attempt to help him, but she couldn't live her life trying to protect his. He had to take responsibility for his choices... as she had to for hers.

When her phone rang, she stared at the screen for long

seconds before picking it up. "Terrence," she said, putting a smile in her voice.

Noah would've realized it was false, but Terrence didn't know her that well yet. He would though, she thought as she agreed to meet him for dinner at his place. She'd go into this with her heart wide open, give him a chance to truly know her, this good, smart man who wanted her.

NOAH WOKE WITH GRITTY eyes and an aching body. He hadn't gone out and picked up a girl last night. Instead, he'd gone running on the beach, the world silvery white under a bright moon, the waves crashing to shore inches from where his sports shoe-clad feet hit the sand.

He hadn't bothered with a T-shirt, just pulled on running shorts and shoes, and then he'd run and run and run and *run* until it seemed he'd left the entire world behind, locked up tight in sleep.

It wasn't true, of course. He was awake and so were the flotsam and jetsam of the world. Including the gangbangers and drug pushers who only came out after the sun set—and who left Noah alone because they were fans. An odd perk of fame, and one he appreciated. His favorite Venice night person was a familiar homeless guy who, night after night, managed to sneak onto the beach to sleep under the stars.

"Hey!" he called out as Noah passed him on the way back to his place.

When Noah stopped, the other man struggled up into a sitting position in his sleeping bag, his deeply tanned face seamed with life and all but covered by a sprawling white beard and mustache and the messy white of his hair. "Why you so crazy? Out here at night all the time, disturbing a man's sleep."

Breath rough, Noah bent over with his hands on his knees. "Just a bad seed, I guess."

"Since you woke me up, you got a dollar?"

"For you, Marshall, I got twenty." Taking the bill from his sock where he'd put it for exactly this purpose, he handed it over. "What's happening, my man?"

"I was creating a symphony inspired by the waves." Marshall tucked away the money. "Now I'm thinking I'll be inspired tomorrow morning by bacon and eggs and sausage. Symphony of Cholesterol."

Noah grinned, knowing that for the truth. Marshall never drank away what money he had, had even turned down a bottle of bourbon last Christmas. "A full breakfast sounds good. I might join you."

The homeless man grunted. "You're not invited. Last time you came into the diner, you had all the waitresses going so crazy they burned my sausages and made my eggs sunny-side up when I specifically said scrambled."

Noah took a seat on the sand, his eyes on the waves rolling in to shore. "Body's gotta eat."

"You got that right." Marshall held out a stick of gum, slid it back when Noah shook his head. "Why do you run so much?"

"Same reason you sit on the beach playing your harmonica long after the world's gone to sleep."

The other man nodded solemnly, rubbing his thumb over the small instrument. "Where's your guitar?"

"Back home. Want to come up so we can jam?" Noah had offered Marshall a place to crash—not in his house, because he couldn't have *anyone* in his house while he slept, while he was vulnerable—but in the guesthouse. The homeless man kept turning him down because he hated walls, hated not being able to taste the wind and breathe the open air.

The only time he'd ever accepted shelter had been during a rare torrential rainstorm.

"Naw," Marshall said to his invite. "I want to work on my symphony. But I'll see you at the diner for breakfast. Seven a.m. sharp. And if those waitresses get my order wrong, I'm eating yours."

Saluting the older man, Noah rose and jogged back to his place. He was so tired by the time he arrived that he slept, though he was still awake in plenty of time to make his date with Marshall and looking forward to it. Whatever path had led Marshall to this life, he had music in his blood—and Noah knew that if not for Fox, Abe, and David, he could've ended up much the same. Lost and without roots and tormented by nightmares until he couldn't bear walls around himself.

Not shaving, he pulled on an old Lakers cap in an effort to shadow his face, then made his way down to the diner on the boardwalk. Marshall was already sitting at a table, having tidied himself up so that he looked respectable. The olive-green weatherproof coat Noah had given him last year was clean, his beard neatly trimmed, and his backpack set beside him. No shopping cart for Marshall, just that ragged backpack.

After getting their food—unburned—they spoke about music and about all the changes Marshall had seen in this area over the years, until the other man got up to use the restroom. Noah picked up the newspaper lying on a nearby table to occupy himself while Marshall was away, seeing too late that it was one of the tabloids. About to throw it back, he caught Kit's name in the sidebar.

Figuring Basil had gotten a payday after all, he turned to the page indicated—to see a full-color shot of Kit standing with her hands in Terrence's, her face glowing. They were beside Kit's car, as if she'd just arrived or was about to leave, and she was wearing a pretty, soft dress in a cool tangerine orange that he knew turned her amber eyes even more striking.

The text read:

It looks like rising star Kathleen Devigny is following in the footsteps of her Last Flight costar, JJ Hughes, in dating not one of her fellow actors but a member of the crew. While JJ is now pregnant with her first child with her cameraman boyfriend, sources tell us that Kathleen's romance with scriptwriter Terrence Gates is only beginning.

This exclusive shot shows her arriving at Gates's home around seven last night. Sadly for Gates, she left at eleven. However, from the rumored smile on his face as he walked her back to her car, the night was a promising one for the talented scriptwriter who already has a Golden Globe under his belt.

Watch this space for more on this developing Tinseltown romance.

CHAPTER 14

THE SATURDAY OF THE gala came around before Kit knew it. It felt strange to her to be dressing for an evening out with Noah when she was now officially seeing another man, but Terrence remained fine with her attending the event. Partly because, as a result of work pressures, they'd only just gone on their third official date, so things were still new, and partly because Terrence knew Noah's reputation.

"He's taking you so his parents won't hassle him about bringing his latest flavor of the night, right?" Terrence had said to her on the phone yesterday, not long after she'd finished a workout with Steve.

Lying flat on her back on the exercise mat, Kit had agreed—Noah's strained relationship with his parents wasn't her story to share.

Now she finished up the old-Hollywood glamour look she'd chosen for the night, her eyes deceptively simple but her lips coated in glossy scarlet. She'd parted her hair in the center and pulled it gently back into a deliberately soft knot, allowing a few tendrils to escape.

Normally she'd have asked Becca to do her makeup and

hair, but given her friend's loyal dislike of Noah, she'd decided on discretion and fallen back on Adreina's teachings. At least with a look this classic, there wasn't much she could mess up.

As for the dress—she rarely wore black, but Noah's family was old-school, and this dress would fit right in while standing out, exactly what an A-list actress was supposed to do.

The latter words were Thea's. "You're hot right now, sweetie," the other woman had said. "But you aren't yet molten, and your place on the A-list isn't set in stone."

Blunt as always when it came to the industry, Thea had gone on to add, "The movies you've got on your slate will get you some traction, but we also need to capitalize on the current level of interest—part of that is continuing to build your image as elegant, stylish, and intelligent."

"Thea, this is Noah's deal."

"It might be his deal, but as a woman you'll be photographed as often, if not more," Thea had reminded her. "The intelligent part is a given since this is a private gala hosted in the home of a renowned art collector. For elegant and stylish, the gown is going to be key, makeup to be decided once we find that gown."

In the end, the two of them had settled on this sleeveless but not strapless floor-length gown that skimmed her body to the hips before opening out into a gorgeous skirt created of multiple layers of material. It draped in a way that meant it had a lovely flow in motion and a stunning line when she was still. The back was a deep vee, but not so deep that she was in danger of looking trashy, while the front neckline was cut straight across at an angle that gave the dress a point of interest suited to the high-class charity/arts event.

Jewels glinted in the light, the only hint of color in the entire outfit coming from her polished green nails and the long emerald-and-diamond earrings borrowed from a jeweler. She acted as his walking billboard; he gave her gemstones she couldn't otherwise afford—courtesy of Thea's contacts.

Thea had laughed when Kit sent her a photo from the nail salon earlier today. "I love it. Kathleen Devigny is still Kathleen Devigny, even when she's going to a stuffy gala. No blending in for you."

Slipping her feet into ankle-breaker Jimmy Choos that exposed her painted toenails when the dress moved, she picked up her simple black clutch and took a deep breath, released it as slowly. "I'm his friend, and he needs a friend tonight."

The intercom buzzed, Butch letting her know they'd cleared Noah through.

"A friend," she repeated again and walked to the door.

She opened it just as a gleaming black limo came to a stop in front of it. Noah exited from the front passenger seat a second later, and all the breath just whooshed out of her. He was always gorgeous, reminding her of a young lion in the summer when his hair turned streaky gold, but today he could've stood in as Prince Charming or as James Bond, depending on the smile he pulled out.

But the smile he gave her was wary.

"Wow." Coming to the door, he stared at her, a sexy, beautiful man in a classic tuxedo that perfectly fit his frame. He was built like a model, she thought suddenly. Lean muscle, wide shoulders, slim hips.

"Wow yourself," she replied after catching her breath. "You do clean up pretty."

Some of the wariness receded. "Shall we go?"

Suddenly unable to bear the strain and distance between them, she said, "Feel in the mood for a friendly wager?"

He tilted his head to the side.

"As soon as the photos of you in this tux start hitting the airwaves, I bet Thea starts getting calls from designers who want to dress you or get you to front their campaigns."

"Not happening. One night does not turn a sow's ear into a silk purse."

She knew the fashion world far better than he did, was conscious it could turn on a dime and that the rules were different for men and women. As long as Noah looked this hot in their clothes when he wore them, the designers wouldn't care what he wore the rest of the time. In fact, the contrast would only heighten interest. "So, bet?"

"Bet. Stakes?"

She tapped a finger against her hip. "If I win, you have to hunt down this specific plant I want for my garden—it can only be ordered from a cantankerous old gardener in Kyoto, Japan who refuses to sell to anyone he hasn't met in person and vetted."

"So let me get this right," Noah said, eyes narrowing. "I'd have to not only *fly to Japan*, I'd have to win the approval of a crusty old man who might kick me out on my ass without a plant?"

"Yep."

"In that case, if I win"—that troublemaker's grin that had been missing till now—"you have to get onstage at the next Schoolboy Choir concert, whenever that might be, and sing a duet with me."

Her mouth dropped open. "And humiliate myself in front of thousands, maybe millions, if the video goes viral? I don't think so."

"You have a good voice."

"For *karaoke*!" She folded her arms. "You'd only be humiliated in front of one old man who won't even care who you are."

"Fine, chicken." Her grim-eyed response made his grin widen. "You just have to sing solo in front of the guys, Molly, and Thea. Song of my choice."

"Done." She set her alarm, then pulled the door shut.

Noah put his hand on her lower back as they moved to the limo, and that was when Kit realized exactly how bad a choice she'd made with this dress. That sexy vee at the back? It meant his rough, callused fingertips would rasp against her skin each time he placed his hand on her back—and no matter the dip in her stomach, the shiver that wanted to ripple over her skin, she couldn't tell him to stop.

If she did, it would make them appear stiff and awkward in photos. That would spark far more rumors than if they acted naturally, one friend agreeing to act as a date for a family event of the other. So she'd suck it up and deal with the fact that in spite of her decision to move on, the chemistry was stronger than ever, electricity crackling over her skin.

"So," she said once they were in the limo, the soundproof privacy screen up, "remind me of everyone in your family."

Bracing his arm along the back of the seat, he undid the buttons on the tuxedo jacket and turned toward her, the crisp white of his shirt stretching across his chest. "My father is a criminal lawyer—Robert."

"Not just a criminal lawyer," Kit interrupted. "He's a pretty big deal, right?"

"Yeah. He's a shark." A shrug. "Mom's Virginia, a political lobbyist turned lady-who-lunches; she sits on countless charity boards to salve her conscience for having no moral compass."

Kit frowned. "Why are you always so hard on your mom?" He didn't get along with his father, but he always seemed far angrier at his mother.

A faint smile that wasn't a smile at all. "Because I'm an entitled brat."

"*Noah.*"

"*Katie,*" he said in the same tone. "Forget about my fucked-up relationship with my parents—it's a hellhole of no return."

"What about Emily? Will she be there?"

"No, she's away at school." A real smile at the mention of his sister. "My aunt Margaret, the one who's spearheading this gala, is my father's much younger sister. She lived with us when I was a child." Shadows darkened his eyes. "Margaret didn't want them to send me to boarding school, but she was only a kid then, still in high school, so she couldn't stop them."

The smile returned before she could say anything.

"But that worked out all right—met Fox my first day at the school." He ran his hand through his hair, messing up the neat strands and exposing a hint of the song lyrics tattooed on his inner wrist. "Aunt Margaret used to visit me once she was in college and could come down without my parents knowing. After she went to Europe for her postgrad, she sent me postcards and letters, presents for no reason."

A pause, his next words quiet. "She got sick soon after that, was in the hospital for a long time. My parents wouldn't let me visit except during official school vacations, so we didn't have as much contact when I was a teenager, but she never forgot me."

As his parents had forgotten him, Kit completed silently, hurting for the gifted, lonely boy become a rebellious teenager. Making the conscious decision to follow a happier thread, she said, "How did you and Fox end up roommates?"

"The school was full of rich kids," he told her, not seeming to realize he was brushing his fingers over her nape.

Kit let it go rather than turning it into a big deal, though it was causing goose bumps up and down her body.

"It was exclusive and out in the middle of nowhere," Noah continued, "lots of trees and playing fields. But they had this policy that no matter who your parents or grandparents were, you had to share a room."

"Some parents must've complained."

"Sure, but the school wouldn't budge, and it had serious high-powered parental support. In the end, most people came around, because the school pitched it as networking from an early age."

Laughing, he shook his head. "I used to say bullshit until Abe pointed out how many of our schoolmates are now in politics, law, other positions of power. I kid you not, one of the kids I used to get into trouble with doing illegal experiments in chemistry is now a head honcho at the NSA—we had a drink last time he was in town."

"Talk about contacts!" Kit said with a shake of her head.

Noah's fingers slid across her sensitive skin again, and at last he seemed to notice what he was doing. His eyes locked with hers, her breath held in her lungs, the moment full of so many words unspoken that it was a crushing pressure in the air. "Fox and you," she prompted softly, because those words had to remain unspoken.

For her own sanity. For the friendship Noah needed.

JAW A HARSH LINE, he said, "I'd never shared with anyone, and Fox grew up with his grandparents, without any brothers and sisters, so we walk in and sit on our beds, staring at each other." Noah could remember the knot in his stomach, the sour taste in his mouth, the cold fingers crawling down his back.

The idea of having to sleep in a room with a stranger, even if that stranger was a boy as small as him, a boy with green eyes and dark brown hair, had almost been enough to thrust Noah into panicked shock. "Then," he continued, "Fox says, 'Did you see we have a pet spider?'"

Kit's shudder was so girlish he smiled. "A pet spider?"

"It was this huge black thing with skinny legs in one corner of the room. We spent an hour watching it spin its web, and we were cool after that." It had been that simple, and yet not. Because that night Noah had a nightmare that left him huddled in another corner, shivering so hard his teeth had clattered against each other; Fox had come over and sat with him, bringing a blanket to cover them both.

That was the moment that had bonded them forever.

It wasn't until he was much older that Noah understood Fox's courage in making the first move by speaking about the spider. Unlike Noah, Fox didn't come from wealth. He'd been dumped at the school because no one wanted him, the school's wealthy environs unfamiliar and scary.

"Boys." Kit shook her head on the affectionate word. "Did your pet spider survive?"

"We kept it safe for a while, but the cleaners came in one day while we were out, and we never saw Mr. Legs again." His muscles began to coil as they turned into the drive that led to the magnificent Beverly Hills mansion that was the site of tonight's gala.

The Tierney estate belonged to a renowned and somewhat eccentric art collector who also happened to be a close friend of his aunt's. "Ready for the circus?" he said to Kit. "I heard Tierney has his own personal mummy."

She reached up to fix his hair, the small intimacy doing things to him he couldn't name. "We can sneak away and go hunt for it if the gala gets too boring."

"Deal."

The limo came to a halt at the bottom of the red carpet, which fell in a cascade down the mansion's museum-worthy front steps and continued on down the drive until it hit the drop-off point at the top of the circular turnaround for vehicles. Beyond was a much longer drive down which they'd just driven, and on either side of the red carpet—corralled behind thick velvet ropes—buzzed a phalanx of black-tie-clad photographers and reporters who'd been given a media pass to the event.

Noah opened his own door rather than waiting for the limo driver and stepped out while doing up the tux jacket, then held out his hand for Kit. She slipped her warm, slender hand into his, and his skin tightened, his body attuned to her on a level that was primal and hotly possessive.

And then she was standing with him, a stunning woman with a heart big enough to forgive him for the worst mistake of his life, to trust him once again with the gift of her friendship. He wouldn't fuck it up this time.

No matter how loud the demons howled.

The cameras had started flashing the instant he exited the limo, but they went insane as he and Kit moved down the red carpet. He kept his hand on Kit's back throughout, loathe to have the other men here believe she was on her own. Because she wasn't. For this one night, she was his.

"Kathleen! Kathleen! Who's your date?" a photographer called out. "What's his name?"

Laughing, Kit turned her face up toward him, then they turned as a couple to the media. The flashbulbs were blinding, questions and exclamations rising in a roar as the photographers and reporters clicked on the identity of her date.

"Jesus," Noah muttered without making a face because he didn't want to ruin the photos, conscious this was an important opportunity for Kit. "It's a penguin suit, people."

"I hope your passport's up-to-date," Kit said on a dazzling smile. "Japan's calling."

"You haven't won yet." Coiled muscles eased, his cheeks creasing in a real smile. "I'm not getting any excited calls from Thea."

"Pfft, the night is young, and you're looking so pretty." She moved with him to one of the official gala photographers on their side of the velvet rope, posing gracefully beside him. Then, bowing to requests, she stepped away to give the other photographers the solo shots they wanted of her and her gown.

Noah pretended not to hear the bloodthirsty mob calling for his own solo shots. This was why he didn't fucking wear suits or brush his hair. It made him too goddamn pretty, though at least he'd grown into his face so that he had a harder edge.

Taking out his phone, he grabbed a few shots of Kit. She blew him a kiss, her eyes bright. Grinning at the resulting image, he asked her to strike a pose. The photographers went wild, clicking along with him. When she finally waved them down and walked over, he immediately placed his hand on her lower back, the silken warmth of her a near-painful pleasure.

"I didn't realize how huge the media presence would be," Kit said to him as they climbed the steps, Kit holding her dress just an inch off the carpet with flawless grace. "You've done me a huge favor, Noah. This kind of exposure…" She shook her head. "Money can't buy it."

"I have a feeling Thea leaked the news we'd be here." Noah had intense appreciation for Thea's smarts as a publicist. "She probably hooked up with Aunt Margaret to offer media privileges to an extended number of photographers." A win-win situation for the charity and for Kit.

Kit bit her lower lip. "Of course she did—I didn't even think about that. Do you mind?"

"Why would I mind? If I can help your career, I will." Sadly, Kit's shining talent wasn't enough—she also had to win the media war, had to become a public darling America and the world wanted to see on-screen. "Speaking of which, you should turn here." Her position on the steps, with the majestic columns of the mansion behind her, would make for a fantastic shot.

"Thanks." Kit's smile hit him right in the solar plexus. "I'm kind of high from the night already—it's fun."

"Yeah, it is," he said, stepping away so she could be in the spotlight. He loved watching her move, loved watching her sparkle. The night *was* fun, but only because she was with him.

When she held out a hand, he took position beside her and they let the photographers snap a few shots of them together.

"Into the cauldron," he said when they turned to continue on up to the entrance. The closer they got to the doors, the harder his muscles bunched, until by the time they cleared the entrance, he felt as if he was made of stone.

CHAPTER 15

HIS AUNT WAS STANDING near the entrance with her partner of many years, Louise. Seeing him, she beamed and walked over as fast as she could in her elegant red gown, a petite powerhouse with golden hair cut in a chic bob, and brilliant blue eyes.

"My favorite boy," she said, giving him a tight hug. "I'm so happy you came. And look at you!" She patted the front of his tuxedo jacket.

"Only for you, Aunt Margaret," Noah said, bending to accept a kiss on the cheek before turning to Kit. "If you don't recognize Kit, I'll disown you."

"Noah!"

Laughing at Kit's scandalized response, his aunt took Kit's hand in her own. "I'm in awe of your talent, my dear."

"The admiration is mutual." Kit's response was warm, her smile lighting up the room. "Everything looks incredible. I hope the gala raises hundreds of thousands of dollars for the foundation."

"Oh, we'll get it," his aunt said, her tone steely. "Even if I have to stand over people to get them to open their wallets for the auction." A wink. "At least I know one donor who won't stiff me."

Noah pretended to look up at the high ceiling as if fascinated by the old-fashioned moldings.

"Don't make me twist your ear, Noah St. John."

Grinning, he hugged his aunt with one arm. "I already transferred the money to the foundation's account. Tonight I'm just going to outbid people to drive up prices for the auction items, then drop out so they're stuck with paying but feeling like they got one over on the brat rock star."

Kit nudged her shoulder to his in laughing agreement while Margaret's responding expression held pure glee.

"That's why I love you. Go on and mingle, you two. Prepare for a few starstruck types—they might be rich, but most can only aspire to bad reality television." She put a neatly manicured hand on Kit's arm. "There are a few people you might want to meet. Noah, make sure you introduce her to Cyril King and Lisa Fei."

KIT RECOGNIZED BOTH NAMES. Talk about money people. Slipping her arm through Noah's as they left his aunt to move deeper into the huge atrium space that made the mansion perfect for gala events, she said, "I'm starting to feel guilty. I came to support you, but I seem to be getting everything."

"Are you kidding?" Noah's upper arm muscles grew rigid under her fingertips. "I'd already be climbing the walls if you weren't with me." He grabbed two flutes of champagne, handing her one and gulping half of his.

"Hey." She put her frown in her voice, not her face, aware they were the focus of multiple pairs of curious eyes. "No getting drunk on champagne." As far as she knew, Noah was always sober in public, but after the motel incident, Kit wasn't taking any chances.

A stormy, dark gray glance that held echoes of the icy cold with which she'd seen him shut down others.

"Damn it," he muttered. "Stop being the voice of reason."

No cold there; he sounded almost sulky.

Lips twitching, she squeezed his arm. "Shall we go say hello to your parents? We can do it quick."

"No." With that flat statement, he turned her to the right. "Let's go talk to Cyril instead. He's a windbag but a funny one most of the time."

However, they'd only gone a few feet when Noah was stopped by an older couple who looked very, very blue-blooded.

"Noah," the lady said with a tight smile that seemed congenital. "It's good to see you here."

"Aunt Althea, Uncle Donald." Ice now, each word dripping with it. "This is Kathleen."

"Charmed, my dear." Another prunish pursing of lips from the woman. "My grandchild tells me you're to be a green… creature in your next movie."

Kit put light pressure on Noah's arm when his muscles bunched again. "Yes," she said with her most dazzling smile, happy to see the male of the pair blink. "It was fun."

"If you'll excuse us," Noah said coolly before his aunt could speak again. "I think I see my mother." As they moved off, he slid away his arm to put his hand on her lower back again. "I'm sorry about that."

Kit felt her eyes threaten to burn at the protective way he was trying to surround her, subtly angling his big shoulders to cut off those who might interrupt them. "Dear Aunt Althea looks like she walks around with a permanent bug up her butt—I'm not about to take anything she says to heart."

Not seeing Virginia St. John, she said, "Where's your mom?"

"Who knows? I just wanted to get away from old Turnip Face."

Kit's shoulders shook. "That's awful."

"Every time I came home from boarding school, she'd visit and she'd look me up and down like a piece of disappointing meat."

"I hate her on your behalf."

His smile reached his eyes. "Can I drink the rest of my champagne?"

"No. You need to keep a clear head so you can outbid everyone without ending up with a hideous souvenir," she whispered as they reached the long table that held the items up for auction. "Look at that piece. Who thinks that's art?"

"I think that plate's worse." He moved his hand slightly on her back. "Looks like a drunk threw up and decided to capture it in porcelain and paint."

"Should I help you drive up the bids?" she said mischievously. "Bet we could get this up to at least ten thousand."

"Aunt Margaret will love you for it."

"Noah."

NOAH'S SPINE STIFFENED AT that patrician male voice. Forcing himself to keep his face expressionless, he turned toward a man who looked like an older version of him—except that

Robert St. John had shorter hair that had turned a pure white and his face was set in hard lines. Noah's face could look like that too, but it wasn't his default face. This was his father's default—if it wasn't, Noah didn't know it, since it was the only face he ever saw.

"Dad," he said, keeping it civil because Kit was with him. "Where's Mom?"

"Virginia is speaking to Althea." Robert turned the glacial gray of his eyes to Kit. "Ms. Devigny, I'm happy to see you here. I know you and Noah have been friends for a long time."

"I'm delighted to be here with him."

Robert faced Noah again—except of course, he never *quite* faced Noah. His gaze was always a little to the left or the right. Robert St. John couldn't bear to look at the son he'd once proudly called his heir.

"I heard your concert tour was a success."

"Yes."

Kit covered the strained silence that followed his curt response. "I attended the New York show, and it was incredible. They blew the roof off."

"Yes, I hear the band is powerful in concert." A faint smile. "I wanted Noah to practice law, but as usual, he's gone his own way."

"Noah, darling." His mother, skinny and sharp and fashionable, appeared around the side of his father. Unlike Robert, she didn't even attempt to look at him, her gaze blank and deliberately unfocused as she rose toward him.

Noah turned his face so her attempt at getting a cheek kiss from him turned into an air-kiss against his own cheek. It was the best he could do for the woman who'd abandoned him when he'd needed her most.

Robert had been a distant figure throughout Noah's childhood, always at court or at his office, but Virginia had been an involved mother. She'd taken Noah to nursery school, picked him up afterward, driven him to swimming lessons, then helped him study so he'd be smart going into elementary school. She'd been the quintessential soccer mom whose world revolved around her son.

Until that son wasn't perfect anymore.

"Introduce me to your date," Virginia said now, her social mask in place.

Noah made the introductions. Kit's gracious warmth softened his own coldness, coldness he couldn't hide. The ice inside him made him feel brittle, as if he'd crack with even the finest pressure.

"I'm so sorry," Kit said just when Noah couldn't take it anymore. "I see a studio exec Noah promised to introduce me to—do you mind if I steal him away?"

Robert and Virginia smiled their acquiescence, but Robert put his hand on Noah's arm when he would've moved past. "I'll call you tomorrow. We haven't had a chance to talk properly for months."

"Sure," Noah said and moved on, having to fight the urge to brush his hand over his arm to rub off his father's touch. Robert had stopped touching him in any way when Noah was just seven years old; these days, on the rare occasions when he did, Noah couldn't stand it.

As for that call, he'd answer it, but only because he owed Robert one for helping out when Molly and Fox had needed urgent legal advice after a massive breach of their privacy during the tour. But any talking would be on Robert's side—Noah's father had no right to any part of Noah's life.

"Hey." Kit leaned in close, her voice, her scent, cutting through the ice as if it didn't exist. "You okay?"

"Yeah." He released a breath he hadn't known he was holding until the exhale eased the pressure on his chest.

"Drink the rest of that champagne."

He'd forgotten he was holding it. "No, you're right. I need a clear head." Placing the flute on the tray of a passing waiter, he grabbed a glass of ice water instead. "Come on, I'll introduce you to Lisa."

"I just said that to get us away." Kit's eyes lingered on his face. "We can sneak out now if you want."

"We have to stay at least until the bidding starts." Finishing off the water, he set it on another tray. "Thanks. I needed a friend back there."

Amber eyes glowed with fierce emotion. "No thanks needed."

The next hour wasn't bad. He liked being able to introduce Kit to people who could help further her career, but that was as far as he needed to go—soon as someone met her, they were drawn into her orbit.

The clear sound of a bell silvered through the air not long after they'd finished a conversation with Cyril King. A minute later, Margaret went up to the podium to make her speech on behalf of the foundation. Noah listened with half an ear, the rest of his attention on Kit; he didn't want to waste a minute of this night he'd been given as a gift.

A night where he could pretend he was good enough to stand by her side.

"If you don't bid during the auction," Margaret said at the end of her speech, "I'll hunt you down and guilt you into writing a check, so you might as well get something for it."

Everyone laughed, the mood happy thanks to the atmosphere, food, and drinks.

The auction began straight afterward, and true to his word, Noah drove up the prices with relentless determination, even acting affronted when he was outbid. He almost went too far with the vomit plate; only Kit's elbow jab to the ribs stopped him from acquiring the monstrosity.

"I think we've done enough," he whispered, leaning down to her ear.

Kit looked carefully around. "It's shadowy with the soft lighting, and we're at the back, while everyone's looking forward. Let's go take a break."

Noah had already spotted the best door; it led deeper into the mansion, and as far as he could tell, it wasn't locked. Almost there, he saw a waitress about to pass by with hors d'oeuvres. "Thanks," he said and grabbed the whole tray. Winking at her when her mouth fell open, he slid out the door Kit had already opened. He saw her pick up a couple of glasses of ice water from a tray that had been by the door before she followed him out.

The corridor was only dimly lit, but he could see another hallway to the left. When they reached the spot, they found it barred by a thick red rope. "Place really is like a museum."

He jumped over the rope, had the pleasure of watching Kit hike up her dress to expose those knockout legs as she climbed over. His body tightened at the sight, his breath caught in his chest, but he ground down the response. He would not ruin his friendship with Kit for sex. Sex meant nothing. Kit meant everything.

"Hey, look." She pointed to a suit of armor down at the end, her voice a whisper. "I wonder if it's one of Tierney's exhibit rooms? Do you think he has the mummy in there?"

Grinning at one another, they walked quickly down the carpeted hallway and into a large room filled with plinths on which stood busts, vases, other objets d'art. Each piece was spotlighted from above, but that was the only light in the room. Not gloomy, more atmospheric.

"Carpet's thick," Kit said, keeping her voice low. "We can sit on it."

"Wait." Noah put down the tray, then shrugged off his tuxedo jacket and laid it on the ground. "Now you can sit, my lady."

She half smiled, half shook her head at him as she turned the coat over so it was the inside surface that touched the carpet. Sitting down, she said, "Your shirt might get dirty, but at least you'll be respectable when we sneak back in."

"Good thinking." He tried not to watch as she kicked off her heels and flexed her feet. The red lines the straps had made on each foot looked as if they could do with a massage, and he almost offered. Only he didn't think he could have Kit's foot in his lap and not betray how much he wanted her.

Not for fucking, for everything.

"Mmm." She bit into a toasted little rectangle of bread topped with what might've been hummus and sun-dried tomato.

Her lips pressed together in pleasure so lush that— *Shut it the hell down, Noah.*

"Try this one." Head bent to the tray, Kit picked up something on a toothpick. "I think it's a prune wrapped in bacon and roasted."

Thankful for the shadows that hid his internal battle, he accepted the dubious-sounding piece of food. His eyes widened on tasting it. "This is seriously good shit."

"I know." Kit ate two before dropping the toothpicks on the tiny pile they'd made on one side of the tray. "I always used to think this place would be creepy at night, but it's kind of fun."

The ensuing fifteen minutes passed by in a heartbeat. Afterward, Noah couldn't have said what they spoke about, only that it felt like it had before—when Kit had smiled at him without masks and he'd been able to breathe. No weight pressing down on his chest, no knots twisting his guts. When he was with Kit like this, he could *breathe.*

"We should go back," she said too soon, and he imagined he heard reluctance. "The auction will be over in a few minutes, and people will notice if you're not there."

Noah didn't think he was the one who was the shining star, but he knew she was right. Someone was always looking for a story. Shrugging into his jacket, he stood in place while Kit went around the back and brushed it off.

"It's not wrinkled enough that anyone will notice, especially with the gentle lighting."

Picking up the tray while Kit grabbed the empty glasses after slipping on her shoes, they snuck back in, leaving the incriminating items on a table by the door and merging smoothly back into the gala.

He received the message from Thea less than a minute after that. "Bullshit," he muttered, staring at the phone screen in disbelief. "You two are punking me, right?"

Peeking when he turned the phone in her direction, Kit grinned. "*Konnichiwa*," she said in an oh-so-helpful tone. "It means 'hello' in Japanese."

He scowled even though he just wanted to watch that silent laughter in the amber of her eyes. "I'm going to murder the damn designer who called her."

"I think he has good taste," Kit said, her smile even deeper. "You rock a tux."

Okay, yeah, it felt good to hear her say that. Worth a trip to a gardener in Japan.

When the music started up seconds later, the final round of bidding complete, Noah could no longer fight his need. Waiting only until there were enough couples on the floor that they wouldn't stand out, he leaned down to Kit's ear. "Dance with me?"

Her lashes lifted, her eyes holding his for a potent moment that hung endlessly in time before she nodded. They moved as one onto the dance floor, one of Kit's hands in his, his other arm around her waist, her free hand on his shoulder, fingers almost brushing his neck.

Noah danced often, onstage and in the clubs he hit with the others in the band, but never had a dance meant more. Swaying to the classical sounds filling the room, Kit in his arms, he felt... happy.

But the clock eventually had to strike midnight, and he had to take Kit home, watch her step inside. When she closed the door, she took the happiness with her.

KIT WAS DREAMING OF Noah's arms around her, music soft in the air and the world beyond nothing but a hazy mirage, when that world intruded with a persistent and highly annoying ringtone. She came awake on a groan. That was her landline. Only a rare few people had the number, and if one of them was calling her at—she cracked open an eyelid—six in the morning, then it had to be important.

Stumbling to the kitchen where she last remembered seeing the cordless receiver, she managed to push the right button to answer it. "Hello." It came out a mumble.

"Go throw some water on your face and get a cup of coffee," Thea ordered. "I'll call back in three minutes."

The dial tone buzzed in her ear.

Kit stared at the receiver, almost sure she'd imagined the whole thing, but then why else would she be holding a phone in her hand while her publicist's commanding tone reverberated in her head. Her *publicist*! Heart slamming into her ribs, she dropped the phone on the counter, flicked on the coffeemaker, and ran to the bathroom. If Thea was calling her this early, it either meant very good news or very bad news.

CHAPTER 16

WATER THROWN ON FACE and teeth quickly brushed for good measure, Kit pulled on her kimono-style blue silk robe over the thigh-length slip she wore as nightwear, stuffed her feet into her favorite slippers, and made her way to the kitchen. It was already light outside, and despite her late night, she didn't feel too ragged.

Maybe because the hours with Noah had felt like a dream, as haunting and as insubstantial as mist—you couldn't capture it, except in your memories, no matter how hard you tried.

Trying not to sink back into the fragile and fleeting perfection of it, she'd just reached the counter when the phone rang again. She picked it up at once. "Thea, what's wrong?"

"Nothing's wrong," the other woman said. "Something could be very right if we manage it correctly."

Exhaling, Kit took a shaky breath. "Next time, tell me that."

"Hey, I called you at six. If it was a problem, you'd get a call at three." Thea sounded chipper as a bird. "So, last night's gala was good?"

"It was wonderful." A beautiful, heartbreaking pretense. "We didn't steal any of Tierney's artwork, and Noah didn't punch any reporters, so the gala can't be the issue."

"Are you kidding?" Thea laughed. "You got amazing coverage *everywhere*. Which is what we need to talk about."

Coffee having finished brewing, Kit poured herself a cup and spooned in a teaspoon of sugar. That was her one indulgence, the single thing she'd never given up, not even for a costume of body paint and Lycra. Life wouldn't have been worth living without her once-a-day treat of sweet coffee.

Drawing in the aroma and moaning silently, she said, "Did we get some exciting interview requests?" It must be prime time if Thea was so buzzed. Kit's own adrenaline kicked in at the thought, her cells jumping.

"Something like that—it'll be easier if I show you. Hold on." Sounds in the background. "Looks like our favorite channel's cycling the story after the ad break. Switch on the television."

Padding into the living room, coffee in hand, Kit brought up the well-known entertainment channel and settled into her sofa to wait as the ads played. "I met a couple of big movers and shakers last night," she told Thea in the interim. "Noah did me a big favor taking me to this shindig."

"I'll say."

Thea's words had just cleared the air when the early morning host came on.

And in today's breaking exclusive, it looks like things are finally getting hot and heavy between bad-boy rocker Noah St. John and Oscar-nominated actress Kathleen Devigny. The two have been friends for years, but last night, they stepped out as a couple for the first time, and boy, did they look good together.

Just between you and me, our sources tell us they've been a couple since the band's sellout tour. We don't blame these two lovebirds for being so secretive, because talk about chemistry! This may be the Tinseltown romance of the year. Stay tuned for more.

Kit stared at the screen, coffee forgotten. It filled with a shot of her laughing up at Noah while he looked down at her. She swallowed, not able to blame the media for jumping to conclusions… because right then, in that moment caught by the cameras, they looked like they adored one another.

Then came a playful image of her blowing him a kiss. Another of the two of them climbing the steps, Noah's hand on her lower back, a final shot of Noah grinning as he took photos of her. The montage made them appear a couple so comfortable with one another that neither the cameras nor the lights caused any anxiety.

Chest hurting, she muted the TV. "We've been to other things together," she said to Thea. "Why is everyone jumping on this?"

"Did you *see* that first photograph?" Thea asked. "It's like you set it up for maximum impact."

"I didn't!"

"I'm not saying you did, but Noah's wearing an impeccably fitted tuxedo. Noah never wears anything but ripped jeans and T-shirts. *Everyone* is gushing about how romantic it is that he cleaned himself up for your first big night out together as a couple."

Kit groaned, dropping her head back on the sofa and pinching the bridge of her nose between forefinger and thumb. "He did that for his aunt, not for me."

"Details, details." Brushing off Kit's comment, Thea continued. "However it happened, it's happened. Now we ride the wave of publicity."

"Why? How?"

"You know why—you're a contender for a number of big roles, but you're being pushed aside by actresses who know how to work the media."

"I know how to work the media." Kit glared at the television. "I just don't want to live my life in front of the paparazzi. And there's Terrence."

"He'll have to cool his heels."

"There's no reason—"

"*Redemption.*"

Kit sat up at that single word, her throat dry. "But the casting director told Harper I wasn't big enough for the role." She'd read for it, was certain she'd impressed the director, so the rebuff had come as a big disappointment.

"Yeah, well, my spies are telling me that you might be back in with a shot. Apparently, you impressed the right people at the gala last night, and this morning's positive publicity has been the cherry on top."

Kit could barely breathe.

Redemption was one of the most incredible scripts she'd ever read, and it was being directed by a multiple-Oscar-winning director who'd made icons out of previously little-known actors and actresses. Even though Kit had earned her stripes in *Last Flight*, the ex-soap-actress tag was a hard one to totally shake off. One hit wasn't enough; everyone was waiting to see if she'd fly high or fall flat on her face.

If she was cast in *Redemption*, even in the secondary role for which she'd read, that was it. She'd be recognized as a legitimate actress, would no longer have to fight so damn hard for every role. "How can your spies know that?" she whispered, barely able to believe what Thea was telling her. "It's six in the morning."

"Do you know why I'm so freaking expensive? It's because I don't sleep and I have spies everywhere." Thea's words were dry. "Just trust me on this—last night was very, very good for your career. Now all you have to do is keep the romance going for another month or so—"

"Wait, wait!" Kit got jerkily to her feet. "There is no romance, not between me and Noah. You know that."

"Of course I know that," Thea muttered. "But for the next month, or at least until they finish casting *Redemption*, there has to be—the money people have to see that you can hold the public's attention in a positive way. If the media's lapping you up, it makes you the next hot thing, and *that* equals free promotion for the movie."

Pacing from one end of the room to the other, Kit shoved a trembling hand through her hair. "But Esra Dali doesn't care about promotion," she said, naming the difficult but brilliant director. "He chooses who he chooses."

"Esra is one of the sharpest operators in the business," Thea retorted. "He's an artist, no doubt about it, and he won't choose a vacuous 'it' girl for his movie, but if it's a contest between two equally talented, equally charismatic actors, he'll inevitably choose the one with the stronger media profile."

A small pause as Thea sipped from what was probably her third coffee of the morning. "He knows he'll lose his backers if he can't make them money—and without those backers and their financing he can't tell the sweeping stories he likes to tell, because those stories require serious budgets."

Shaking all over, Kit put a hand over her mouth and tried to think. "You know Noah, Thea," she said at last, her stomach a lump of ice. "He isn't a one-woman guy." It hurt her to say that, hurt her to remember all the women he'd slept with. Broken glass thrust directly into her veins couldn't have hurt that much.

"Then you have to convince him to behave for a few weeks," Thea ordered. "Because while this publicity could make you, it could also tank you. If he's caught with a group-ie, you go from being one half of Hollywood's hottest couple to the woman scorned."

The brutally pragmatic words sent Kit to her knees, but Thea wasn't finished. "You'll get pity while he'll come out the stud. Because the world's not fair, and a woman who 'can't keep her man'—as I promise you the story will be spun by the tabloids—is not someone people want to emulate or to follow. You'll become toxic until I can clean up your image, and that'll take time."

Kit's head felt stuffy, her eyes hot. She wanted to argue with Thea, but she knew the other woman was right: the world *wasn't* fair. Everyone wanted their silver screen idols to be winners in real life too. Even her superhero movie might tank if people began to pity her. Kickass superheroes didn't get dumped.

And still… "No, Thea," she whispered, her throat raw. "I won't use Noah that way." It wasn't his fault this had spun out of control.

"He's your friend—"

"No," Kit said again, conscious Thea was operating with a handicap. She didn't know Kit and Noah's history, didn't know that not only would Kit not force Noah into an untenable position, she wasn't sure her heart could take the charade. She was too afraid it'd start to believe the illusion was real.

"Kit, this is serious."

"I know. I'll take my chances." She'd started out in the movies in a low-budget film—she'd do that again. No matter how much damage this did to her image, she was still an Oscar-nominated actress. *Someone* would hire her, and even if her career trajectory took a dip, it wouldn't be forever. She'd make it back out.

Strong thoughts, but as she hung up, her mind raced like a rabbit, her skin hot. She'd worked so hard for her career, and it was all about to go up in smoke. Heat suddenly turned to ice. The cosmetics contract she was relying on to get her out of a huge financial hole wasn't yet final... and there was every likelihood Noah would pick up a woman again tonight.

Kit pressed her fists to her closed eyes but couldn't stop her mind from thundering ahead, couldn't stop her gut from roiling.

The blowback would begin the instant Noah's latest sexual conquest hit the tabloids. Chances were high she'd lose that contract. Nobody wanted to buy anything from a loser.

Eyes gritty, she wondered how it had all gone so wrong.

NOAH WAS OUT BY the pool listening to music, hoarding the memories from last night, and fixing a broken string on his oldest Breedlove guitar, when his phone chimed. Seeing

Thea's name on the screen, he put it on speaker so he could continue to work while he spoke with her.

"Hey, doll," he said, grinning as he used a term that was so *not* Thea. "David want something?"

"No, I want something."

"Yeah? What can the PR goddess want with a mere mortal?" Frowning in concentration, he checked the tension. "I already did my quota of publicity."

"It's about Kit."

All at once, she had his absolute attention. Propping the guitar against the table on which his phone sat, he took the phone off speaker and put it to his ear. "What about Kit?"

As Thea spoke, he felt his lips curve. "That's fucking great," he said after she told him about Kit being in the running for *Redemption*.

"Only if you can keep it in your pants."

Hand clenching on the phone at the razor-sharp words, he said, "You'd better explain that."

When she did, he just stared out at the cold, clear water of the pool. "You're serious? If we don't pull off the happy-couple routine, it could crash her career?"

"The damage potential is high." Thea spelled it out for him.

Elbows braced on his thighs, Noah wondered exactly how pissed Kit was at him right then. "What does Kit say?"

"She'll probably fire me for going over her head, but I'm not a publicist because I'm a quivering lily. This could hurt her badly, Noah." The sound of messages coming in on what might've been Thea's computer. "She says she doesn't want to use you, but it would be mutual. Schoolboy Choir fans are just as excited about the hookup—I've been watching it trend across social media since the news hit."

"I don't care about my profile or the band's." Noah fisted his free hand, bones pushing white against skin. "If Kit needs me, I'm there."

"*Can* you keep it in your pants while you're officially together?" Blunt as an ax, Thea kept going. "Because if you can't, then I have to start putting out denials and you two have to laugh off any relationship rumors. We can mitigate the damage at least. If only you and Kit hadn't looked so cozy—*Oh fuck!*"

Noah sat up. Thea rarely swore. Whatever the situation, she handled it. "What?" he asked. "Goddammit, Thea, *what?*"

"Did you two sneak off for your own little picnic last night?" Thea sounded like she was gnashing her teeth. "It looks like a waitress followed you, got a photograph. It's not the best shot, but added to the red carpet photos and the waitress's story of how 'adorable' you two were being, this makes damage control a pipe dream. No one's going to believe a denial, and it'll all turn to shit the instant you're seen with another woman."

"I'll do it," Noah snarled. "I won't have Kit exposed to the fucking vipers."

"You have to be sure, Noah," Thea said. "You have to be dead certain you can stay faithful to her for the entire time you're together. At least three and a half weeks to a month—*Redemption* might be cast earlier, but whatever happens, you have to keep it going long enough that it looks real."

She took a breath before continuing. "At that point, I can extricate you both with a little fancy footwork. You and Kit will decide you were more suited to being friends after all, and as long as you keep everything friendly and you both start dating new people around the same time, it'll all blow over."

"Yes, I'm sure." If he had to, he'd take the sleeping pills he hated. Given the bile-inducing side effect, he'd long ago decided he'd rather anaesthetize himself with random fucks since he got about the same amount of sleep either way. But if it would protect Kit, he'd take the pills.

"All right, I'll talk to her," Thea said at last.

"No." Noah knew Kit, knew this had to come from him. "I'm going to drive over to her place. We'll call you once we've sorted things out between ourselves."

CHAPTER 17

NOAH DROVE TO KIT'S in his Mustang, the top down. The gleaming black convertible had two silver stripes front to back and was even more distinctive a vehicle than Fox's Aventador.

He saw the TV vans and photographers milling around her gate the instant he hit her street. Kit clearly hadn't emerged yet because the media had that bored air to them that shouted disappointment. All that changed the instant a blond paparazzo spotted his car.

A lightning strike of camera flashes.

Taking a deep breath, he slowed down instead of blasting through the paps with his horn blaring. They actually allowed him to turn so that his car was in front of Kit's gate, likely because that gave them a shot of him heading to see her, but then they swarmed.

He braced his arm on the door, a lazy grin on his face that he'd perfected long ago. People didn't look too deep when they saw that grin, figuring that was who he was. "Lovely morning isn't it?" he drawled into the microphones thrust at him.

Grins all around.

"Noah!" shouted one TV reporter. "Is it true? You and Kathleen are a couple?"

Smile deepening, he slipped off his sunglasses. "You want to get me in trouble this early in the day, Jessa?" he asked, playing the reporter like a fish on a hook.

"Come on, Noah, give us something."

"No comment." He laughed to take the sting out of it, slipped his sunglasses back on. "I might have one after I talk to a certain gorgeous woman, but you have to let me through first."

They drew back, sensing juicier news to come if they gave him what he wanted. Hoping that news wouldn't be a black eye, he roared down the drive after Butch opened the gate, the bodyguard's flinty gaze ensuring no one dared attempt to sneak in behind Noah.

Kit threw open her front door as he brought the convertible to a stop in front of the house. Around the corner and distant from the gate, they had absolute privacy.

Stalking out to meet him as he vaulted out of the car, she put both hands on his chest and shoved. "What the hell did you think you were doing?" Her eyes sparked fire at him. "I saw you on the security cameras! You just turned this ridiculous rumor into an unkillable monster!"

"It had to be done," he said, standing his ground. "Thea says if we—"

"Thea called you?" She gritted her teeth. "I'm going to fire her. I don't care if she's my friend."

"No, you won't. Because she's the best in the business and she's right."

Ignoring his words, she stormed back into the house, her jeans-clad legs eating up the ground.

He followed, knowing where she was heading even before she used the kitchen entrance to step out into her garden. Deciding to let her stew in private, he found the green tea he knew she kept in an upper cupboard, brewed it up for her in the little ceramic pot with a metal handle. He was probably fucking it up, but it was the thought that counted right?

Putting the pot and the tiny Japanese-style handleless teacups on a tray, he grabbed a bunch of cookies from her stash and took the tray out to her. She was weeding with bare hands, her jewel-green nails bright against the weeds and her gray T-shirt as old and soft as his black one.

He put the tray on the wooden picnic table and poured her a cup. Taking it to her, he hunkered down by her side and held it out.

"You are not pacifying me with tea."

Shrugging, he sat down with his legs stretched out in front of him and drank it himself—or tried to. "Ugh. Still just as disgusting."

"It is not disgusting. It's the best *sencha* you can get." She grabbed the cup from him and took several sips of the hot liquid. "What was that? By the gate?"

"That was me being your friend."

Putting the cup back in his hand, she continued to weed. "That was you being a troublemaker." She went to pull something out, seemed to realize it wasn't a weed, and patted the soil back in place. "Now everyone's going to expect us to be a couple."

"They already did."

"Thea might have been able to defuse that."

175

"Not fast enough." He offered her more tea.

She emptied the cup, then sat on the earth, her eyes no longer on the garden. "You can't keep it up, Noah." It was a strained statement. "Playing the adoring boyfriend."

He'd never had any fucking trouble adoring Kit. "I will. I promise you that." When she looked away, he continued to speak. "I've never promised you anything before, Kit—that's because when I make a promise, I don't break it." And he'd known he couldn't give her what she needed. Not then. Nothing much had changed. He was still an asshole, but he *would* protect Kit. That was his motivation, and fuck if he'd mess it up. "I won't let you down."

Her gaze was raw with emotion when she finally looked at him again. "I don't know if I can do it."

Her pain was like knives plunging into him, slicing through his gut to leave him open and bleeding. "I can't give you what you need in so many ways," he said, ripping his heart open for her, "but I can help your career. I can do that. Let me, Kit. Please." He'd never begged for anything, but he'd crawl on his hands and knees for this small chance at redemption.

Eyes stark, Kit shook her head. "How can I accept that?" A rasped whisper. "How can I use my friend?"

"You're not using me." He dared lay one hand against her cheek, his fingers brushing the rich silk of her hair. "I'm offering to help. That's what friends do, right? Support each other. Let me support you in public. Let me be that guy." *Even if I can never be good enough to be your guy.*

Kit's throat moved. Not saying a word, she dusted off her hands and got up, went to the table. "Come and drink some tea."

He took a seat, allowed her to refill his cup. Pouring another one for herself, she sat on the other side of the table. "Harper called ten minutes ago."

"Yeah?" Not about to drink the tea but holding the cup for its warmth, his own skin chilled, he said, "What did she say?"

"Same thing Thea did. I'm apparently on everyone's radar all at once. She's had multiple 'feeling things out' calls—no one ready to commit, but people letting her know they're watching to see how I conduct myself in the spotlight."

Noah put aside the tea and took a cookie. It was sugar spice and it was delicious. "Pisses you off doesn't it?"

Renewed fire in her eyes. "Hell yes. I'm a good actress who busts her balls and barely gets a little grudging recognition, but then I go out with a random musician and boom, I'm hot property?"

"Ouch."

"You deserved it." She bit into a cookie, chewed. "Will you humiliate me?"

The quiet question erased the laughter, made his blood go cold. "No," he said. "Never. I promise you that."

He knew why she was having trouble believing his promises; he might've never said the words out loud when they'd been friends the first time around, but it had been implied. A promise not to hurt. A promise to care. A promise to love.

"Kit." He wanted to reach for her hand, but she'd curled it into a fist in a silent rejection. "What I did? I'll regret it for the rest of my life. Never again will I hurt you on purpose. You have my word."

"The groupies? Can you resist them?"

"I've never had a problem resisting them." He didn't pick

up women because he was attracted to them or because he had a giant ego he needed to massage.

At Kit's open disbelief, he thrust both hands through his hair. "Whether you want to trust me or not, you have to. There's no other option unless you want to destroy everything you've spent years building."

KIT KNEW HE WAS right. It was infuriating, but he was right. She could lose her entire career because the media and the public were fascinated by a relationship that could never be. The idea of starting from close to scratch again, of going through all the rejections and closed doors, it was hard to think about. But just as hard was remembering the pain Noah could so carelessly dish out.

He'd said he wasn't going to humiliate her, but how could she believe him, given his track record? She couldn't. All she could do was trust in their friendship. Because one thing she did know about Noah—he didn't let his friends down. Come concert time, he was always onstage no matter what he'd gotten up to the night before.

"All right," she whispered. "But only until *Redemption* is cast. Whether that's a yes or a no for me, things should have cooled down enough that Thea can finagle a breakup that leaves us both in a good place."

She kept on speaking before he could reply. "Everyone understands friends to lovers doesn't always work. As long as you don't get caught with a woman in the interim, we should be fine."

Noah's face was strained, and she had the feeling this was hurting him, but she couldn't sugarcoat things. False truths would only hurt them both in the end. As it was, she wasn't sure she could survive pretending he was hers for even a short three or four weeks. It was like being handed the most wonderful gift in the world, only to be told it wasn't really yours. It was just on loan. You couldn't touch, couldn't have. Just pretend.

"Deal," he said and took a deep breath, then released it. "If we want to keep the media on our side, we have to give them a bite."

Kit felt her jaw muscles lock but nodded. "Let's drive out, grab a coffee."

"I've got a better idea. How about I take you to breakfast at Pierre Baudin?"

"I think you have delusions of grandeur," she said, relieved to be back on a normal footing. "That place is booked up months in advance." Even though it had only opened six months ago, Chef Pierre Baudin's cafe and restaurant was quickly becoming "the" place to see and be seen.

Noah's eyes sparkled. "Watch and learn." Pulling out his phone, he made a call, said, "*Bonjour, mon ami.*" A pause. "Fuck you, JP, you know that's the only French I know." It was said with the ease of a man who knew the person on the other end wouldn't take offense. "Yeah, yeah. So, can you fit in my girl and me today?"

My girl.

The words stabbed at her.

Kit forced herself to breathe past it. She'd have to do that in public, couldn't afford to betray just how much the charade was hurting her. The media saw everything, and if this was going to work, she had to put on the performance of her life.

"Thanks—and oh yeah, we come with a paparazzi entourage who'll splash your place everywhere you want it splashed." Hanging up on a stream of what sounded like curses on his birth, Noah grinned. "And we're in."

"Since when do you know temperamental chefs who've taken restaurants to the coveted third Michelin star? And what's with calling him JP?"

"Remember the whole boarding-school-as-networking thing? JP was there—his full name is Jean Pierre Baudin." He scowled. "Christ, that means my father was right."

"Ah well." She patted his hand. "At least he need never know that you networked your way to a table at *the* hottest place in town." Getting up, she said, "Let me change." While Noah could turn up in disreputable jeans and a plain black T-shirt, his feet clad in heavy black boots with more than one scar and scuff, she had to be done up to the nines or the gossip blogs would immediately start printing tut-tutting stories about how it was a shame she'd let herself go.

Life really was unfair.

CHAPTER 18

THE NEXT THREE DAYS were surreal. Kit had had no idea just how many people had secretly been hoping for a hookup between her and Noah. "It's like this giant underground network of Noah and Kathleen shippers," she said to Thea and Molly when she met the two women for coffee later that week. Becca hadn't been able to make it, so Kit planned to catch up with her the following morning.

Today, she, Thea, and Molly were at a cafe down the road from Thea's office, seated around a sunny outdoor table. The odd photographer had snapped a shot, but for the most part, they were left alone. Kathleen Devigny with girlfriends wasn't as good a score, financially speaking, as Kathleen Devigny with Noah St. John.

"They call themselves the NoKats."

Mouth falling open at Thea's response, Kit shoved her sunglasses to the top of her head. "*NoKats?* Are you kidding me? We already have a nickname?"

"You always did," Thea said, sanguine and in control as always, her sleek black hair in an elegant twist at the back of her head and her golden-skinned face expertly made up. "It was low level, nothing worth bothering about. People love shipping fantasy couples, and most of the time it doesn't go anywhere."

"But—"

"All these years while you hung out with Schoolboy Choir," Thea said, slicing into her blueberry muffin, "you had to know fans were starting to imagine things."

"Why with Noah?"

"The chemistry, babe," Thea said after chewing and swallowing a bite of her muffin. "But it wasn't just Noah. The AbKats are bummed. The KatiDid and DeFox groups already threw in the towel since Molly and I had the bad form to come between you and David and you and Fox."

Eyes narrowed, Kit glared at a laughing Molly. "Your sister is making this up to screw with me, right?"

But Molly shook her head, her brown eyes teary with laughter and her creamy skin flushed. Pushing her beautiful tumble of black hair behind her ears, she spoke through her amusement. "Thea showed me one of the forums on the way here." A hiccup as she tried to catch her breath. "I reckon the AbKats are still holding out hope you'll dump Noah for Abe."

"Oh for God's sake." Kit wished she'd ordered wine rather than iced green tea. "And who the hell came up with NoKats? At least you and Fox got Foxy."

"Fox hates it, but I tell him at least it's better than Folly." Molly's eyes danced as she reminded Kit of her suggestion. "David and Thea don't have one though. How come?"

"Because I'm a PR specialist who doesn't like to be in the media myself," Thea said. "I quashed that little bug before it sprouted."

"You couldn't do the same for the NoKats?"

"Sorry, Kit, but the NoKats and co were good for your brand." Thea checked an incoming e-mail. "They were just waiting to believe. Now they're lighting up the Internet."

Eating a bite of the carrot cake she'd split with Molly, Kit put down her fork. "This is getting out of control." Panic beat at her—because instead of dying down, the attention only seemed to be gathering steam. "We're never going to be able to walk away without damage."

"It's early days," Thea said without the least tension in her voice. "You're new and shiny. My spies tell me another new and shiny couple is forming in the wings as we speak—in a blatant attempt to steal some of your limelight—so you'll get a breather soon."

"Who?" Molly leaned forward, then winced. "Damn it, I'm supposed to stop with my celebrity-gossip addiction."

"It's not gossip." Thea patted her sister's hand. "It's intel. And this manufactured hookup is going to be between Abigail Rutledge and Garrison Stone."

Kit sucked in a breath. Abigail was the rumored frontrunner for the lead role in *Redemption*, and Garrison was said to be a shoo-in for lead male. Lowering her voice, she leaned toward the other women. They instinctively dipped their heads toward her.

"I didn't want to jinx it by saying anything," she whispered. "But Harper told me this morning that Esra might be considering me for the female lead rather than the secondary role." Her heart thumped at even the idea of it.

"Oh my God." Voice low but excited, Molly squeezed Kit's hand.

Thea smiled, no hint of startled excitement on her face.

Spies, Kit reminded herself. Thea had spies everywhere. "But if Abigail's got Garrison on her arm…"

"Pfft," the publicist said after eating another bite of her muffin. "Garrison's doing Abigail a favor because she once did him one, but they have no chemistry. Zero. Zilch. If I was their PR manager, I'd have nixed the idea. They're only going to show the world—and Esra—exactly how bad they'd be as an on-screen couple."

"Are you sure?" Kit frowned. "Abigail is an excellent actress and Garrison is brilliant."

"I could be wrong," Thea allowed. "It has happened once or twice in known history." A wry smile. "Which is why it's good you'll be at Zenith with Noah this weekend."

Kit's stomach flipped. The outdoor festival was out of town, which meant everyone would expect her to share Noah's bus. Zenith's location made any other option impossible.

So far, she and Noah had gotten away with public "dates" and one night where he'd stayed in her guest bedroom, but there'd be no way to avoid the intimacy forced by the festival.

"Is it really worth it?" she said to both women.

Molly, who knew all about her history with Noah, touched her hand again, this time with the gentleness of a friend attempting to offer comfort. "Noah's really happy to be able to help you. I think he's…"

Thea sighed when Molly faded off. "Seriously you two, give it up. Information is my job. I know you"—a glance at Kit—"and Noah actually had a thing a while back, but since you kept it private, I didn't interfere. Clearly it didn't end well?"

Kit nodded, unable to say anything further.

But Thea was smart and she'd had her own bad breakup. "If it was caused by what I think caused it, then I give you major props for not cutting off his balls and throwing them in his face."

"He didn't cheat," Kit said, because to cheat, you first had to make a commitment. Noah had never given her that.

Theirs had always been a mirage of a relationship.

STANDING ON THE MAIN stage at Zenith on Friday morning, Noah plugged his guitar into the amplifier, checked the settings, and played a short solo—or tried to—to test the sound. A screech of feedback had him stopping with a wince. "Maxwell!" he yelled to the crew chief, who was working out in front of the stage. "You trying to blow out my eardrums?"

"If I was," the bearded man yelled back, "they'd have gone boom!"

"Yeah, yeah." Noah hunkered down to look at the various cables and connections, saw the problem just as one of Maxwell's people came up and fixed it.

"Sorry, man," he said to Noah. "Totally my screwup."

"Forget it." Shit happened. That was why Schoolboy Choir was out here this morning checking everything. They'd kick off the festival tonight with a big show, then do another set Saturday afternoon. The festival officially ended Sunday at midday, but Friday night and Saturday were the big events.

Zenith was one of Noah's favorite festivals. This stage and the two smaller stages to the left and the right, open fields between them, were the only "buildings" around for what appeared to be miles. People brought their own tents to camp in, and the city supplied sanitation and medical facilities, while food trucks were plentiful.

Unlike other festivals that often descended into mud and alcohol-fueled fights that messed with the music, the organizers had done a great job of keeping Zenith wild—sometimes crazy wild—but trouble-free year after year.

Part of it had to do with the fact the festival was out in the middle of nowhere, which tended to create more of a tight atmosphere. The other factor was that it was a long haul to get here—the only people who made it this far were the true music fans. And they came in their thousands.

The grounds wouldn't open for another four hours, but long lines had already formed at the gates as people waited to grab the perfect spot for their tents and catch some of the warm-ups.

"Yo, Noah," Abe called out from where he stood by the keyboard. "You ready to try a run-through?"

"Yeah, let me just check this is good first." This time it was pure, raw music that poured out of the speakers.

A cheer came from the direction of the far-off gates.

He smiled. "We got an audience boys, so let's make it good."

"I always make it good," Fox said with a slow grin, cupping his hands around the microphone but keeping his head turned so his distinctively gritty voice wouldn't carry. "Always."

"All talk," David said from the back, playing a quick beat that ended with a clash of the cymbals. "You know the quiet ones are the doers."

"You white boys keep on talking." Abe ran his fingers over the keys of his keyboard. "Meanwhile, the brother over here will smoke your asses."

"Who you calling a white boy?" David said before bringing down the sticks in a fury of sound that cut off abruptly as he did that thing where he could simply shut down the drums.

Noah came in with his guitar right on cue, Abe flowed in, and then they all stopped and Fox's voice roared out over the microphone.

It was like they'd never had the post-tour time off, the meld was so flawless. Over a month they'd gone without playing a proper set, and now it felt like coming home. He caught Abe's grin, heard the sheer joy in Fox's voice, sensed it in the flourishes David threw into the beat, felt it in the way his own fingers caressed the strings.

It was blood in his veins, the music, the energy that made his heart beat. Up here, with the music burning up the air and his closest friends in total synergy with him, there was no pain, no anger, no hopeless rage. There was just the sweet, pure beauty of music in every cell of his body, making him pure too.

Fingers moving over the strings, he let the music fill him. He used a pick occasionally when he was going to town on a seriously hard rock number, but even then, he'd been known to use his fingers. He liked the direct connection to the strings, and his fingertips had long ago become callused enough to take it.

Today he brought the song to an end with a guitar solo that had Fox grinning and calling out, "Hell yeah! Noah is in the *house!*"

Noah only became aware of the riotous cheers from the early birds when the last note faded from the air. Shoving his hand through his sweat-damp hair, he grinned a hello at

Genevieve. The bass player was joining them for this concert and, having worked with Schoolboy Choir previously, had come smoothly into the mix when she arrived halfway through the song.

Happily married with three kids, Genevieve liked performing but didn't want the pressure that came with being part of a band. Being a session musician suited her, and having her here freed Abe up from having to do double duty and lay down the bass line since Noah couldn't play lead guitar and bass at the same time. The band had a few bass players they worked with for live performances, but Genevieve was their favorite.

"Sounds like we're good to go," Noah said to everyone. "We could leave now, go relax."

Fox raised an eyebrow, David grinned, and Abe began the intro into another song while Genevieve had a rock-and-roll smile on lips she'd painted electric blue.

Laughing, Noah fell into it, and they played just for the fun of it, Genevieve working with them. Fox slung on his own guitar partway through, and the two of them dueled it out while Abe carried the song with his voice, then David challenged Noah and they had one hell of a jam session.

"Fuck, man," Noah said afterward, his T-shirt sticking to his back. "How the hell do you keep that going?" Drumming was one of the most physically draining positions in a band.

David gave him a shit-eating grin, his teeth flashing white against the warm golden-brown tone of his skin. "I'm just in a good mood."

"Oh, shut the hell up," Abe growled. "Just because you're getting laid on a regular basis doesn't mean you have to rub our faces in it."

David grinned harder. "Dry spell, huh? Sucks to be you."

As the two exchanged more insults and comments while Genevieve looked on, Fox crouching down to talk to Maxwell about something to do with the mike, Noah guzzled a bottle of water and felt warmth spreading in his veins. Tonight he wouldn't go home with some random groupie. Tonight he'd go home with his girl.

Yeah, it was pretend, but that didn't mean he couldn't enjoy the beauty of it. Imagining Kit waiting backstage for him like Molly waited for Fox and Thea did for David on the days she could fly in to meet him, it made Noah's insides twist into knots that didn't hurt. They ached instead, and the ache was a good one.

Rubbing at his eyes, eyes grainy from lack of sleep, he pulled off the guitar. "I'm going to crash for a couple of hours." At this point he was tired enough that he might actually get some sleep. "We hooking up for dinner?"

Fox nodded from where he was still crouched on the edge of the stage. "Catering truck's coming in around four."

They'd go onstage at six, so it was better they eat earlier. "I'll see you then." Taking his guitar with him because he'd fucking kill anyone who damaged the stunning instrument, he headed to the back of the stage and down. This entire area was blocked off from the public and lined neatly with equipment trucks and other behind-the-scenes stuff.

Schoolboy Choir's tour buses were parked side by side behind all that, a buffer zone between them so the noise wouldn't be too bad. Kind of a moot point for an outdoor concert, but the buses were insulated against noise, so it worked. He got into his bus using a thumbprint scan, and putting down his guitar soon as he was inside, kicked off his boots and socks before tugging off his sweaty T-shirt, leaving it all in a pile by the door.

His belt and jeans he tore off on his way to the back of the bus, and then he was falling flat on his face in bed, so exhausted after not sleeping in much more than short fits and starts over the past week that his mind just shut down.

CHAPTER 19

KIT ARRIVED AT ZENITH around three that day to find it already buzzing. Fans had set up multicolored tents as far as the eye could see, and the food trucks that lined the area were doing a brisk business. Everyone seemed in a cheerful mood, and though the live music hadn't yet started, people were singing among themselves.

Having been driven around to the back, she stepped out and looked for a familiar face. Molly had told Kit to give her a call if she couldn't spot the crew, but right then she saw Maxwell, his black Schoolboy Choir T-shirt tucked over his beer gut and into his jeans as per usual. However, not as per usual was the busty blonde snuggled to his side.

They kissed as Kit watched, not sure quite what she was seeing. Maxwell was very married and had always seemed crazy for his wife, with whom he had two teenage boys. Kit wasn't sure she could handle Maxwell cheating. It would be like losing a sacred touchstone that told her some people *did* make it.

The crew chief looked up and noticed her just as she was wondering if she should head in the other direction. Beaming, he came over, one arm around the shapely woman who was dressed in thigh-high boots over skinny jeans teamed with a black leather jacket and a fitted Schoolboy Choir T-shirt. Unlike Maxwell's, the woman's tee had a scoop neck that exposed impressive cleavage.

"I heard you were coming in this afternoon." Maxwell kissed Kit on the cheek with the ease of long familiarity, his salt-and-pepper beard ticklish. "I don't think you've ever met my wife, have you?"

Oh. Smiling as relief kicked her in the ribs, Kit held out a hand. "It's great to finally meet you. Kim, right?"

"Yes." A warm, big-hearted smile. "You were the best part of *Primrose Avenue.*"

Kit's own smile deepened at hearing the name of the soap that had been her first long-term gig. "Thank you." Yes, *Primrose Avenue* had been a bit of a millstone around her neck when she wanted to transition into the movies, but it was a good show for what it was, and she'd enjoyed working on it. "Are you here for the whole festival?"

"Yes. Our boys are out front in a tent, and we're under strict instructions not to so much as look in their direction the entire weekend," Kim said, her voice reminding Kit of Adreina's. "Maxwell may have street cred because he works with the band, but according to our youngest, it's 'total loser zone' to have your parents attend the same festival as you."

Kit laughed at how well the other woman mimicked her son's no doubt disgusted tone. "I'm here till Sunday too," she said. "Maybe we can talk more."

"I'd like that."

Maxwell dropped a kiss on his wife's head, so obviously in love it was adorable. "You looking for Molly or for Noah?"

"Molly." Kit felt light-headed at the thought of being shut inside a bus with Noah. "I figured she could show me the ropes."

"She's in her and Fox's bus." Maxwell jerked a thumb toward the buses Kit could see parked not far away. "Fox is with David, so you girls can chat without interruption."

Kit didn't take him to task for calling her a girl. He called Schoolboy Choir his boys. No one argued. "Thanks." Leaving Casey to deal with the car, her luggage to be stored in the trunk until later, she let Butch walk her to the bus.

"I'll be fine if you and Casey want to go get a bite or something," she said to the bodyguard. "I'll probably talk to Molly for a bit, then find Noah."

Butch didn't look convinced. "This would be a great place to snatch you if the creep's here, and thanks to all the publicity about you and Noah, he probably is. I'll stay until Noah's with you."

"Okay," Kit replied. "You're the expert." Part of the reason she'd hired Butch despite the fact she couldn't really afford him was that he was so damn good at his job. Leaving him to stand watch, she knocked on the bus door. Molly opened it a second later and, crying out, engulfed Kit in a warm Molly hug. "You're here! I thought you wouldn't make it till five. Come in!"

It was the first time Kit had been in one of the band's buses, and she was surprised to see that it was relatively roomy. "Nice living area." She put her handbag on the small counter that fronted a compact utility kitchenette tucked into a corner.

"It works," Molly said cheerfully. "Want a tour? It'll take like thirty seconds."

"Sure."

"This is my study." Molly pointed out a cute little desk and chair positioned in one corner of the living area, almost but not quite directly opposite from the sofa. That sofa was angled so that it faced the television screen hung on the same wall against which sat Molly's desk.

"The facilities." Molly took her through to the very back of the bus. "Shower's not too bad, actually. Tiny, but that can be fun." A wicked grin.

"I think living with Fox is a bad influence on you."

Laughing, Molly slid aside the door to the bedroom. The bed within was neatly made up with pretty white-on-white sheets and fluffy pillows; the high windows along two sides let in light while preserving Molly and Fox's privacy.

"The windows are reflective," Molly told her. "We're kind of paranoid."

"Don't blame you." Kit wrapped an arm around the other woman's shoulders, still angry on her and Fox's behalf after the ugly invasion of privacy that had happened during the band's tour.

Slipping an arm around Kit's waist, Molly hugged her back. "I'm good, promise," she said before she broke the hug to show Kit the built-in closet. "Helps to know the pathetic creep who recorded us is behind bars." A glance at Kit. "Speaking of which, the cops have any luck with the stalker?"

Kit shook her head and took a seat on the bed. "I'm still getting letters and cards."

"Damn. I was hoping he'd have fallen off a cliff and disappeared by now." Molly sat with her, folding up her legs. "How are you doing?"

"Fine—really." Kit reassured the other woman. "The stuff he's been sending in is relatively vitriol-free for him, but it could be that he's stewing and waiting to make his move." Anger had her clenching her hands on the edge of the bed. "I've been photographed with both Terrence and Noah lately, and the police psychologist is worried that could push him over the edge."

The police team kept in regular touch with her, the men and women who dealt with celebrity-stalking cases having seen the sometimes-fatal results firsthand. No one was taking this lightly, especially given how far the stalker had already gone by breaking and entering. "When I say it's less hateful stuff, I'm comparing it to the more abusive messages, but his current letters, even the present he sent a month back, it's still creepily possessive and jealous."

She shuddered. "He sent me a fine gold chain with a small locket, said he'd 'noticed I wasn't wearing my favorite neck-lace' in photos and he was worried I'd lost it." Kit touched the bare skin of her throat. "The creepy thing is that I did lose it—while shooting the superhero movie."

Molly's eyes widened. "You think he stole it?"

"I can't imagine how—there've been no other signs that he can get on set. Nothing else stolen or missing, no psycho messages." The hairs rose on the back of her neck at even the faint possibility that he might be one of her colleagues.

"I think he really does just notice even such tiny things about me, and the way he talks, it's like we're intimate." Oddly, it wasn't the sexual messages that creeped her out the most. Those always seemed like he was trying too hard. "He says things like how we're meant to be together, how no one will ever understand me like he does, how he's the only one I can trust with my secrets."

Molly shivered. "It's like he wants to put you in a box and keep you."

"Yes, that's it exactly." Kit rubbed her hands up and down her arms.

"I don't know if Noah had a chance to tell you," Molly said, "but the band hired extra security. Plus the entire crew knows to be on the lookout for anyone acting suspiciously."

Cold wiped out by the warmth of knowing she was among friends, Kit fell back on the bed. "Thank you." Such small words to hold so much emotion. "I'm going to enjoy this weekend—I made a decision after buying my place that I wouldn't allow the stalker to ruin my life."

"You're so strong, Kit. This stalker has no idea who he's up against." Molly's words were fierce. "And I can't wait to have fun with you here—I know things have been tough with the whole Noah situation."

Breathing in and out with conscious focus, Kit stared up at the ceiling. "I have to share his bus, Molly." The paparazzi were buzzing in every nook and cranny; there was no way she could hide out anywhere else.

"He's been amazing with everything so far," Molly reminded her, her voice soft and hopeful. "It might not be so bad."

Kit had, quite frankly, been surprised at Noah's cooperativeness. He'd accompanied her to places where photographers could snap them, been good-natured about the ravenous media interest when she knew full well he had a temper if someone pushed into his personal space. And, most importantly, he hadn't even appeared near a club, much less picked up a girl.

The tabloids and magazines were already agog with stories of how he'd been "tamed" by love, of how "silver screen star" Kathleen Devigny had pulled off the coup of the century by quietly stealing the heart of rock's gorgeous bad boy. If even half the media hype about her and Noah's relationship had been true, Kit would've been ecstatic. Too bad it was a tissue of lies and fantasy.

"I should go find him now." Throat dry and stomach jumpy, she forced herself to sit up. "Some photographer's probably got a camera trained on this bus, and while a short visit to say hi to you won't look odd, they'll start to wonder if I stay too long."

"I can open Noah's door for you if he's out." Molly got off the bed. "We all decided we should be able to get into each other's buses."

Rising herself, Kit said, "Abe?" She knew everyone was still worried about the keyboard player's mental state, though he appeared to have gone stone-cold sober after his dangerous on-tour binge.

"That's part of it, but it just makes sense." Molly led her to the front of the bus. "We're family on the road, and we keep an eye on each other. Maxwell can also get in, because seriously, the idea of Maxwell selling us out is so ludicrous it's not even funny."

"Did you meet his wife?" Kit stepped out of the bus in front of Molly. "I adore her already."

"She visited during the tour," Molly said with a smile as she pulled the door shut so it'd lock. "They're so sweetly in love it

197

makes me happy each time I think about it." Her face lit up without warning. "Fox, I thought you and David were working on those lyrics you wanted to get right."

"Done." Fox drew Molly into a luscious invitation of a kiss, one hand cupping her face, before he turned to hug Kit. "Have a good drive down?"

Kit had just begun to reply when she heard someone calling Molly. The other woman looked over her shoulder. "It's Maxwell. I think he wants me to play intern for a minute."

Leaving Kit with Fox, Molly ran over to help Maxwell grab a bunch of cables out of the back of a truck. "How is he?" Kit asked Fox in a soft murmur.

The lead singer's expression turned grim, his dark green eyes close to obsidian. "Bad. He isn't sleeping, Kit. I don't think he's slept the past two, maybe more, nights."

Hands fisting by her sides, Kit fought off images of the motel room lit by a garish neon glow. "Because of me?"

"Far as I can figure out, he uses those random fucks as sleeping pills," Fox said bluntly. "He hasn't had that outlet. He finally crashed just after eleven this morning, and I told everyone not to wake him. We don't need him until right before we go onstage, and he can grab energy drinks prior to performing."

"What do you mean he uses the groupies as sleeping pills?" Kit said, still stuck on the first part of his sentence.

Fox ran a hand through the chocolate brown of his hair. "Not my story to tell, sweetheart. But you need to know enough to understand that you have to make sure he sleeps. Otherwise he'll have a fucking heart attack or something from sleep deprivation." He glanced over at Noah's bus... just as it opened.

A tousled blond head stuck out, sleepy eyes landing on Kit. "Hey." Noah's real smile was a thing of beauty.

Walking over, his feet bare and his body clad only in a pair of disreputable ripped jeans she recognized from the other day, he drew her into his arms, nuzzling his chin over her hair. She knew it was just for show... except maybe it wasn't, not this time. He was all warm from sleep, drowsy eyed and yawning against her.

Giving in to temptation, she slid her own arm around his waist and, Fox's warning strong in her mind, said, "Let's go back to the bus so you can grab some more shut-eye."

"I'll catch you both later." Fox walked over to Molly and Maxwell after bumping fists with Noah.

Not far off, Butch gave her a salute, waiting until she was at Noah's door before he faded off into the crowd. She knew he'd be back as soon as he'd checked out the area, but for now she didn't need the protection. Noah nudged her up into his bus, then came up behind her, pulling the door shut.

Kicking something accidentally, Kit found they were his boots. They'd been abandoned not far from the door, along with a crumpled black T-shirt. She leaned down and picked up the tee, had to fight the urge to bury her nose in it; she loved the way Noah smelled, and that hug outside had only made her need worse.

Stomach tensed against the stupid butterflies that refused to get the memo that she was over Noah, she tried for a stern tone. "This is *not* going to work if you throw your clothes around on the floor."

Still smiling that lazy, sleepy smile, he grabbed the tee and chucked it onto the sofa, the layout of his bus the same as

Molly and Fox's except there was no desk tucked into the corner. "There, now it's not on the floor."

She tried not to smile. "You're dopey with sleep deprivation. Go get some more rest."

Jaw cracking in a yawn, he took her hand and tugged her to the bedroom. "I can't sleep, but I'll lie down if you sit with me and tell me stuff."

"What stuff?"

"Any stuff."

Pushing him down onto the bed, she slipped off her heels, then climbed on beside him. He was lying on his back, his arms folded under his head and his eyes, those so often unreadable eyes, turned toward her.

Unable to look into the storm gray lest she betray too much, she busied herself getting into a seated position with her back to the wall that acted as the headboard. The idiotic butterflies dipped and dived at being so close to him, his gorgeous body laid out in front of her.

Noah was built beautiful, his chest bare of hair except for a thin trail that began below his belly button and disappeared into jeans that hung sexily low, exposing the lickable vee of the muscles on either side. There wasn't a lot of ink on the front of his body. Lyrics down his left side in vertical lines, a quote that spoke to him across his ribs on the other side, and a small, stylized sun on his left shoulder.

She couldn't see his back in this position, but she knew it bore a finely detailed phoenix so stunning the artist in question had asked Noah to pose for a photograph that adorned the front of the artist's book. That phoenix rose from the flames, defiant and glorious, and after guessing just how deep

Noah's scars went, Kit had come to realize the phoenix was Noah.

Only he hadn't quite escaped the forces trying to haul him back down.

I can't save him, she reminded the heart that still ached for him. *Not if he won't help save himself.*

Swallowing the lump in her throat, she said, "I had a one-on-one meeting with Esra Dali." She'd held the news inside all day because Noah was the only one with whom she wanted to share it.

"No shit?" A smile that just destroyed her. "You got the part?"

"Not yet. But he asked me to come in next week and read for him again, this time with Garrison opposite me." The Abigail-Garrison show was now on the road, and they were doing better than Thea had predicted, so things weren't yet in the bag.

"Kit, that's amazing."

Noah's excitement was genuine, she knew that. He'd always been her biggest champion, right back from when they'd first become friends. The fact he'd broken her heart didn't alter that, didn't erase all the things he'd once been to her... still was to her. "Thanks," she said, wanting to shake him and kiss him at the same time. "I'm cautiously excited."

"So," Noah said after a short pause, "what did Gates say when you told him about us?"

CHAPTER 20

KIT RUBBED A HAND over her face. "Terrence and I aren't an item anymore. I wanted to tell him the truth about everything, but... I didn't."

She'd still been on the sofa the morning after the gala, staring at the muted TV, when Terrence had called her. He'd said he was watching the same report, asked her if the rumors were true, if she'd ended up in Noah's bed the previous night.

Kit had gone to deny it, to reassure Terrence that it was all media hoopla, when he'd continued on to ask if she'd "dumped" him for "that manwhore," if she'd "lowered herself to the gutter." He'd added that he hadn't thought her so "cheap."

His voice had been colder than she'd ever heard it, so much anger in it that she'd felt the hairs rise on the back of her neck. Maybe it was just a flash of temper, but maybe it was a side of Terrence she didn't know—and his extreme possessiveness was especially troubling when they'd only gone on three tentative dates.

Kit's mind had suddenly filled with the stalker's letters. He'd used the word "whore" liberally too, though always in relation to Kit. Chilled, she'd snapped at Terrence that he had no right to speak to her that way, and that if they hadn't been over before, they were now.

Afterward, she'd felt guilty at suspecting Terrence of being her stalker, but she couldn't shake off the chill, not even after he apologized via text message since she refused to answer his calls.

"Hey," Noah said, voice quiet. "I'm sorry. I know you liked him."

"I did," she admitted, dropping her head back against the wall. "But don't feel bad. The way Terrence reacted to the news about us, it made me realize that maybe the man I know from work wouldn't be the same man in private."

Noah rose into a seated position, one knee raised, his arm braced on it. Gently gripping her chin in his fingers, he said, "Gates touch you?" Danger glinted in his eyes, deadly intent in his voice.

"No. We spoke on the phone." The shields around her heart pounded to nothing by his proximity, his protectiveness, and driven by a wave of love that simply would not die, she closed her hand over his wrist. "Fox told me you haven't been sleeping."

He dropped his hand from her face, broke her hold.

No major change in his expression, but she knew him, had spent hours studying his face over the years when they'd circled around each other... and in the months when they'd been more than friends. She knew before he spoke that the shutters had come down, that he was about to give her an answer that told her nothing.

"I've always had trouble sleeping." A shrug. "I don't want to take sleeping pills, so I catch naps when I can—like today. I make up the sleep."

No, she thought, he didn't. He was always wired. For a while, way back at the start, she'd thought he might be using, but she'd come to know that Noah didn't do drugs. He just didn't get enough sleep, turning jittery and almost too "bright" when the lack came to a head.

He appeared okay right now, but she knew Noah was adept at putting on a persona. "Noah," she said. "Are—"

"I'm fine," he bit out, then seemed to consciously force himself to relax. "I'm fine," he said in a less sharp tone. "Just a few nights of insomnia. I'll probably crash tonight."

The emotional shutters had turned into a wall in front of her eyes. She wanted to shove at that wall, to batter it down, but battering against it when Noah didn't want her inside would gain her nothing but broken bones. "I'll have to spend the weekend in this bus," she said as the butterflies finally went still, curling inward in an effort to protect their fragile bodies.

"That's sorted." Noah grinned, no tension now that she'd backed off. "I have a sleeping bag over there and I snuck in a single airbed I can pump up." He pointed to the right, and she saw the neat package of the airbed—so compact he could've easily brought it and the small air pump next to it into the bus without anyone being the wiser.

"I'll even pump it up for you," he said with a straight face.

She should've said they were friends, could share the bed, but she couldn't. She wasn't that strong. If Noah was in a bed with her, she'd either curl into him or scream at him while pounding her fists on his chest.

Why don't you want me?

Why all those other women but not me?

What do I lack?

Her anger was as powerful as the other emotion inside her heart, the one that whispered he was hers. Despite everything, it kept saying he was hers. Delusional heart.

Falling back on a mask that wouldn't appear a mask, she arched a single eyebrow. "Haven't you heard? Kathleen Devigny does not *do* airbeds, darling."

"Well, I'm not too important for it." A grin as he shoved a hand through his hair. "It'll fit in the living area with a little maneuvering so you can have the bedroom. Just chuck out some clothes for me to change into after my shower."

Kit rolled her eyes and kept her mind resolutely off the fact Noah would be wet and stripped to the skin bare yards from her. "It's not like I'm going to lock the door and dance naked in here. You can come in."

She must've been a really good actress because he laughed at her quip, and for one instant, they were simply two friends who happened to be sharing a joke.

Nothing more.

IT WAS STILL LIGHT when Schoolboy Choir got ready to take the stage, the sky streaked red and orange and indigo with sunset. Noah found himself in the unfamiliar position of preparing to head out to the stage with a woman by his side. He was used to picking up women after shows, but he never had anyone with him before a concert.

It had always seemed as if that would be an intrusion. He liked to get his head in the game, fully into the music pre-show. He didn't want to talk to anyone except the guys sometimes. He certainly didn't need a groupie coming on to him, expecting him to be happy about it.

So after grabbing a bite once he got up properly and showered to wash off the sleep, he'd been itchy for alone time. Except the media jackals were out, their cameras trained on the bus. Kit couldn't leave so soon after their "romantic reunion," as described online, so they'd been stuck together.

"Noah," Kit had said ten minutes into it, "I'm going into the bedroom to read. Do what you need to do."

Then she'd disappeared.

He hadn't believed it for at least five minutes, but she hadn't come back out, and when he'd peeked in at her, he'd found her sitting cross-legged on the bed, reading a script and marking it up as she went. Returning to the front room, he'd grabbed his iPod, his headphones, and settled in.

Often he played the guitar preshow, but today he'd just listened to stuff. Some of it was their own, some of it sung by his favorite bands, a scattering of it classical. No one expected him to listen to that last, but he liked the purity of it at times, liked figuring out the meaning behind the music. When the music beat in his blood, it cleared out everything else.

Too bad that didn't work while he was asleep. He'd tried it more than once.

Now, bare minutes before showtime, he was getting ready to walk out the door with a woman. It was strange… but good strange. He'd been complaining to Fox about not having a girl of his own, and here she was. Just for a weekend, but she was his, and she *got* him; she understood that he needed the music and she wasn't threatened by it.

When he'd finally come out of the music and gone looking

for her, she'd been frowning at her script. Glancing up with an absent look in her eyes, she'd said, "Is it time?"

"Ten minutes."

She'd taken those ten minutes to change into skinny black jeans that hugged her ass in ways Noah really shouldn't be noticing, paired with black ankle boots and a silky red T-shirt that faithfully caressed her form. The vee in front barely exposed any cleavage, and the design was simple, but the way the fine material hinted at the possibility of a lacy black bra beneath...

Blow-off-the-roof sexy wasn't an adequate description.

She'd also done something to her hair so that it was all tousled and rolled-out-of-bed hot, her lips plump and red, her eyes smoky.

"Holy hell," he'd said, enjoying the look but missing his Kit. The woman who stood in front of him was Kathleen Devigny.

Then she'd winked at him and there she was, his Kit. "What do you think we've been doing in the bus all this time, Casanova? Gotta give the right impression."

Allowing the memory of that moment to fall away because the reality of Kit with him was so much better, he glanced back to where she stood on the living area level while he'd stepped down to open the door. "Ready?"

"Rock on." She handed over his guitar. "I'll be your adoring girlfriend slash mega groupie."

Guitar in one hand, he stepped out with a grin on his face that was real, twisting sideways once he was down so he could grab her hand as she came out. He didn't care about the cameras, just wanted to touch her. He could do that now without crossing dangerous lines because Kit thought it was all make-believe.

But when he wrapped her hand firmly in his and held it against his thigh, he meant it. And when he tugged her close to his side and leaned down to nuzzle at her hair, he meant that too. As he did his words when he released her hand to wrap his arm around her shoulders. "I'm glad you're here."

Eyes suddenly dark, Kit looked away as she slid her own arm around his waist. Her silence was a kick to his fucking heart. But the pain was nothing compared to having her tucked up against him. He didn't deserve her, would never deserve her, but for this short window of time, he could pretend and live an impossible dream.

"It's interesting being on the back end from the start," she said at last. "The energy is intense." A squeeze of his waist that he wasn't expecting and that made his heart do weird things inside his chest. "*You're* intense."

"You didn't even come near me. How do you know I was intense?"

"That bus is luxurious but small. I could *feel* you being all intense and rock-god-like."

Heart continuing to do weird things, he nuzzled his chin into her hair again. "Yeah well, thanks for the patience."

"No, I get it. I hole up like that when I'm readying myself for a big scene." Another squeeze of his waist that made him feel all odd deep within. "I don't want people talking at me, expecting to get a response. All I want is silence in my head so my skin can settle."

Noah just wanted to kiss her. She got it, got everything.

NOAH WAS SO WARM and strong against her, his scent making her want to bury her face against his neck, draw it in. And he was being so physically affectionate, nothing anyone would expect from him... so maybe, a stubborn kernel of hope whispered, maybe it was real?

Don't fall back down that cliff, Kit. He'll destroy you.

Even as that reminder sliced pitilessly through the hope, Kit accepted the bleak truth that Noah would always be the one. She might one day love another man, but it would never be like what she and Noah could've had together. The promise between them, it had been something most people never experienced. It was broken now, shattered so badly nothing could put it back together, but when it had been whole, it had been beyond beautiful, a priceless gift.

Noah could've been her heart.

Instead, he'd be her friend with whom she could never quite have a real friendship. And he'd be the man she'd have to kiss before he went onstage in a couple of minutes. She'd have to act the doting girlfriend she'd teased him about being, the two of them kissing and snuggling like a couple in the first flush of love.

She'd thought she was ready, had convinced herself it would be just another scene from this movie they were playing out for the cameras.

Only it hurt so much that her first kiss with Noah would be fake.

Walking up onto the back of the stage with him, she smiled at Molly as the other woman appeared with Fox. She hadn't seen Abe, or David and Thea yet, but they had to be nearby. Turning into Noah, she took a deep breath. "You know what we have to do, right?"

He raised a hand and cupped her cheek, his fingers in her hair as he leaned in to press his forehead against hers. Holding her just that way, as if she was precious, he said, "You know something?"

"What?" she whispered inside the cocoon he'd created.

"We just gave them the money shot."

She blinked, startled out of her upsetting thoughts.

Noah had been photographed with women, but he'd never been photographed being tender with any of them. Kit knew, because despite her best intentions, she couldn't ignore reports about him. Noah never cupped a woman's face so sweetly, never smiled at her while stroking his thumb over her cheekbone, never tugged her close against him as he whispered in her ear.

"I'll take care of you, Kit," he said, his lips brushing her ear while his fingers wove deeper into her hair. "I won't let the vultures steal pieces of you."

Kit swayed into him, told herself it was all part of the show. "Thanks."

"Make sure to cheer for me," he ordered as he drew back, "maybe throw your panties onstage too—aimed directly and only at me."

She shoved at his chest, though she was feeling all warm and hopeless inside. Warm because he was being the Noah she loved, the Noah who *did* look out for her, the one who'd never hurt her. Hopeless because this Noah was just as real as the Noah who'd so cruelly crushed her heart.

"You wish," she said, digging up a smile. "If I ever throw my panties onstage, it won't be for some pretty guitar player."

"Oh, ouch." Laughing as the crowd started to chant for

Schoolboy Choir, he blew her a kiss and, slipping his guitar over his head and across his body, ran on with Fox. David and Abe ran up from the other side at the same time, and the crowd went crazy.

Genevieve slipped on more quietly after saying a quick hello to Kit and Molly.

Cupping the mike with both hands in that way he had of doing, Fox said, "You guys ready to party!" while Noah plugged in his own guitar, as was his habit.

A thunderous roar of sound was the crowd's reply.

The band responded by launching into a hard rock anthem that had the attendees throwing up their hands and jumping up and down. Heading down the steps and around to the special section in front of the stage to join Molly and Thea, Butch, Casey, and the other security personnel making sure they were safe, Kit allowed herself to get caught up in the music, allowed herself to watch Noah.

For the first time since they'd met, she didn't have to hide anything.

So she watched him move, listened to him play, and felt her heart thunder as loud as the crowd. "This is amazing!" she said to Molly and Thea.

"I've done the festival before, but never like this!" Thea took a few photos with her phone as she spoke, tweeted them. "I'm tagging you," she said to Kit. "Retweet."

"Always working." Laughing, Molly pretended to confiscate Thea's phone while Kit obeyed the retweet order, then took photos of her own to share.

Thea bared her teeth at Molly's efforts. "I want everyone to know how my gorgeous man is rocking the festival already."

"Hey." Molly elbowed her sister. "That's *our* men."

When the other woman took out her own phone, Kit laughed. Molly had a single social media account that she rarely used, but today she sent out a photo of Fox making love to the mike, captioning it: *My guy owning the stage at Zenith. #love*

Simple. Perfect. So much what Kit wanted to write, but those words would haunt her when this illusion ended; she couldn't put her heart out there for the universe to mock. So on the photograph she sent out into the world of a wildly talented man with storm-gray eyes, she just wrote: *Noah rocking #Zenith!!!!!!*

CHAPTER 21

THEY'D KICKED OFF THE festival with a fucking boom, Noah thought as he came backstage after the final set. Not thinking about his actions, he hauled Kit close and pressed the side of his face to hers. "I'm starving."

She laughed. "You're also sweaty."

Her hands landed on his bare skin, his T-shirt now the property of whoever it was who'd caught it when he'd thrown it out into the crowd. The intimate contact burned, sending a shock of sexual need through his body.

He pulled back with a jerk that had Kit's eyes going wide before she blinded him with a Kathleen Devigny smile. "The cameras are still on," she said without ever losing that smile. "Take my hand if you can't stand for me to touch anything else."

She could've kicked him and done less damage. Grabbing her hand, he squeezed. "It's not what you think."

Her smile remained high-voltage, but her eyes, they were hard and hurt at the same time. "You've been very clear, Noah. Don't worry, I'm not getting the wrong idea. I know you don't want me."

He almost laughed because wanting Kit was so much a part of him, there was no Noah without it. But his laughter twisted inside him. Holding Kit's hand tight, he said, "We're all having pizza together. I just need to quickly shower off the sweat."

Kit nodded and they walked to the bus. Soon as he pulled the door shut behind them, she released his hand—or tried to.

He held on. "Don't."

She shook her head. "It's fine." A tight smile. "I really am not getting any ideas." Sliding out her phone, she waved it at him. "Van messaged. We dated last year, remember? He's asking if you and I are serious."

Noah winced as his fantasy shattered. Kit wasn't his. He had no right to stop her seeing other men. Releasing her hand, he said, "What're you going to tell him?"

"Nothing." She looked down at her phone, fingers moving across the screen. "You and I are officially a couple, and I have to keep up the fiction or this is all for nothing." A quick look up, a quicker smile. "Won't be forever."

Noah's body grew rigid. "Two minutes," he said and ducked into the shower.

KIT BRACED A TREMBLING hand against the counter of the kitchenette, trying to breathe past the pain in the center of her chest, an agony of knives stabbing at her from the inside out, stabbing so hard they were punching through rib and muscle to make her bleed.

Every time she thought Noah couldn't hurt her any more, he did it again.

She swallowed convulsively, squeezing her eyes shut to hold back the tears that threatened to choke off her air. She could hear the shower turning on, knew it wouldn't last long. Noah had to be starving after that show.

Breathing through her nose, she forced down all the emotions tearing at her, as she'd learned to do while filming the traumatic scenes in *Last Flight*. Her character had undergone torture, loss, agonizing emotional suffering, and sometimes the crushing power of living those emotions had threatened to take Kit under. She'd had to learn to compartmentalize, to shift from a wrenching scene to a joyful one, the shooting schedule not always cohesive or chronological.

Now she used every skill she had to bring herself back under control.

Hearing the shower cut off, she released a quiet, deep breath, was waiting with a slight smile on her face when Noah stepped out... and almost doubled over from the punch to the stomach that was his damp body. He'd wrapped a white towel around his hips, but water trickled from his hair down his pectoral muscles to kiss its way over his ribs and past his ridged abs to disappear into the softness of the towel.

When he turned to head into the bedroom, she saw the phoenix, stunning because it was on the masculine architecture of Noah's body.

Wrenching away her gaze with a harsh reminder that he couldn't bear her touch, she slid her phone out of her pocket and skimmed through her e-mails. There were a couple from Harper telling her there was no news on *Redemption*, but that no one else—namely Abigail—had been signed either. The race was still on.

Right then a message popped in from Thea's intern, copied to Noah and Thea. It was a roundup of all of Kit's and Noah's media mentions today. The efficient young woman had included a file of clippings of the main articles, even screenshots of tweets and other posts online.

#NoKat was trending worldwide, thanks to the "money shot" Noah had engineered.

Kit knew she shouldn't; she'd been in the business too long not to know the Internet could wound, but she couldn't stop herself from doing a search on that hashtag. She didn't know what she was expecting, but it wasn't what she got.

Did you see that?! I TOLD you he was into her! #NoKat #Forever
OMG, so romantic! Why can't my boyfriend look at me that way? #NoKat #Romance #SCFans
Okay, I was bummed when Noah hooked up with her, but yeah, he looks happy, so #NoKat, I'm on board.
Even my cold and bitter heart is melted. #NoKat #SCFans
That is the most romantic thing I've ever seen. #NoKat #Happy #Staytogetherforeverplease

The sentiments were repeated over and over and over again. A lot of women were crushed that Noah was taken, but most found it romantic that the bad boy had apparently reformed for his girl. Meanwhile, the band's male fans were chest-poundingly proud that "their" Noah had hooked up with such a "hottie."

Kit wanted to scream and laugh at the same time. Yeah, she was hot. So hot that Noah was physically repulsed by the idea of any sexual contact with her.

"Hey." Noah stepped out of the bedroom. "Just let me pull on my boots."

She watched him do exactly that. He'd changed into a fresh pair of black jeans that were just as disreputable as the ones he'd been wearing earlier and a plain black T-shirt. As far as she could see, he'd just run his hands through his hair after rubbing it dry with a towel and left it at that. And he was flat-out gorgeous.

NOAH PUT HIS ARM around Kit's shoulders after they left the bus. She didn't resist, sliding her own arm around his waist and acting the smitten girlfriend, but he was conscious of her tension. No one else would be able to tell, but he could sense it through his skin, feel it in his gut. He'd hurt Kit because he couldn't handle his own reaction to her, and he didn't know how to fix that.

How could he tell her about his fucked-up psyche without betraying everything?

He couldn't.

All he could do was try to be the best friend he could be in his own messed-up way. Putting his lips to her ear, he said, "I'm sorry," then took a breath and slit open a vein. "I'm so damn happy you're here, with me."

Fuck, it was hard to just lay himself out there. "I like having you in my space, near me." Loved the smell of her soft skin and hair, the way she felt against him, her smile. "I don't want to push you away, but there's stuff inside me that"—another harsh breath—"that just screws me up sometimes."

Her hand clenched on his T-shirt. He wondered if she remembered she'd given him this tee. It was plain, but it had a tiny guitar stitched at the bottom on the right. The guitar

217

was in black, hardly visible, but he'd always liked that tiny, secret detail.

She didn't say anything in answer, but her hand opened and she kind of... petted his side. It was just a small motion, but it spoke louder than any words she could've said. Unable to fight the need, he took advantage of the situation to cuddle her closer.

If it could always be this way, if he never had to think about sex, if he could fix his brain so it didn't hunger for the same thing that destroyed him, he'd beg her forgiveness on his hands and knees and find a way to put a ring on her finger that would never ever come off.

Only that was such an impossible dream that he might as well wish for wings.

"You hungry?" he asked as they reached the marquee set up to one side of the "behind-the-scenes" part of the festival grounds. The scent of hot cheese and all the other good stuff that equaled pizza made his stomach rumble.

"I actually am—I danced the entire concert."

Seeing Thea tug David into a kiss not far from the marquee, Noah wolf-whistled. David grinned and didn't stop the kiss, one hand cupping the back of Thea's head, the other on her ass. She wasn't in one of her professional outfits but in a tiny sparkling dress that left her long legs bare from high up on her thighs, her straight black hair out of its usual twist.

No question that Thea was hot, but all Noah saw when he looked at her was a highly competent publicist who could chew up and spit out most of the paparazzi before she had her first cup of coffee in the morning.

"I'm happy for them," Kit whispered as they neared the marquee. "They fit."

"Yeah, they do." Noah nodded at Abe as the keyboard player appeared from the other side of the tent. "There was a good chance David would've ended up a sad, lonely old man if she hadn't taken pity on him."

Close enough to hear, Abe snorted. "I need a hella sexy woman to take that kind of pity on me," he muttered. "I think David's the one laughing now."

"I don't know who's more smitten, David or Thea."

Noah heard a tone in Kit's voice that he'd never expected—mingled want and envy. The latter wasn't sharp, hard. It was soft, poignant, and it made him want to give her things, make her happy. "You know he sent her a pink teddy bear when we were on tour?"

Kit's smile was huge. "Really? How do you know?" Utter delight in her tone.

"I caught him walking back into the hotel with it tucked under his arm," Noah said, wondering if Kit would like that kind of a gift. He'd never have thought so before this conversation—she was so put together, so stylish.

Except now she sighed and hugged herself. "That is ridiculously adorable and romantic."

Abe had wandered off toward the table where piping hot pizzas were being set out, cooked courtesy of some kind of a portable oven, but Noah turned to Kit. "You don't have teddy bears in your house." He paused. "Do you?"

"No, but no one's ever given me one."

Noah had had a fucked-up childhood, but he remembered a teddy bear that his nanny, Josefina, had given him before he was packed off to boarding school.

"To keep you safe," she'd said in the Spanish she'd taught

him, her eyes wet and dark. "He will be your friend."

Josefina never knew that the bear didn't make it to board-ing school. Noah's father had taken one look at it as Noah climbed into the car that was taking him to the school and pulled it out of his hands. No son of his, he'd said, was going to go to school clutching "an infantile toy."

Noah had tried to hold on to the only piece of certainty he had, that soft brown bear representing love and safety, but he'd been a small boy against a much bigger man. His father had thrown the bear onto the driveway, then told the driver to go. The bear had been crushed under the wheels of the glossy black Rolls-Royce.

Shaking off the memory and wondering what Josefina would make of him now, he glanced at Kit. "I thought your parents did the 'throw money and toys at the child' kind of parenting?"

Kit bit down on the plump softness of her lower lip. "I didn't mean I didn't have soft toys. I did... but no one ever picked one out for me especially—Mom or Dad wrote the check on my birthday or Christmas, and the store employees came in and set up the toy display." She shook her head, mouth twisting up at one corner. "I sound so spoiled."

"No, I get it." His nanny's inexpensive gift had meant more to Noah than anything his parents had given him after it all came out. Josefina had still cared about Noah even though he wasn't perfect anymore, and that had made all the difference.

"You two gonna eat?" Having navigated his way back to them, Abe held out a plate with a whole giant pizza.

"Oh, that looks like heaven." Kit took a slice, managed three bites in the time it took Noah to wolf down a whole piece.

Seeing a table clear up, he grabbed it for them and the three of them took a seat, the plate of pizza in the middle and fresh bottles of beer and water dropped off by one of the catering staff. Nudging aside the beer without a word, Abe stuck to water, and Noah and Kit kept him company.

Noah knew Kit'd had a lot of trouble with Abe's drug issues, but she'd never not been supportive when Abe tried to stay sober. She'd been partially responsible for convincing him to enter rehab the second time, but Abe hadn't been ready, had relapsed. This time though, there was a sense of intense resolve about the other man.

"Fuck, this is good," Abe groaned, picking up another slice.

Noah nodded as around them, the marquee pulsed with the voices of musicians and crew, the throb of music from the closest stage pumping through the earth.

"Hey, Abe!"

Rising at the call from Genevieve's husband, Abe finished off his slice and went over to catch up with the bass player and her artist spouse.

"Perfect timing." Fox put a plate full of miniature desserts on the table and, swinging around Abe's chair, sat with one of his arms on the back while he used the other to pick up a chocolate tart.

Noah took a piece of cake while Kit decided on a cookie.

"Where's Molly?" Noah asked his bandmate.

Fox was very protective of his fiancée—she was getting more used to the limelight, but she still wasn't as comfortable in it as they were, probably never would be.

"With Maxwell's Kim." The lead singer used his thumb to point behind him to the left. "They're talking about an old archaeological site Molly's researching for one of her work contracts."

Still hungry, Noah got up. "You want more pizza?" he asked Kit and Fox both.

When they shook their heads, he went to grab a couple more slices. It was on the way back that a woman put a hand on his forearm. Her fingernails were hot pink and tapered, her hand slender. When he looked up, he didn't recognize the face, but he recognized the look. The petite blonde was giving him an invitation bright and clear.

"Hi," she said, twisting a lock of her hair around her finger. "You want to party?"

"No."

Kit's gaze met his as he closed the distance to their table. There was a pinched look to her eyes that didn't fit her, wasn't her. As he watched, it smoothed out, her expression settling once more into that of Kathleen Devigny, the A-list actress dating a rock star, not Kit, the woman who was friends with Noah.

CHAPTER 22

KIT HAD NEVER BEEN so glad to get away from a crowd. The strain of pretending had turned into a throbbing pulse in her left temple, her skin stretched thin and tight over her bones. But the flip side was that she was now alone with Noah in a very small space.

"I think I'll go to bed," she said as soon as Noah pulled the door shut. "Been a long day."

"I'll just grab the airbed and the sleeping bag."

She went into the tiny bathroom to clean off her makeup so they wouldn't be in the bedroom together, and when she came out, it was to see Noah in the living area pumping up the airbed. He was down on one knee, his T-shirt stretched over his back and his hair falling over his forehead.

"Good night," she said, her heart bruise growing darker at the sight of this man who could've been her forever. Only of course that wasn't true. Noah had never given himself to her, never asked her to be his.

I don't want to push you away, but there's stuff inside me that just screws me up sometimes.

Yet other women put their hands on him without concern.

He *allowed* it, would do so again as soon as this charade was over. Kit had tried so hard to understand, to move past the way he'd flinched from her, but she wasn't superhuman. Rejection hurt. And watching another woman so casually touch him? It eviscerated.

He looked up, storm-gray eyes holding her own, all those words forever unspoken between them. "Good night, Kit. Dream sweet dreams."

"Always," she said, but when she got into bed after changing into a camisole and pajama pants, she twisted and turned and slept in snatches. The dreams she had were filled with music and with a man whose smile she couldn't forget.

She woke at six a.m. Rubbing at gritty eyes, she walked out into the living area to see the airbed deflated and folded up in a corner, the sleeping bag neatly rolled up beside it. No sign of Noah. In the bathroom, she threw cold water on her face, came fully awake with a jolt.

She'd just stepped out of the bathroom when the bus door was pulled open and Noah jumped inside. His hair was plastered to his head, his T-shirt and running shorts to his body. Water ran down his face.

That was when Kit realized the fine drumming she could hear was rain hitting the bus roof. "You'll freeze," she said, grabbing a towel from the little built-in cupboard next to the bathroom. "Get those shoes and socks off."

He obeyed, bending his head so she could rub the towel over the blond strands of his hair. "This'll wreck the festival if it doesn't stop," he said, the words muffled by the towel.

"What's the weather report say?" She knew he'd have checked; Noah did things like that.

"Forecast to clear by eight. Cross your fingers they're right."

Having dried his hair so it was no longer dripping, she ordered him to strip off his T-shirt, then went around and dried his back. It wasn't until she came around to his front, his eyes looking down into hers that she realized what she was doing. Her camisole was thin and he was bare to the waist, all golden skin and ridged muscle and ink. He didn't want her, but that didn't matter to her body.

Her nipples tightened.

Shoving the towel at him, she turned away. "Dry off. I'm going to grab a change of clothes for you." She barely resisted the urge to wrap her arms protectively around herself.

Kathleen Devigny did not hide.

It took her only a couple of minutes to find him some clothes, the closet was so small. After putting them outside the bedroom, she shut the door and got changed herself. She'd intended to wear a dress, but with the rain, she hesitated. In the end, she decided to hope for the best and pulled on the summery yellow strapless sundress that had a cute blue print. She'd pair it with her ankle boots and a hip-length leather jacket she left on the bed for now.

A deep breath, the mask firmly back on, she opened the bedroom door.

Noah was at the kitchenette, damp hair roughly finger-combed and body clad in the old blue jeans and black T-shirt with a faded silver print on the back that she'd found in the closet. Looking up, he smiled. "You want some cereal?"

God, that smile. "Yes," she said as her stomach dipped despite all her admonitions to the contrary.

Picking up a large box, he poured a multicolored waterfall of sugary rings into a bowl.

"Really?" She raised an eyebrow. "Why don't you just give me a candy bar and be done with it?"

A wink. "That's for me." He put a smaller, unopened box on the counter. "*This* is for you."

It was her favorite kind.

Gripping the butterflies in a tight fist lest they escape and forget all the painful lessons she'd already learned at Noah's hands, she opened the box and poured the flakes into a bowl. He poured milk over it, and the two of them ate in silence. Pretending there wasn't this great pulsing thing between them, this unfinished promise that hurt so much. Pretending they were normal.

"What time did you go for your run?"

A shrug. "Around five maybe."

"It must've still been dark."

"Best time to run. Everything's quiet and most of the vultures are asleep."

Fox's warning vivid in her mind, Kit said, "How much sleep did you get?"

"A few hours." Nonchalant words.

She put down her bowl. "Now you're lying to me?"

His jaw got that hard line that never augured anything good. "Leave it, Kit. I told you I have bad nights sometimes."

"Leave it? Noah—"

"*Leave it.*"

Noah had never yelled at Kit. Never. He still hadn't. But the cold whip of his voice made her flinch. She'd heard him use a similar tone against people he didn't like or those who were getting in his face, but he'd never used it on her.

At first she was hurt—and then she got mad.

Coming around the counter, she stood half a foot from him, arms folded. "You think you can do that to me?" she asked, her fury as hot as his was cold. "Just freeze me out with the famous Noah St. John temper?" So angry it felt as if her skin glowed red-hot, she shook her head. "It doesn't work that way. Friends care. I *care*." He knew that; what use was hiding it? "You're running on a razor-thin edge."

His eyes glittered, unrelenting stone and icy mists. "What're you going to do? Hug me and make it better? Wave a magic wand to make the insomnia disappear?"

Kit gritted her teeth, but she couldn't quite control the scream that wanted to erupt from her throat. "I sure as hell don't intend for you to give yourself a heart attack from sleep deprivation or endless running just so I can get a part!"

She slashed out a hand. "We're done. We'll break up in a big dramatic deal, and you can pick up one of those women who allow you to get some sleep." Yes, that hurt, that fucking hurt, but this was Noah's life they were talking about.

"*No.*" He grabbed her upper arms, hauled her close. "I promised you I would do this."

Shoving at his chest, Kit tried to pull away, but all she succeeded in doing was taunting herself with the muscled heat of him under her palms. "I'm releasing you from the promise."

NOAH WANTED TO SHAKE her, but he'd never chance hurting Kit. "I won't release myself. I *need* to do this."

"This isn't your redemption, Noah," she said, her eyes so passionate with emotion that they seemed to glow. "You don't need to do this to save our friendship. I'm being your friend now."

"If you're my friend, then you let me do this." *Even if I can't give you anything else, I can give you this.* "You damn well let me do this, Kit."

"I won't watch you drive yourself into the ground!"

"I won't. I'll take a pill tonight. I'll sleep." The nightmares would ravage his drugged mind, but it'd be worth it. "I'll sleep. I promise."

Her expression altered, the anger suddenly intermingled with so many other emotions that he couldn't separate them out. "Why won't you talk to me, Noah?" she whispered, placing one hand against his cheek.

The touch was hesitant and he hated that, hated that he'd made her afraid of touching him in friendship, in affection. Raising one of his own hands, he held hers against the stubbled roughness of his cheek. "You know me better than anyone else in this world." Fox knew the details of one thing Kit didn't, but Fox didn't know his heart, not like Kit.

"I don't know why you hurt." A harsh whisper. "Why you hurt so much that you do things that make you deeply unhappy."

Sliding his hand into her hair, he tugged her against him, held her stiff, angry body close. And didn't want to let her go. Not today. Not tomorrow. Never. "Be with me," he whispered, knowing it was the most selfish thing he'd ever asked of anyone in his entire life. "Be with me."

Kit froze against him, a flesh and blood statue.

"I can't be what you need," he whispered against the side of her head. "But be with me anyway."

Kit's body stayed rigid, her breathing so quiet he wasn't sure she *was* breathing. Noah knew he should release her, call back the words he should've never spoken. But he stayed silent and he held her tight, right against the twisted, scarred, selfish heart that beat only for her.

FIFTEEN MINUTES LATER, AND Kit didn't know what she was going to do. Being with Noah, having him for her own, it was all she'd ever wanted, but not this way, not when he couldn't even sleep from the strain of being faithful. It sounded so stupid to put it that way, but how else could she explain it? Noah seemed to get a kind of peace—fleeting though it was— from his random hookups that she couldn't give him.

"Kit."

Glancing up from where she was sitting on the edge of the bed, having just put on her boots, she saw him in the doorway. He'd thrown on a leather jacket over his black tee, and it just intensified the rock-star vibe. But his eyes... his eyes were vulnerable.

"Rain's stopped," he said.

Unable to bear looking into those eyes that asked her for things that might break her, she got up and tugged at her own leather jacket. "We'll look like those twin couples."

"Yours is brown and sleek, mine is black with buckles and zippers everywhere. Totally different." He shifted out of the doorway, angled his head toward the front of the bus in a silent invitation.

"Where are we going?" she asked as they stepped outside and he wrapped one arm around her shoulders. Around

229

them, the festival grounds were damp and still sleepy. The first show wouldn't kick off till nine, and Schoolboy Choir wasn't on until four that afternoon.

"Just for a walk."

He'd gone running and now he wanted to go for a walk. If she was with him, she wouldn't need Macho Steve, the Evil Personal Trainer, Kit thought wryly. But walking with Noah in the cool morning light was fun. They went out back, behind the buses and the other vehicles. The fields seemed to stretch out endlessly, but once you got over a little rise about a ten-minute walk away, it turned into woods.

Into those woods they walked, just the two of them and the birds and the bodyguards who hung back enough that Noah and Kit had privacy. "Why are Butch and Casey following us?" Noah was more than tough enough to take on the coward who got his rocks off by stalking her.

"I'm not taking any chances with your safety," Noah said, his body suddenly all hard edges. "I don't ever want you in a situation where you feel helpless and alone."

His words, his care, dealt another smashing blow to her already shaky defenses. No, she told herself, he's not good for you. Yes, said her heart. Just yes. "My Spidey senses haven't gone off lately," she said aloud. "I don't think he made it to Zenith."

"Yeah, well, better safe than sorry." He glanced back, lifted a hand in a wave of acknowledgment. "Butch and Casey are good guys—and they know not to get too close."

Kit went to make a joke about getting caught in flagrante delicto, but then the reality of her and Noah stabbed at her and she couldn't.

Be with me, he'd said.

There was no mistaking what he'd meant. He was asking her to make the pretense real, asking her to be his.

I fuck everything female that moves. I don't want that with you.

He'd meant that too. He did not want to sleep with her. That continued to hurt, but she knew it wasn't as simple as a lack of sexual attraction—their chemistry was as real as the brutal pain he'd caused. There was something else, the same something that kept him awake at night, that made him do self-destructive things like pick up women who cared nothing for him and about whom he didn't care.

Be with me.

The memory of the raw words made her breath catch, her heart ache. "You looking forward to the show today?" she asked, needing time to understand him, understand herself, understand *this.*

In a way, there was only one answer. But that answer might destroy them both.

"Always." Noah grinned. "I like performing—I'm a peacock at heart."

Kit felt her eyebrows draw together over her eyes. "And that's why you once hung out with me in my garden for an entire week, without the least desire to go show off?" That had been the best week of her life... though Noah hadn't spent the nights at her place. He'd gone home, probably picked up groupie after groupie while she was building cotton candy romantic dreams.

Another stab of pain, another reminder that if she agreed to be with him, she'd live in constant fear that he'd break, go back to his promiscuous ways. But then he nuzzled at her with a smile lighting up his face, and her stupid, irrational heart melted again.

"Yeah well, even a peacock needs the occasional break." He pointed out an eagle overhead, its wings majestic. "Seriously though, I like the rush of performing, but it's good to have the downtime. That's when the music comes."

Kit nodded. "It's the same with me and acting." She loved being in front of the camera, putting on another skin, but then she needed to be herself, to be "quiet," to recharge and find her center.

That morning they talked about music, about drama, about so many things except the three words Noah had spoken that changed everything.

Be with me.

CHAPTER 23

THINGS WERE HOPPING IN the backstage area by the time Kit and Noah returned. After grabbing coffees from the catering truck parked outside the marquee where the festival organizers had put on a breakfast spread, they headed toward Molly and Fox's bus, figuring the other couple would be up.

"Kathleen!"

Kit froze, that sultry female voice with its faint trace of a Venezuelan accent intimately familiar. "*Mom?*" Turning, she stared at the leggy woman with masses of expertly tousled black hair striding toward her.

Adreina Ordaz-Castille was dressed in black leather pants that appeared painted on, spike heels that left sharp little divots in the rain-wet earth, and a designer black shirt that hugged her body and was unbuttoned enough to expose the upper curves of her breasts. Her jewelry was chunky silver and turquoise. She was exquisite and sexy both.

A trail of slack-jawed men gazed after her in hopeless want.

Kit couldn't quite keep herself from glancing at Noah to gauge his reaction to seeing her mom in the flesh. Males tended to forget themselves in the orbit of the magnetic sexual allure that was Adreina Ordaz-Castille.

Noah's eyes were wide, his muscles bunched, but not with worship.

Kit blinked. "Why are you freaking out?"

"It's your mom," he said under his breath. "I'm pretty sure she's going to shoot me."

A silly, turbulent twisting in Kit's stomach at the realization that he looked at Adreina and saw only her mom, she said, "No, my mother loves rock stars." Adreina had dated plenty of them before settling down with Kit's dad.

"Mom, what are you doing here?" she said when Adreina reached her.

Her mother kissed her on both cheeks before answering, the scent of Adreina's perfume a familiar embrace. "Your father and I are here for the festival."

"Oh, right." Kit didn't know why she was surprised; her parents were very active on the celebrity circuit, and this edgy festival was starting to gain serious media cred. And Adreina did still love rock stars, even if only to watch them perform. "Where's Dad?"

A familiar silver head appeared around the corner a second later. Parker Ordaz-Castille had two cups of coffee in hand from one of the festival trucks. "Hello, honey," he said, drawing Kit into a hug after giving Adreina her coffee. "Noah, good to see you again."

The two men shook hands. Following that, Kit's mother put one hand on Noah's shoulder and leaned in to brush her lips over his cheek. Adreina touched easily. The boys Kit had dated in high school and college had often taken it the wrong way, believing it a come-on. It wasn't.

Noah, however, still had that wary look on his face, clearly braced for parental disapproval.

"How did you get backstage?" Kit asked her parents, the funny, twisty feeling inside her refusing to subside.

"We know people." Parker winked.

"Oh, look!" Adreina waved at someone. "There's Naomi. We'll see you later, darling."

"Sure, Mom." Relieved it was over, Kit turned to Noah. "See, no biggie."

He was scowling. "What the hell? If I had a daughter and she was dating a guy like me, I'd take him out back and threaten him with a shotgun to make sure he treated her right."

Kit's mouth fell open. "You?"

"Yeah." He folded his arms, his scowl growing heavier. "Jeez, Kit, he didn't even tell me to be good to you. That's bullshit."

Realizing he was dead serious, she bit the inside of her cheek to keep from smiling. "Where did you pick up this chivalrous instinct?"

"My father," he said, the sneer that usually accompanied any mention of Robert St. John missing from his voice. "He's a son of a bitch, but he brought me up to look after any women under my care."

"*Under your care?*" Kit raised an eyebrow. "Chauvinistic much?"

He shrugged. "Yeah, well, maybe it is, but I'm not changing. My imaginary daughters are *never* dating musicians. Ever."

Stomach somersaulting at the idea of little girls with Noah's features and talent, she shook her head. "Noah St. John, bad boy of rock and concerned father of imaginary daughters. Hell hath frozen over and become an ice rink."

"Come on, smart-ass." He slung an arm around her shoulders again. "Let's go find a seat out front so we can watch Esteban. Maxwell has rug things we can use since the grass won't have dried out yet."

Kit fell in with his plan. Not only did she like Esteban's music, she knew he was a good friend of Noah's. She had a feeling Schoolboy Choir and Thea had had a great deal to do with getting him on the bill at the festival. Yes, he had a morning slot, a time when people were still getting themselves together after a late night, but he *had* a slot. His performance would be reported on by the bloggers and other media here, clips would be posted on social media, and so on.

Grabbing a spot beside a wild-haired guy sitting up in his sleeping bag, Noah pulled her down between his legs. She settled with her back to his chest and tried not to sink into his warmth, his scent, *him*. Whispers and camera clicks sounded from around them, but no one tried to intrude into their space.

Part of the draw of Zenith was that the musicians blended into the crowd, hung out and danced like regular people. It was an unspoken rule that they weren't to be mobbed. Kit didn't know how long that would last with the festival getting bigger and bigger, but it held today.

Then Esteban walked onstage. Just a dark-eyed singer and his guitar and his voice. Listening to the smooth, heart-tugging cadence of it, Kit felt herself becoming boneless against Noah. "He's a real musician, like you guys. No tricks."

"Yep." Noah's lips brushed her ear as he spoke. "I was thinking—that song I wrote. Esteban would do it justice."

She knew he was talking about "Sparrow." "No." Scowling at the idea that he'd even consider giving it to anyone else, she twisted around to look at him. "That's meant for you."

"It's not a Schoolboy Choir type of song," he said again.

"Have you even talked to the others?"

Hauling her back against his chest, Noah wrapped her up in his arms. "Stop fighting with me and listen to the music."

She did, but she wasn't finished. She didn't know why Noah was being so stubborn about "Sparrow" when he and the other guys messed around with all kinds of stuff as they put together an album. Maybe, another part of her whispered, *because* the song was so close to his heart. If it didn't make it onto the next album, or if the other guys didn't like it, he'd be devastated.

Kit knew Abe, Fox, and David would like it; she just had to convince Noah to sing it for them.

"I like this one a lot." Noah's lips brushed her ear again, his breath warm and his body so strong and powerfully male around her own.

Breasts swelling against her bra, Kit fought off a responsive shiver as her battered heart begged her to stand firm on one beat... and to give in on the next.

Be with me.

SCHOOLBOY CHOIR'S AFTERNOON PERFORMANCE went off with a bang. Dressed in rock-appropriate knee-high boots and a strapless dress in glittering gold that barely covered her butt and had caused Noah to suck in an audible breath when she walked out of the bedroom, Kit had just as much fun this time around as she'd had the night before.

Beside her, Molly cried when Fox sang the song he'd written for her, the one with which he'd proposed onstage during the tour.

Kit couldn't help but feel a stab of envy.

Molly and Thea were so lucky. Their guys were theirs—no questions or doubt. Totally devoted. Fox saw no one else when Molly was in the room, and David's face just lit up when he found Thea in the crowd.

Kit wanted that for herself. And she wanted it with the gorgeous man onstage who wanted to be with her... without being with her.

"Hey." Molly, her curvy body clad in a sexy halter-neck dress, wrapped an arm around Kit's back as the band segued into another song. "What's the matter?" Gentle words, a tone that held infinite care. "The situation with Noah?"

Kit nodded and left it at that. The rest was too painful, too private, to share. "Noah said there was going to be a party tonight."

"Yeah." Molly spoke against her ear to be heard over the thumping pulse of the music. "Plan is to party with the crowd a bit, then move on back to the marquee."

That was exactly what they did when night fell. Kit laughed and danced with the concertgoers and her friends... and Noah, his hands possessively on her hips as he danced behind her. Heart in her throat and skin so sensitive the tiniest brush of his arm against her own made her inner muscles clench, Kit was barely aware of Butch and Casey's watchful presence.

When their group did finally make it to the backstage marquee, the party continued on.

"Oh, *shit.*"

Noah's quiet but vehement exclamation had her looking up at him. They were standing against one "wall" of the marquee, her back to his chest and his arm around her waist as she nibbled on the hot, salty fries she hadn't been able to resist—dancing was exercise, right?—and he drank a beer.

"What is it?"

A nod. "Sarah."

Her eyes widened. The only Sarah she knew who'd get that kind of a reaction from Noah was Abe's ex-wife. From whom Abe had parted in a very, very messy divorce. She'd come after him with the kind of anger a woman only showed when she was either a vindictive money-grubbing bitch or she'd been terribly hurt.

Kit's bet was on the latter. Because while Sarah had always been a little standoffish, Kit had also seen the other woman looking at Abe with a hopeless, painful longing in her eyes. That didn't explain why she'd hooked up with some other guy only months after their separation. To hurt Abe? Or maybe to try to get over a man Kit would bet Sarah hadn't truly wanted to divorce. Then again, you never knew what went on inside another couple's relationship.

Following Noah's line of sight, she spotted the tall woman with lush brown skin speaking to Esteban. Of mixed Puerto Rican and African American descent with a Japanese ancestor thrown into the mix, Sarah had highly distinctive features. Kit had always found her to be one of the most beautiful women she'd ever seen—it wasn't cookie-cutter beauty, but striking. You remembered Sarah.

Her hair was all wicked curls that Kit loved, but Sarah often wore it straightened, as it was tonight. As for her body, it was a knockout. She had both serious curves and serious tone to her. In modeling terms, she'd be a plus size. In real-world terms, she was the kind of woman who, in another time, would've been a pinup.

The last photo Kit had seen of Sarah had featured her with a baby belly, but then had come the sad news of a stillbirth. Hurting for her, Kit had sent a condolence card and flowers. She hadn't been sure Sarah would welcome a visit since they'd never been as close as Kit already was to Molly, despite the fact she'd known Molly for a shorter period. It was as if Sarah had always had a wall around her, a cool, remote distance that made getting to know her difficult.

"Where's Abe?" she asked, putting the rest of her fries aside on a nearby table.

Noah swept the room with his eyes. "On the other side." He looked down at her.

She nodded. "You go make sure he stays there, and I'll talk to Sarah." She would've gone over to say hello anyway, but now she'd be running double duty. No one wanted Abe and Sarah to meet up. The last time that had happened, it had been in divorce court, and from what she'd heard, the atmosphere had been both volcanic and glacial.

Noah swigged back his beer. "If you see the others, give them a heads-up."

"I will." She left with a brush of her fingers against his.

Making her way to Sarah's statuesque form, the other woman dressed in a gorgeous red dress that hugged her curves, she smiled at Esteban when he spotted her first. "Your set was wonderful," she said to the darkly handsome man.

"Thank you." A glance from her to Sarah and back. "You know one another?"

"Of course." Kit held out her hands. "It's good to see you, Sarah."

Esteban was pulled away by Thea at that moment, the other woman smiling at Sarah and Kit both before she led the singer toward a group of people Kit recognized as industry heavyweights.

Sarah returned Kit's squeeze of her hands. "I kept meaning to call you," she said in her lovely contralto. "Thank you for the flowers, the card. It meant a lot."

"I was so sorry to hear about the baby." Giving in to instinct, Kit hugged the taller woman.

Sarah stiffened for only a second before hugging her back. "Sorry," she whispered hoarsely when they drew apart, her dark brown eyes wet, haunted. "I'm still raw about it."

Kit just squeezed her hand again.

"They did too, you know." Quiet words. "David, Noah, and Fox. They sent me flowers." She shook her head. "I didn't expect it, those four are so tight. I know they think I'm a bitch after the divorce and everything, but they still…"

"They knew you for a long time." Sarah and Abe had been married for two years before their separation and eventual divorce.

A smile that wasn't a smile. "I don't think we ever really knew one another. My fault, but none of that matters now. Please thank them for me when you see them. And… thank Abe too."

Accurately reading Kit's surprise, Sarah said, "No, I wasn't expecting it, either."

"I'll tell them," Kit said when Sarah didn't continue, obviously done with the topic. "Sarah, I have to ask—what are you doing here?" Schoolboy Choir was the headlining band, no way to miss that piece of information.

Sarah wrapped her arms around herself, rubbing at her bare forearms. "My fiancé, Jeremy Vance, is backing Stir Crazy."

A band that wasn't as big as Schoolboy Choir but that was starting to make its mark. "Oh." It hadn't been a surprise to Kit that Sarah had ended up with someone else in the industry. After so long with Abe, she must've formed deep friendships of her own. "Well, I guess you and Abe can't avoid each other forever."

Sarah's smile was tight. Lowering her head and the volume of her voice, she said, "I heard about Abe's drug overdose on tour." Lines fanned out from the corners of her mouth, her shoulder muscles stiff. "Is he back on them?"

Kit shook her head. That "drug overdose" had actually been extreme alcohol intoxication, but she didn't know if she had the right to tell Sarah that since the band had kept it out of the media. Abe's problems with drugs were old news and no one paid it much mind. "He's clean," she told Abe's ex-wife. "You know how I am about drugs—I wouldn't tell you that if it wasn't true."

A visible relaxation in Sarah's features. "I'm glad. I—" She cut herself off. "I tried to be there for him for so long, Kit."

"I know." Kit touched Sarah's forearm. "No one thinks you gave up." Sarah had gone through the wringer with Abe, had helped him through relapse after relapse. Kit didn't know what had finally caused Sarah to walk away, but she knew it had to have been brutal to break the will of a woman so strong.

Taking a deep breath, Sarah said, "You were incredible in *Last Flight*. I read online that you might be making another movie with the same team?"

Kit nodded, and they spoke about the movie business for a bit. Sarah wasn't involved in it except on the periphery, since Jeremy dabbled as a producer of teen-oriented movies when he wasn't backing bands, but she had a keen interest in all aspects of the entertainment industry. Kit was just starting to think disaster had been averted when she felt the hairs rise on the back of her neck.

Turning, she saw Abe coming toward them with Noah behind him. Catching her eye, Noah shook his head. Abe, it seemed, was hell-bent on seeing Sarah.

CHAPTER 24

"Y OU'RE HERE," ABE SAID to Sarah when he reached her.

With Abe being such a big guy, most women looked ridiculously delicate next to him. Not Sarah. She looked hot and sexy and as if she could take him. Except right now her spine was stiff, her expression holding a fragility Kit had never before seen.

Not sure what to do, Kit fell back with Noah. "Shall we leave them alone?" she whispered.

Eyes grim, Noah leaned down to murmur against her ear. "I caught a glimpse of her fiancé in the crowd. Have to make sure Abe doesn't go off on him if he appears."

"Abe's over Sarah. Why would he go off on Jeremy Vance?"

"Why do you think he's over Sarah?"

"Er… huge, ugly divorce and countless groupies?"

"Yeah well, things aren't always so simple." Dark gray eyes locked with hers.

Abe brushed past them right then, breaking the moment. "Go," Kit said to Noah. "Make sure he's okay." Abe might be sober, but if anything was going to push him off the ledge, this would be it.

As Noah went after the keyboard player, Kit returned to Sarah. "Are you okay?" she said, seeing the strain on the other woman's face.

A jerky nod. "I have to get some fresh air."

"We'll go out together."

But before Kit could lead Sarah to an exit different from the one used by Abe, Jeremy Vance appeared out of the crowd. "Darling," said the distinguished man with his artfully silvered black hair and aquiline features, his skin tanned a flawless gold. "I was looking for you—I have someone I want you to meet."

Arresting blue eyes landed on Kit, Vance's lips curving. "Kathleen Devigny. I don't think we've ever met in person. A pleasure."

Kit made small talk, then watched helplessly as Jeremy led Sarah away. The other woman had put on a good face, but whatever it was Abe had said to her, it had hit deep and hard. Noah was right—their marriage might be over on paper, but it wasn't over in their hearts, no matter if they appeared to have moved on.

Hurting for them both, she looked around until she spotted a couple she knew and went over to join them. When Noah returned, he tugged her into a slow dance on the improvised dance floor.

"Jesus," he muttered, holding her close. "Abe's fucking torn up. I didn't know what to do, so I grabbed David. He's always been able to calm Abe down."

Kit could see that happening—David was so stable. "Where are they?"

"David took him for a walk." He tightened his arms around her, his hard, muscled body moving just enough to tantalize. "We'll keep him away from Jeremy Vance for another two hours and that's it. No drama."

"Two hours?"

"Sarah told Abe she and Jeremy are leaving via private chopper tonight." He ran his hand down her back, his cheek pressed against her temple. "Now, will you dance with me, Kit?"

The way he held her—there was such tenderness in it that he confused her all over again.

"Yes," she said, surrendering to the magic of this weekend.

And every beat of her heart, it whispered... be with me.

AN HOUR AFTER THE best dance of his life, Noah was sitting on the couch watching a rerun of a football game and psyching himself up to take a sleeping pill when there was a bang on the side of the bus.

"I'll see what it is." Kit, dressed in a short nightgown over which she'd wrapped a kimono-style robe that reached her ankles, ducked out from the kitchenette where she'd been grabbing a glass of water.

She was so fucking beautiful.

That he could've handled. He'd have screwed her and moved on. But Kit, she had a heart and that heart cared about him. He didn't understand it, but he was going to hold on to her care as long as humanly possible.

"Wait." He beat her to the door. "No chances, okay?"

A scowl darkened her face at the reminder of her stalker, but she nodded and stepped back, letting him open the door.

The cause of the disturbance was clear even in the post-midnight darkness. Abe had another man shoved up against the bus, one arm to the guy's neck and his fist cocked back to smash into the man's face.

Jumping out barefoot, Noah slammed out his hand and caught Abe's fist before it would've pulverized the other guy's mug. He didn't care about the stranger. He cared about Abe. The keyboardist was dangerously strong—if he'd landed that punch, he could've done serious damage, ended up in jail for grievous bodily harm.

The security guys Noah had hired to spell Butch and Casey were as big, but they were following orders and staying in position on either end of the bus. He'd made it clear they weren't to leave their posts for anything short of an emergency. All Kit's stalker needed was a single opportunity, a momentary lapse in their concentration.

He was aware of Kit jumping out and flying toward Molly and Fox's bus next door. Abe, meanwhile, was pushing against Noah's hold, causing Noah's biceps to bulge and his body strain to hold position. "Fuck it, Abe, pull back," he gritted out as the man Abe was holding against the bus began to choke.

"Abe, stop!"

Only at the ragged feminine cry did he become aware of another person in the shadows. She'd been kind of crumpled against Fox's bus, which was why Noah hadn't noticed her at first, but now she tugged on Abe's arm. "Stop!"

Shit, it was Sarah. That meant there was a good chance the man Abe was trying to kill was her fiancé. Noah had never understood Abe and Sarah's relationship, but he'd felt Abe's muscles flicker at Sarah's voice, so he didn't tell her to back off.

"Abe!" Sarah cried again. "*Stop it!*"

Making a wordless sound of rage, Abe wrenched back just as Fox appeared. The man behind Noah began to cough and rasp at the same time. "I'm going to fucking call the cop—"

Abe roared and would've come toward the idiot if Fox hadn't body-slammed their bandmate into the side of the bus. Leaving the lead singer to handle Abe, Noah turned to the man—what the hell was his name?—and said, "Shut the fuck up."

The patrician-faced man flinched at Noah's ice-cold voice but squared his shoulders nonetheless. "I'm pressing charges."

"Yeah?" Noah wanted to sock the asshole himself. "You do that and I'm going to release the security-camera footage of Sarah's face and how it got that way." He'd glimpsed the bruises, the bloody lip when she came over to try to stop Abe.

Jeremy Vance, that was his name, swallowed. "There's no footage."

"You sure? After that shit the last asshole tried to pull with Molly and Fox? There sure as fuck are security cameras pointed at all external areas." It was no lie—the cameras were mounted discreetly on different parts of the buses.

The shithead looked unsure. "Your primitive friend isn't worth my time," he said at last in a voice that screamed wealth and breeding.

It had zero impact on Noah; he came from the same cesspool.

"Sarah." Jeremy Vance settled his suit coat as if Abe hadn't almost torn off a sleeve. "Come here. We're leaving."

Noah glanced over his shoulder to see Kit standing with her arm around Sarah, who was still in her party dress. Abe's ex-wife was shivering, her eyes huge with shock. When Abe ripped off his jacket and threw it at Kit, she caught it, put it gently around Sarah.

"*Sarah.*" Jeremy's tone was what another man might use calling a dog.

Abe shoved out again, Fox slamming him back down. Turning to Jeremy, Noah said, "Leave now, or I'll break your face myself. Come near Sarah again, and I won't stop Abe from killing you." And because he understood what held value for men like Jeremy, he added a final icy warning. "You ever even *whisper* about charges against Abe, and I'll make damn certain you're known as the wimp who pounds on women—I'm sure that'll go down great on the charity board and country club circuit." He curled his lip. "I not only know your world, I'm part of a family that fucking rules it." Noah might hate his parents, but he had no compunction about using their connections if those connections would protect a friend.

It was the least Robert and Virginia could do for the son they *hadn't* protected.

The bastard paled and walked off at last. Noah didn't think he'd say a word about this, but he was glad to see Thea appear with David, Molly obviously having run to get the other couple.

"What happened?" Thea asked, taking in everything at a glance, her phone already in hand.

Neither Abe nor Sarah said a word, so Noah filled Thea in as much as possible given what he'd seen. Sarah's face told its own story.

Going up to Sarah, Thea said, "You'll hate me for this, Sarah, but I'm going to take photos of your face." She did it before the other woman could object.

Sarah flinched, her trembling becoming full-out shaking. "I don't want anyone to see." It was a thin whisper.

"No one will." Thea's voice was fierce. Reaching out, she cupped Sarah's bruised face in gentle hands. "This is your insurance against the bastard. He won't be coming near you again."

Sarah gave a jerky nod.

"Let's get you inside," Molly said to Sarah and waved everyone into her and Fox's bus.

Staying behind to lock his and Kit's bus, Noah went over to one of the bodyguards. "Did anyone else come this way? Anyone with a camera? Crew or others who might've seen what happened?"

The tall, heavyset former wrestler shook his head. "No one. I saw the woman and that fuckwit head down from the party tent, and I kept an eye on them since they were cutting through your area. Seemed like they started arguing a few feet from your bus, then they were in the shadows and heading away from this section." His jaw went grim. "I didn't see him hit her or I would've intervened—counts as an emergency in my book."

"Mine too."

"Abe was about a minute behind them. I heard the sound of his voice and then he hauled the other guy back to slam him against your bus." Touching a finger to his earpiece, the guard said, "We've got some partiers coming this way. I'll head them off."

Leaving him to it, Noah stepped inside Fox's bus and pulled the door shut. He couldn't see any of the women, realized they must be in the bedroom. Abe was pacing across the small distance of the living area, his anger as hot now as it had been outside. "The bastard fucking *hit* Sarah," he said, his voice trembling with rage. "You should've let me turn him into paste."

"Yeah, and watch your ass rot in jail." Shoving a hand through his hair, Noah held Abe's furious eyes. "I would've done the same thing, man."

"Yep."

"Yeah."

Fox's and David's immediate agreement seemed to take some of the steam out of Abe. Shuddering, he rubbed his face with both hands. "Can you check she's okay?"

David went and tapped lightly on the closed bedroom door. Thea appeared in the doorway a second later and, pulling it half-shut, came with David. She was dressed in a just-above-knee-length robe in silky blue-gray tied securely over her nightgown, her feet bare and her face naked. Regardless, she was fully armed and ready to do what needed to be done.

"Sarah's okay," Thea said to Abe just as Molly exited the bedroom.

"Fox," she said, "could you grab some ice from the party tent? We need it for her bruises."

"On it." Fox left at once while Molly went to make Sarah a cup of tea.

"Sarah doesn't want to press charges," Thea added, "and that's her choice. I'll keep a record of everything in case Vance ever decides to make trouble."

251

"Has the bastard got her stuff?" Abe said suddenly. "Sarah always carries a purse. I didn't see anything on her."

Noah frowned. "Hold on." Stepping outside, he looked carefully around until he located the spot of shine that had caught his eye as he came in. It was a sequined red clutch. Grabbing the slender thing, he took it inside. "Here."

Abe took it, and for a second, the big guy looked shaken and vulnerable and lost. "She's weird when she doesn't have her purse. It's like her security blanket."

Tugging it gently from his grip, Thea took it to Sarah.

Fox returned half a minute later with ice in a large glass that Molly wrapped up in a hand towel and took into the bedroom.

"Okay," Thea said when she and Molly returned to the living area of the bus, "tell me what happened so we can figure out what someone might've seen, what kind of story they might sell to the tabloids."

"Vance was in a black mood," Abe said flatly. "I could see it, decided to follow to make sure she was okay. Then he hit her."

"Did anyone see you leave?" Thea asked, her eyes on her phone.

Abe rubbed his face again. "I don't know. I wasn't paying attention."

"Jim—one of the bodyguards—says he wasn't followed," Noah told Thea. "I don't think this'll hit the tabloids."

"If it does, I'm going to spin it as jealousy, two men fighting over a woman." Thea's tone brooked no argument. "Sarah stays under until her face heals. I will not have her further abused, this time by the media."

"She can stay here tonight," Molly said softly. "Fox and I left the party early, so we've already had a couple of hours of sleep." She leaned into Fox's embrace as the lead singer stroked her hair.

"We'll make sure she gets home," Fox said. "And that she has someone with her."

Thea nodded as Molly pressed a kiss to Fox's jaw before going to pick up the tea she'd left to steep. "I better take this to her. She's still shocky."

Meanwhile, Thea got on the phone, pulling her assistant out of bed and giving her rapid-fire instructions about watching all possible media outlets for anything concerning Abe, Sarah, or Vance.

Leaving her to it, Noah looked at Abe. Fox and David stepped close enough that the four of them could talk, but Abe wasn't in a talking frame of mind. David, however, had that stubborn look on his face—the drummer was the quietest of them in many ways, but when he dug his heels in, he dug them in.

"Look man," he said now, "whatever's up with you and Sarah—"

"Nothing's up," Abe ground out. "She was being hit. I stepped in. I would've done it for any woman in that situation."

"Yeah, fine." David folded his arms. "But this is Sarah, and the last time you two were together, you went down the rabbit hole."

Abe's jaw was granite. "The drugs weren't Sarah's fault. She never touched the stuff, hated that I did. Fuck, she even flushed my stash down the toilet when she could find it."

"I know," Fox said, "but being with her did something to you." Putting his hands on his hips, he held Abe's gaze. "And being with you didn't make her happy either, so just be careful."

Hands fisted, Abe didn't say anything.

"Fuck it." Noah grabbed the keyboardist's shoulder. "We're just trying to look out for you. We'll look out for her too, make sure she's all right." They'd closed ranks around Abe during the divorce, but this was simple human kindness.

Abe gave a jerky nod. "She doesn't have any family."

Noah hadn't known that, felt a sudden stab of guilt at how he'd judged Sarah for being so possessive and clingy of Abe when they'd been together. Young and alone in a vast city, he couldn't blame her for wanting to hang on to the one person who was hers.

"We'll take care of everything," Thea said, having finished her phone call. "Noah, I need you and Kit to hog the media spotlight, make sure no one feels the need to go digging up other juicy news about the band."

"No problem." He didn't think Kit would mind. "I'll be dropping her home tomorrow, so that'll give the vultures plenty to salivate over." He felt Fox's eyes burn into him as Thea nodded and returned to the bedroom. The lead singer didn't say anything until after Kit, Thea, and Molly had come out of the bedroom, having left Sarah tucked up in the bed.

Molly stayed in the bus in case Sarah needed anything, while Kit and Thea went across to Noah's bus to get a cup of coffee. David took Abe for another cooling-off walk; the levelheaded drummer was the best person for it.

"You and Kit," Fox said quietly, the two of them standing between the buses. "What's happening there?"

Noah was the one who folded his arms this time. "None of your business."

"Screw that, Noah. What I said to Abe? Applies double here—you broke her heart."

Noah flinched at the pitiless words. Fox was the only one who knew what he'd done to Kit, having seen her directly after she found Noah in bed with the groupie. "I won't hurt her again," he said to the man who'd been his best friend since they were seven.

"You sure?" Fox raised an eyebrow, dark green eyes unforgiving. "I've seen the way she looks at you—the way *you* look at her. Don't try to bullshit me that you're both acting."

Noah didn't have an answer for that. He knew he was taking advantage of Kit. "I haven't lied to her."

"Have you told her everything?"

"No. She doesn't need to know." Noah would go to the grave keeping that information from Kit. "Don't you tell her," he said, fisting his hands in Fox's T-shirt and hauling the other man in. "Don't you fucking say a word."

Fox shoved him back. "You think I'd do that?" It was a low snarl.

Thrusting his hands through his hair, Noah blew out a breath. "Fuck. No." He drew deep drafts of the cold air. "The idea of her knowing..." He shook his head, unable to describe the humiliated anguish it caused in him.

"I get it," Fox said quietly. "But this is Kit. She was your friend first, is still your friend. Maybe you should trust her."

CHAPTER 25

KIT WOKE WITH HER heart thumping. A glance at the watch she'd left on the built-in nightstand told her it had only been two hours since she'd gone to bed. Sarah had been asleep by the time everyone returned to their buses, and they'd made plans to meet in the morning in case Fox and Molly needed any help getting the other woman home without tipping off the media.

Rubbing at her eyes, she figured it must've been a very late partier outside who'd woken her. She couldn't hear music any longer, but people were no doubt up and about. She'd just turned onto her side when she heard it—a low, harsh sound, like an animal caught in a trap and unable to escape. Shoving aside the thin comforter she'd pulled over herself, she jumped out of bed and ran to the living area.

Noah was lying on the air mattress, having kicked off the sleeping bag. Dressed in black boxer briefs, he was curled up on his side, his hands fisted and his teeth gritted so hard that she could see bone white against skin, muscle and tendon taut enough to snap.

Dropping to her knees beside him, she said, "Noah. Noah!" When he didn't wake, that horrible sound still coming from his throat, she put her hand on his bare shoulder and shook. "Noah, wake up!"

Nothing.

Oh no, he'd taken the sleeping pills. He'd done it in front of her, after showing her the bottle. "There," he'd said, throwing them back dry. "I'll sleep. Happy?"

She *had* been happy, thinking he'd finally get some rest. Now she realized she'd made a terrible mistake. "Noah," she said, shaking him again. "Noah, wake up, *please*. Noah." Crying now, she shook and shook, but he wouldn't wake from his drugged nightmare.

Not knowing what to do, she ran to the bedroom and grabbed her phone, found Fox's number. Fox had known Noah the longest, might understand what this was. "Fox," she said when he answered the phone on the first ring. "Noah won't wake up and he's having a horrible dream."

"I'm on my way."

"Just you!" she said before he hung up. "Not Molly." She loved the other woman, but she wouldn't let anyone but Fox see Noah like this.

"Just me."

He was at the bus door—which Kit had opened—within half a minute after hanging up. Coming inside and pulling the door shut behind him, he said, "Did he take something?"

"Sleeping pills." She pointed to the bottle on the counter of the kitchenette. "Nothing strong. I checked. It's just meant to make him drowsy so he'd drift off." She stroked back Noah's sweat-damp hair. "Noah, please wake up."

Fox didn't say anything. Hauling Noah up, he hit him across the face hard enough that it had Kit jerking back.

About to shove the lead singer away from Noah, she suddenly realized Noah had stopped making that trapped, painful sound. "Noah?"

He shook his head slightly, but his eyes remained heavy. Settling behind him, she tugged so that he leaned against her. "Noah, it's Kit."

"Kit."

Wrapping her arms around him from the back at the mumble, she just held him. "It's me, I have you." Her eyes met the smoky green of Fox's. "You've done this before." He hadn't even hesitated in hitting Noah—he'd known it was the only thing that would work. "Will he be all right?"

Fox, his face grim, grabbed Noah's chin. "Noah. You there?"

A faint nod.

Getting up, Fox said, "I'm going to put on some coffee. Pour it down his throat when it's ready. Don't let him fall back asleep."

"I won't." Wiping the heel of one hand over her eyes, she said, "Noah, did you tell Fox about 'Sparrow' yet?"

A slow scowl on Noah's face. "Shuddup."

Wet laughter shook her body. "Make me."

"Kit." He raised a hand, closed it over her forearm. "Pretty Kit."

The scent of coffee filled the air. Going to the door, Fox said, "He'll stay a little dopey for a while, so don't take advantage. I'm going to leave so he can focus on you—it should help." With that, the lead singer was gone.

Kit tugged hard on Noah's hair when his eyes began to close. "Stay awake."

"Mean Hallucination Kit."

"Going from pretty to hallucination?" Easing him down, she went to quickly grab some coffee.

It only took her a few seconds, but his eyes were closed by the time she came back. "Hey!" She couldn't bring herself to hit him, so she pulled his hair again. "I'm going to tell Fox about 'Sparrow.'"

His eyes flicked open. "Hallucination Kit's not nice."

"No, I'm not." Putting down the cup, she pushed and tugged until he was upright enough that she could get behind him again, cradling his back against her chest. "Noah!"

He muttered grumpily at her, but she didn't care. Not so long as he was awake and not locked in whatever hell it was that had held him captive.

God, she loved him.

There, she'd said it, even if it was only in her head. She loved him. Damaged and beautiful and talented, he was the only man she'd ever loved, no matter if he'd stomped on her heart.

"Drink this coffee," she ordered after blowing on it to cool it down.

"Coffee from Mean Hallucination Kit," he mumbled, letting her put the cup to his lips.

She got half a cup down him. He spoke in disjointed pieces between sips. Sometimes he made her laugh, but mostly she was so worried about him that she focused every ounce of her attention on keeping him awake. "I am *never* letting you take sleeping pills again," she said at one point, rubbing her cheek against the bristled roughness of his.

"Hate sleeping pills," he muttered, able to hold his own coffee cup now. "Make me scream."

Kit froze, caught in a moment when she knew she could have the answer to every question she'd ever had about Noah.

Don't take advantage.

Fox's light comment suddenly held a deeper, darker meaning. Kit opened her mouth, about to give in to temptation… and couldn't. Because whatever she discovered this way would be tainted and would always taint anything they built, whether it was a continuing friendship or something deeper.

Swallowing the questions, she kissed the side of his temple. "Finish drinking your coffee."

"Enough." He put down the nearly empty cup. "I'm jumpy." A yawn cracked his mouth, but he kept his eyes open. "Pretty Hallucination Kit."

Not lucid, she realized, just a touch more coherent. "Pretty Drunk Noah."

He started laughing as if that was the most hilarious thing he'd ever heard. "Not drunk," he said at last, a heavy scowl on his face. "Sleeping pills. Hate sleeping pills."

"I know. I'm sorry I made you take them." She hadn't understood, hadn't realized the terrors that haunted him. "I won't do it again."

He patted her forearm. "'S okay." Another yawn. "I want to sleep."

Kit went to tell him to stay awake, but a glance at the phone she'd dropped nearby told her it was nearly dawn. Maybe he could sleep now? "Will the bad dreams come?" she asked, hoping she wasn't inadvertently crossing a line.

He shrugged. "Maybe. But need sleep."

Kit eased him down. "Okay, but I'm going to dump ice water on you if you won't wake up when I shake you."

"'Kay." A frown, lines between his eyes. "Alone."

It took her a second. "Okay." She picked up the sleeping bag and put it over him, then went into the bedroom. If Noah needed to be alone to get rest, then she'd give him solitude—but she'd still keep a careful eye on him.

NOAH WOKE WITH COTTON wool in his mouth and a bladder that was about to burst. Stumbling to the toilet, he shut the door and did what needed to be done, then turned to the sink and threw water on his face. The shock of cold brought a few of his senses back to him.

That was when he noted the bruise on his left cheekbone.

Opening the door, he said, "Kit?"

She poked her head out of the bedroom. "You're awake." A brilliant smile, her gorgeous hair tumbling over the vivid blue of her robe.

"Did I fall flat on my face?" He indicated the bruise.

"No." She winced. "You kind of ran into Fox's hand."

Fuck. He'd taken the fucking pills. "How bad?"

"You wouldn't wake up, but once you did, you were quite funny." A crooked smile. "You called me Mean Hallucination Kit."

He felt his gut turn to lead. "What else did I say?"

"Nothing, except for telling me what you thought of certain bands and how you hated sleeping pills." Her eyes, bleak and dark, went to the bruise on his face. "I'm sorry, Noah. I didn't know the pills would lock you into a nightmare."

The lead grew heavier. "You saw my nightmare?"

She nodded.

261

"What did I say?"

"Nothing." She held his eyes. "I didn't ask you and you didn't say."

He finally took a breath. "Thank you."

Kit shook her head. "Don't thank me. I pushed you into this." Wrapping her arms around herself, she rocked slightly on her feet. "You can't go on like this, not for three more weeks or however long it takes."

"We've had this argument." He grabbed her wrist. "I can do it." He couldn't have her give up on him.

"I know you can." Tugging at her wrist, she tried to extricate it, but when he refused to let go, she stopped attempting to pull away. "I want you to move in with me."

He stared at her. "What?" Having his own space, his own bolt-hole, had always been critical.

"You've slept over before," she pointed out. "You might've been blind drunk the last time, but the other times you were sober."

He'd snuck out and run for hours each of those nights, fallen asleep out of exhaustion. It had only been for a fitful few hours, but he had slept. "Why do you want me to move in with you?" He had to know what she expected, because there were things he simply couldn't give her.

She touched his bruised cheek, her fingers featherlight. "You asked me to be with you."

His entire world trembled.

He knew he should call back that request. It was beyond selfish. But his throat, it wouldn't work.

"If we're going to make a relationship work *in any way*," she said, "we have to figure this out."

"I'm almost twenty-eight years old, Kit. If I could figure it out, I would have by now." He turned into the tender warmth of her hand.

"I bet you've always tried to do it alone, haven't you?" She didn't wait for an answer. "We do it together this time."

Noah wanted to say she was wrong, that it wouldn't work, but he *hadn't* ever tried to figure this out with someone else. Even with Fox, they'd only discussed it that one time when he'd been a scared seven-year-old boy. Never again.

And there lay the crux of it. "How can you fix something if you don't even know why it's broken?" Because he wouldn't tell her. The idea of Kit knowing? It savaged him.

"I know something really bad happened to you," she whispered. "Bad enough that one of the toughest men I know is still haunted by it."

He flinched. "I'm not tough." If he had been, he would've gotten over this long ago.

"I'll be the judge of that." Her wrist still in his hand, she said, "Will you come home with me?"

"Yes," he said, a desolate nothingness inside him.

This would fail. When it did, so would all the hope inside him that one day he might be normal, might have the right to love Kit.

CHAPTER 26

LATE AFTERNOON THE NEXT day, Kit smiled and flirted with the cameras as she and Noah drove through the gates of her home in Noah's convertible. He'd be returning to his place later to grab clothes and other things, but given the situation with Abe and Sarah—and since this media circus was inevitable—they'd decided to handle it together.

The funny thing, Kit thought as Noah laughed at something one of the photographers had yelled out, was that she no longer cared about either the movie or the cosmetics deal. Her career was important to her, but the most important thing in her life was in the driver's seat, and he was badly, badly hurt inside. Kit didn't think she was a magician, didn't believe she could heal him, but she could love him.

Maybe it would help a little.

Maybe it might even be enough to stop him from continuing on the self-destructive path he'd been walking to this point.

"Kathleen! Give us a smile!"

She gave the photographer what he wanted, wondering why anyone cared what she was doing and who she was doing it with. She knew it was good that they did, that it helped her make a living doing the work she loved, but today she just wanted to be alone with Noah.

However, it took them another five minutes to get through the gates. Reaching the house not long afterward, the two of them got out in silence. Kit glanced reflexively into the backseat of the convertible. "Noah, did you leave that gift in there?"

"No." Frowning, he went to pick up the card stuck to the package, which was wrapped in gold paper.

"Wait." She took off the thin, colorful silk scarf she was wearing and passed it to him. "In case there are fingerprints." She was probably being paranoid, the gift something a fan had managed to drop in during the media fracas outside, but she had to be sure.

Using the scarf to pick up the card, Noah opened it with care. The dangerous ice in his expression answered her silent question. When she went around to his side, he wrapped his arm around her while holding the card out of reach. "You don't need to see this. It's the same ugly bullshit."

"I have to see it. I have to know what's in his sick head so I can protect myself."

A muscle jumped in Noah's jaw, but he brought the card close enough that she could read it. As usual, the message wasn't handwritten but made up of words and letters cut out of magazines and newspapers.

You slut. I bought these chocolates for you, but now I hope you choke on them. How dare you cheat on me with that asshole rocker? Wait until I get my hands on you.

A shudder going through her, she closed her eyes. But only for a second. "Come on. Fox made me invest in full security coverage at the gate after that pap tried to get him arrested." At the time, she'd whimpered at the further cost, but now it might give them their first glimpse of her stalker. "Butch is an expert at the system."

Noah made the call to the bodyguard, who'd remained by the gate.

After updating Butch once he arrived, Kit led both men to the security room inside the house. First, however, she ducked into the kitchen and found a paper bag into which Noah could drop the card and gift-wrapped package.

"I'll pass that on to the cops," Butch said.

Placing the bag beside him in front of the security screens, he quickly brought up the relevant footage. But no matter how carefully they examined it, no one appeared to drop anything into the backseat.

"It could've been done as you slowed down to turn into the gate, where the cameras don't reach, or anywhere else you stopped—even at the traffic lights," Butch said. "Remember that group of fans that congregated against the car to take photos? Plus you picked up coffee from a drive-through." Butch's expression was dark. "I clearly wasn't watching closely enough."

"It's not your fault." Kit touched his arm. "You were watching for physical threats, not this kind of cowardice."

Noah looked at the video again, eyes narrowed. "I am never again driving the Mustang with the top down when I have you in the passenger seat."

"Yes, you are." Kit scowled at him. "Don't let the creep get to you—that's what he does." Already he'd forced Kit into crushing debt. That, she hadn't been able to avoid, but she wasn't about to allow him to steal such small pleasures from her or Noah's life.

"I'll go help Casey with the sweep, make sure the bastard didn't get in." Butch picked up the paper bag. "And I'll get this to the cops ASAP."

Tugging her close after the bodyguard left, Noah held her with one arm, burying the fingers of his other hand in her hair. "That's it. I'm never moving out."

Kit smiled despite the circumstances. "Wait until I want you to watch *Dancing with the Stars* with me."

"Oh Jesus, *Dancing with the Stars*? Really? I thought you were a football kind of woman."

"I can like both." Laughing at his expression, she said, "You hungry?"

"No, you?"

"No." She tapped a finger on her lower lip. "Why don't you go grab the rest of your stuff? It's not like the paps are going to leave when it gets dark."

Reaching out to tangle his fingers with her own, Noah said, "Want to come with?"

Kit's pulse kicked. She had to fight to keep her voice from betraying what his invitation did to her. "Yes."

THANKS TO A TRAFFIC jam caused by a Mercedes that had rear-ended an Aston Martin, with both drivers deciding to be assholes about it, it took Noah forty minutes to get to his place. He'd already had stuff on the bus, as well as his instruments, and they'd all been shipped to Kit's, but there were a few other things he needed.

"Sorry about the mess," he said to the one woman who mattered. He still didn't understand why it was so hard for him to have Kit here, but it was. Even now, after he'd specifically invited her to accompany him, his muscles were tight, his chest aching.

"It's not as bad as I expected." She stepped around a bunch of autobiographies he'd left stacked on the carpet beside the sofa, which faced the entertainment area. "I do think the mold in that takeout box is probably growing legs by now though."

Picking up the box, he threw it at her. She caught it reflexively. "Ew!" But then she looked down, eyes going wide. "Hey! This is fake."

"Abe gave it to me for my birthday. Since I live on takeout, he figured I should have an appropriate piece of art."

"This is art?" Appearing dubious, she looked at it carefully from every angle before placing it on the coffee table. "I didn't know Abe hated you."

Grinning, he headed to the other end of the house to grab what he needed. His place was spread out all on one level, but it wasn't open plan. He liked doors and walls, which was fucked-up, because he *didn't* like being locked in. But if he had to be inside, he wanted it to be in small spaces where he could see everything at a glance.

His room in his parents' home had been huge, a suite far too big for a small boy. Unlike Kit's toy store of a room, his had been filled with educational items, charts, and books. He'd had his own desk and computer and a rotation of tutors who were on twenty-four-hour call should he have a question about the homework they'd assigned.

His father had him studying toward the SATs before he was five years old—and since study questions were the one time his father had all the time in the world for him, Noah had *liked* it. If things hadn't gone to hell just over a year later, he'd probably have turned into a suit-and-tie-wearing robot like his old man. Christ.

As he chucked things into a duffel, he was aware of Kit moving around in the living area—and also aware that she hadn't gone any deeper into the house. Respecting the boundaries he'd set... and that just felt weird. He'd never brought her here, but now that he had, he wanted her to feel at home. "Hey, Kit!"

"What?"

"Go left, then out through the first door on your right, before the wall of glass. You'll like it."

FOLLOWING NOAH'S INSTRUCTIONS, KIT finally ventured out of the living area. She hadn't wanted to intrude, conscious Noah wasn't sure about having her here. That hurt, but it was a small enough thing and one she couldn't cling to if she wanted to give them a real second chance. Instead, she concentrated on the fact he'd invited her to come with him today, went through a narrow door... and into someone's attempt at a Japanese garden.

She laughed, so delighted she couldn't hold it inside. "This is terrible!" The plants were all wrong, the placements having none of the peaceful elegance of a garden meant to promote serenity.

"Hey!"

Following the insulted sound of Noah's voice, she found he'd stepped out onto a balcony farther down the house. "I did my best!"

Kit grinned and leaned down to tug up a few weeds. He kept confusing her. He didn't want her here, but this garden? It was an attempt at creating a piece of her inside his home— because his garden was walled in by wings of the house. As if he was holding her heart inside his protection.

Her chest filled with emotion.

"Who looks after this while you're on tour?" she asked him when he came over. "They haven't been doing a good job." Nothing had been trimmed, the weeds rampant.

"No one. It's set up with sprinklers, but after a tour, it tends to be a bit of a jungle." He ran his hand over her hair.

Startled at the unexpected contact, she looked up into those eyes of darkest gray. "What?"

"It's nice, seeing you here."

She was still trying to process the words when he turned on his heel to return to his bedroom. As if he'd shown her too much and needed walls between them.

Rubbing a fisted hand over her breastbone, she watched him until he disappeared, and she told herself to have patience and hope. If she didn't have both, she might as well give up now.

But even as she told herself that, a small, secret part of her remained curled up in a self-protective ball. Because Noah had hurt her once already. So much. And that self-protective part of her wasn't sure he wouldn't hurt her again, wouldn't betray her again.

NOAH HAD STAYED OVER at Kit's before, but it felt different now. Awkward. He wasn't sure what they were doing, what he should be doing, but he knew he didn't intend to mess it up. "Hey," he said, walking into the kitchen about twenty minutes after they'd arrived back at her place, having once more navigated the paparazzi gauntlet.

There'd been a few loitering at his place too, but most had made the right call and parked out at Kit's. They were still out there, even though it was now after eight and there was little chance either he or Kit would venture out, given that they'd just returned from Zenith.

"Hey." Kit's smile was like goddamn sunshine, going straight through his skin to own him. "Want to help me cook?"

"Sure." At least it'd keep him busy so he didn't fuck up. "What do you want me to do?"

"Grill stuff."

"I'm your man." He was even pretty good at the grilling thing. "Where's the meat?"

"Fish."

He tried to control his face, but she laughed. "You are so transparent. I thawed a steak for you. Fish for me." She held up a thin bamboo spike. "I'm putting together some vegetable skewers to grill too."

Having helped her carry the small bowls of vegetables and a cutting board out to the patio area off the back of her kitchen, he put everything on the small wrought iron table she had out there, then pushed up the lid on the grill. Her Japanese garden was off to the left, but she'd planted plenty of lush greenery here too, cocooning the space in whispering quiet.

271

As he got the grill going, she sat at the table and put the skewers together. They were colorful with bell peppers and things, and he was actually looking forward to eating them.

"I made a marinade for the vegetables," she said conversationally as she worked. "With honey and spices and my secret ingredient."

Noah's lips tugged up at the corners. "Did David teach you?"

"Busted!" Her laughter filled the air, filled the hollow spaces inside him.

There was more laughter as they finished making the meal, more smiles, until nothing was awkward. He felt like he was home. The food was good, but the best thing was sitting out here under the early evening sky with Kit across from him.

Too bad the simple pleasure of it couldn't last. His mind began to race as they finished clearing up, a rat on a wheel. What the hell was he going to do when it was time to sleep? He wasn't about to take the pills, and his other "drug" of choice was now permanently off the menu. The only thing he could do was run, but he wasn't going to leave Kit alone in the house when her stalker was back.

So do push-ups or sit-ups until you exhaust yourself enough to catch some shut-eye, he ordered himself. *Do* not *screw this up.*

"You know there's a *Dancing with the Stars* special on tonight, right?"

He groaned, his worry about sleep momentarily erased. "You're really going to make me watch?"

She bumped him with her shoulder. "I'm *inviting*. If you'd rather do something else, I don't care."

Laughing at her fake-insulted tone, he said, "Since when are you passive-aggressive?"

A wink as she grabbed a packet of frozen blueberries from the freezer and poured a handful into a bowl. "This is war." She held up the bag. "You want some?"

The invitation made his breath get all hard and jagged inside him. He'd never eaten frozen blueberries before Kit introduced him to what was one of her favorite desserts. And now here he was again, being given a second chance. "No, I'm good." Trying to breathe normally, he followed her to the lounge, sprawling beside her as she took a seat on the sofa with her legs curled under her.

Since she hadn't told him to stop doing it, he stretched out his arm along the back of the sofa and played with her hair.

Reaching back, she tugged off her hair tie so that the fall of silken strands cascaded over his hand. "You sure you don't want a blueberry or three?"

"You twisted my arm." He twined her hair around his fingers. "Gimme."

She popped a couple into his mouth. Their eyes connected.

The intro to the show came on a second later, breaking the incipient tension of the sweetly intimate moment.

Noah had never had so much fun watching random famous and semi-famous people try to dance. He had to admit he had a new and serious respect for a few of them for putting themselves out there, but mostly he was horrified. "Spandex? Wasn't that made illegal like two decades ago?"

Elbowing him, Kit spluttered with laughter. "Stop it."

"Fuck me, he's wearing *sequins.*"

"Rock stars have been known to wear sequins."

"No rock star in his right mind has ever worn sequins in that—" His mouth fell open. "Is that a codpiece? For real?" Snorting, he said, "No way except in his dreams is his dick that big. He's probably got two bananas in there."

Face going red as she tried to hold in laughter, Kit ended up against him. He curled his arm around her, realizing he didn't have to fight his need. She'd said they could try, and he liked having Kit's warm, laughing body next to his.

She stayed against him, and every so often when he made a particularly deplorable comment, she'd lightly hit his thigh and tell him to behave. Every other time a woman had touched his thigh, it had been about sex. The first couple of times Kit did it, he tensed, but then it was okay. It was Kit and they were watching a silly show on television that she inexplicably liked. It was normal.

He hadn't been normal for a long time.

CHAPTER 27

KIT WORRIED ABOUT NOAH when they headed to bed, but she didn't want to push him on the sleep issue after the disaster with the pills. Not to mention she didn't want to end his first day here with a fight. Smiling good night, she spent an hour awake and worrying before finally drifting off—only to wake three hours later. It took her sleep-muddled brain a minute to realize what had woken her: noises from Noah's room.

Getting up, she pulled on her blue robe and went out to look for him. His door was open, but there was no Noah inside. A whisper of wind along the hallway told her where he'd gone. She padded to the door that led out into the garden, found him sitting on the outdoor bench in his boxer briefs, his head between his hands and his elbows on his thighs. She could see his face in the soft light from the solar-powered paper lanterns she'd hung out there.

The naked anguish in his expression threatened to break her.

Pulling back before he saw her, she pressed her spine against the wall, swallowing repeatedly and blinking in an attempt to get the burning in her eyes under control. Only when she was no longer in danger of breaking down did she step out. "Can't sleep?"

His head jerked up. "Shit. I woke you."

"Want to go for a run?"

He stared at her. "It's two thirty in the morning."

"So?" Turning to go back into the house, she said, "I'm getting changed."

"You hate running."

"Doesn't mean I can't do it."

He knocked on her bedroom door half a minute after she'd closed it. "Kit, it's fine."

Having already pulled out her running shorts, she opened the door. "Noah, we're in this together. You watched *Dancing with the Stars* with me. I'll go running with you. Now go get changed." She shut the door in his face.

"*Kit.*"

"I'm awake now and I'm going running. Your choice if you want to join me."

An infuriated sound came through the door, but she heard him moving to his room, and when she stepped out in her running clothes, her hair corralled into a ponytail, he was there. "We can run around inside your property," he said, holding up a hand when she would've objected. "This stalker guy watches you. We can't take the risk that he's out there and he has a gun."

She threw up her hands. "I don't think he can run that fast, but whatever." At least this mortgaged-to-the-hilt estate had enough land to make for a good lap.

NOAH PUT HIS HANDS on his hips, eyes narrowed. Kit never said things like "whatever" in that tone of voice. "What's wrong with you?"

A growling sound. "When did I say I was a morning person?" With that, she turned and headed out. "Pull the door shut and set the alarm."

Glad she was thinking smart and not relying blindly on her security guys, he input the code to arm the security system, then pulled the door shut. It locked automatically behind them. Kit was in front of him, warming up. Noah never warmed up—he just ran until the nightmares couldn't keep up, but today he stretched to keep Kit company. When they began to run, it was to head down a pathway that wove through the trees on her property.

It took him a minute to figure out the right pace. Kit was fit, but his stride was longer and he ran far more than she did. Running was hands down her least favorite form of exercise. It should've irritated him that he had to slow down for her, but he liked having her beside him, liked that he wasn't alone in the dark. The fact that she chose to be with him even when she didn't like running?

Yeah, that did all kinds of things inside him.

"You going to build a pool?" That, he knew, had been a significant downside to this property, but she'd bought it anyway because she'd been in a hurry. Not content with ejaculating on her bed, her disturbed stalker had slipped love notes under the town house door. She'd had to get out.

"When I have the money," Kit replied.

"I have the money."

"I'll pretend you didn't say that."

The night wind rippling through his hair, he set his jaw. "If we're going to live together, I get to contribute." He *wanted* to contribute, to do things that turned this from her place to theirs, entangling them together on another level.

"Right now we haven't even lived together a single day. Let's talk when it's been a year."

"Two months."

Kit snorted. "Eight."

"Six."

"Fine."

He grinned. "What kind of pool do you want?"

Slanting him a glance, she said, "Shut up and run."

He laughed and they ran, the night a starlit quiet around them. They passed one of the security guys, kept going with a nod of hello. It took four circuits around the property before Kit stopped at her front door. "Enough?" she said, her breath jagged and her hands on her knees.

"Yeah." He usually ran for hours, but then he was usually alone. Running with Kit had been different—he didn't know if he was tired enough to catch some shut-eye, but at least he no longer felt as twisted and black inside. "Let's go in."

HE DID SLEEP. NOT much, but about the same amount he did after exhausting himself—or by fucking out his rage. Not that it had exactly been the latter when he screwed those random groupies. There was a twisted version of male pride involved too, but he didn't have to think about his fucked-up psyche today. Because today when he woke, it wasn't with the taste of disgust in his mouth but to the scent of coffee.

Wandering out of the bedroom without bothering to pull on jeans over the black of his boxer briefs—Kit had seen it all before anyway—he yawned as he stepped into the kitchen. "I thought you'd sleep in."

She didn't look away from the box she was reading. "Can't. Body clock."

"What's that?" Leaning on the counter, he stole her coffee and took a deep gulp.

"Waffle mix."

His stomach rumbled.

Glancing across the counter, her lips began to curve before her expression morphed into a scowl. "You look terrible."

KIT WAS LYING—NOAH looked gorgeous. His hair was all rumpled, his shoulders golden and sleek with muscle, his upper body far too beautiful for her peace of mind.

And his eyes, those gray eyes, were full of light.

"Gee, thanks, Katie."

"No waffles for you."

"Hey, come on!" A grin that made him impossibly more beautiful. Putting down her coffee mug, he came around the counter, and damn it, he wasn't wearing jeans. "I bet I can convince you otherwise."

When he put his hands on her hips and tugged her forward, she slammed the box of waffle mix against his chest. "Stop right there, mister." Her stomach was flipping, her skin hot.

He wrapped his arms around her instead and leaned in to press his forehead against hers. "Good morning."

"I hate mornings," she said, trying to keep her voice strong. It was difficult—she'd never seen Noah like this. In a good mood, yes, but never this good. He seemed to be smiling with his whole body. If this was what she got to wake up to every day, she might just come to like mornings.

"I'll make the waffles from scratch," he said, his cheeks creasing.

Her mouth fell open. "Since when can you cook?"

"I didn't say I could cook. I said I could make waffles." Moving one hand to her face, he cupped her cheek, that heartbreaker smile still on his face. "I had a job in a diner once, remember? Not long after the guys and I first came to LA. Anyway, the cook taught me."

"Female cook?" she asked and saw the answer in his wicked smile. Affecting a scowl, she pushed at his shoulders, had to fight not to keep stroking the hot silk of his skin. "Let's see these famous waffles." She didn't really want him to release her. Being close to Noah when he was like this... it made her want to laugh and cry at the same time.

He rubbed his thumb over her cheek before letting go. "Where's your flour?"

"Same place as your pants," she muttered and, when he threw back his head and laughed, couldn't help her own smile. "Go put on clothes or you might burn something important."

Still grinning, he returned to his bedroom and came back out wearing only a pair of jeans she recognized—hard not to when the denim had a tear just below his butt and threadbare patches all over. "Do you wear those outside?"

A shrug. "I wore them onstage during the tour."

Jealousy bit into her with sharp little teeth. Stomach tensing, she shoved away the nasty, vicious emotion. Being jealous of all the women who wanted Noah—who'd been with him—would destroy the two of them before they ever had a shot. She had to let it go, but it was hard. So damn hard.

"Found it!" He held up her flour container with a triumphant look on his face.

Smiling, because how could she not with him here, looking at her that way, she helped gather the other ingredients. He was just finishing up the batter while the waffle iron heated when her cell phone rang.

Glancing at the screen, she saw it was her agent. "Harper?" she said, figuring it had to be bad news if the other woman was calling her at six thirty in the morning. "Hit me with it."

"Esra Dali just called." Harper's voice was ebullient. "Wants you in for a screen test at ten."

Kit gripped the edge of the counter. "You sure he wasn't drunk?" she asked, trying to keep her heart from racing and failing spectacularly. "Pretty early for a call."

"He keeps crazy hours. You make sure you get your butt down to the studios by ten, otherwise I'll disavow all knowledge of you."

"Where do I need to go?" Writing down the details, she hung up to see the gorgeous rocker in her kitchen pouring batter into the waffle iron.

It was as wonderfully surreal a sight as the words she spoke. "I have a screen test for *Redemption*."

Noah's face lit up. "Fuck yeah."

AN HOUR AND A half later, after they'd polished off the waffles and she was in her garden, meditating to put herself into the right mind-set for the screen test, Harper called back. The normally cool and collected agent was beside herself.

Thanks to Kit's suddenly red-hot profile, the cosmetics company had sent in a revised offer that extended her proposed contract to include all international markets. "I don't see any nasty clauses this time," Harper said, "though I'm flicking it to the legal eagles to check. You should be signing on the dotted line tomorrow if all goes well."

Kit hung up to the knowledge that her financial problems were close to over and that, if all went well, her career was about to shoot into the stratosphere. She should've been as ecstatic as Harper, but…

Her eyes lingered on Noah where he sat against the cherry blossom tree, lazily strumming his guitar while she sat cross-legged on a yoga mat a short distance from him. The music didn't bother her when she meditated—she liked it, liked him nearby. But even when physically close, it felt as if he stood an ocean apart from her.

It wasn't the sex. She hungered for Noah until she couldn't breathe, but if sex hurt him to the point that it had become a weapon he used to self-harm, then she'd find a way to deal. No, what caused her pain was that he didn't trust her enough to tell her what had caused the still-bleeding wound on his soul.

Lifting his head, he met her gaze, and in his eyes she saw a future with a man who was her best friend, but a best friend who'd keep his secrets, keep part of his soul forever hidden from her.

Could she live with that?

CHAPTER 28

NOAH PUT THE TOP firmly on his convertible before he and Kit left for the screen test. He said it was to protect her hair, but Kit's expression told him she knew that was a load of BS. Noah waited for her to argue, but his mind was made up: no way was he permitting the stalker to ruin a day that could mark a watershed moment in her career.

Though she shook her head at him, she didn't try to make him change his mind, and they rolled out of the drive a couple of minutes later to the flash of cameras. The vultures were all hoping for some kind of an exclusive to fuel the current media feeding frenzy.

"What the fuck do they think we'll do?" he said to Kit once they'd made it out. "Strip naked and dance together in front of the gate?"

"Will Taylor."

Noah groaned. "He doesn't count." The country music star hadn't only been caught with his pants down while he fucked his mistress during an island getaway, he'd then been photographed standing stark-naked in front of a hotel window while a different woman gave him a blowjob. Turned out he'd thought the window was reflective. "In fact, you can never use Will to score points in any conversation. It's too easy."

"At least he was wearing his cowboy hat," Kit said with a laugh. "It would've been *seriously* embarrassing if he was caught bareheaded."

"Stop right there. I don't want to think about what another guy was wearing while a groupie sucked him off."

A sudden silence from the passenger seat, no riposte. And he realized what he'd said. He'd never been photographed, but how many groupies had sucked him off? He couldn't remember their names, probably hadn't ever known them, their faces a blur and their mouths doing things to him that made his body respond though his heart remained frozen.

Most of the time, it had felt as if he was standing outside his body, watching someone else be touched. The times when he *was* present, that was when the rage came out, when he turned brutal. He'd never hurt a woman, but on the rage nights, he made sure to pick a woman who made it clear she could take it. Then he used her, shoving her out after he was done. That was who he'd been for a long time: a bastard who didn't really see women as anything other than objects he could use to drown out the nightmares.

Then had come Kit.

"Sorry." It was a blindingly inadequate apology, but he didn't know what else to say. He couldn't erase his past. If he could, he'd have done it as a child, wiped the memories from his mind so he could have a chance to grow up normal.

"Don't say that." Kit's soft response was unexpectedly fierce. "This won't work if you feel like you have to keep apologizing." Her hands were white-knuckled fists on her thighs. "We have to start fresh, start now."

Noah knew it wasn't going to be that simple—their history was what tied them together. He also knew that part of the problem was that he'd given those women something he wouldn't give Kit.

His hands flexed on the steering wheel, his entire body tense.

If he slept with Kit, he'd end up either in the cold or in the grip of rage. Those were his only choices, and he didn't want to stain their relationship with that ugliness. But… would it be so bad if it would make Kit happy? He always knew when the rage times were coming, so he'd just pick a cold time.

She'd never know—he was apparently decent at sex. Not the long, lazy act he'd seen in on-screen romances or read about. The hard, fast stuff. It was mechanical on his part, but none of the women had ever complained.

Muscles locked tight, he decided he'd do it tonight.

It'd be worth it to strengthen the bond between him and Kit.

"Turn here." Her voice broke into his thoughts, chipped away at the ice. "Security should have our names."

Following her directions to the right parking area after they were cleared through the studio gates, he slid the car into an empty spot. As he went around to meet her by her side of the car, it was with his own emotions under lock and key. "You'll knock 'em dead."

A shaky smile. "Now that we're here, I'm scared," she whispered. "This is the biggest opportunity of my career."

"No one else could do justice to this role." He'd read the script on the flight back from the music festival, knew it was made for Kit. "Just remember that. And if all else fails, imagine Abigail Rutledge lording it over you at the premiere."

Kit's eyebrows drew together. "Not happening."

"That's my Katie," Noah said and drew her into a hug. He wasn't really a hugger, but Kit was, and truth be told, now that he'd started the hugging thing with her, he kinda liked it.

Taking a deep breath after he released her, she smiled and gave him two thumbs-up. "See you when they set me free. Probably be an hour at least."

"You fine going in there alone?" She'd asked Butch and Casey to stay at the house today.

"Yes. Esra's got a couple of stalkers of his own—harmless types who keep trying to get in, steal his stuff as souvenirs, rather than anyone who wants to hurt him, but it means his area is always secure." She nodded toward the security guard on the door that was her destination. "Okay, better go."

"Break a leg." He watched her walk through the door.

Rather than waiting in the car, he went for a walk and managed to find a small coffee stand. Grabbing a plain black coffee, he made his way back toward the area where he'd parked and saw that the mock street to the left was now swarming with crew. He was leaning against a wall watching them set up a rain scene when he felt someone's eyes boring holes into the side of his face.

Hackles up, he turned his head. *Aw, shit.* It wasn't the stalker. It was the guy Kit had been dating before she and Noah got together: Terrence Gates. "Hey." Noah straightened away from the wall. "I guess you want to punch my face."

"For starters." Arms folded, Terrence glared at him through the clear lenses of his metal-framed glasses. "You don't deserve her."

"No, I don't." That was simple fact. "But she's mine, and I'm not about to give her up."

Terrence's already hard expression turned stony, his hazel eyes like chips of granite. "Yeah, well, I'll be there to catch her when you let her down. Losers like you always do."

Noah's blood boiled, but he grabbed the fury in an iron fist, squeezed. Kit wouldn't thank him for making a scene at her place of work. "You'll be waiting one hell of a long time," he said lightly, unable to stop himself from adding a cocky smile designed to piss Terrence off.

The other man stepped forward, arms unfolding as if he was going to take a swing. Noah wasn't about to allow that to happen. "You want to take me on?" he said in a frigid tone. "Fine. Choose your time and place, but it sure as hell won't be at the studio." They were surrounded by people with phones, many of whom would love to make a few extra bucks by selling a shot to the tabloids. "Someone's probably already gotten a snap of you approaching me."

Terrence stared at Noah for a minute longer before turning and walking away. He'd unfisted his hand, but his shoulders remained bunched up. Though Noah tried to stay pissed off at the guy, it proved impossible—Terrence had a right to be angry. Yeah, the scriptwriter had apparently been a dick after the gala photos came out, but jealousy could do that to a man. All indications were that prior to the gala, Terrence had treated Kit with utmost care.

Noah, meanwhile...

He crushed his paper coffee cup and threw it in a nearby trash can, then walked back to the car. There was a small yellow flyer on the windshield. Probably a sneaky promotional attempt by a small-time movie company hoping to catch the eye of a studio bigwig. Everyone had to hustle.

Not against such self-starting behavior, he pulled the flyer out from under the wiper blade and turned it over. "*Fuck.*"

Printed on the yellow paper was a black-and-white photograph of him and Kit. It had been taken at the festival and had the look of a professional shot. If he had to guess, he'd say it had been printed off a news or magazine site. From what he could tell, it had originally been a shot of Kit sitting in the circle of his arms on the Zenith grounds, a smile on her face and his head bent toward her own.

On this copy, however, the stalker had scrubbed out most of Noah's face with a black marker until he'd torn a hole in the paper. He'd then switched to red ink to write the word "WHORE" across Kit's face.

About to crush the fucking thing into a ball, he remembered what Kit had done and dug around in his glove box, found a plastic bag he'd stuffed in there. He placed the flyer inside, then put the whole thing in the glove box. He didn't want to tell Kit about it and ruin her hopefully amazing day, but he had to so she'd know the creep did in fact have access to the studio lot.

He wanted to demand he come along with her every day she needed to be here, but knew she'd never stand for that. At least she'd have Butch and Casey with her. Damn it, how had the fucker known she and Noah had left the guards at home today? The most likely explanation was that the stalker had made it a point to learn the faces of Kit's security staff, been confident no one was watching the car.

Glancing around, Noah saw crew from the outdoor shoot walking this way and that. A lantern-jawed action star was standing talking to a bearded director. The actor and Kit had dated just over a year ago, and according to what Noah had picked up, the breakup had been anything but amicable. Kit and Action Dude had barely had two dates when the fuckwit leaked their "hot and heavy relationship" to the media. Apparently, it had all been pure fantasy—and Kit had broken things off at once.

Terrence stood not far off, arguing with a short, plump woman over something.

Those two were hardly the sole or even the best suspects. Action Dude was banging a centerfold-turned-reality-star now—and lapping up the attendant media coverage. As for Terrence, the jealousy-laced venom had continued to pour forth even when Kit had been dating the writer.

Still, stalkers were mentally unstable, so that didn't automatically take Terrence off the suspect list. He could've thought to scare Kit to force her to rely on him. And the action star could be banging one woman while obsessed with another. Noah would make sure the bodyguards knew to keep an eye on both men if they were nearby.

But there were so many others around, any one of whom could've become obsessed with Kit after she smiled at him politely, or maybe said "thank you" for a cup of coffee. That's all it took for the deluded to create a whole life, a whole relationship inside their head. That gaffer or that set-construction guy, or even that overweight character actor, it could be any of them.

Frustrated, he turned to face the door through which Kit had disappeared. It opened at the same instant to reveal the woman at the center of his thoughts. Her face was expressionless. Noah knew that could mean either very good news or very bad news. Taking his cue from her, he stayed silent as they got in the car and drove away.

"So?" he said once they were safely out of the lot and away from prying eyes.

A squeal erupted from the passenger seat. "Esra loved me! He was trying to pretend he was cool and not really into me, but I could see the fireworks going off in his head. He told me he's seeing Abigail this afternoon, but I think he just wants negotiating power when it comes to the contract. I *nailed* it, and we both know it!"

Kit finally stopped to take a breath. "We spoke for twenty-five minutes afterward, and it was serious, in-depth script talk. He asked me if I could work with Garrison given the politics if Abigail doesn't get the job, and I said I'm a professional."

Another gulped breath. "I can feel it, Noah. Only reason it won't be mine is if he plays politics, and I don't think he will. Esra might be an arrogant SOB, but he's a brilliant one who won't put his name on anything about which he isn't passionate." She blew kisses over to Noah. "And thanks to you, Abigail and I are even on the publicity stakes, so that's become a nonissue."

"You're the best, Kit. Period." He loved seeing her like this, so happy and excited and confident. "Let's pick up a bottle of champagne on the way home, have it chilled for when the news comes."

"No." A severe sound. "There's being confident, and then there's jinxing things."

"Right." Laughing at her adorable scowl, he guided the Mustang into a turn. "I keep forgetting how superstitious actors can be."

"Don't knock it. I was once in a small live performance of the Scottish play." Shivering, she hugged herself. "Never again. That play is genuinely haunted."

Reaching out, he flicked her nose. "And you, Katie, are genuinely cute."

"Say that again and I'll bite you."

Much as he wanted to keep the upbeat mood, he knew he had to tell her about the flyer. As she'd said, she had to know to protect herself. Jaw and neck muscles tense, he said, "Your stalker has access to the lot."

Silence from the passenger seat, then an exhale. "What did he do?"

He told her. "You don't need to look at it," he said when she would've reached for the glove box. "I haven't hidden anything."

Nodding in a trust that made him feel like he'd won the lottery, she leaned back in the seat. Her voice, when it came, was more focused than angry or scared. "It makes sense that he's in the business."

"Why?"

"When my place was broken into? It was while I was at a small party at the house of a camerawoman from my *Primrose Avenue* days. Not a lot of people knew I was gone. I guess he could've just been watching my place, but that wasn't the only suspicious incident." She tapped her finger on her knee.

"Once, I came back to my trailer on set and it felt as if someone had rifled through my purse. Nothing was missing, so I figured I was just being paranoid, but I changed the locks on the gate, the house, and the car anyway, despite the cost. A few days later, I found scratches on my car lock, as if someone had tried to use a key."

Noah gripped the steering wheel with bruising force. "You tell the cops this?"

"Sure—and studio security at the time. But you know how many people there are on a lot at any one time." Pragmatic words. "It's a miniature city. And since I didn't get any threatening notes or anything stalker specific, I figured it must've just been an opportunistic thief."

"You're taking this a lot better than I am." He wanted to strangle the creep.

Patting his arm, she said, "I've had a lot longer to get past the angry stage. These days I concentrate on being smart, on not giving him any opportunities, *or* my emotional energy." She relaxed into her seat. "Have you spoken to Abe since we got back?"

"This morning after breakfast." The keyboard player was not in a good headspace, and Noah had intended to bully him into coming over so he wouldn't be alone with his demons, but someone had beaten him to it. "He's staying with David and Thea."

"Sarah?"

"She wanted to go home, but Fox and Molly convinced her to stay with them. Her face needs to heal so she can go out, and they're worried because her ex has keys to her place." After the way Jeremy Vance had hurt Sarah, no one wanted to take any chances by leaving her alone in a space he could access.

"I've met guys like him before," Kit said, tone grim. "They're cowards who wait till they get their victims alone."

Noah nodded, in full agreement with her about the spinelessness of any man who'd hit a woman. "Thea went in quietly with a security guy and collected clothing and other personal stuff for Sarah, and she's arranging for the locks to be changed. It has to be done under the radar, so it'll take a few days."

In the meantime, Sarah would stay out of public view and Abe would stay with friends who understood his triggers and how to defuse them. "One piece of bad news—Thea had a couple of calls from reporters who heard Abe and Sarah and Vance came face-to-face at the festival. They're sniffing around for a story."

"Damn, that's the last thing either Sarah or Abe need." Kit shot him a determined look. "Let's distract the paparazzi with the promise of a money shot, have them too busy salivating over us to worry about an ex-couple."

CHAPTER 29

NOAH HAD NO ARGUMENT with Kit's suggestion. If this was what he could do to help his friend, then it was what he'd do. "PDA?" he suggested, figuring he could pull something like he had at the concert, closeness that wouldn't make either one of them uncomfortable.

Kit twisted her lips. "No, let's go be cute together."

"I don't do cute." He shuddered. "Don't start expecting me to buy you soft toys or other sweet shit." But since she really wanted a teddy bear, he'd get it for her. It'd be kind of adorable to see Kit go all soft and happy over a cuddly toy.

"So romantic." The words were dry enough to parch the desert. "That's why it's going to be catnip to the paparazzi. 'Noah St. John Tamed'—I can just see the headlines."

He pretended to gag. "I never knew I was signing on for fiendish and painful torture."

Laughter from the passenger seat. "You come up with an idea then. I've never consciously played the media this hard before."

"We get caught making out in a car."

"In broad daylight? I don't think anyone will buy that from

me." A pause, her next words soft and nearly soundless. "And if we're going to have a first kiss, I want it to be private."

Noah stopped breathing for a second. He didn't know how to kiss. Having anyone's face close to his, it was too personal, too much an invasion. When he fucked women, he took them over. A kiss though, it would bring them into him too, leave a mark. He preferred distance. Maybe that was fucked-up, but in the grand scheme of things, it was a minor detail.

"Your turn," he said, his gut all tense. "No PDA, no cute, no making out."

"I could get caught standing with my hand over my belly," Kit said with a gleeful laugh. "That would be so much fun, except people might take me seriously and there goes *Redemption*."

Noah didn't laugh. "You want kids?"

"Yes." A pause. "I know you don't, but I really do."

"Before, what I said, I was just thinking of some poor kid stuck with me for a dad." He'd have screwed that up royally. "With you, it'd be different." He already knew Kit would rock the motherhood thing, and when he was with her, he was a better man. If they ever got to the point where they could do the kid thing, she'd teach him how to be a good father, and he'd listen—he never wanted his kid to hate him like he hated Robert St. John.

"Yes, well, we can talk about all that later." Kit's voice was odd, but then she snapped her fingers. "I have it. Let's go to Disneyland. You don't have to be cute—the location is cute all by itself."

"Rock stars don't do Disneyland—gotta think of the brand, Katie." He took her light punch on the arm with a grin. "We go to Six Flags and ride the fucking roller coasters."

"Only lunatics ride things that make them scream in terror."

295

NALINI SINGH

HE GOT HER ON a roller coaster. She screamed like a banshee and threatened to murder him when he laughed. Wrapping an arm around her shoulders once they got off, he pressed a kiss to her temple and bought her cotton candy. "That should sweeten you up."

"My hair must be a mess."

It looked like she'd just tumbled out of bed. Not liking the idea of anyone else thinking that, he took off his cap and snugged it on her head before stealing some of the sticky sweet stuff she was picking off in little tufts.

"This is evil," she said, eating another tuft. "Macho Steve will kill me tomorrow."

"We could just go for an extra run," he said at the name of her personal trainer. "Or another roller coaster ride."

Elbowing him, she pointed at a ride to their left. "Who would be insane enough to go on that? Listen to the screams."

He looked at her, smiled. Narrowing her eyes, she tried to back away. He held her in a pretend stranglehold as he led her to the line. Later, after they'd survived the ride, he bought her a small blue teddy bear with a missing ear, as if it had been torn off in a scuffle. It was sitting forlornly at the back of a shelf like someone had shoved it back there until they had time to clear him away.

Noah knew he should buy Kit an undamaged, pristine bear, but he bought the bear with the missing ear. "I couldn't leave the little guy."

Kit's face threatened to crumple. "*Noah.*"

Wrapping her in his arms to hide her from the world, he couldn't stop his stupid grin. "Shit, did I just do cute?"

A jerky nod. "He's adorable. I love him." Then, to his surprise, she hid the bear back in the gift bag rather than holding it so the photographers would see it as they walked out.

It meant too much, he realized in staggered shock. Meant enough to protect. A bear with a missing ear and slightly dirty fur, imperfect and ragged... just like the man who'd bought him.

KIT GOT THE PHONE call as they were driving home from the theme park. *Redemption* was hers. "Harper's negotiating the final deal, but she says the terms look okay at first glance," she said after hanging up, still not sure she hadn't hallucinated the entire conversation. "I'm going to be one of the leads in an Esra Dali movie."

"The role was always yours."

She just wanted to kiss him. He was always so firmly on her side.

Trying to think of a way to distract herself, she said, "Did you get those mugs for the guys?" He'd laughed and said he was buying glittery pink princess mugs for Fox, Abe, and David as gifts. Kit had gone gift hunting herself, buying things for Becca, Molly, and Thea, as well as her cousin's young children. She'd also added something happy and sweet for Sarah, figuring the other woman needed a smile.

"Yeah," he said, then groaned. "Shit, I forgot to grab a gift for Emily. The little brat will pout for days if she finds out I got the mugs for the guys and didn't get her anything."

Aware he loved the "little brat," Kit smiled. "I have you covered. I got her a teacup for her collection."

"You really like her, huh?"

"Of course I do. She's a sweetheart." Kit petted the adorable bear sitting in her lap. Trust Noah to get her something so perfect, something he'd chosen specifically for her. "I got you something too."

"What?" A curious look. "Spill, Devigny."

Grinning, she reached into the backseat and found the small package. "Shall I open it for you, or do you want to wait till we're home?"

"I never knew you were such a tease."

She laughed and opened the package to reveal a glittery pink princess mug stamped with the letter N. "I couldn't have you feeling left out."

"Gimme that." He swiped for it.

"Nuh-uh." She wrapped it safely back up. "I'm not having you throw it out the window. I want a picture of all four of you drinking from these mugs."

He grumbled, but she caught that heartbreaking, lopsided smile that made it clear he loved that she'd bought him a gift, and her heart, it went all liquid inside her chest. First what he'd said about children, and now this...

Noah was devastating her defenses one by one.

THEY CELEBRATED HER CASTING with champagne and a homemade dinner where Kit talked off Noah's ear about the script, and he just grinned and listened and told her again that the part had always been meant to be hers.

His belief in her was one of the things that had first made her fall so hard for him. She'd grown up being told by the world that she was inferior to her parents—there had been the "fugly" comments of the tabloids while the gossip magazines and bloggers had been more sly, calling her "awkward" and pointing out her ordinary teenage acne as a "brave fight" she was undertaking.

Other people hadn't been as subtle. As a child, then a teen, she'd overheard more than one guest at her parents' home say uncomplimentary things.

"You'd never believe the ungainly child was Adreina and Parker's daughter."

"I don't know, maybe she'll grow into those limbs. If she doesn't... poor child."

"Fugly is right."

The adult Kit understood that those people had been vicious, sharpening their claws on a vulnerable target, but being constantly negatively compared to her parents wore away at a person. She'd never said that aloud to anyone but Noah, wary of appearing the "poor little rich girl." But he got it. He knew it wasn't about ego but about identity.

Kit didn't want to be labeled as Adreina and Parker's daughter. She wanted to be Kathleen Devigny, who was her own person quite apart from the two larger-than-life people who had created her.

"You are," Noah had said to her the first time she admitted her frustration. "The world won't know what hit it when Kathleen Devigny takes it by storm."

She loved him for that and for his talent and his heart that was bigger than most people knew. He'd never told her, never mentioned it in even a single interview, but she knew he donated a large percentage of his income to charity. The only reason she knew was that she'd been in his hotel room one day when she'd picked up a piece of paper that had fallen to the floor. As she was putting it back on the table by the phone, she'd inadvertently read a few lines—enough to tell her the letter was from his accountant, itemizing donations made on Noah's behalf. All the ones she'd seen had related to children.

Complex, beautiful, talented man, she thought, her heart hurting. She loved him, but she knew he was broken. Perhaps permanently.

"Let's go sprawl on the couch and finish off this champagne," he said after dinner.

Kit nodded because, broken or not, he was hers and she wouldn't give up on him.

They'd just taken a seat on the sofa, Noah's arm around Kit's shoulders, when she got a text from Harper. Her mouth fell open. "Give me the remote." Grabbing it, she switched channels.

"*Blue Force?*" Noah groaned as the iconic theme music came on. "I watched *Dancing with the Stars*. I should get to choose today."

"I'm on it." She snuggled close to his side. "It was taped three years ago, just before the series was put into temporary deep freeze—Harper just found out a few minutes ago that this is my episode."

"Why the fuck would Harper put you on this piece of—" Clearly catching her warning glance, he smiled. "I must've been thinking of another show. This is pure genius."

She made a disbelieving noise but stayed against him. "This was before *Last Flight*. I was still on *Primrose Avenue* and trying to break out into serious drama. These guys gave me a shot, so don't you ever mock the show."

"Yes, ma'am." He ran his fingers over her shoulder. "What're you playing?"

"A murdering junkie." She grinned at the open disbelief on his face. "Wait till you see me—you won't recognize me."

Ten minutes into the show and there she was, lying in a dirty bed in a crack den, her face scarred by the pockmarks junkies created by digging into their skin, her hair matted and greasy. Her teeth, too, were yellow and cracked.

"Why would they spend all that time making a gorgeous woman look like a hard-core addict?" Noah muttered. "Why not just hire an actual junkie?"

"Watch, it's a good episode." It charted the descent of an Ivy League educated heiress into drug addiction and murder. "I get to be glamorous in some of the other shots, but I think I did my best work in the crack-den scenes."

Noah watched quietly with her, and she could tell that despite his disdain for the show, he'd become hooked on the plot. Content and happy, she wasn't prepared for him to suddenly jerk to his feet. Unbalanced, she braced one hand against the sofa cushion. "Noah?"

"I can't watch this crap anymore," he said and strode out.

Kit stared after him. She knew she should be hurt, but she was just confused. Sure, *Blue Force* was a spinoff of a spinoff, but it wasn't trying to be anything but what it was—a quick police procedural that acted as brain candy after dinner. The writing was smart, plus the anchor cast had great chemistry. And it wasn't as if Noah was a snob with this kind of stuff— she'd seen DVDs of action movies at his house, many of them far more cheesy than *Blue Force*.

Shrugging and deciding he was just in a mood for some

reason, she returned her attention to the show but couldn't focus, becoming more and more frustrated as the minutes passed. What was wrong with Noah, and why wouldn't he talk to her?

Unable to let it go, she switched off the TV, then went looking for him. He was in the garden, beer in hand as he sat on the weathered wooden bench by the outdoor table. From the two other bottles lined up on the table, he'd started as soon as he left her. "Planning on getting blind drunk tonight?"

Looking up at her furious question, he laughed, but the sound held little humor. "This barely qualifies as alcohol." He put the half-full third bottle on the table and got up. "What I'd like to do is get drunk on you."

Frowning, she held her position just outside the doorway, not about to allow Noah St. John to intimidate her. "You're drunk," she said, putting a hand on his chest and pushing when he came too close.

"No, I'm not." He backed her up against the house, placed his hands palms-down on either side of her shoulders. "You don't hate the taste of beer, do you, Kit?"

"No, but—"

He kissed her.

Her parched, starving nerve endings shrieked to life. She'd dreamed of Noah's touch for so long, and now he was finally, *finally*, touching her. He tasted of the crisp bite of beer and of Noah. Just Noah.

She had no defenses, no shields, no way to protect herself.

Fingers curling into his T-shirt, she rose toward him. He deepened the kiss, thrusting his tongue into her mouth as he fisted a hand tight in her hair… and a hint of reason infiltrated her mind. This was all too sudden, too fast, too aggressive.

Not romance.

Not passion.

Anger.

Lashes flicking up, she saw his eyes on her face. Flat. Remote. He wasn't involved, she realized, her pleasure turning into this ugly coldness that made her feel dirty inside. He was kissing her, but he wasn't the least bit involved. She could've been a mannequin for all he cared.

Tearing away from him, she wiped the back of her hand over her mouth. "Why would you do that?" she whispered, her entire body shaking. "Why would you hurt me that way?"

His eyes glittered. "You seemed to be having a good time."

She wiped the back of her hand across her mouth a second time, bleeding inside. Enough, she thought. *Enough.*

He'd fucked another woman in front of her and she'd managed to forgive him, had given him another chance, but she wasn't a self-flagellating doormat. "Get out," she said quietly.

CHAPTER 30

"SINCE YOU'VE BEEN DRINKING," she added, "I'll call you a car. But you *will* get out."

His face was stone, eyes about as soft as concrete. "So that's how hard you'll fight for me?"

She trembled, her hand fisting. "How about you fight for me for once?"

Not giving him a chance to answer, she shook her head. "You don't trust me with your secrets, you mess with my head, you make me feel ugly and unwanted, and you ask why *I* won't fight for *you*?" Anger smashed into hurt, the jagged shards splintering through her. "Fuck. You."

Noah's face set into an impenetrable mask. It was the same look he'd given his parents at the charity gala.

Hardening her heart against him, protecting herself against the pain he could so carelessly inflict, Kit said, "You did this. Whatever the pain inside you, tonight *you* made the decision to drink and to do that to me." But alcohol or not, he wasn't drunk, had known full well what he was doing.

"I'm not leaving you with that creep out there."

Kit gave him a humorless smile. "I'll survive. I damn well did while you were busy fucking every groupie from here to God knows where." Her words made him flinch, and a small, vengeful part of her felt good that she'd hurt him too.

And *that* made her hate him a little, that he'd turned her into this vindictive bitch. Not wanting to say anything else, words that would make her hate herself too, she walked into the house and grabbed her phone. She felt Noah come in, go into his room. He was outside with his duffel when the car drew up, Casey at the wheel. The bodyguard and driver was meant to be on a break, but she'd asked him to do this as a favor, not trusting any other driver not to use it as a payday.

Locking the door the instant Noah was out, she determinedly refused to cry. Instead, she called Fox. "I threw Noah out," she told the lead singer. "Make sure he doesn't do anything stupid." However much she hated him at this instant, she couldn't forget the night that had begun this journey, how she'd found Noah in the motel room.

"I'll take care of it," Fox said in his distinctive grit-laced voice. "You okay?"

"No." Everything hurt.

"You want Molly to come over? Sarah'll be fine on her own—she's steadied since we got back."

"Thanks, but I think I need to be alone right now." Get her head screwed on straight. "Look after him." With that, she hung up and went back out into the garden.

Seeing the beer bottles Noah had left out there made her angry all over again. Picking them up, she took them inside to the sink, poured out the beer that remained in the third bottle, then ran the water so the smell wouldn't linger and took the bottles out to the recycle bin. After which, she returned to the garden.

305

Except she couldn't find peace here, not today. All she kept seeing was Noah. All she kept feeling was him, his lips pressed against hers and his eyes so bitterly cold. "No *more*, Kit," she whispered. "You can't help a man who doesn't want to be helped." She loved him, would probably always love him, but it was time she accepted that being with him would slowly destroy her.

She was done.

NOAH RIPPED UP THE stupid little cherry blossom tree he'd planted in an effort to recreate Kit's garden inside his home and slammed it against the opposing wall. He missed, hit the wall of glass. The dirt slid down in smudged streaks, but he didn't stop to watch; he was already ripping up the other plants. He'd put down smooth stones like she had in certain places in her garden, and now he picked those up and threw them at the glass. It smashed.

The sound was right, was an echo of what was happening inside him.

He picked up another stone. Then another. And another.

By the time he ran out of stones, he'd broken every single pane of glass that had previously provided a view from the house into the garden. Shards glittered under the small lights that had come on automatically when he stepped outside. He'd put in those lights because he knew Kit often sat in her garden at night. He'd liked to imagine her here, a cup of green tea in hand as she relaxed after dinner.

"You done?"

Jerking around, he saw Fox leaning in the doorway that

led into the garden from near the living area, his arms folded and his expression unreadable.

"How the fuck did you get in?"

"You gave me a key," Fox reminded him. "I wouldn't have come inside on my own except you weren't answering the door."

Chest heaving and hair falling over his eyes, Noah stared at his friend. "It's eleven at night. You didn't just decide to leave Molly and Sarah alone and drive over here."

"Sarah's asleep and Molly's talking to her best friend on the phone." Fox's eyes watched him without blinking. "I'm going to make you some coffee."

Noah didn't go inside. He destroyed what little remained of the garden. When he was done, no one would've guessed that there'd once been a pathetic little garden here. No one could see his fucking heart, all stunted and hopeful and over-grown with weeds.

"Here." Walking out, Fox thrust a mug of coffee into his hand.

Holding his own cup, the lead singer looked around. "Feel better?"

"Go to hell." Noah threw the damn coffee against a wall. It made a satisfying crash of sound, the coffee dripping like blood down the white stucco.

Fox didn't look at the new damage. "Kit called me."

Skin going tight all over his body, Noah stared at the cof-fee-stained wall. "Why?"

"She thought you might do something stupid." Fox took a sip of his coffee. "I don't think she was thinking about garden destruction."

Noah fisted his hands. He wasn't going to talk about Kit to anyone.

"What did you do?"

"None of your fucking business."

"Fair enough." Fox drank more of his coffee. "Do I need to punch you in the face?"

Glancing at the other man, Noah shrugged. "It's done. Over."

Fox's eyes looked black in the light as he held Noah's gaze. "Bullshit."

"Fuck you."

"Now that we're past that, we're going to talk."

Snorting, Noah swiveled on his heel and went to walk inside. Fox blocked him. Noah shoved at his shoulder, Fox shoved back, and then they were throwing punches, Fox's mug falling unheeded to the rucked up dirt and dying plants. If it had been Abe, Noah would've been in trouble—the keyboard player was big enough that his size was a distinct advantage in a fight.

Fox and Noah, however, were evenly matched. He landed a punch for every one of Fox's. His fist smashed into Fox's cheek, the other man's slammed into his jaw, making his teeth crash down on the side of his tongue and the hot taste of blood fill his mouth. He retaliated with a punch to Fox's ribs that made the lead singer double over.

Reacting to the hit, Fox headbutted him in the gut, taking him to the dirt.

And Noah stopped thinking.

WIPING THE BLOOD OFF his face with a towel some time later, Noah looked in the mirror. "You fucked up my face, man."

"Shut the fuck up," Fox snarled from the kitchen area.

When Noah walked in, the other man threw him a bag of frozen peas that had probably been around since the Ice Age. Noah didn't even know who had put it in his freezer. Fox was holding another bag of some frozen thing against his eye.

Noah chose to use the peas against his jaw. Unlike Fox, he didn't have a black eye. He had a jaw that felt as if it had come to within a hairsbreadth of being broken, a cut above his left eye, and another one on his cheek. His mouth wasn't in the best condition either.

"You look like shit," he said to Fox.

"Thanks, princess. You look great." His hair damp from the water he'd thrown on his face at the sink, the lead singer pointed at Noah. "You're calling Thea."

"Not happening. Let the tabloids make up some bullshit story about how the band is splitting up." The fact they'd been in a fight would be pretty damn obvious as soon as the two of them were caught on camera. "She's probably asleep anyway."

"Thea doesn't sleep, and you're a chickenshit."

Noah didn't deny it—Thea was goddamn scary when she got mad. "I don't see you calling her."

"Bastard." Stabbing in their publicist's name on his phone, Fox put it on speaker. "Noah and I punched each other," he said when she answered. "Our faces look like crap."

"Of course you did, and of course they do," she muttered. "It's not like I enjoy having a peaceful life." A small pause and rustling noises followed by a masculine murmur in the background.

"David says he's going to punch you both in the morning." Thea actually sounded like she was smiling. "I'll make a preemptive strike, say you fought after a few too many drinks, then kissed and made up. Long as they have a reason and you don't give them a juicier option, we can ride it out."

She made a small hmming sound. "It's not like they can sell the line that you were fighting over Kit—not when Fox is so openly crazy for Molly." Thea's voice softened on the last part. "And rock stars are expected to behave badly once in a while, so this is actually good for your image. Leave it to me."

After hanging up, Fox went straight back to the conversation that had led to the fight. "You screwed up. Why?"

"It's what I do." Noah put down the bag of frozen peas, felt his jaw. In one piece at least.

"How long have we been friends?" Fox's tone was dead serious. "Over twenty years. You don't get to bullshit your way through this."

"What, you want to have a heart-to-heart? Shall we paint our nails together while we're at it?"

"You love her," Fox said, stealing all the air in Noah's lungs. "You've loved her for so long, and now you're just going to give up? That isn't the boy I knew."

Noah sucked in a breath at Fox's oblique reference to their childhood. "Don't go there," he said quietly. "Never go there."

"Is keeping your secret worth giving up Kit?"

"Yes," he said on a wave of gut-twisting pain. "I'll lose her anyway if I tell her." It was torn out of him, the serrated edge in every word ripping him bloody. "I can't stand how she'll look at me." How his father had looked at him.

His mother had stopped looking at him altogether.

"You don't know that." Fox threw down the bag he'd been holding against his eye. "She loves you too."

"So much she threw me out." That hurt, that she'd thrown him out the first time he'd fucked up... except it wasn't the first time, was it? He'd more than fucked up the night in the hotel suite when he'd orchestrated that ugly little play that had devastated her.

He could still see the stark, shocked pain in her eyes, still hear the dull sound of her heels on the carpet as she ran out of the room.

Shoving a hand through his hair, he collapsed into a chair. "I was so angry at her," he whispered through a throat gone raw. "For expecting me to be normal."

"You sure she's the one expecting anything?" asked the man who'd known him since he was a boy who just wanted to be like everyone else. "Or is it you?"

CHAPTER 31

WHEN HER PHONE BEEPED, Kit gratefully abandoned the script she'd been trying to read since throwing Noah out. It was a message from Becca: *Hey, I know it's late, but I'm out with some girlfriends not far from your place. Want to join us?*

Kit didn't usually go out so late, but that was because she'd been on back-to-back early-morning shooting schedules. She had no reason to be up early tomorrow. And what else was she going to do but stomp angrily around the house?

Sounds fun, she messaged. *Where exactly are you?*

Becca texted back the name of an upscale bar located a short fifteen-minute drive from Kit's place. After stripping off her clothes, Kit slipped into a short and shimmery dress in beaten gold, let down her hair, and slid her feet into sky-high heels. Five minutes in front of the mirror and her face was done.

Becca would probably play with it in the bar's bathroom anyway. The makeup artist couldn't help herself—she constantly tweaked all her friends' looks, but since she was so damn good at it, no one minded.

Turning, Kit checked the back of the dress in the mirror— there wasn't much, the two sides held together by chains of *tiny* pearls that just asked for a man to break them. Below that, the fabric hugged her hips without being so tight as to look ridiculous. Sweeping her hair down her back again, she made sure the front was sitting well. The shoulders merged into a kind of a cowl-neck that softened the otherwise clean lines of the dress.

It didn't need jewelry.

Since Casey was back from his delayed break, she asked him to drive her while Butch sat in the passenger seat. Another two guards remained behind to watch the house. Thank God she could now actually afford them—but much as she liked all the men, she wished she didn't need the entourage of security.

Damn her stalker.

"Thanks, guys," she said as Casey opened her door in front of the bar. "I'll be fine inside. It's pretty busy."

Neither guard looked happy, but they nodded. The three of them had long ago come to an understanding that while she'd take their advice, she'd call the final shots. Right now, she just wanted to hang out with women who weren't close enough friends to pick up on her mood. Becca usually would of course, but if she'd been at the bar for a while, she was probably happily buzzed by now.

Walking in, she immediately found Becca's group. A pretty, bubbly foursome, they were ensconced in a relaxed seating area around which circled several hopeful men. At least one had made some headway, was whispering sweet nothings into the ear of a blonde Kit couldn't recall meeting before. Becca, meanwhile—dressed in a short black dress paired with black boots striped in blue—was firmly rebuffing all advances.

Seeing Kit, the makeup artist jumped up and hugged her tight. "Congratulations again, babe! I've been waiting all day to hug you." Another squeeze. "*Redemption*! What a coup!"

It was impossible not to smile. "To say I'm happy about that is an understatement." She tugged gently on a strand of Becca's hair—gone was the pink bob, replaced by a vibrant blue one. "I like this. And"—frowning, she leaned in—"are those tiny feathers on your eyelashes?"

Laughing, Becca closed her eyes so Kit could check out the falsies. "I bought them at that place we went to before the superhero movie sucked up our lives." She hauled Kit down into a seat beside her, her dark eyes sparkling. "Tell me *all* about your meeting with Esra Dali! I've heard he's a bit of a smoldering dish!"

Partway through Kit's recap, Becca ordered a celebratory bottle of champagne. Since Kit had already had champagne with Noah, she only drank half a glass, just enough so that Becca wasn't disappointed.

Then she danced with her friend and the others, steadfastly ignoring the men who tried to put the moves on her. She was happily physically exhausted when she and Becca finally left the bar arm in arm. They were the only two left of the original group. The other women had all hooked up with men from the bar.

Of course a few of the paparazzi had gotten wind of Kit's location and were camped outside, including her personal English pest.

"Ditched Noah already?" Basil called out.

"You ever hear of a girls' night out, Basil?" That explanation ought to keep a lid on the breakup for another day or so. Not much breathing room, but enough for her to find her footing and armor herself before she had to face the jackals.

"Don't suppose you'd give your friend a kiss, love?" Basil asked, ever hopeful. "Secret lesbian love affairs sell, you know."

Feeling Becca tense up, Kit smiled at her friend before turning to Basil—she knew how to deal with him, while Becca didn't usually come face to face with the paparazzi. "Sure, Basil," she said, pausing just long enough that the photographer all but stopped breathing in anticipation. "I'll do naked yoga for you while I'm at it."

All the photographers cracked up, a number needling Basil, who was like a cockroach. He just kept going.

"A flash of your knickers, then. While you're getting into the car."

Rolling her eyes, Kit walked over to the car with Becca. Casey was already out, with the door open. "Hop in," she said to her friend. "Make sure you don't accidentally flash the cameras. They'll find a way to use it."

Yawning and leaning against her, Becca said, "You really don't mind giving me a ride?"

"You're my friend—what kind of question is that?" Ushering the shorter woman into the car, Kit told Casey where Becca lived and they drove off.

"*Did* you break up with him?" Becca asked sotto voce, proving she wasn't as drunk as she appeared to be—or that even drunk, she knew Kit far too well.

Kit couldn't bring herself to say it. "It's complicated," she replied.

Becca patted her on the arm, her nails beautifully polished in blue with black stripes. "Trust me, honey, you deserve better than some manwhore out to nail as many groupies as he can."

Kit's spine went stiff. "Don't talk about him that way."

Pulling back, Becca said, "Oh, wow, sorry." A tight smile. "I was just doing the girlfriend thing. You know, the 'all men are dicks and the ex is the biggest dick of all' post-breakup talk?"

Exhaling, Kit dropped her head back against her seat. "I know. I'm sorry for snapping at you." Becca had commiserated with her in much the same way after the action-star debacle—it was Kit who was behaving oddly, so mixed up that she didn't know what she was saying or doing. "I just…"

Becca touched her hand. "You can talk to me, you know. Makeup artists are like priests—the seal of the confessional, only it's of the makeup chair."

Trying to laugh but failing, Kit dropped her head on the other woman's shoulder. "I'm not ready yet." She wasn't sure she'd ever be ready to talk to anyone about Noah.

"One thing I know," Becca said, "you'll be fine. You're beautiful and talented, and any man would be lucky to have you."

Too bad the only man she wanted didn't want anything to do with her.

Kit didn't voice the painful thought aloud, and when her friend waved good-bye to Kit from the doorstep of her apartment, Kit smiled and waved back. Then Becca was gone, and Kit was once again alone in the car with Casey and Butch.

None of them spoke the entire drive home.

Once there, she let the two guards do a thorough sweep of the house before she locked the door behind her and stripped off. Sweaty from the dancing, she had a shower, then put on a slip in midnight blue. The decadent sleepwear was courtesy of her pre-stalker and pre-debt days.

The sheets into which she slid were a much more prosaic cotton.

But though she was tired, she couldn't switch off her brain; she kept going over what had happened in the hours before Noah pulled his hurtful stunt. It had started so well. Then Noah's mood had just *turned*. Yes, he was moody, but he'd never before been so erratic. Frowning, she tried to figure out if she'd said something that had hit him wrong, but she hadn't even been speaking when he'd gotten up from the sofa.

The television had been on, *Blue Force* running as she— *Blue Force*.

Sitting up, Kit tried to remember the scene that had been on right before he got up and walked away, but her memories were all jumbled up. She could barely remember her own part.

Shoving aside the comforter, she ran into the kitchen where she'd left her laptop. She flipped up the lid, navigated to the website of the television station that featured *Blue Force*. "Come on, come on," she said, hoping the site had been updated with the episode they'd played tonight.

When it asked for her password, it took her two tries to get it right, her heart was racing so hard. Then she was in and there it was, the episode of *Blue Force* she and Noah had been watching. Skipping ahead to what she thought was roughly five minutes before Noah had walked off, she watched carefully. The scene was a flashback to the first time Kit's character had tasted cocaine. Nothing unexpected, nothing that could've triggered Noah's anger or drinking.

She was chewing her lower lip in frustration when that scene cut to another one. She hadn't paid too much attention to it at the time because it linked to a background plotline unconnected to the crime in this episode. Two well-dressed people were talking about their child, hoping he was all right. The woman cried, said, "I can't bear knowing he's out there with God knows who. My sweet baby."

The scene cut away again to a bleak-faced and exhausted-appearing detective staring at a bulging folder. Pinned on the front of it was a photograph of a little boy with shining blond hair and a gap-toothed smile.

A younger colleague interrupted the detective, and it was back to the Ivy Leaguer-turned-junkie storyline. Blood chilled, Kit clicked away from the site and to a major search engine. She started to search for anything on Noah's childhood. Had he been kidnapped? Held for ransom?

Kit's stomach lurched. Because from what she'd seen, the *Blue Force* storyline hinted at far more than a simple kidnapping. The mother was worried about what was being done to her little boy.

"No, no," Kit whispered and continued to search. She knew it was futile—if there was anything to find, the tabloids would've found it long ago. But she couldn't help herself.

She even tried using his mother's maiden name to widen the search. Nothing.

Hand trembling, she put it to her forehead and forced herself to take deep breath after deep breath before she hyperventilated. But her mind, it raced. How could the kidnapping of the scion of a powerful family be erased from existence? Sure, Robert St. John would've been a high-powered lawyer even when Noah was younger, but you couldn't just wipe out media attention.

Unless the police had never been called, the ransom quietly paid.

She found a bottle of water in the fridge and guzzled a third of it before trying to think through the whole thing. Usually if a ransom was paid and the child returned, it was because the kidnapping was a businesslike transaction. No way would Robert St. John have allowed his son to be missing for days without putting every possible agency on the trail of the kidnappers.

Something was wrong with her theory.

Buzz.

Jumping, she answered the gate-to-house intercom. "Butch?"

"Hey, Kit. I don't know what's up with you and Noah, but he's at the gate. You want me to let him in?"

Gut in knots, she said, "Yes." She wasn't sure she was in any shape to speak to him, but it seemed like a big mistake to send him away. Whether she let him stay depended on what happened next. Because what she'd said still applied: his pain didn't give him permission to deliberately hurt her. No matter how much she loved him, she wasn't getting back on that particular roller coaster.

Shrugging on her robe, she closed the browser on her laptop and went to open the front door. The night was cool and starlit—and quiet. When she failed to hear the sound of the Mustang's powerful engine after more than half a minute, she got back in touch with Butch. "He's not here yet."

"Walking," the bodyguard told her. "Fox dropped him off."

319

Kit returned to the doorway. Noah finally appeared in the drive a few minutes later, tall and making her heart ache… and with a face that looked like it had gone a few too many rounds with a fist. Temper flaring, she ran out to him and grabbed his jaw in her hand.

"Ouch."

She softened her hold but not her glare. "Come inside so I can see what you've done to your face."

"I was heading that way." One of his hands landed on her hip, that familiar cocky smile back on his face. "You gonna throw me out again?"

"We'll see." She led him into the house and shut the door. Examining his face in the hallway light, she saw he'd taken quite a beating. "Fox look like this too?"

"Worse."

She made a dubious sound in her throat, conscious Fox would probably tell Molly exactly the same thing when he arrived home. "What is it with guys and fists?"

A shrug as Noah dropped his duffel on the floor. "I put frozen peas on it."

"You want me to applaud?"

"Yeah." A grin, followed by a wince. "That bastard hit me in the mouth."

She could see the split upper lip, the slightly swollen lower one. "Yes, well, I wanted to do that myself today, so he did me a favor."

"I fucked up." Raising his hands, he cupped her face, his smile fading as his throat moved. "It had nothing to do with you. I just took it out on you because… Because I knew you'd forgive me."

Her eyes burned. "I love you," she whispered and pressed her fingers to his lips when he would've spoken again. "I love you, but I won't be an emotional punching bag."

CHAPTER 32

NOAH HAD NEVER FELT like more of a bastard. Kit's words couldn't have hurt more if they'd been designed for it—but he knew she hadn't done that. Her whispered declaration had been too raw, held too much pain. "I'm sorry," he said, pressing his forehead to hers. "I'm so sorry."

When he felt wet on his hands, he realized she was crying. "Please don't. Please," he begged. "Kit, *please.*"

Her hands closed over his wrists as she swallowed repeatedly. "Want to go for a walk in the garden?"

Choking on a burst of laughter, he said, "Okay."

"What's so funny?"

"I wrecked my garden," he admitted. "It was pathetic anyway."

"*Noah.*" Her mouth fell open. "That was a lovely garden! How bad? Maybe I can—"

Shaking his head, he said, "I really did a number on it. Beyond redemption, I'm afraid."

"I'll plant you a new one."

Noah wasn't used to putting himself out there. He'd been protecting himself for a hell of a long time. But Fox was right—

he was the one who'd screwed up here, not Kit. It was time he acted like a goddamn man and not the scared little kid he'd carried inside for more than twenty years. "Or I could sell my place," he said, speaking past the huge clawing fist around his heart. "Of course, then I'd be homeless."

Kit's hands tightened on his wrists. "We have to figure this out first," she whispered, and the claws punched in, drawing blood. But then her lips curved. "If you were homeless, I'd buy you food and get you coffee. You could sleep on the sidewalk outside the gate."

The fist eased open. "Very funny." He wiped his thumb over her cheekbones to get rid of the remnants of her tears, aware it wasn't going to be as easy to fix things between them. Kit had let him in the door, but the wound he'd caused tonight wouldn't heal quickly... if it healed at all.

He went out to the garden with her, staying silent as they walked through the neatly tended pathways. When he reached down to weave his fingers through her own, she curled hers around him, but there was a stiffness to her.

"Noah," she murmured a couple of minutes later, "I watched that episode of *Blue Force* again."

Nausea swamped him, along with a wave of black rage. His fingers threatened to tighten to crushing pressure. "Why?" The single word came out as harsh as broken stone.

A quiet glance that was more of an answer than any words she could've spoken. She'd looked because she loved him and she was trying to find a way to help him.

"What did you figure out?" he asked, every muscle in his body so rigid he felt as if he was made of thousands of pieces of steel wire.

"Were you kidnapped as a child?"

He laughed, and it was a broken sound. "That would've been simpler." Tugging Kit against him, he thrust the fingers of his hand into her hair and cupped the back of her head as he pressed his cheek to her temple.

He could feel the tremors running through his body, couldn't make them stop, the past he'd spent a lifetime trying to bury suddenly shoving at his mind. He'd never, *never* wanted Kit to know, but she was starting to suspect. Whatever she'd imagined, it couldn't be as bad as the truth, but he realized at that instant that he couldn't live with having her guessing, having her hurting for him as she imagined scenario after scenario.

He didn't know if this was better. It made him feel sick to even think about.

She ran her hands down his back. "Noah, I'm sorry." Her breath against his neck. "It's all right. We don't have to talk about it right now."

He couldn't stop the damn shaking, and he couldn't let go of her. It felt as if he'd throw up, but his body was ice-cold at the same time. When he tried to speak, nothing came out. He was that child again, that small six-year-old boy who couldn't escape from under the suffocating body of the man who was hurting him.

Shaking so hard now that he felt as if he'd break apart, he turned his nose into Kit's hair, breathing her scent in an effort to forget the acrid, sweaty, ugly scent of that bed, that room, that man.

"Noah." Kit's voice, a little thready but resolute. "Noah, it's Kit, and we're standing in my garden after having a really big fight." She stroked his back again. "Your face looks like you ran into a brick wall. Three times."

He wanted to laugh, couldn't manage it.

"Does it hurt here?" She petted his back gently. "I didn't even ask if you guys kicked each other around."

"No," he managed to rasp out. "Fists only."

"Glad to see you two have standards." Her voice steadied with his response, as if she'd just needed to hear him. "The real question is whether you rolled around in the mud after you destroyed your garden."

Her hair was soft against his chin, her body slender and yet curvy in all the right places. He could smell that fruity shampoo she liked, the one he'd used once and felt as if he'd been emasculated. On her, it was perfect. And her skin, it had its own Kit scent. She was the most beautiful woman he'd ever met, and it had nothing to do with her face.

I love you.

I love you, but I won't be an emotional punching bag.

He knew at that instant that he hadn't just hurt her. He'd come very close to abuse of the kind that left no bruises but hurt just as bad. "I'm sorry," he said again, the tremors still rocking his frame. "Forgive me."

"It's okay, Noah."

No, it wasn't okay, and he knew she wasn't fine with it, but right now she was so worried about him that she was giving him a pass.

"Fuck!" Wrenching away from her, he strode into the garden.

He half expected her to follow, but she didn't. Instead, she let him walk into the darkness and when he came back ten minutes later, having conquered the shaking but with his body covered in a cold sweat, she was waiting for him on a picnic blanket she'd laid out on the mossy grass, her head on a pillow as she looked up at the stars.

Coming down beside her, he laid his head on the pillow she'd placed next to her own. It was automatic to stretch out his arm so she could use that as her pillow instead. He had a stupid fucking romantic dream of waking up one day with his arm all numb because she'd slept on it through the night. Yeah, he was screwed.

She accepted his silent offer while, above them, the sky glittered bright. "That's part of why I love this place," Kit said to him. "It's far enough away from the lights that you can actually see the stars."

Noah had spent more than one night awake staring up at the night sky. "You know that group of stars?" He gestured up. "That's called Pegasus."

"How do you know that?"

He shrugged. "I was up late and bored one night, so I started looking stuff up online and kind of got into it." For a while, he'd thought about buying a telescope, but he didn't want to take away the magic by making the stars too real; he'd rather just look at them as sparkling pieces of light, clean and untainted.

They lay there in silence for a long time, and the claw was back around his heart when he found the courage to speak. "It happened when I was six years old."

The shaking threatened to start again.

Nails digging into the palm of the hand he had by his side, he clenched his jaw and breathed short and shallow in an effort to fight it. "My father had this friend." Noah tried to say the name, but all that came up was choking bile.

He swallowed it down, kept going, aware that he was destroying his future with Kit—what woman would want a man who'd had *that* done to him? He'd been made less than a man before he even had the chance to grow up.

"My family and the friend's family used to spend summers together in houses side by side on Cape Cod." Noah's chest was so painful now that it was as if his rib cage were crushing his internal organs. "He had a son around my age, so my parents thought it was the perfect arrangement. Emily was only a few weeks old, and she stayed with the nanny, and the other boy and I were sent off to play while the adults socialized."

Kit curled her fingers around the hand he had beside her head.

He held on tight, knowing he'd soon enough have to let her go forever. "Only it wasn't always like that. Sometimes my dad wanted to work and my mom wanted to go out for a coffee with the other boy's mom. So my father's friend would volunteer to watch us boys." His breath was a wheeze now.

Oh, don't coop the kids up with the nanny. She can't keep up with two growing boys anyway. I'll make sure they stay busy and out of trouble.

Noah could still hear that voice in his head, so jovial and friendly. He'd trusted that man because his father had trusted him. The man was a dad too. Dads were to be trusted.

"He hurt you and his son," Kit said softly. "You don't have to give me details, Noah. I can imagine."

It was an out, and one he should've grabbed on to, but if this was the last night he was to spend with Kit, then why not give her the whole ugly truth? She deserved it after all the crap he'd put her through. "He never touched his own son. Only me."

327

Noah forced himself to breathe. "He'd send his son to play in the backyard and then he'd…" The memories threatened to drown Noah in suffocating blackness. Staring up at the brightest star in the sky, he got the rest of it out before he could no longer speak. "He did pretty much everything you can do to a small boy with no defenses."

He heard a wet sound, realized Kit was crying again.

Curling his arm inward, he held her against him. Again, he'd made her cry and it wasn't over. Somehow he could still speak, and the words, they came out one by one, each a razor blade slicing his vocal cords. "Afterward, he warned me that if I ever told, he'd cut my parents' throats in the middle of the night and do the same things to Emily that he'd done to me. He said that even if my parents survived, they'd send me away for bringing the monster to their door."

"That fucking bastard." Kit's hand was a fist on his chest, her voice thick and harsh.

He crushed her closer, the tremors in his body having turned stiff until his muscles and bones felt like those of an eighty-year-old man. "I was only six, and he showed me the knife he'd use to cut my parents' throats. So I didn't tell."

To this day, Noah didn't know if he'd have been believed if he *had* told. "That summer, he did it again and again and again." Noah's father had brought a lot of work with him, and Noah's mother had so many friends to see after having been on bed rest for most of her pregnancy; they'd thought nothing of leaving Noah with the man who was thought to be a friend. And the man's wife had thought him a great guy for offering to babysit so she could accompany Noah's mom on her visits.

"Even after we returned home," Noah continued before he couldn't, "I didn't tell anyone. He'd convinced me that he was a real monster, that he could get to my family no matter where we lived." Huddled and shivering under his blankets, he'd barely slept as he waited for evil to crawl through the window. "It was only when my parents started making plans to spend the next summer with the same family that I broke. I had a screaming tantrum, saying I didn't want to go."

"What happened?"

"Time out." He smiled grimly. "My father told me I was too old for such theatrics and left me alone in my room to think it over. What I did instead was go into his study and use the key hidden under his lamp to unlock the drawer in which he kept his gun."

Kit's gasp was loud.

"I knew how to use it." How to load the bullets if it was empty, how to release the safety, how to brace himself for the recoil. "My father'd taught me—we're all 'real men' in the St. John family. Guns and hunting and women." His father had always had a woman on the side, all part of the proud St. John tradition.

Bitterness in his mouth, Noah fisted his hand in Kit's hair. "My father walked into my room an hour after he'd left to find me pointing the gun at the window."

Kit went as if to rise up, but he couldn't bear to see the disgust on her face, so he used his grip in her hair to keep her down. Not resisting, she stayed.

"To his credit, he didn't yell. Instead, he asked me why I had the gun. I told him it was to shoot the monster so he couldn't hurt us." Noah could still see his father's face as Noah finally told him about how the monster liked to do "bad things" to Noah: a mix of shock, pain, disgust… and shame.

Noah sometimes liked to imagine the latter two had been directed inward or at the man who'd done the crime, but Robert St. John's later actions had made it clear the disgust and shame had been directed solely at Noah. "To cut a long story short, my father told me we wouldn't be going to the Cape, I gave him the gun, and two weeks later, after a discreet medical examination to make sure there was no permanent physical damage, I was shipped off to boarding school."

This time when Kit jerked up her head, he couldn't keep her down. Turning his face away, he stared out into the garden.

"What about counseling?" she said, horror in her tone. "Did they even talk to you about—"

"No." After the medical exam, no one in his family had *ever* again discussed the events of the summer of his sixth year. "My mother couldn't even bear going with me to the doctor, and my father… he looked at me and was ashamed of me because I'd allowed it to happen."

"You were just *a child!*" Open rage in Kit's voice as she sat up beside him, her knees brushing his side. "They didn't report the man, did they?"

"No. I spent my first year at boarding school having nightmares about him hunting me down." It was after a screaming nightmare that Fox had tried to comfort him and he'd spilled the whole truth. His best friend had responded by putting a chair under the doorknob so no one could get into their room, and together they'd rigged up a noisemaker across the window.

"Tell me they didn't just let that monster walk free," Kit pleaded.

"On my eighth birthday, my father gave me a cutting from a newspaper. It was the man's obituary." Putting one arm under his head, he chanced looking up at the stars again, Kit in his peripheral vision. "It wasn't until I was older that I searched online and discovered the man had been found in his study at home, dead of a self-inflicted gunshot wound."

"Suicide. He did the world a favor."

Noah wanted to laugh. "He did nothing. My father used to defend small-time mobsters, did you know that? The kind of men who'd do him a solid, no questions asked."

"You think he had the bastard killed?"

"I know he did." Noah was certain Robert St. John had done it because that man had dared shame the family name, not because he'd hurt Robert's son. "When I turned eighteen, after a big-ass party my mother threw because that's what she does, my father found me fucking some random debutante. Later that night, he slapped me on the back and said, 'Good to know that asswipe didn't ruin you, boy. I hear the pussy begged for his life.'"

CHAPTER 33

I F NOAH'S PARENTS HAD been in front of Kit right then, she'd have slapped them both sideways. They'd sent away a traumatized, scared boy without offering him any help. What must he have thought when he was shoved out of the family home? When he was *abandoned?*

Just like the monster had predicted.

"It wasn't your fault," she said softly, conscious those beautiful gray eyes hadn't met hers since he began speaking. "You know that, don't you?"

"That night? The one of my eighteenth birthday party?" Noah said instead of answering. "It was the first time in eleven years my father asked me if I'd like to go on a hunting trip with him and the rest of the males in the extended family. Every other boy had been going since he could hold a weapon."

Kit had never hated anyone as much as she hated Robert St. John right then. "That makes him an asshole. It *doesn't* make any of what happened your fault."

He still wouldn't look at her, but he moved one hand to touch her lower back, the contact hesitant. "I don't like sex," he said, the words blunt and hard. "I fuck women because it

332

makes me feel like a man, and for a short time afterward, I can forget that I had my manhood taken from me."

Kit didn't know how to deal with this—Noah's pain wasn't something that could be fixed with kisses and hugs or love. This was a down-to-the-soul wound, one that was still bleeding. But she knew one thing, and that was that she loved Noah. "Bullshit."

His eyes finally flicked to her, the dark gray unreadable. "You never say bullshit."

"I'm saying it now." She held his gaze. "You're one hell of a man—that bastard hurt you, but he did not make you any less a man."

Jaw tight, he broke the eye contact. "Yeah, okay."

Gripping his jaw, she made him face her. "What if it was me?" she asked him. "What if it had been a child Kit in that room instead of you? Would you consider me any less a woman?"

"No, of course not." His fingers dug into the flesh of her hip. "But I'm a man, Kit. I was brought up to be the man of the fucking house. To take care of the people who were my own and to gut anyone who dared hurt any of them, *and I couldn't even protect myself.*"

"Noah, you were six years old." Kit was speaking, but she knew her words were hitting a stone wall of rage and self-recrimination and indoctrination. "Girl or boy, no six-year-old can protect themselves against an adult. The hurt is the same, regardless of the gender, and deserving of the same care."

That held true no matter the age of the abused, but right now, she had to focus on the fact Noah had been a child—she might actually stand a chance of getting through to him if she made him consciously think about the fact he was pitting a small boy against a full-grown adult.

Her attempt didn't work.

"I should've shot him," Noah said. "That's what my Dad said the day he found me with the gun. After I told him, he said I should've shot the bastard."

"I want to shoot your father right now," Kit ground out. "Jesus Christ, that man has no business being a father." Her parents might be feckless and self-involved, but the one time she'd had a bully come after her in school, they'd marched in and torn the principal a new one, then confronted the bully's parents. "Where was your mother in all this?"

"Shopping, tanning, taking Emily for walks in her stroller, anything to get away from the reality of a defiled child." A vicious smile on his face. "She can't look at me, did you notice?"

She had. Now that she knew why, she wanted to pound Noah's mother into dust, just crush her out of existence. "That's on her." Kit's voice shook with sheer fury. "It's the job of a parent to be there for their child, to kiss the hurts and fight the monsters. It sucks that yours failed at that." She reached out to brush back his hair.

When he grew stiff, she nearly withdrew, but gut instinct forced her to keep going, keep running her fingers through the golden strands. If he wanted her to stop, he'd pull away.

He didn't.

Inch by inch, second by second, his muscles eased until she braced her back against a tree, stretched out her legs, and coaxed him to put his head in her lap so she could continue to play with his hair. "Have you ever spoken to anyone about this?"

"Fox knows."

"No, I mean a counselor, or—"

"No. And that's not going to change."

"Noah—"

"*No.*" He closed his eyes, one knee drawn up on the picnic blanket and shoulder muscles bunched again. "I'm not going to spill my guts to some shrink. Not now, not ever. It'll end up on the front page of a tabloid the next day."

That tone was one she'd rarely heard from him, but it always meant a hard, bright line beyond which he would not negotiate.

The worst thing was that she couldn't even argue with him. She was sure there were trustworthy psychologists and counselors out there, but they kept records and those records went into computer systems or into filing cabinets, and Noah was a high-profile man. All it would take was a single nosy receptionist or file clerk who couldn't keep the news to himself or herself, and it *would* end up in the tabloids, front and center.

Oh, the articles would be clovingly sweet, giving lip service to Noah's courage and strength, but all the while, they'd be ripping him to shreds by bringing up the most horrific time of his life over and over and over again. He wouldn't be able to escape the knowledge in people's eyes, and knowing Noah as she did and having just heard what he believed about masculinity and strength, she knew that would destroy him.

What she didn't know was if he'd walk away from her too, now that she knew.

For this moment, he lay there quietly as she stroked her fingers through his hair, his eyes closed. She didn't know when she realized the rhythm of his breathing had changed.

He was asleep.

Eyes wide, she almost halted in her soothing strokes, caught herself before she could interrupt the rhythm. If Noah was finally sleeping, especially after what he'd just told her, she wasn't about to wreck it.

She didn't know how long she sat there, lazily stroking her fingers through his hair, but the night was beyond quiet when he stirred.

"Wassasleep?" he mumbled, the words running together.

"Yes." She stretched out her stiff legs when he rolled over to lie on his front, a pillow under his head. "You want to stay out here?"

"Hmm."

Getting up, she went inside and grabbed a thick afghan throw to put over him. The nights could get cool, and he was already on nothing but a picnic blanket. She was tempted to stay beside him, but she wouldn't take what he wasn't ready—or able—to give. From what she'd picked up after all these years of knowing him, Noah never actually slept with another person.

She tucked the throw into place and was about to leave when a strong hand encircled her ankle. Looking down, she saw that he was still in the same position on the pillow, his head turned away from her. Yet when she tried to tug away her foot, his fingers tightened.

Lips curving in a shaky smile, she said, "I need to go find a sleeping bag. You might like the cold, hard ground, but I prefer luxury."

A stroke of his finger over her skin before he released her.

Returning inside, she gave herself a moment to cry and to punch out her rage on the pillows. She *hated* Noah's parents right now, maybe even more than the man who'd hurt him.

Heart still thumping after she'd washed off her face, she dug up the sleeping bag she'd bought for a camping trip Becca had organized a couple of years ago. Putting it aside, she changed out of her slip and robe, and into warm microfleece pajamas. By the time she returned to the picnic blanket, Noah seemed totally out of it. Moving quietly, she rolled out the sleeping bag and getting in, turned on her side so she could look at his face.

Even in sleep, there was a tension about his features that said he didn't rest easy.

Reaching out, she stroked his hair again until the strain seemed to lessen. She kept it up until her own eyes were so heavy and gritty that she fell asleep with her hand lying by his head, golden strands brushing her fingertips.

NOAH WOKE IN THE hazy gray of early morning, but for once, he felt no sense of constriction, of being trapped. It took him a couple of seconds to realize he was outside in Kit's garden... and that Kit was curled up on her side in a sleeping bag next to him.

Everything came racing back: what he'd told her, what she'd said, the way she'd touched him.

His heart thudded in a raw combination of anguish and shame and hope. She was still here, so maybe she wasn't going to kick him to the curb. Maybe.

Moving very, very carefully, he ran a single finger over her cheek. She made a frowning face and snuggled down. He knew he should let her be, but he couldn't. He had to know how she'd look at him this morning. So he did the same thing again, pressing a little bit harder so it wouldn't tickle.

This time she didn't frown, just kind of settled under the touch.

When her eyes opened a few minutes later, he had to fight not to look away. He had to see, because now, while she was unguarded, that's when he'd see how she really felt. Later, she'd hide any disgust because she was a good person, a kind one. At this instant, she was vulnerable and he'd take advantage of that vulnerability to see... to *know*.

At first, all he saw was drowsy grumpiness. "I was sleeping."

"I know." He kept his hand on her cheek. "I wanted to wake you."

"You know I'm not a morning person," came the mutter before she yawned, her gaze clearing.

And then she truly looked at him... and he saw what he'd always seen when Kit looked at him: no shame, no pity, no disgust. Just Kit's stunning amber eyes looking at him as if she saw something of value in him.

"So?" she said with a scowl. "You woke me. Now entertain the beast."

He felt his cheeks crease. "I don't feel sleepy. It has to be at least five hours since we fell asleep."

"Since *you* fell asleep." She poked him in the chest. "I was stroking your hair, remember?"

He did remember. The strokes had been soothing and caressing and just... caring. He'd never had that, never let anyone close enough to show care. "That was nice. Will you do it again?"

"I might." A sparkle in her eyes, she turned her head to press a kiss to his palm. "But for now I'm going back to sleep."

He didn't think she'd be able to fall asleep, but he'd forgotten how often she had to sleep at odd times because of shooting schedules. She was out again in minutes, but that was okay. He could deal now that he'd seen her eyes, seen that she still saw him as Noah, the man she wanted, and not Noah, the boy who'd been helpless in that Cape Cod room all those years ago.

He didn't know where they'd go from here, but for this one morning, everything was all right, and he could watch Kit while she slept beside him.

KIT GROANED AS SHE walked into the kitchen after her shower. "I hate camping."

"I kind of liked it." The freedom, the night air around him, the stars above and Kit beside him. It was all he needed.

"Hmph."

"Come here, Grumpy Guts." He held up a plate with a fresh waffle doused in syrup.

Eyes lighting up, she hopped up to sit at the counter and didn't even protest when he insisted on feeding the food to her, taking a bite now and then himself. "Here." He handed her a mug of coffee when he saw her glancing around for a drink.

"Mmm, my favorite blend." Breathing deep, she took a sip. "More waffle."

Laughing at her tone, he opened the waffle maker to take out the one he'd started cooking partway through their demolition of this one. He got most of the second one since Kit declared herself full after a couple more bites.

"Can we talk about stuff?"

He felt his back stiffen at the careful question. "Yeah." It came out harsh.

But Kit's question wasn't what he'd expected, wasn't about what had happened to him as a kid. "You don't like sex, but what about the rest?"

"Jesus, Kit, you know I've been around the block. I've probably done everything they write about in Penthouse and then some."

Kit scowled at him over the lip of her coffee mug. "If I come up with something you haven't done, will you do it with me?"

"Yeah, why not?" If she was still willing to be with him, he'd give her everything he could. "But babe, you'll be eighty before you unearth anything I haven't done."

"Uh-huh." She sipped her coffee. "Have you ever had a massage from a lover, given one yourself?"

He stared at her, blinked. "No."

A smug smile. "Oh, what's that I hear?" She cupped a hand at her ear. "It's the sound of Noah St. John eating humble pie. Why yes, Kit," she added in a deep voice, "this humble pie is mighty delicious."

"Smart-ass." He grinned. "I thought you were talking about sex stuff."

"It falls on the spectrum—that's why they call them massage parlors."

"Are you going to offer a happy ending?" She was right; it all came down to sex.

Another scowl. "I'm not that kind of girl." A pointed finger. "And you owe me a massage tonight."

He went to reply, shut his mouth when he realized that a massage would give him permission to put his hands on Kit. For a while at least, it wouldn't be about sex. It would just be about touching her, and he wanted to do that. He'd always wanted to touch Kit. "I guess I'd better buy some oil."

CHAPTER 34

KIT HAD NO IDEA what she was doing. Noah needed a counselor, but since he refused to even consider going to see one, they had to stumble through this on their own. Part of that meant reading everything she could online about abuse survivors. She did that during the day while Noah hooked up with David and Abe to go see a set of drums David was thinking of buying.

The first thing that became clear was that Noah's belief that as a male, he should've been able to protect himself, wasn't unusual. According to the help sites and forums, even small boys picked up and internalized the wider world's ideas about "real men." How those ideas had savaged Noah broke Kit's heart.

In his case, his parents' actions had further solidified his beliefs. Robert and Virginia had made him feel like he was the one who'd done something wrong, boarding school a punishment. "Bastards."

Breathing past her fury, she continued to read.

When Becca called her midway through the day to ask her if she wanted to hang out, Kit said, "I'll take a rain check this time, okay? Thanks for thinking of me though."

"Of course! I know breakups can be hard."

"We're back together," Kit told her, hope a fiercely optimistic candle in her heart. "Wish us luck."

Becca paused before saying, "Good luck, Kit." Her voice was quiet. "I'm sorry, I still don't think he's good for you—but if you love him, I'll back you."

"You're a good friend." One who'd been there for her from her *Primrose Avenue* days and who'd seen her in the aftermath of the first go-round with Noah. Kit couldn't blame Becca for her view on Noah, but neither would she let even the closest friend influence how she saw the complicated, talented man she loved.

Hanging up after a lighthearted conversation about monster makeup, Kit continued to read. Enough to know that she could really screw this up. She was so scared of getting things wrong and messing up everything. And she couldn't talk to anyone without betraying Noah's confidence.

No, wait. She sat up straight. *Fox knows.*

Grabbing her phone, she called the lead singer. "Noah told me," she said and didn't elaborate. "He won't go to a counselor, Fox."

"Yeah, I know." Fox blew out a breath. "You're going to have to figure this out between the two of you."

"I don't want to mess up." Already she'd made a mistake in not actually asking him if he wanted to exchange massages. "I don't want to hurt him."

"He doesn't want to hurt you either," Fox said. "He's done a piss-poor job of showing it to date, but that guy will walk on hot coals for you if you ask. So I figure you two have a better starting place than most."

Kit tried to hold on to that thought as she did some more reading. Harper called around midday and told her she had a meeting with the *Redemption* people tomorrow, which she noted down. But otherwise, her day was quiet. Even the media coverage about Noah and Fox's fight was relatively low-key.

It totally fizzled out once Fox joined the other guys on their drum-kit-buying slash just-hanging-out trip and a blogger uploaded photos of Noah and Fox laughing together after Fox offered Noah a bag of frozen peas. The two were also pretending to throw more punches.

Kit had to admit that photomontage made her smile too.

They're such guys sometimes, she messaged Molly, attaching a link to the article.

The other woman replied quickly. *Fox stole those peas from our freezer. I was planning to use them for dinner!*

Laughing so hard her shoulders shook, Kit sent another message. *Did he tell you Noah looked worse?*

Of course!! :-)

Kit decided to call Molly, and the two of them had a good laugh before the conversation turned serious. "Sarah's doing laps in the pool," Molly told her. "I think she's more comfortable here now, but she really wants to go home."

"I can understand." Kit would want to be in her own space too. "Has Abe been by?"

"No, but he messages me or Fox several times a day to check on her." Blowing out a breath, Molly said, "I had my phone on the counter earlier and Sarah saw his message on the home screen."

"Oh." Kit worried her lower lip. "What was her reaction?" After what she'd seen at Zenith, she had no idea what was going on between Abe and Sarah—*or* what had gone on in their marriage and divorce.

"It's strange, but she looked shocked… and kind of sad." Molly sounded like she was moving around as she spoke. "Thea says Abe's been extra quiet and uncommunicative but that he's staying stone-cold sober."

"Good." At least if drugs and alcohol were out of the equation, Abe and Sarah could finally talk. "Is that your other phone ringing?"

"Drat. It's a work call."

"Go grab it. We'll catch up later." After hanging up, she threw together a quick salad for lunch, then continued her reading.

NOAH PICKED UP DINNER on his way back home from what had turned into an impromptu jam session at David and Thea's, and they ate out in the garden—at his suggestion. He was really comfortable out there, Kit realized, another idea bubbling in her mind.

"So when's this massage thing happening?" he asked an hour after dinner.

Surprised and happy he'd brought it up himself, she smiled. "You sure you want to do it?"

"Yeah. I bought this stuff." Going into the house, he came back out with a bottle of organic vanilla oil for sensitive skin. "I figure your skin's softer than mine."

"It looks great," she managed to get out, though her stomach was full of butterflies. The idea of having Noah's hands on her, those guitar calluses deliciously rough against her skin…

Breathe, Kit. This is just a massage. That's all it can be.

The point was to teach Noah that sensual touch didn't always have to lead to sex, that intimacy could be built in other ways... that he could give her physical pleasure in other ways. The latter sounded selfish, but the things Noah had said, his behavior, it all pointed to the fact that should he be unable to give her pleasure, he'd take that as a failure on his part, and that failure could lead him to some very dark places.

Kit was going to do everything in her power to keep him from going there.

"Do you want to go first or shall I?" she asked after spreading out a blanket in the center of the living area, Noah having shifted the coffee table out of the way.

"I'll do you," he said without hesitation.

Butterflies in full fury, she nodded and, going down to her knees on the blanket, took off her T-shirt while Noah came up behind her. Her yoga pants, she was definitely keeping on. She didn't know whether to take off her bra or not, decided to leave the decision up to him. "You can unhook the bra if it gets in your way," she said as she lay down on her stomach.

Noah didn't say anything, but she felt his warm, strong presence behind her, heard him twist off the cap on the oil, sensed him pour some onto his palm. Vanilla scented the air. Then his hands were on her, and the rough, warm feel of them brought tears to her eyes. She'd waited so long for him.

NOAH PUT HIS HANDS on Kit's shoulders, careful not to use too much pressure. She was so fragile in comparison to him,

345

her skin delicate. He immediately found he couldn't work properly from the side. "I'm going to straddle you. Okay?"

"Just don't try to bridle me for a ride."

Chuckling, he straddled her on his knees and ran his hands over her shoulders.

"Harder, Noah. I won't break."

He obeyed the request in small increments until she let out a groan at the sweep of his thumbs on either side of her spine and kind of went all lazy and loose-limbed under him. Realizing he'd found a sweet spot of pressure, he kept it up as he went down her back.

When he reached her bra, he unhooked the clasp and kept going. Her back was flawless, one of her best features. When she wore those dresses with a plunging back, he just wanted to stroke her like she was a cat. Today he had full permission, so he indulged himself.

"What about you?" she mumbled at one stage.

"I like doing you," he said, running his hands up her back. She moaned again. "'Kay."

There wasn't much conversation after that; Noah sank into the sensory experience, into the feel of Kit's body under his hands, the scent of vanilla in the air. He'd had women offer him massages before, but he'd always said no. He'd certainly never wanted to return the favor. It had all been wham-bam-get the fuck out of here. Yeah, he was no prince.

But with Kit he *wanted* to linger, wanted to touch, wanted to just do the things that gave him pleasure. No expectations, no demands.

His body hadn't gotten the memo though, his cock hard as rock at the physical stimulus of having Kit's ass so close, her upper body all but naked in front of him. Gritting his teeth, he continued the massage; it wasn't until a while later that he realized Kit hadn't said a word for over half an hour.

"Kit?" he said softly.

No answer.

Putting his hands on either side of her head, he leaned down to check her face. Her eyes were closed, her breathing even.

He grinned. She was so not going to be pleased with him when she woke up and realized he'd massaged her to sleep on the floor. He, on the other hand, felt like a smug asshole.

Grabbing a blanket, he covered her. Then, thinking of how it had felt to sleep with her outside, he found an extra pillow and sprawled on the blanket by her side. He didn't really sleep, the demons vicious tonight, but that was all right. Every time they howled too loud, he stroked Kit's bare back until the simple human contact silenced the voices.

CHAPTER 35

NOAH COULDN'T HELP KEEPING a wary eye on Kit over the next few days. He kept expecting her to turn around and give him a look of disgust—and though he *knew* Kit would never be so cruel, he couldn't stop the demon voices. Those same demons sent him running into the darkness night after night so that he wouldn't have to deal with his failure as a man with her.

He made sure not to wake her, and he stayed on the property, running countless laps. No matter how fucked-up he was, he wasn't going to leave Kit vulnerable again. If she called out for him in the night, he'd be within reach. Protecting her was the one thing he *could* do.

On the fourth day after the massage, the two of them having barely been in the same room since, he returned home from a songwriting session with the guys to find a furniture truck parked outside the front door. Casey and Butch were standing watch as two hulking men unloaded the truck.

Scowling, he headed over to where Kit stood in the doorway, dressed in a green tank top and black shorts, old tennis shoes on her feet. "You didn't tell me you were getting a delivery." He'd have made sure to be nearby. Her stalker might have gone quiet, but he hadn't given up; Kit's agent had received a letter meant for Kit only two days earlier.

"Nothing you haven't seen before," Harper had muttered over the call Kit had put on speaker. "Usual poison and delusion. I'm adding it to the file."

Now Kit skewered him to the spot with her eyes. "Did you want me to put on my running shoes and hunt you down?"

He winced. "Shit. Sorry."

"You can make it up to me by helping to move this inside. I told the truck guys to leave it here—don't want strangers in the house."

"Yeah, sure." He realized she'd ordered a bed—the frame was in three parts as far as he could tell, the mattress a good one, but there were other parts he couldn't quite understand. "Where are you going to put this?" She did have spare rooms but kept them closed off unless she had a guest over.

Kit didn't immediately answer, instead waving off Butch and Casey when the bodyguards offered to help after they'd escorted the truck to the gate. "Noah and I will take care of it. Thanks, guys."

Once everyone was gone, she said, "We're taking it into the garden."

"The garden?"

"Uh-huh."

Figuring he might as well indulge her, he began to carry through the pieces. She helped with a few odd-shaped ones, but he was able to handle most of it on his own. "Years of shifting gear," he told her when she made a comment about how much weight he could lift. "I tend to get antsy day before

349

a show, so I help the crew." It kept the thoughts from circling in his head.

"Well, I approve," she said with a slightly wicked smile. "I've always liked your arms."

"My arms?" Having brought in the last piece, he put it down, then held out his left arm. "It's an arm."

Kit danced her fingers over it. "A sexy arm. All muscle and sinew."

"Huh." He shrugged—if Kit had a thing for his arms, he could live with that. "So, we putting this bed together or what?"

"Yep."

He ended up stripping off his T-shirt a half hour into it since manhandling the pieces under the sunny sky had gotten him sweaty pretty quick. He was aware of Kit's eyes on him, but she didn't initiate contact of any kind. Gut tight, he tried not to let that bother him, but it did. He'd seen her with other men she'd dated—she liked to touch.

"You take a vow of chastity or something?" he finally said, trying to make light of his need for contact... for reassurance that she still wanted him.

She looked up from where she was sitting on the ground, screwing in a bolt to keep the fancy iron frame of the bed in place. "I want to talk about that." Her teeth sank into her lower lip as she tried to tighten the bolt.

"Scoot." Crouching down, he took over the task. "You have really girly muscles, Katie."

"Thank you very much." Sitting with her hands behind her, she said, "You okay to talk?"

No, he was never okay to talk about that.

Kit passed him a second bolt. "I won't push you," she said gently. "But Noah, we have to communicate at some point."

"Damn it," he said, twisting the bolt too hard and almost snapping it off. "Why can't we just leave it? I don't particularly want to keep going over a time I'd rather forget." Not that the nightmares would permit that.

"I don't want to talk about the past but about the future."

He frowned. "Yeah, what?"

"The reason I haven't touched you today is because I don't want to screw up," Kit said frankly. "You're the most beautiful man I've ever seen, but the idea of you flinching from my touch hurts so much."

His jawbones ached, he'd clenched his teeth with such strength. "I'm sor—"

"I didn't say that to make you feel bad." Moving with none of her usual grace, she went around to the other side of the bed and began to loosely fit in the bolts so he could do the final tightening. "I'm trying to be honest, and I need you to be too—neither one of us wants to hurt the other." A look across the bed, a question in the amber of her eyes.

"Hell, Kit, hurting you makes me feel like a bastard." He shoved a hand through his hair. "I don't want to be that guy." Never again wanted her to feel like an emotional punching bag. Even the thought of those words made nausea roil in his gut.

"And I don't want to be the woman who makes you feel trapped or broken." She shifted to slot in the bolts needed on the next part of the bed while he came around to tighten the ones she'd already fitted. "So we have to talk."

Noah didn't talk about stuff like this. Even before the incident with the gun, his father had never talked about feelings or any of that shit; Noah had always believed that to be the right way. Men were men and they shut up and dealt with things. Still, Kit was a woman, and women liked to talk. So maybe he could meet her halfway. "What do you want to know?"

"Does it weird you out if I admire your body?" Her cheeks pinked, her gaze brushing over his pecs.

He started to grin because hell, he was a man and the woman blushing while she surreptitiously scoped out his body was the seriously smokin' Kit Devigny. "I like the way you look at me."

That part was easy to say, but he had to force out the rest. "You're a woman. You're Kit." Smile fading, he twisted the wrench. "I got a bit of a rep as a homophobe a few years ago because I punched a guy who hit on me, but I don't give a fuck who anyone fucks or if they like to do a three-way every Thursday. I'm just—I can't handle male attention if it's directed at me." The reaction was visceral and violent.

"I get it," Kit said, her tone normal. No whispers, no tip-toeing. Just blissfully normal.

His shoulder muscles began to unknot. "So yeah, since you're a hot chick, your lechery doesn't weird me out."

"A hot chick?" Laughter. "Smooth, St. John."

"I try." No longer nauseated, he found his grin again. "You do realize this is equal-opportunity leering? I get to check you out too."

"Do your worst." The final bolt sliding in at that blushing challenge, she went to the leftover pieces and said, "This is a canopy."

He tightened the bolt. "Like to go over the top?"

"Yep."

Grabbing the instructions, he read them through quickly, nodded. "Got it." They spent the next couple of minutes unwrapping all the pieces and making sure nothing was missing. "So is that all you wanted to know?"

"No, the touch thing," Kit said as she held up a piece so he could bolt it into place. "I need to know what's always okay with you."

"Shit, Kit, I don't think about stuff like that." Moving behind her, he went to put his hands on her hips, hesitated... then did it. He grabbed her hips tight, nuzzled a kiss to her neck.

She shivered. "Hey, no fair. I can't move while I'm holding up this thing."

"I know. Makes it more fun." Running his jaw along her shoulder, he tugged playfully at her earlobe before breaking away to put the piece in place so she wouldn't get tired arms. "You don't"—he coughed—"mind if I touch you?"

If the ugliness in his past wasn't enough, he'd covered himself in dirt over the years. He had no idea how many women he'd screwed, and he couldn't remember the majority of their faces. No way to paint that into a pretty picture. "I'm clean," he blurted out before she could reply. "That's the one thing I didn't mess up."

Kit's response was quiet. "I'm glad."

A concrete block fell on his chest. "I should've kept my mouth shut, huh?"

"No." Kit held up a bracing piece so he could lock it into place. "If I'm asking you to be honest, I have to be honest too." She ran a hand through her hair, her other hand still holding up the piece. "I know those women didn't mean anything to you, but I don't like thinking about them."

Noah thought of how he'd feel if he saw Kit fucking some other guy; his head pulsed red-hot with rage. "Yeah, I get it."

He wanted to push her on the touch question but couldn't bring himself to repeat it.

"And I love your touch, Noah." She went to pick up a small piece, came back. "You and I, we're starting from scratch, from the moment we decided to be us." Her eyes held his, beautiful and haunted. "I will walk anywhere with you, but the one thing I ask is fidelity. Don't cheat on me. That's my line in the sand."

Stark and painfully honest, her words sank into his bones, branding him. "I won't," he vowed. "I've got plenty of other self-destructive behaviors I can indulge in instead."

It was meant to be a joke. It fell flat.

"Don't be flip." Kit scowled. "And you didn't answer my original question about what touches are always okay."

He got another piece of the canopy into place. "I don't know." Shrugging, he went to elaborate before his brain kicked in and ordered him to keep his mouth shut.

"Just say it. I might not like hearing some of it, but I need to know."

Fuck, she was killing him. "I didn't really do much touching," he admitted. "It was mostly slam my cock in, get off, and that was it." Even with a blowjob, he'd rarely done more than just unzip his jeans. And the stupid-ass hotel-room stunt he'd engineered? He'd braced himself on his arms so he barely touched the woman anywhere else on her body. "No foreplay, no wasting time."

"Wow, and women still kept flocking to you?"

"Go figure." Noah had never called himself the greatest lover on the planet, but some groupies got off on the hard, cold fuck that was his specialty.

"What about kisses?"

"Romantic bullshit," he muttered, then paused. "But you know, since you're my girl and all, I guess I could get into it."

Kit's eyes were sparkling when she looked up, and he knew she'd forgiven him for the cruel mockery of their first kiss. "Be still my heart."

"Smart-ass." Grabbing her with an arm around her neck, he pulled her close. Her hands landed on his bare chest, and when he lowered his head, her lips were still parted in the beginnings of a laugh.

The kiss was romantic bullshit... and he found he liked it. Liked the way he could feel her smile, the way her fingers curled into his chest, the softness of her. Shifting until he'd backed her up against the house, he braced one arm over her head, put his other hand on her jaw, and kissed her. He knew he was probably not doing it right, but it felt good and Kit didn't seem to mind his lack of skill.

When their lips parted, his heart was thumping and her pupils were dilated, her breathing shallow. "I vote for more romantic bullshit."

He grinned at the husky comment. "Meet you on the couch after dinner."

Pushing playfully at his chest, she said, "Let's get this bed up first."

They did finally complete the bed. Turned out Kit had bought some kind of fancy waterproof canopy cover that looked like fabric.

"Mostly we can keep it like this," she said, tying off the curtains to each of the four poles. "On the rare occasions it rains, we can close the curtains."

"What about the stars?" What was the point in sleeping outside if you couldn't see the stars?

"The top peels back." She showed him how, and suddenly, the bed had a direct view of the sky, that sky bordered by a frame of curlicued metal.

Throwing himself down on the mattress, he put his hands behind his head and nodded. "I dig it."

Kit came down on the bed beside him, but when she would've lain down, he unfolded an arm so she could put her head on it. He curled it back around her, and they lay there in the sunshine for a while until it got too hot.

"It'll be great at night," he said after they went inside, having closed the canopy to protect the mattress from the heat.

"Glad you think so. I got it for you."

He paused in the act of lifting a juice bottle to his lips. "What?"

"You seem to sleep better in the garden."

It was true, but he'd figured that was a fluke. Not wanting to disappoint her though, he decided to try it out that night.

Six uninterrupted hours after he'd put down his head, he lifted it up. It was the longest stretch of nightmare-free sleep he'd had in years. Even once he shrugged off the grogginess of such a long sleep, he had no particular desire to get out of bed. Yawning, he lay there and listened to the birds that lived in Kit's garden and wished she was nearby so he could try some of that romantic bullshit again.

When he asked her to sleep with him on the bed in the garden the next night, she agreed, and yeah, there was some messing around. Kisses mostly. It was normal and romantic, and he actually felt like a goddamn man when he made her moan in the back of her throat.

Maybe this would work, he dared think. Maybe they could make it.

CHAPTER 36

KIT WAS FEELING GUARDEDLY optimistic. Not only was Noah sleeping at least a few uninterrupted hours a night, he was working with her to figure out the physical stuff. She'd thought it'd be awkward and hard, but it wasn't. It was fun, like they were teenagers, cautious and not quite sure what was okay and what wasn't.

Noah had really gotten into the "romantic bullshit." Turned out the bad boy of rock liked kissing. Kit had never been so thoroughly kissed in all her life. The night before, he'd pinned her down on the bed outside and, one hand gripping her jaw, kissed her until she'd all but melted into the bed. For a man who'd avoided kissing before, he'd sure picked it up fast.

"I love him so much," she confessed to Becca when she met her friend for a coffee a week later, a surely silly smile on her face.

Becca laughed, her makeup relatively low-key today, though her hair remained that gorgeous, vibrant blue. "In that case, I'm happy for you, you sappy goof. I will, however, still stab him in delicate places if he hurts you."

Reaching over, Kit touched Becca's hand. "It's different this time, trust me." Noah remained the same man, but he was no longer using his defenses to block her out, sabotage their relationship. This was the Noah she'd come to know in their hotel room conversations—the sensitive, complicated, talented man who'd written a heartbreaking song about a sparrow with broken wings.

She understood that song now, knew how deeply personal it was, though to anyone who didn't know his past, it would simply be a sweet, sad, *beautiful* song.

"Hey," Becca said with a wry smile. "Boys come and go, but girlfriends are forever, right? I'm not going to mess with our friendship by dissing Noah when you love him."

"I want you two to like each other—give him a shot, okay?" Kit knew this "boy" wouldn't be going anywhere. He made her heart sing.

"Just for you." Becca poked her cake fork at Kit. "Are you two coming to my birthday dinner? Crap, I think I forgot to e-mail you. It's tomorrow night."

"I feel wounded! Forgotten already." Kit slapped a hand over her heart. "What time? Where?"

"Nothing fancy. My place. We'll do takeout, and since I forgot to order a cake, we'll eat random cakes I pick up from the grocery store. Seven p.m. to probably around ten thirty as a whole bunch of us have to be on set by eight the next day."

"I'll be there." Kit crossed her fingers that Becca and Noah would hit it off. "And I'm going to make sure you have a proper birthday cake—chocolate-frosted vanilla, right?"

Becca's smile was so sweet it belied the tough attitude she so often put on. "Thanks, Kit. I should've known I could count on you."

NOAH GAVE KIT A dubious look when she told him her hope that he and Becca would find common ground. "Becca is never going to like me, Kit. It's in the girl code or something."

"Just be nice to her," Kit said, picking up her phone to call a caterer friend who owed her a favor—and who happened to have a baker on staff.

"Yes, ma'am."

He *was* actually nice to Becca, to the point that the makeup artist seemed to be thawing a little. Kit actually saw the two of them in conversation not long after Becca cut the dual-layer cake Kit's caterer friend had managed on short notice, and Becca had a genuine smile on her face. Relieved she wouldn't have to run interference between her man and one of her closest friends, Kit had a great time at the party.

Returning home with Noah around eleven that night, she stretched in the hallway. "That was a good night."

The only awkward moment had come when Terrence turned up.

"*Oh, shit,*" Becca had mouthed from across the room. Later, when she'd had Kit alone, she'd been so apologetic. "I totally forgot you two had a thing before you got together with Noah. Do you want me to ask him to leave?"

Kit had assured her friend that it was fine, but the situation had been strained. Terrence had barely spoken to her, and it made her sad that he was still so angry with her—though she did think he was taking things a bit hard when they'd only been on three actual dates. They'd been friends for years before that; surely he understood that she hadn't meant to hurt him?

His behavior seemed unusually possessive, but Kit couldn't bring herself to believe Terrence was her stalker. Still, she'd be extra careful around him, especially since Jade was still excited about Kit doing the project with the two of them. Kit had expected Terrence to veto it, but according to Jade, he wanted Kit for the role.

Not that she'd know it from his personal treatment of her.

"Hey." Noah rubbed the lines between her eyebrows. "Why the frown?"

Kit shook her head, not wanting to bring up Terrence. She'd sensed the animosity between Noah and the writer, figured they must've run into each other when she wasn't around. "I'm glad you and Becca are getting along."

Taking her hand, he tugged her to her bedroom and leaned in the doorway while she slipped off her heels. "Yeah, dodged that bullet. Phew." He pretended to wipe his brow. "Any guy worth his salt knows you're toast if you get on the wrong side of the girlfriends."

Kit laughed. "How did you do it?"

"Told her I was crazy about you." Smiling lips, dead serious eyes.

Her heart squeezed so hard she could barely breathe. "I have to change," she said, the words coming out husky.

Stepping inside the room, he braced his back on the wall by the door. "Can I watch?"

Kit's breath froze in her throat at the unexpected question, the heat in Noah's gaze searing. "I... Okay." Gripping her nerves in a tight fist, she walked over to him and, turning to give him her back, swept her hair over one shoulder. "Unzip me. Please."

A rough breath, his lips brushing her nape before he began

361

to tug down the zipper slow and easy. He touched her nowhere else, but by the time he'd finished, she had goose bumps all over her body. Keeping her back to him, she returned to her original position beside the bed and slid off the long sleeves of the midthigh-length black dress.

A single push at the hips and the soft fabric fell to pool at her feet.

He groaned. "You're wearing a garter belt with thigh-high stockings."

Yes, she was. Not simply because she liked the way they felt on her body, but because Noah had once let it drop that he found the look hot. It had been a passing comment while they'd been watching a movie, but she remembered everything when it came to him.

"These old things?" she said and, stepping out of the dress, bent down to pick it up. She was hotly conscious of Noah's eyes on her ass as she walked into the wardrobe and hung the dress in the section where she put clothes that needed dry-cleaning.

A deep inhale while she was hidden from him, a slow exhale, her pulse a drumbeat.

Going back to the bed using the same unhurried stride, she put one foot on the mattress and unclipped the stocking from the garter belt. The stocking was baby fine and, to be honest, not really necessary in LA. But again, it was all about playing to Noah's fantasies.

She rolled down the stocking with care, inch by inch. Tugging it off her foot, she dropped it to the floor and started on the second. No rushing, no visible self-consciousness, just a woman slowly, sensuously teasing her lover as she undressed for him.

Though Noah hadn't moved from his position by the door, his thumbs hooked into the front pockets of his jeans, his breathing was audible. Her own heart thumped hard as stone against her ribs. It was so loud by the time she finished taking off the second stocking that she couldn't hear Noah anymore. Dropping the ball of airy material to the carpet, she put both feet back on that carpet and went to undo the tiny hooks that fastened the lace of the garter belt around her hips.

It was erotic black, the same color as her panties and the demi-cup bra she wore on top. All a matched set.

Her hands trembled as she removed the lace and dropped it on the bed.

She'd just lifted her arms back to unhook her bra when Noah moved. She saw it out of the corner of her eye, stumbled when his weight hit her, but he had his hands tight on her hips, kept her upright.

"Noah," she gasped, feeling the hard push of his cock against her lace-covered butt.

"Now, Kit," he said harshly. "Now, while I only have you in my head."

Kit didn't argue. If Noah thought now was the time, now it would be. It wasn't as if she wasn't burning up for him. "Yes," she said.

He turned her to the wall, pushed her forward. It was rough but controlled, Noah's hands holding on to her until she'd braced her palms against the wall. Her chest heaved, her breasts swelling against the cups of her bra. She made a low, needy sound in her throat when he pulled down the scrap of her panties... and then they just tore, the ribbon ties on either side snapping like they were made of paper.

She felt his hands moving behind her, heard the sound of a belt buckle being opened, the metallic rasp of a zipper being lowered, braced herself for him. She was ready, her body melting, but at that moment, a dark, twisted fear invaded her heart. He was taking her from the back, the way he'd no doubt taken many of those other women. Was that all she'd become? Did he even remember who she was anymore?

Something ripped.

A condom wrapper.

"I'll keep you safe," he ground out.

Her panicked heart interpreted that to mean he was keeping a barrier between them. Part of her knew that was stupid, that he was doing the right thing, but her panic grew and grew. She couldn't bear it if they did this and—

His hands back on her hips. Spinning her around, strands of her hair sticking to her cheeks, he grabbed her face in his hands and kissed her so hard that their teeth collided. But that was okay, that was better than okay, because he had his eyes open and he was looking at her and he knew damn well who it was he held.

"Kit," he said, stroking his callused, gifted hands down her body and lifting her just enough that he could thrust into her.

Hard. Fast. Deep.

A guttural scream ripped out of her. She'd thrown out her hands for balance when he spun her, clawed at the wall as he pulled out then slammed back in. Barely able to hold herself together, she put her hands on his face, on that part of him he so rarely allowed anyone to touch, and held him, their eyes locked together and their breaths colliding as he pounded her into the wall.

The scent of him was hot, masculine, and Noah. Just Noah.

Her body knew his, wanted his, and her heart, it was his.

Her orgasm was inevitable. The last things she saw were Noah's eyes looking into hers, the dark gray wild. His body slammed into her one final time and went rigid, his fingers digging into her flesh and his chest crushing her breasts.

Her hands never left his face.

And she heard him say "Kit" again a heartbeat before the world became nothing but a wrenching kaleidoscope of pleasure.

NOAH SHUDDERED THROUGH THE clawing, violent pleasure of his orgasm. It gripped him, shook, but what held him even more tightly was Kit's touch on his face, her skin against his.

Legs shaky afterward, he pulled out of her and got rid of the condom by trying to chuck it in the neat wicker trash basket Kit kept on one side of the room. He was fairly certain he missed, but Kit could be pissed with him for that later. Right now he just wanted to hold her.

Tumbling them both onto the bed, Kit's eyes dazed when they opened, he braced himself over her just enough that he wasn't crushing her. Her breasts, still cupped by black lace, moved against his chest, and her breath kissed his face. She lifted a trembling hand, stroked his jaw. It felt good, felt fucking great.

"You can have the romantic bullshit now," he said, being the hard man when the truth was that he needed the romantic bullshit.

Lips curving in a smile that rocked his world and eyes heavy lidded, Kit stroked her fingers back to play with his hair as she put her other hand on his biceps. "Thanks," she said and, when he kissed her, kissed him back slow and lazy.

He sank into the kiss, sank into her, feeling good after sex for the first time in his life. It hadn't been some cheap hate fuck. Not the women, he'd never hated them. It was himself he'd hated, his anger directed inward.

This, tonight... it didn't feel like that.

He didn't hate what he'd done, didn't want to escape it. He wanted to linger, wanted to wallow, wanted to wrap himself in this moment when he'd given his woman what she needed. Squeezing her breast as they kissed, he caught her moan in his mouth, squeezed again.

She squirmed under him, but her fingers stayed lazily playful just above his nape.

Lowering himself even more heavily onto her, he tugged down the cup of her bra and filled his hand with her warm flesh. Her nipple was stiff against his palm, her skin silky. Even softer than the skin of her legs as they rubbed along the hair-roughened skin of his.

They lay tangled and lazy in bed, kiss after kiss, the air hot and humid between them and his hand on her breast.

"Let me take off my bra," she murmured when her lips were swollen and wet and her body so aroused that he could smell the erotic musk of her in the air.

He lifted himself off her but didn't go far. She had to twist to get the bra off, and he enjoyed every small movement. The instant the lace was gone, he came down on her again, this time with his chest flush against her breasts and his hands interlacing with hers on either side of her head. His cock unerringly found her slick heat.

She arched, moaning. "Again?"

"Yeah." He felt good tonight, felt normal, no demons howling in his head. "You got protection?" He'd only had the one condom in his wallet

Kit ran a foot up his calf. "In the bathroom cabinet."

He groaned, not wanting to get up and out of bed to go grab it. "It's meant to be in the bedside drawer for a reason."

Rubbing up against him, she wiggled one hand free to run a finger down the line of his throat as the tip of his cock touched the scalding heat of her. His eyes all but rolled back in his head. A little more of this and he was done. Especially if she kept stroking him, petting him, dropping kisses along his jaw and down his throat.

"I'll go get it," he said, not moving.

She hooked her legs over his hips. "Okay."

"*Kit.*" He was trying to be a good guy here, but she wasn't exactly helping. "Move another inch and I'll be inside you."

Lashes lifting, she sank her teeth into her lower lip... and moved that inch.

The air left his lungs, his hips slamming forward almost of their own accord to bury his cock to the hilt inside her. She was so goddamn hot, so fucking wet. "Oh, Jesus."

Not about to question her trust when he'd never felt so good in his life, he began to move again. He'd intended to go slow, intended to make it last, but his body had other ideas. No way would this be slow, not with Kit holding him so possessively inside her while her kiss was pure heat and tenderness.

"Noah, do that again," she moaned after he pulled out almost all the way, only to thrust back in.

His cock pulsing at the sign of her pleasure—yeah, his dick

was a teacher's pet, wanted all the gold stars—he gave her what she wanted. Again and again and again.

AN HOUR LATER, THEY somehow stumbled to the outdoor bed and fell asleep, sticky with sweat and sex.

CHAPTER 37

K IT WAS STILL FLOATING in a dream world midmorning the next day. She'd always known she'd enjoy getting physical with Noah, but she'd never imagined *that*. It hadn't just been the orgasms. Those were incredible, her body yet buzzed from them. No, what she'd loved the most had been all the unexpected "romantic bullshit" afterward.

Just lying tangled up with Noah while they kissed and laughed and talked.

They'd done that after the second time too, and she'd fallen asleep to the feel of his kiss against her shoulder as he spooned her.

The fact he'd slept the night through was the cherry on top of the entire thing. "Careful, Kit," she murmured to herself. "One night doesn't fix everything." What had happened to Noah couldn't be so easily overcome. It was a scar on his soul, and the two of them would have to learn to deal with it day by day. But—she smiled—it looked like there were going to be a lot of good days mixed in with the bad.

Buzz.

Startled from her happy thoughts by the sound of the intercom, she answered it to find Butch on the other end. "What is it, Butch?" If she had a visitor other than a friend, she'd have to change quickly out of the old cutoffs she was wearing with a sleeveless amber-colored top.

"Your friend, the makeup artist with the blue hair, is here. I figured you'd want her sent up, right?"

"Yes, thanks." Hanging up, she finished putting her hair in a ponytail and went to the front door to open it. She waved to Becca when the other woman stepped out of a red sports car of the same model as Kit's black one.

"I didn't expect to see you today," Kit said, happy for the company. Noah had gone out to pick up a purchase, and she wasn't meeting Harper and Thea till this afternoon. "Aren't you at a shoot today?"

"I'm on break. I had to bring you something!" Becca ran over on high-heeled black boots. She'd paired the boots with a short and tight black skirt, her top a fitted white tee over which she'd thrown a fake fur vest in black with sparkles. On her head was a jaunty hat also in black.

Reaching Kit, she opened her hand.

Gold glinted in the sunlight.

"My necklace!" Kit picked it up. "Oh my God, where did you find it?" A rare, thoughtful gift from her father, Kit had cherished the fine necklace with its diamond pendant in the shape of the comedy and tragedy masks that symbolized the dramatic arts. She'd lost it after forgetting to leave it at home one day, had believed it stolen.

It was the necklace for which her stalker had sent her a "replacement."

"It was in a corner of the makeup trailer I'm in for this

movie—same trailer as with the superhero flick," Becca said. "I realized that's where I always put my makeup kit after I worked on you in your trailer between takes. My best guess is that the necklace fell into it and then fell out when I opened the kit."

"I'm just glad you found it." Hugging the other woman, she invited her in.

"You alone?"

Kit smiled. Clearly the Noah-Becca relationship would require more work. "Yes. Noah's gone to pick up a guitar he just bought." He had an ever-expanding collection—a large part of which was now housed in one of her formerly spare rooms, and the thing was, he used them all.

"These were made to create music," he'd said to her once. "Not to be hung up in a museum or a rich man's showroom."

"Let me grab my purse and phone." Becca zipped back to the car before coming into the house.

Leading her to the kitchen, Kit set the coffee to brewing, then used the shining brushed steel of the fridge as a mirror to put on the necklace. As she did, she thought back to the day it had gone missing and remembered that she'd been extra careful. Not wanting to lose it, she'd put it in a little toiletries bag, which she'd then placed in a cupboard built into the wall.

It didn't have a lock, but since the cupboard otherwise held light snacks, she hadn't thought anyone would bother to search there, even if they got into the trailer.

"Hmm," she said to Becca. "I don't think this fell into your makeup kit."

Her friend froze in the act of eating a cookie she'd grabbed out of the jar on the counter. "You don't think I took it?"

"No, oh my God. Of course not!" Kit was horrified Becca would believe that even for a second. "I was thinking that whoever stole it might have stashed it in the makeup trailer since there's always so much traffic there and, for some reason, couldn't come back."

"Yeah, could be. We did have a lot of new people on that movie." Becca smiled. "So how's the whole stalker deal? Still creepy?"

"It sounds so old-fashioned, but having Noah here really helps." Kit felt her heart just grow big and hot inside her chest at the touch of his name on her lips. "He makes me feel safe. I know the stalker won't try anything while Noah's around."

"Wow, lot of faith in a guitar player."

"He's far more than that," Kit said, walking over to check on the coffee. "Just give him a chance."

A shrug. "Sorry. I'm always going to think you deserve better."

Kit didn't want to have this conversation again, and this time she decided to be honest with her friend. "Don't do that, Becca. Don't put him down." She knew Noah would never allow anyone to bad-mouth her in front of him, and she hated hearing Becca do that to him. "I love him, and he's going to be a part of my life."

"So I should get with the program or get out?" The other woman put down the cookie and got off the breakfast stool. "I expected better from you than that you'd be one of those women who ditches her friends once she has a new cock."

"*Becca.*" Shocked by the vitriol, Kit came around the counter. "Why would you even say that? We've been hanging out just as much as always. You know I cherish my friends."

The other woman folded her arms. "I know you used to talk to me about the stalker and your contracts and how much this house was sucking your income and all that real stuff. *I* was the one who helped you when the stalker first appeared. *I* was the one who held your hand when you made the first police report." Becca's cheeks were red, her breath quick and harsh. "Now you tell Noah everything and treat me like nothing."

"That's not fair." Kit waved her hand in a wide gesture, accidentally hitting the small glass bowl in which she kept her keys. It went to the floor, shattered, her keys falling out. She didn't stop to pick them up. "We spoke so much because we were together on set every day." First on *Primrose Avenue*, then later on *Last Flight* and the superhero movie. "Of course we see less of each other now that we're working on different projects. That doesn't mean we're not friends."

Becca shrugged off her hand when Kit would've put it on her shoulder. "He's a whore, Kit and you're a whore for sleeping with him."

Flinching, Kit stepped back. "That's enough." It was far beyond anything a friend should ever say. "I don't know what's wrong with you, but I think you should go before you destroy our friendship."

"Don't call me the next time the stalker leaves a gift in your car. Personally, I think he's wasting elegant Florentina Chastain chocolates on a woman who thinks Noah St. John is a good catch."

Furious, Kit was about to physically throw Becca out when her blood ran cold. *No one* but Kit, Noah, Butch, and the police detective handling her stalking case knew about the chocolates.

Even if she was misremembering, she knew she wouldn't have said the name of the chocolatier to anyone—she hadn't even opened the package at the time. It was only forty-eight hours ago that the detective had mentioned the name in a call to her. He'd been checking if maybe she'd had any contact with that particular store, or if any of the employees were familiar to her.

"How do you know about the chocolates?" she asked Becca, a sick, heavy feeling in her gut.

When Becca's expression went white, her lips not moving, Kit lifted a hand to her mouth. "Why would you do that?" It came out a shaken whisper. "Why would you help some creep terrorize me?" The two of them had been friends forever, had trusted one another with so many of their secrets and dreams. "Why, Becca?"

Becca didn't answer, just reached into her purse and pulled out a small, sleek gun. Kit stared at it. Of course the security guards wouldn't have thought to search her. She was Kit's good friend, had often come to the house... when she could've left a door ajar or a window open for later access. Not here, not with the alarms, but back at the town house, where the stalking had first begun.

"I don't want to kill you," Becca said in a voice that held anger and panic both. "I never wanted to hurt you."

"Then why did you bring the gun?" Kit felt as if she were looking at the world through a freeze-frame, everything hanging in time. "Why are you pointing it at me?"

"The gun's for *him*, for that fucking whore who made you so cheap." Becca's pitch was high and sharp, but her hands didn't tremble. "You're *my* friend. *Mine*. He's got no right to you."

Kit suddenly remembered how someone had wrecked Schoolboy Choir's dressing room a couple of years ago when they'd done a set as part of a charity concert. The guys had figured it was a drunk fellow musician, but Becca had been backstage at that concert, acting as makeup artist for a soloist.

Kit put that incident together with Cody's slashed tires the night of the wrap party, the dog feces that had been thrown at the house of a female director with whom Kit had begun a friendship before the director moved to work on a project in Europe, as well as the way Becca was always busy when Kit invited her to join Kit, Molly, and Thea for coffee or lunch, and knew the police, everyone, they'd been wrong.

The stalking had nothing to do with sex or physical attraction. It had to do with a pathological kind of friendship on Becca's part. If Kit was right, Becca hadn't been helping a male partner—this was too personal. That meant the sexual part of the stalking had been window dressing meant to hide Becca's gender and true aim: to be Kit's one and only friend.

"Where did you get the semen to smear on my bedspread?" It had been done literally a minute before Kit walked into the house, on dark blue sheets that would've made the stain obvious, even if the stalker hadn't left a card next to it.

Becca had been in the town house the day before, seen the sheets, could've easily broken the lock on the window through which the stalker was found to have entered. As for the timing, Becca had been texting with Kit as Kit walked home from the party she'd been at that night—a party which Becca had left earlier on some excuse Kit couldn't now remember. Kit had told her she'd be home in five minutes if Becca wanted to drop by.

Now the smaller woman shrugged. "Saved the condom from a wannabe actor I fucked who has a thing for you." A small smile. "He did me because he thought it would get him close to you. I figured he'd make a good fall guy if the DNA was ever traced—the dipshit even has a poster of you on his wall. Smoking gun, right?"

That was when Kit realized just how deep this went, how much planning had been involved. "You must really care about me," she said, playing to Becca's pathology though terror threatened to freeze her to the spot. "Not many people care in this industry."

"That's what I've been trying to tell you." Becca dashed away a tear. "I'm the one who's always looked after you. I made you beautiful on *Primrose Avenue*, then made you perfect for *Last Flight*. You would've never gotten that Oscar nod without me, but did I ever crow? No. I was happy for my friend. I wanted the best for you."

"I know. I understand." In truth, Kit was the one who'd recommended Becca to the *Last Flight* crew, and from that credit had flowed other work offers for the makeup artist.

Becca smiled shakily. "Good. I don't want to lose our friendship over this. Once I get rid of Noah, we can go back to how it was."

She waved the gun as Kit's entire soul screamed. "Let's go sit in the living room and wait for him. We'll drive out and bury the body in the desert and you can say he got drugged to the eyeballs and ran off with a groupie." A sudden frown. "Don't scream or I'll shoot you. Your bodyguards are too far away anyway."

Kit decided she *would* scream, but she'd wait until Noah was back. She would not let Becca hurt the man she loved more than anything.

CHAPTER 38

NOAH WAS TALKING TO the older guy from whom he'd bought the mint-condition blond Gibson when his eye caught on the magazines on the man's coffee table. "You into makeup as well as guitars?"

The bearded and tattooed biker and musician stroked his white beard. "Yeah, right. Those are my granddaughter's— girl wants to work in the movies creating aliens or something." He threw up his hands. "I tell her she should do beautiful women, but she just says *Grandpa*, then starts talking about brow ridges and facial prosthetics and..."

The other man was still talking, but Noah had tuned him out. Something about the topmost magazine was bugging him. Picking it up, he scanned the cover. Nothing he was interested in; it looked like a small trade magazine for those in the makeup industry. It didn't even feature anyone he knew, so why was he—

The letters. The fucking letters.

The magazine used a distinctive font on the cover, the same as in several of the letters used in the card the stalker had attached to the box of chocolates left in the backseat of Noah's Mustang.

Becca

He shook his head to dislodge the thought. Just because he didn't get along with Kit's friend was no reason to suspect her—and anyway, the stalker was a man. Still, it might point them in the right direction.

"...so I said, sure honey, whatever you want."

Tuning back into the other man's monologue, Noah grinned and nodded. "Women, huh?"

"Can't live without 'em." Winking, the bearded male held out a hand. "Pleasure doing business with you."

"Same."

Getting into his car for the drive back home, Noah decided to call Kit, tell her his idea about her stalker's likely connection to Becca's side of the industry. Maybe it was a guy who'd worked on Kit at some point. When she didn't answer her home line or the cell, he figured she must be out in the garden. Speaking of which, he'd intended to pick her up a plant... but he had a sudden compulsion to get home, that damn magazine nagging at him.

He'd surprise her with the plant later, he decided and drove on, going as fast as he dared.

Arriving at the gates, he rolled through after activating them using the remote Kit had given him. He saw Butch keeping an eye on things, stopped to say hello. "Any problems?"

"Nah. Kit's got her colorful friend with her though, so you might want to make yourself scarce. I don't think that one likes you too much."

"Becca?" Noah's muscles tensed. "How long's she been here?"

"Couple of hours." Butch frowned. "What's wrong? Did I screw up?"

"We might all have screwed up." Noah thrust a hand through his hair. "Kit wasn't answering her phone when I called a half hour ago." The garden theory still applied; they could be out there talking, but Noah didn't want to take the chance.

Getting out of the car, he said, "Let's go up quietly. If they're in the garden chatting, no harm, no foul and Becca never has to know I suspected her."

Butch nodded. "I'll radio Casey, tell him to keep an eye on the gate while we go in."

It felt as if it took them forever to reach the house. Splitting up, they went around on either side, careful to avoid the windows, though Noah made sure to take a quick glimpse inside as he crouched by each. He wanted to think he was being an idiot, but his heart was thumping, adrenaline flowing, and then he looked through the living room window and rage roared through his blood.

Kit was sitting stiffly in a chair while Becca sat across from her in an identical chair. Nothing wrong with that except for the fear on Kit's face. Becca had to have a weapon.

Continuing around the house, he met Butch on the patio, told him what he'd seen. "It has to be a gun or Kit would've tried to overpower her." Kit was taller, had more muscle.

Face grim, Butch said, "Our one advantage is that we know the situation and there are two of us, three if I pull Casey in—or we can alert the cops, have them bring in an extraction team."

"No, we do it quickly. She's clearly unstable, might decide to shoot Kit while we set things up." He would not leave Kit in danger and afraid. "Wait," he said, a sudden thought blazing

379

in his head. "Why is she still here?" If Becca's intent had been to hurt Kit, she could've done that as soon as she arrived, then taken off.

"Probably waiting for you."

Their eyes met on the heels of Butch's flippant mutter.

The bodyguard swore softly.

"So," Noah said, "she wants to shoot me." They could use that. "Is your marksmanship good enough to get her through a window?"

"Were any of the windows open?"

"Shit. No."

"Can't take the risk the glass will slow down or skew the bullet enough to give her a warning—even a split second could change everything." Butch slid out his weapon. "You go through the front door and I'll go through the back," the bodyguard said. "I can get behind her and disarm her while she's distracted by you."

That sounded fine except for one thing. "Kit won't just sit there and do nothing." Because Kit fucking *loved* Noah. "She's going to get in the way when Becca tries to shoot me, could get hurt." An unacceptable risk.

"Find a way to alert her that you know what's happening."

Noah rubbed his forehead, trying to think clearly. The next few minutes were going to be the most important of his entire life. Because if anything happened to Kit…

KIT JERKED AS HER cell phone rang again. "You should check that. If it's one of the guards and I don't answer this time, they'll get suspicious."

Grabbing the phone, Becca swiped to answer. "Hi, Butch," she said, her voice bubbly and cheerful. "Kit's in the ladies' room, but she told me to answer if you or Casey called. Is someone at the gate?"

A short pause.

"Oh, okay, I'll tell her. Do you want her to call you back?" Another pause. "All right. Bye." Hanging up with a smug smile, Becca said, "I could've been an actress, you know. A really good one. But I make other people pretty instead. I made you the prettiest of all."

"You did." Kit had managed to keep Becca calm over the past two hours by reminiscing over their friendship, though all the memories were now forever tainted. "What did Butch want?"

"Oh." Becca waved her gun. "He said the exterminator you called to take care of the sparrow's nest in your rain gutter came by to say he'd forgotten his ladder extension thingie or something like that, so he'd be back in three hours after another job." Becca made a face. "You gonna kill the birds? That's kinda cold, Kit."

Kit's heart thumped, her face threatening to flush. Because no sparrow had made a nest in the rain gutter of the house, and if one had, Kit certainly wouldn't exterminate it. She did, however, have a lover who'd written what was her favorite song of all time, despite its haunting sadness.

A car engine sounded on the drive not long afterward, drawing steadily closer. It stopped, a door was shut. The front door opened within seconds. "Kit!"

"Answer him." Becca pointed the gun at Kit's face on that low-voiced command. "Or I'll mess you up until you won't need makeup to play a horror villain."

Kit didn't care about her face. She cared about Noah's life. Hoping that she'd read things right, that Noah wasn't about to walk into an ambush, she said, "In here!"

"I'm going around the back!" Noah called out. "I got you some plants. I'll off-load them in the garden."

Kit rubbed her hands on her thighs, realizing Noah was trying to get her out of this room with its limited access routes. "I should go back there to meet him."

"You're with your friend. No reason for him to get suspicious."

Kit thought fast. "I never sit in here with anyone who visits. I'm always either in the kitchen or in the garden."

"You could be showing me stuff from your closet, or I could be doing your makeup."

Shrugging, Kit went for another Oscar nomination. "Sure, I guess. Only, the bedroom's before this room, so when he doesn't see us in there and he sees the broken bowl in the kitchen…"

That seemed to decide Becca. "Get up." She nudged at Kit with her gun. "Stay in front. Do or say anything stupid and I'll blow your brains out."

"I thought we were friends."

"We are, but you need to prove your loyalty to me by not warning that piece of shit who thought he could take you from me."

Kit's hands fisted, the urge to plant one in Becca's face increasingly strong. "I won't. We've talked. You know you mean too much to me, my career means too much to me, for me to throw it all away."

"Good. Now we just have to finish—"

Kit dropped to the floor the instant she was outside the doorway. She heard a scream, heard the thunder of the gun going off, smelled gunpowder in the air as something slammed to the ground.

Terrified Becca had made good on her threats and shot Noah, she turned to find Noah and Butch had pinned the other woman to the floor. They must've both been in the corridor, on opposite sides of the door.

"Are you hurt?" she asked, looking from one to the other. "Noah, Butch!"

Taking a zip tie from his inner coat pocket, Butch put it around a screaming Becca's wrists while Noah held her down.

"We're good," Noah said at the same time. "Your ceiling will need a little repair work though."

She looked up, saw the hole. Relief was a cool river crashing over her. "Hope the sparrow is safe."

Noah grinned. "Tough things, sparrows. They can survive just about anything." Releasing Becca once she was contained, he came over and tugged Kit up and into his arms.

"You were fucking amazing." He squeezed her tight. "The plan was for me to haul you out of the way so Butch could take her down, but then you did that drop and we could both focus on her."

Holding on to him with all her strength, she said, "My character's best friend in *Primrose Avenue* was taken hostage by a deranged ex once. I got to save her and she had to fall to the floor to give me the chance to shoot him."

Noah's chest rumbled against her as he laughed. "And they say you can't learn anything from soap operas."

Crying and laughing, Kit didn't look as a screaming, ranting

Becca was taken outside by Butch to wait for the cops. She knew the other woman was disturbed, needed help, but she couldn't be generous right now—she was too angry and chilled by the remnants of the fear Becca had created in her. She just needed to hold on to Noah, and he clearly needed to hold on to her.

That's how they stayed until the cops came.

THE REST OF THE band, as well as Molly and Thea—Sarah having returned to her home now that the locks had been changed—descended on the house in the next hour. Thea was already handling the media calls so Kit didn't have to, while Molly and David made a late lunch for everyone as the rest of them sat at the kitchen table talking over the shocking turn of events.

"That's serious premeditation," a grim-faced Abe said when Kit explained the disgusting incident with the semen on her bed.

"Scary fucking premeditation." Noah's voice was without mercy. "I hope they lock her up for a long time."

"Not much doubt of that," Fox said, his eyes glittering with barely withheld fury. "She had Kit at gunpoint."

"And she's got a record." Thea, who'd been in the garden, talking on the phone, came back inside. "That last call was from one of my police contacts—Becca stalked someone before, back in high school."

The publicist went to David, leaning into him as he slid his arm around her. "No charges filed, so it didn't come up in a background check, but the victim called in once news of

Becca's arrest hit the media. Becca went at her with a broken bottle."

Kit put both hands over her face for a second to get her breathing in order. "No charges?"

"The victim and Becca used to be best friends, and Becca had lost her dad not long before the incident." Thea's phone buzzed again. "Since Becca didn't actually manage to hurt her and was leaving town anyway, the friend decided not to pile on the hurt." Pressing a kiss to David's cheek before she put the phone to her ear, Thea walked back out into the garden.

Noah held Kit close to him, as he had since it happened. "Thank God she's off the streets and out of your life."

Feeling sad for her friend but also angry and relieved it was all over, Kit just soaked in Noah's warmth and listened to the others talk. Thea's phone was going nonstop, the publicist popping in and out to keep them updated as comforting food smells filled the kitchen. One of Noah's guitars inevitably ended up in his arms while David made do with a couple of utensils against various surfaces, and Abe clapped a rhythm as Fox sang one of their older hits.

It was just what she needed. Blissful normality.

CHAPTER 39

S HE SLEPT THAT NIGHT in Noah's arms under the starlit sky and woke to find him awake. "Did you sleep?" He'd held her in his arms through the night, made her feel so deeply safe, but she could tell his demons had been at him again. "Be honest with me."

"Four hours," he said with a smile that didn't reach his eyes. "Pretty good for me."

Rising up on her elbow, she brushed his hair off his face. "Hey," she whispered. "There was a time when spending a night in your arms was a pipe dream for me. We're doing it, making it."

Noah flexed then fisted the hand of the arm he had under his head. "I just feel so goddamn pathetic sometimes." The words were spit out. "I'm a grown man who wakes up shivering after a nightmare. What the fuck?"

Kit had that sense of flying without a chute again, stumbling her way through this. So many things she didn't know, but one thing she did: she loved this man and he loved her. "I didn't have nightmares," she told him. "Thank you for keeping the monsters at bay."

Some of the tension leached out of his body, the steely gray of his eyes softening. "You're kinda cuddly in bed, Katie." A hint of a smile. "I can't move an inch without you following."

She made a face at him. "You complaining?"

Squeezing her hip, he grinned. "Never. Cuddle up to me all you like. I can take it."

Kit laughed and knew they'd survived this hurdle. "Come on. I'm starving." She'd barely eaten last night, her nerves still jangling. "What do you say to waffles again?" Movie diet be damned.

"I say I make better waffles than you."

"I say you're right, so get moving."

"Yes, ma'am."

Falling back a little on purpose just so she could watch Noah's ass in the white boxer briefs that were all he wore, Kit smiled. For the first time since the stalking began, there was no weight of fear on her, no edginess. She felt light and free. And the fact Noah was with her, that he trusted her with his secrets? Yeah, that made everything better.

"We're doing this," she whispered again. "We're making it."

THE NEXT THREE NIGHTS were wonderful. The fourth was so bad Noah pushed her away and went inside to grab his guitar. She heard him plucking at the strands as she lay in bed alone—and she decided that would never work.

Getting up, she made them both coffee, then left him to his brooding—though not until after she'd kissed his sullen face. "I love you," she said with another kiss. "Even when you're a bad-tempered, surly rock star."

Scowling, he didn't say a word, but when she returned home around six that night after a shoot with the cosmetics company, it was to find an iPod waiting on her pillow. When she slotted it into her music system, Noah's voice singing the haunting words of "Sparrow" filled the air. It made her cry and then smile, because she recognized the gentle beat in the background, the gritty voice that joined Noah's on the chorus, the expert piano playing.

He'd finally shared the song with the guys. Not just shared it but recorded it.

Listening to it five more times in a row, Kit messaged him: *It's my favorite. I'm crying, it's so beautiful.*

His response came seconds later: *Was doing weights with David. I keep forgetting how fucking fit he is and then he wipes the floor with me. Damn smug drummers. And yeah, I figured "Sparrow" deserved to be recorded after it helped us defeat the psycho bitch. I'll be home soon. Stop crying.*

Sliding away her phone, Kit allowed herself to think of Becca. Part of her would always mourn the loss of their friendship, and one day she might even find it in herself to visit Becca in the facility where she was being held, but she'd never be able to forgive the other woman for the terror she'd caused.

However, that was over and done with, and Kit didn't intend to allow it to further steal her time or emotional energy. She just wanted to treasure her true friends, and most of all, she wanted to be with Noah, to create a life with him. With that thought in mind, she pushed up her sleeves and decided to surprise him with a homemade dinner.

NOAH FELT GOOD. HE'D felt like shit this morning, but then Kit had told him she loved him even when he was a bad-tempered, surly rock star and his mood had started to lift. Part of him couldn't help but worry that she'd decide he was too much work—her affectionate scowl this morning had been just what the doctor ordered.

Then he'd gone to see the guys and finally fessed up about "Sparrow." He'd had a serious fucking case of nerves before he started to sing it for them, but all three had loved it. In Fox's eyes, he'd seen an understanding of the hidden meaning of the song, but there had also been a quiet pride.

Fox understood what it meant for him to release "Sparrow" into the world.

David and Abe, who didn't know about his childhood, had blown out their breaths almost in sync.

"Goddamn. That's powerful, man," Abe had said quietly, then added something Noah would've never expected the keyboard player to say. "It made me think of Tessie, like she's flying free just like that bird in the song."

Noah's heart had clenched in visceral pain. "Yeah." It was all he'd been able to say; he knew how deeply the death of Abe's baby sister had scarred Abe, and to think his song had given the keyboard player a measure of peace was a priceless gift.

David had just nodded and picked up his sticks to beat out a deep, gentle rhythm that fit the song. Fox had grabbed his guitar, and Abe, in whose house they'd been sitting, had taken the dust covers off the grand piano he hadn't touched since the day Tessie died.

They'd recorded it raw using Abe's equipment, and Noah had driven back home to leave the song for Kit before hooking up with David. Feeling pumped and as if he'd released all the toxic stuff that had built up inside him, he dumped his gym gear in the back of his car and thrust a hand through his shower-damp hair. "You and Thea want to swing by for dinner?" he asked David, who was parked right next to him.

"Nah, I have to go play trophy husband at a big dinner meeting Thea has with some too-stylish-for-you magazine people." David's grin belied his words.

"Watch that goofy fucking smile. You have an image to maintain," Noah said, but he was happy for his friend; David had been crazy about Thea forever.

Just like Noah had been about Kit.

David pointed a finger at him. "I don't have the bad-boy image. What are you going to do about that now you've shacked up with Kit?"

"Tell everyone to bite it." He had no intention of giving the media bad-boy fodder ever again—not unless it involved being caught making out with Kit in scandalous locations. That, he was definitely up for.

Laughing, David bumped fists with him, and they got into their cars to head off in opposite directions. Noah was listening to Esteban's latest LP when he stopped at a crosswalk to let an older couple get across.

He was tapping a beat on the steering wheel and smiling at the thought of going home to Kit when his eye was caught by the man and the golden-blond child who'd just stepped onto the crosswalk from the other side. The man was holding the boy's hand, the boy dragging his feet. It was a familiar scene that Noah had probably witnessed a thousand times over his lifetime, but today, it made nausea churn in his gut, his hands clamping tight on the steering wheel as a haze of red filmed his vision.

Unclipping his seat belt, he began to open the car door, convinced the child needed to be rescued... but then the man said something and the child's face lit up. Bouncing on his feet now, he spoke excitedly, and then the two were on the other side of the crosswalk and walking away.

Noah's heart still thumped, his throat dry.

It was only when an impatient horn sounded from behind him that he pulled his door shut and started driving again. He didn't know where he was going, but it wasn't home. He felt too fucked-up to go home. Ending up on a sea-facing outlook, he stared at the Pacific Ocean crashing to shore until gray turned to dark and all he could see were the headlights and fading taillights of cars along the Pacific Coast Highway.

Sweat pasted his T-shirt to his skin, his hands still clamped on the steering wheel. Finally peeling them off, he shoved open his door and got out. Nausea cramped his gut again without warning. Bending down instinctively, his hands on his knees, he threw up. There wasn't much in his stomach, just a bottle of the electrolyte-laden sports water David had given him.

After that, it was just harsh, dry retching that felt as if it went on forever. He was half aware of a phone ringing in the distance, but he couldn't focus on that, his entire concentration on getting his spasming muscles under control.

It seemed to take forever.

Grabbing a fresh bottle of water from the pack he had in the back, he rinsed out his mouth and threw some water on his face, then stood facing the warm wind until it had dried him off. His phone, when he checked it after getting back in the car, showed him Kit's name on multiple missed calls and text messages. She had to be worried since he should've been home hours ago.

Feeling like a shit, he sent her a text message: *I'm fine. Don't wait up.*

He switched off the phone after sending it so she couldn't call him. He couldn't talk to Kit right now. He felt filthy, dirty, ugly, just as he'd felt when he'd been a boy the same age as the boy he'd seen on the crosswalk. That wasn't what had set him off, however. No, he'd finally realized the reason for his insanity—the man's shirt.

It was the exact same shirt the bastard had worn the day it began.

He hadn't realized the pattern was burned into his memory, not until today.

After drinking the rest of the water, he threw the empty bottle on the passenger seat and started up the engine.

Once again, he didn't know where he was going; he just needed to drive. But when he ended up in the parking lot of a strip joint splattered with graffiti, the garish neon lights flashing on his windshield, it wasn't a surprise. This was where he fit, a place where no one would expect him to be a better man.

He had no right to someone like Kit, no right to touch her, hold her. He'd ruin her. Better he stay in the darkness.

Switching off his engine, he opened the car door.

CHAPTER 40

KIT HAD GONE FROM worry to panic to fury in the space of the past few hours. When Noah didn't make it home by the time he should have, she'd figured he and David must've ended up hanging out. She hadn't started to really worry until he was an hour late. That's when she'd sent the first text message, to no response.

Feeling fear walk cold fingers up her spine, the memory of the incident with Becca yet fresh in her mind, she'd called David, discovered that Noah had left the gym long ago. She'd tried to be logical, to not panic as she called and messaged him, but had just started thinking she needed to check the hospitals when she received his response.

I'm fine. Don't wait up.

The cold arrogance of the message stunned her. Not about to take it lying down, she called back at once—to be told Noah's phone was either switched off or out of range. Kit had a very good idea which was true.

So angry she could barely think straight, she put on her running shoes and pounded out her anger on the pavement. Noah still wasn't back by the time she returned, and all the

393

food had gone cold. Showering, she changed into shorts and a tank top, and making herself a plate, took it out into the garden.

The peace of it soothed her, and made every part of her hurt with stabbing pains. Because if Noah had hit a wall at some point today, then things could well be far worse than him just acting like an asshole to her. She might wake to tabloid reports of him getting drunk or breaking up a place... or fucking some random woman.

Anger burned her throat.

Putting down her fork, she dropped her face in her hands and breathed deep.

"Kit."

Her shoulders grew stiff at that familiar male voice, her emotions caustic. Too furious to look at him, too afraid of what she might see, she forced herself to pick up her fork and eat a bite.

Noah slid onto the bench beside her, moving until his thigh and arm pressed against her own. She smelled sweat, as if he hadn't showered after the gym, but the rest of it was just Noah. No alcohol, no clinging tobacco smoke, no perfume.

"How mad are you?"

"Depends." She stared out into the garden. "What did you do?"

"I went to a seedy strip club and sat in the parking lot telling myself that was what I deserved. Not a home, not with you. Just a dirty place I couldn't ruin with my ugliness, with people who couldn't give two fucks about me."

His words made her hurt for him, but she was braced for a blow herself, waiting for him to tell her the rest. Because she'd hit her limit. She'd told him her line in the sand. If he'd crossed it, she wouldn't be able to forgive him. Not this time.

"I opened the car door to get out," Noah said, breaking her heart, "and then it hit me what a fucking idiot I was being. I was about to let what that bastard did destroy the best thing in my life. I was about to permanently damage my relationship with a woman who loves me even when I'm a surly, bad-tempered and moody son of a bitch. So I pulled the door shut and hauled ass home."

He put his hand on the back of her neck, and the touch was oddly tentative for Noah. "So, how long are you going to be mad?"

Relief was a roar of blood through her veins. Not pulling away from his touch because, even with anger lingering inside her, she knew he'd take that as a rejection, she said, "I'll let you know when I'm not mad anymore."

He groaned. "Open-ended? That's cold, Katie."

Dropping the fork onto her plate, she turned to face him, and then she did what she'd wanted to do since the instant he'd told her he'd shut the car door and come home. She wrapped her arms tight around him. "That's for coming home," she said as his own arms wrapped around her so hard she could barely breathe. "The mad is for making me worry and for thinking you couldn't come back to me just because the demons were awake."

He shuddered out a breath and then, without prompting, told her what had set him off. "Dumb, huh?"

"No. It just caught you by surprise." She glared at him. "What're you going to do the next time something hits you sideways?"

The answer was immediate and so sure she believed it. "Find you."

"Good." Pulling back, she looked up into his face. "We need a pool." She didn't want to wait six months, wanted Noah to know his place was right here. With her.

His eyes filled with that luminous, astonishing light, his smile delighted as he held her face in his hands and pressed his forehead to hers. "Infinity?"

Melted by that smile no one else in the world ever saw, she fisted her hand in his T-shirt. "I saw one with waterfalls that I like."

"We can get waterfalls." A tender kiss followed by a wicked one. "As long as you promise to wear string bikinis and stand under the water."

"It could be arranged."

Still smiling, he said, "I need to shower." He ran his hands down her arms. "I've made you sticky too."

"Want to shower together?"

His eyes widened, and she realized this too would be a brand-new experience for her debauched rock star.

"Yeah," he said with a slow smile. "Will you soap my back?"

"If you ask nicely."

NOAH HADN'T EVER SHOWERED with a woman before. Watching Kit pin up her barely dry hair, her sleek body naked, he started to think he might just like this. Then she turned on the water and stepped in, shooting him a playful look over her shoulder, and he *knew* he liked this.

Stripping off his own clothes, he got in behind her and bent to kiss her neck, his hands on her hips. He knew she was still technically mad at him, and he deserved it, but she loved him too. Even when he fucked up, she still loved him.

He could always come home.

She wouldn't kick him out just because he was imperfect. The only thing he had to do was take care of her heart, a heart she'd entrusted to him. He could do that—crossing her line in the sand held absolutely no appeal when on this side stood his Kit who wanted to build a home with him.

"Hey," she said in mock reproof when he ran his hands up to cup her breasts. "I thought you wanted to shower?"

"I am showering," he said, feeling young for the first time in an eternity. "With a gorgeous woman I intend to lather up." He took her fluffy loofah from her, on which she'd squeezed some girly-smelling body wash, and began to run it over her body.

Leaning back into him, Kit let him do what he wanted, and what he wanted was to worship her. She smiled up at him, and for the first time in his life, a sexual situation was playful. He held the eye contact, kept returning to it, and he had fun. When she stole the loofah from him and tried to cover him in her perfumed body wash, he threatened her with all kinds of revenge.

Laughing, she swapped the loofah for the bar of plain soap he preferred and began to soap him up. He wasn't sure he'd like that part, but he did, because... well, because it was Kit. It was as simple as that.

Sinking into her, he pressed her to the wall and kissed her. She was still smiling and he tasted it as they kissed, as he ran his hand down her stomach to slide two fingers through the liquid-soft flesh between her thighs. He hadn't lied—he wasn't very good at the foreplay stuff, hadn't really ever done it before her, but he wanted to touch Kit, wanted to explore with her.

"Tell me what you like," he said, bracing his other arm above her head.

She shivered as his fingers brushed a particular spot. "*Oh, that's good. Do that.*" There were more whispers after that, more smiles, more kisses.

At one point she gripped his wrist and said, "Noah, oh *please* don't move."

He didn't move. He just upped the pressure.

Back bowing, her breasts lifted up as if for his delectation, Kit came on a little scream. Noah's cock was pulsing, but he was kind of addicted to seeing Kit orgasm, so he decided to continue his education in foreplay by pressing one hand to her lower back and bending his head to her breasts.

He licked, he sucked, and after a while, Kit's gasped breathing turned even more ragged. "Can I touch you here again?" he asked, cupping her between her thighs. She'd pushed him away earlier, saying it was too sensitive.

A moan as he rubbed his stubbled jaw over her breasts. "After that orgasm, you can do whatever you like, Noah St. John."

Feeling like a damn god, he stroked his fingers deep into her, listened to her answers to his carnal questions, and had the reward of feeling her clench convulsively on his driving fingers as she came again with shocked suddenness.

Yeah, that was hot.

Drawing out his fingers from her possessive grasp, he lifted her up against the wall and entered her with his cock. He was hard as stone, and with Kit so honey slick and sated around him, he could've pounded her balls-deep and it would've been fine. But Noah found he had an unexpected patience today.

His balls might be turning blue, but damn, his cock liked being inside Kit.

It was a long, slow session full of romantic bullshit, and afterward, when they were drying off, Noah realized he'd made love to Kit. Not fucked her, not had sex. Made love. He'd always thought that was a dumb phrase, but not today. Today it felt exactly right.

Towel wrapped around her body and tucked over her breasts, Kit came over to him and, linking her hands with his, said, "We're going to be okay."

"Yeah," Noah said. "We are." He was still going to fuck up, but since he wasn't about to hurt Kit, wasn't about to give her up, the fuckups would be manageable. And if she kept smiling at him that way, as if he delighted her... Yeah, well, maybe he wouldn't fuck up that much after all. "I love you, Kit. I will always love you, and I will never mess this up."

It was a vow.

EPILOGUE

TWELVE MONTHS LATER AND Noah was in Kyoto, Japan, paying up on his wager. He'd even made it a point to learn about the red tape he'd have to clear to get the plant back home. But, though this was his forfeit, he wasn't alone on his walk to possible humiliation at the hands of a cantankerous gardener. His lover and best friend walked beside him as they went down the narrow and twisting street at the end of which lived a seventy-year-old man with the reputation of being a bad-tempered *oni*, or Japanese demon.

Dressed simply in skinny blue jeans, canvas sneakers, and a striped blue-and-white tee, her hair pulled back in a sleek ponytail and large sunglasses on her face, Kit nonetheless looked like a movie star. A very famous movie star whose work in *Redemption* was getting serious buzz even while the movie was still in postproduction.

"What?" she said, turning to him with a smile.

Lifting their linked hands, he kissed her knuckles. "Just admiring the most talented woman I know."

"Says the man who wrote the megahit song not only of the year but of the decade." She wore her delight for him on her sleeve, just as she admitted her love for him without hesitation when asked by the media.

In claiming him so unabashedly, in making it clear she was *proud* to have Noah St. John as her man, she'd healed things inside him that had been broken so long he'd thought they'd stay that way forever.

"Yeah, that little sparrow's doing well." It was a song that still made him hurt, but alongside the pain, he felt a quiet pride—in a way, in setting "Sparrow" free, he'd set himself free too. "There, isn't that the right place?"

They looked carefully at the kanji the hotel concierge had written out for them, compared the characters against those on the gate. Taking a deep breath when they proved identical, Noah raised his hand to knock.

THREE HOURS LATER AND Kit had never laughed so hard in her life. The little old gardener had turned out to be a fan—not of her, of Noah and Schoolboy Choir. Over the moon that Kit wanted one of his plants, he'd invited them to stay for dinner with him and his utterly sweet wife. After which he'd offered Noah not sake, but an alcohol so potent it smelled like paint thinner to Kit.

Then the gardener had proceeded to drink the bad boy of rock under the table.

Grinning as she poured a thoroughly drunk Noah into a cab while carefully handling the plant, she got them back to the hotel and up to their room.

"Love you, Kit," Noah mumbled, nuzzling at her as she keycarded their door open and put the plant safely on a little table nearby. "Got your plant."

"I love you too, but you need to get in bed before you fall asleep against the door." She managed to push and prod him to the sprawling bed.

Falling flat on his face, he lost consciousness.

It struck her then. This was exactly how it had all begun. With her getting a drunk Noah into bed. But that was the only parallel. This time she pulled off his boots, managed to get off his belt and jeans, even his T-shirt and, after removing her makeup and changing, slipped into bed beside him.

As she pulled the comforter over both of them, she thought back to that night and knew she could've never imagined this one. Not just tonight, but all the nights that had led up to this. Noah, her stubborn rocker, had not only kept his word, he'd kept his word so well that the tabloids had thrown up their hands in disgust and stopped following him.

Oh, he was still plenty bad. Put him onstage and he was pure sex and heat and a broken guitar or two. But when he came off that stage, he looked only for "his girl," for Kit. All that energy and drive he'd spent on hurting himself? It had now become a fidelity and a devotion that made emotion choke her.

When Noah St. John decided to love, she thought as she snuggled up to him, he went all the way. "I'm so lucky to have you," she said, pressing a kiss to his jaw.

Thick lashes lifted, a moment of pure clarity in the dark gray as Noah wrapped his arm around her waist. "Meant to ask you to marry me, put the ring in the plant soil, but gardener made me drunk. He's so small. What *happened?*"

Half laughing, half crying at his adorably astonished expression, Kit kissed his jaw again. "You can ask me tomorrow morning."

Cuddling her close, he said, "Will you say yes?" It was a sleepy mumble.

"Yes," she whispered on a smile of pure happiness as he fell back asleep. "I'll say yes."

I hope you enjoyed Kit and Noah's story! If you'd like to read a special extra scene featuring them, swing by my website www.nalinisingh.com and join my newsletter. You'll receive the extra scene as part of your Welcome newsletter – and keep an eye out for future newsletters, as I often send out free short stories, deleted scenes, and sneak peeks.

Talking of sneak peeks, I'm already at work on Abe and Sarah's story and should have it in your hands in 2016. If you'd like to read other stories in the Rock Kiss world, check out Rock Addiction (Molly and Fox's story), Rock Courtship (David and Thea's story), and Rock Hard (featuring Molly's best friend Charlotte). An excerpt from Rock Courtship is included on the next page.

Any questions or comments? You can contact me at any time through the e-mail address on my website. You can also find me on Twitter *&* Facebook *– xo Nalini*

SPECIAL EXCERPT FROM

ROCK COURTSHIP

SINCE HE'D SACKED OUT FOR SO LONG, David didn't have much time before he had to head to a downstairs conference room for the interviews. He'd steeled himself for the inevitability of coming face-to-face with Thea, but the sight of her still threatened to gut him.

Scowling, she strode over on sky-high red heels worn with a sleeveless and tailored black dress that ended just above her knees. "Did you put ice on that eye?"

He made himself speak, act normal—he'd become pretty good at that after the length of time he'd loved her. "Yeah, past few hours."

"What about last night?"

He shrugged.

Her glare could've cut steel.

Thankfully, the first reporter arrived a second later, and David spent the rest of the time making light of his new and hopefully short-lived notoriety. Interviews complete, he slipped away while Thea was talking to Abe, and once in his room, used his phone to do some research.

He had no idea how to write a memo, and if he was going

406

to do this, he had to do it properly. The only question was, was he going to do this? Putting down the phone, he got up and, going to the living area of the suite, got down on the floor and began to do push-ups. It was an easy motion for him regardless of his bruised ribs. Like most working drummers, he had to stay highly fit or he'd never last an entire concert.

He usually put in gym time every day, often went running with Noah or Fox, or did weights with Abe. Today, the familiar, repetitive motion of the push-ups cleared his mind, helped him think.

He only wanted Thea with him if she wanted to be with him.

Thea had made it clear his interest wasn't reciprocated.

But, as Molly had reminded him, Thea also had a first-class bastard of an ex. David didn't know exactly what had gone on between Eric and Thea, but he could guess, given that Eric had publicly flaunted a new fiancée within two weeks of the breakup. A silicone-enhanced airhead who simpered and giggled on Eric's arm and didn't have an ounce of Thea's feminine strength.

If fate had any sense of justice, the bimbo would divorce the fuckhead a year down the road and take Eric for every cent he was worth.

So, he thought, pumping down on his arms, then pushing back up, his body held in a punishingly straight line, it could have just been his timing that had led to her rejection. He'd waited six months after the breakup—until he'd thought Thea was okay, but what if she hadn't been at that point? He knew exactly how good she was at putting on a professional, unruffled face.

Hell, he'd once seen her handle a press conference with panache when two hours earlier, she'd been throwing up from food poisoning. What if she'd still been pissed off with the entire male sex that day in her office? Was it possible she'd have rejected any man who walked in and asked her out?

He paused, body tensed to keep himself off the floor as hope uncurled inside him. Because Thea hadn't dated *anyone* since the breakup. That wasn't just wishful thinking: he'd accidentally overheard her business partner at the PR firm, Imani, talking to another mutual friend on the phone a week before the band left LA—he'd been in a conference room early for an interview, the door open to the corridor where Imani was on the phone.

He should've called out and let her know he was inside, but he hadn't been listening at first; it was hearing Thea's name that had caught his notice. And then he couldn't not pay attention.

Imani, happily married to a surgeon, had apparently tried to set Thea up with a colleague of her husband's, only to be stonewalled. "I know Thea's over Eric," the other woman had said, "but whatever el slimeball did, he might have put her off men permanently." A sad sigh.

David wasn't sad about Thea not dating. He was ecstatic. Because it made it easier to believe that it had been his timing at fault. Like Imani, he didn't have any fears that Thea was still in love with the dickhead—no, she was too smart to put up with that kind of bullshit. That didn't mean the bastard hadn't hurt her; a woman as strong and as independent as Thea rarely allowed herself to be vulnerable, and David had a feeling her ex had used that rare, beautiful trust against her.

Fuck, but David wanted to kick the shit out of him. But more, he wanted to make Thea happy. Even if it meant taking a beating himself.

Getting up off the floor, he grabbed his phone and began to type out a memo on the tiny screen. It took him hours of drafting and redrafting to make sure it said exactly what he wanted it to say. He was still working on it when the band headed out to the concert location—where he saw the last person he'd expected.

Thea, now dressed in sleek black pants that hugged her butt and a soft, silky T-shirt of midnight blue under a dark gray blazer that nipped in at the waist, had come to say good-bye to Molly since the two women had missed each other that morning. Narrowing her eyes when she saw him, Thea ostensibly spoke to the entire band—but he knew the words were directed at him.

"If you want me to continue putting out fires for you," she said, "do *not* do anything that interrupts my vacation." A blistering look that was very definitely focused on David. "And next time someone tells you to put ice on a bruise, you listen!"

Then she was gone, her luggage already in the trunk of the car that was taking her to the airport for her flight to the Indonesian island of Bali, home to her parents and little sisters. He watched her step inside the car, its taillights fading far too quickly into the night.

Even then he didn't send the memo.

No, he waited until the minute before the concert was about to begin before pushing Send and turning off his phone. At least this way, he wouldn't be able to torment himself by checking for a response until after the show.

THEA HAD BARELY SUNK INTO the comfort of a cushioned armchair in a quiet corner of the airline's frequent-flyer lounge when her phone chimed. Putting down the glass of champagne she'd allowed herself in anticipation of the first real vacation she'd taken in over a year, she picked up her phone. It was impossible for her to simply ignore it—hazard of having a profession where a single leak or news report could change the trajectory of an entire career.

You never knew if it would be for good or for bad until it happened.

Seeing the message was from David, she felt her abdomen tense. He'd hardly spoken to her today, not that she could blame him. She'd been so worried about that eye of his that she'd snapped at him twice when all she'd wanted was to grip his jaw and check for herself that he was okay. He'd probably written her a nice, polite apology for not contacting her as soon as he was picked up by the cops... Only the thing was, Thea had had it up to here with David being polite to her.

He was polite to her when she had meetings with him and the rest of the band. He was polite to her when she called to ask him his views on particular publicity options. He was polite to her when she joined the band for dinner as a friend and not their publicist. He was *always* polite.

And nothing else.

Her hand clenched on the phone. If he'd been that way from the start, she wouldn't have known any different, but David hadn't just been polite to her when she came onboard the Schoolboy Choir team. He'd been sweet and funny and warm. So many times toward the end of her relationship with Eric, when her ex-fiancé had done or said something that hurt her, it was David she'd called.

She'd never told him the real reason why she was calling,

had always made it about work, but he'd made her feel better nonetheless. It had taken her several months to realize David was shy, but it wasn't the kind of shy that left him tongue-tied or lost. He just needed a bit of time to get to know people, warm up to them. When he did, his loyalty was etched in stone, his support unconditional.

That support had helped her deal with far more than he knew.

And now… he was polite and reserved and she *missed* him. So many times, she had to fight the urge to take hold of those strong, solid shoulders and shake him, tell him to stop it!

Even though he was meant to be a client and nothing else.

Bracing herself for the horrible, polite message to follow, she opened his e-mail. Her mouth dropped open.

He'd sent her a memo.

And it had nothing whatsoever to do with the bar fight.

Reasons Why You Should Give Us a Shot

Introduction: In this memo, I, David Rivera, explain why you, Thea Arsana, should seriously consider entering into a relationship with me.

First, let me address what I believe is your main reason for not dating me: that I am a client. This can be easily remedied. You own an agency in partnership. Your partner, or, if Imani has no space on her books, one of your senior associates, can take over the Schoolboy Choir account. If you'd prefer not to move the account, you can have Imani vet anything that has to do specifically with me. (Speaking as a member of SC, we want you, no one else.)

Second, while I admit I am a couple of inches shorter than you and two years younger, I have absolutely no hang-ups about either. I don't think such a small age difference matters, and I'm fairly certain my maturity levels are acceptable. I point out that I, too, am an eldest child. As for the height thing—I seriously love those heels you wear. Never will I be so stupid as to demand you wear flats.

Not when watching you walk in heels is one of my all-time favorite things to do.

I'm also in good shape. I realize I'm not as pretty as Noah, or as built as Abe, or have a dimple like Fox, but I have been told I have good teeth. Therefore, I'm not physically deficient.

Third, I think you're hot. Extremely, combustibly hot. If I could, I'd keep you in bed for a week running, naked and mine, and I'd still not have enough. I think every part of you is hot, but I'm particularly turned on by your mind and your legs. You should see the fantasies I have of seducing your mind with my words while I stroke my hands over your legs, rub my fingertips along the inner skin of your thighs.

You don't mind calluses, do you, Thea? They come from drumming so intensely over a long period. All that physical work also means I have plenty of stamina. I can go as long and as hard as you want, or as slow and as deep, or any combination thereof. Hard and deep. Slow and long. Hard, deep, long? I can do that.

Your choice.

Or if you prefer it gentle and lazy, I can do that too.

(Though we'd probably have to burn things down to a simmer with a hard, fast bout or three first.)

I'd be careful as I stroked you, but I'm afraid my touch would be a bit rough, a fraction abrasive, especially when I reach between your legs and use my fingertips to squeeze that pretty, plump, hard little—

Thea closed her eyes, took a deep breath. It didn't do much good, her chest heaving and her pulse a brutal thud against her skin. Mind filled with the potent erotic imagery he'd conjured up and thighs tightly clenched in a futile effort to contain the sudden throbbing ache in between, she stared up at the ceiling of the lounge.

All she saw was David's hand on her thigh, the small scar he had across the first knuckle of his right hand a slash of white against the dark gold of his natural skin tone. His arm was hard with strength and dusted with tiny black hairs, muscle and tendon flexing under his skin as he teased and played with her clit using those callused fingertips before thrusting a single finger deep into—

She squeezed her phone so hard that she heard the case crack, her body rigid and nerves gone haywire. When it was over, she collapsed into her seat in stunned shock, glad that the curved shape of it and her position in a seating arrangement right in back had hidden her from view of the others in the lounge.

He'd made her orgasm.

With nothing but the pressure of her thighs on her needy flesh and his words. The damn man had figured out her weak point and he'd aimed his missile right at it: her mind.

ACKNOWLEDGMENTS

A SPECIAL THANKS TO Leena and Dave Shalloe for their help with beta reading and particularly the musical aspects of this book.

Thank you also to Sharyn and Jayshri for your wonderful feedback, and to Ashwini for being all-around awesome.

As always, any mistakes are mine.

ABOUT THE AUTHOR

NEW YORK TIMES AND USA TODAY bestselling author of the Psy-Changeling, Guild Hunter, and Rock Kiss series **Nalini Singh** usually writes about hot shapeshifters and dangerous angels. This time around, she decided to write about a beautiful, charismatic guitarist with a dark past. If you're seeing a theme here, you're not wrong.

Nalini lives and works in beautiful New Zealand, and is passionate about writing. If you'd like to explore the Rock Kiss series further, or if you'd like to try out her other books, you can find lots of excerpts on her website: www.nalinisingh.com. *Slave to Sensation* is the first book in the Psy-Changeling series, while *Angels' Blood* is the first book in the Guild Hunter series. The website also features special behind-the-scenes material from all her series.

6-16

CPSIA information can be obtained at www.ICGtesting.com
Printed in the USA
LVOW11s1536150616

492730LV00007B/566/P

9 781942 356356